I0772376

# Fire Line Generational Burst

**Marques Bowden**

Cover Art By
Sidra Iqbal

Edited by
Hoffman Smith
Rothesia Stokes

# Special Thanks

First, I would like to thank my lovely wife Brandi for putting up with my intense desire to write. Also, my gang/family of kids, nieces, and nephews: Bryson, Dorian, Britynn, Akia, Tariq, Zafir, Kimaja, KyAsia, Elijah, Isaiah, Lyric, and my youngest son Dreadon AKA Dragon. Daddy loves you and hopes you will see the value of these stories in the future. I also want to thank the countless people who helped, inspire, and influence me to pursue writing for the enjoyment of all. Finally, I would like to thank the ancestors known and unknown that pave the way for Foundational Black Americans to survive; to tell our stories our way and to continue to influence the world with our presence.

# Chapter 1: Refreshed Outlook

It has been about a year since Malik has saved the woeful teenagers from being sexually exploited and robbed of their innocence and freedom. The winds of change flow constantly like cold, melted ice from a mountain to a river. As Malik stands outside his luxury apartment, many thoughts flow through his head.

"The city seems a little quieter now," he reflects. "However, I still feel uneasy about the future. I was able to stop the Elite 8, but only briefly. On top of that, I lost so many people along the way…"

Malik looks down at his hands. Seemingly ignoring the orange coloration of another Atlanta skyline sun rise. His thoughts continue to flood his mind like a monsoon, dwelling on the constant tug of war of accomplishment and unresolved agendas.

Suddenly, a ring interrupts his intrinsic moping. Malik quickly snaps out of it and wiggles through his pocket to find his phone. Again and again, the phone continues to ring. Then, with a simple swipe from his thumb, Malik answers the phone.

"Hello?" "Um… um… is this, Malik Wilson?" the apprehensive voice questioned. Cautious, Malik responds promptly while controlling his emotions to what may be to come. "Yes ma'am. May I ask who this is?"

Then an awkward pause intensifies the moment as Malik grows a little more impatient. "Hello? Are you still there?" Malik asks as he patiently waits for a response. "Did you know Dr. Willis Hauss?" "Hauss? *This is getting strange…* Who is this?"

Then, the phone rattles a bit, signaling the shy and nervous actions of the woman on the other side of the line. Afterwards, courage compels the young lady to blurt out her reason for the call.

"My name is Audrey. Audrey Hauss." "Audrey Hauss… So that means…" "Yes, I am related to him, Dr Hauss was my grandfather."

Amazed, Malik takes a moment to settle down; meanwhile, he reassesses the direction of the conversation then begins to generate follow-up questions.

"He never mentioned any family." Malik responded, "So how do I know you are who you say you are for 1…and how did you get this number?"

Again, the phone shakes for a moment before the young woman is able to regain her nerve.

"I can't explain everything on the phone…and I know you must think this is some sort of prank or joke. I can only show you. If you can meet me, I can explain everything." "How can I trust you?" Malik responded. Then, the young woman confidently responds with a few surprising words.

"You can't. I know, but I know of a Moor that works behind the shadows. I know my grandfather spent his life studying those guys… and I know he confided with someone before he died."

Immediately, Malik recognizes the words in between the lines. The death of a mentor still lingers in his subconscious like an odor. Yet, this mysterious woman claims to be related to the late patriarch.

"Ok," Malik relinquishes, "Where do you want to meet?" "There's a small coffee shop outside of downtown. We can meet there at 10:00. Is that good with you?" "Yes…" "Ok, thank you and see you then." 'CLICK'

Malik puts up his phone, then stares once again at the skyline, manipulating a plan of action before meeting the young woman.

*"That seems too convenient…"* Malik expressed, "Hauss never mentioned any family. He didn't have pictures of them or anything. However, I can't overlook the fact that she knows something as well as how much those Elite 8 guys kept tabs on him. Perhaps…well, I won't know until I investigate."

Malik then goes inside his apartment and grabs his clothes. As he opens the closet, his leather jacket stares at him like a lingering memory. He chuckles, then whispers to himself while he gets dressed.

"I sure did have many battles in that jacket," Malik reminisces, "Despite taking down some of their premier members, it seems like this war is far from over. *I guess it's safe to say that, as black people, we were not enslaved in a split second. So, our liberation won't be as quick either.*" Malik presses his jeans then makes final adjustments to his shoes before heading out of the room.

Before leaving his apartment, he makes sure he grabs his phone and locks all of the windows in his apartment. After a quick look around, Malik walks out of the room, locks the door, then proceeds outside towards the meeting place.

While walking downstairs towards the outside of the building, another ring vibrates through his pocket. Malik immediately searches his pocket to grab his phone. As he views the screen, he sees a familiar name and number. With a quick swipe of his thumb, he answers the phone.

"Hey there sis, what's up?" Malik answers, "How's Jacksonville?" "It's beautiful out here. The weather is just as hot as Atlanta, but a lot more rain and humidity." the young lady responds.

For the past few months, Emma has been staying with her grandparents, meanwhile learning the ways of her ancestors while purging away the poison fed to her throughout her upbringing.

"That's great." Malik continues, "How are the grandparents? I miss them and I should visit them again." "Well," Emma adds, "They're very loving and supportive. Grandmother is very strict when it comes to my training though. She says it's necessary for me to learn how to connect with our past to purge through the future." "Well, she's right Emma. Most of our power comes from who we are. Without that understanding, there's no fuel to our fire." "Yeah, but before I was… well, you know…"

There is a brief pause on the phone as Malik walks out of the building to walk towards the rendezvous spot.

"It still feels strange, Malik. I mean, yes, I was powerful before. It seemed like power was in the palm of my hand. Now, I feel caged up, unable to grasp the simple concepts of controlling our power, let alone understanding who I am." "It'll come sis. TRUST ME!" Malik emphasizes, "Sometimes these concepts don't come when you want them to. Just trust the process and, more importantly, trust yourself."

Emma smiles at the other end of the line as the words of encouragement revive her confidence. "Thanks Malik. I appreciate that." "You're welcome. By the way, I need to go soon. I'm on my way to meet someone." "Oh…" Emma snickers sarcastically, "Meeting a woman, I see." "Yeah, but not like that. She said she had some information." "(SIGH) What woman doesn't?" "Well, for one, she claims that she's Hauss' granddaughter… and that she knows about… us." The tone of the conversation quickly turns to that of great intensity. Emma then ends the conversation with a wise and prudent word of caution. "Be careful Malik. I remember that the Elite 8 has people in places you would never expect. Regardless of what she tells you, keep a constant watch of what you say to this woman." "Thanks sis. Take care of Grandma and Granddad for me ok, I'll talk to you soon." "Ok, bye Malik (CLICK)"

Malik looks at his phone, then takes a deep breath to debrief himself of the conversation.

*"Emma is right. Although I could easily see her intentions, I can't risk showing my eyes without exposing my identity. I need to find out what this woman knows."* Malik puts his phone back in his pocket and then stroll towards the coffee shop.

10 minutes later, Malik makes it to the coffee shop. He enters the establishment and makes his way towards the register.

"Good morning, sir." the cashier greets, "How can I help you?" "Yes, can I have a Verde Blood Orange Tea please?" Malik orders. "Absolutely, will that be chilled or hot?" "Hot please." "Very well, that'll be $3.46 please." Malik pulls out his wallet then gives the cashier his black card. "Ok, thank you very much sir. Your order will be ready in about 2 minutes." Malik nods and smiles as he goes to the waiting area.

As he waits for his order, Malik scripts his potential conversation to prepare for the questions he wants to be answered. *"Ok, so she claims to be Hauss' granddaughter. I'll need proof of that. Plus, there has to be a reason why she is coming for me. I need to know how she knew of our relationship and why she has reached out."* DING. The sound signals to Malik that his order is ready. "Here you go sir. Enjoy and thank you for stopping by." Malik nods and smirks as he finds a seat.

Malik sits down and takes a sip of his freshly brewed tea. Anticipating the meeting, Malik dwells more into deep thought.

*"I don't like this at all. I don't know what to expect, or why am I taking this so seriously?"*

Then, a strikingly beautiful woman enters the coffee shop. She is slender, average height (about 5'8'') with the shape of a supermodel, a strut that commands attention, and skin so pure and dark you can see the reflection of the sun.

She goes to the counter to order her drink. Malik is taken back by the sight of the woman. Most men would have rated this woman as a 9 out of 10. Malik, on the other hand, is so dumbfounded by the sight of this woman that he almost forgets the purpose of this meeting.

As if the woman can sense the eyes of curiosity, she scans the establishment before looking towards Malik's direction. She winks at him before she gets her coffee.

Soon, the stunning woman walks over to Malik and addresses him. "Hi, you must be Malik," she says, "I'm Audrey. Pleased to meet you." Malik gets up, shakes her hand, and then sits down.

# Chapter 2: Missing Pieces

Despite his will, Malik finds himself constantly distracted by the presence of Audrey. Her demeanor and femininity rival that of Super Models. She appears to act inconspicuous of the attention, but her shyness hides a confidence that could demand action or attention.

Once they sit down, Audrey begins to brief her grievance towards Malik.

"Thanks for meeting with me. I know you must be very busy with your website," she states. "Not a problem," Malik responded, "So what can I do for you?"

Audrey then looks in her bag and scrambles to locate something of value. Moments later, she pulls out several pictures and a book. The book looked old, worn down, and covered with the dust of time. However, it was the pictures that drew Malik's attention.

"That picture… it looks just like…" Malik took a moment to pause and to regather himself. "This picture has the distinctive markings your grandfather once shared with me." The picture is of a sword. Not just any sword: this sword has a broad, long, and curved blade with a leather-covered hilt. Most striking is the guard, shaped like the form of a dragon with the carving of the Dracocernentia in the center. Despite this revelation, Malik kept the information limited to avoid any suspicion of his alter ego.

"Wow," Malik played along while concealing his real motives, "Those relics look really old but authentic. Where did you get these?" "Well, my mother kept them in her attic for years. She almost destroyed them because she felt that my grandfather spent more time on his research than with his family." "Which reminds me, when was the last time you saw your grandfather?" Audrey paused for a while; then her eyes became as full as the universe. Gazing into Malik's eyes, before she could muster up the words to explain their awkward meeting.

"I was only about maybe 9 or 10 when I last saw him." she responded, "At that time, my grandparents were strangely going through a divorce. My mother was so upset with him that we never saw him after that." "A divorce...*after all of that time together? Doesn't seem right.*" Malik thought as he continued to listen to the young lady. "When my grandmother died 5 years ago, my mother and I would organize her things so that we'd always have a way to remember her. Yet when my mom came across these documents, I urged her to keep them." "Urged?" "Yes… I wanted to know what was so important that my grandfather couldn't be with his family."

Despite the story having holes, Malik dwells with empathy for this stranger; meanwhile, attempting to offer comforting words by sharing bits of information about himself.

"I was adopted by an abusive man, who would always criticize me and put me down. His wife did the best that she could, but… she died of cancer about a year and a half ago." "I'm so sorry," Audrey responded, "It must have been really rough for you." "Well, it was for a while, but someone was there to help me through my tough times." Audrey sighed for a bit, understanding the relationship Malik had developed with Hauss. "So, that's why you were so close to him." she deduced, "In a way, I envy you." "I wouldn't be so sure about his intentions Audrey," Malik said while steering the conversation back to the focal point. "I think that your grandfather found something that would've changed the world." "I guess… which reminds me of why I asked you to meet me here."

Malik sits up straight in his chair, bracing himself to whatever Audrey is preparing to throw at him. "So, what is it?" "I want to know what these pictures mean. I want to know why my grandfather spent his life pursuing such ridiculous stories and legends," Audrey admitted, "I want to know about these pictures." "So why do you think I know?" Malik questioned, "I mean, yes he was a mentor and a friend, but these images here… this is something that goes deep. WAY DEEP."

Then, Audrey grabs both of Malik's hands, gives a look that could melt ice cream into milk, and smiles. "What can I do to convince you to investigate these pictures for me? It would mean a lot to me and my family; plus, we can finally get some closure." she pleaded, "Don't you want the same for my grandfather? Your friend?"

As if ensnared by emotions and a beautiful face, Malik suddenly remembers how Hauss gave him the documents and list of overseas colleagues he'd worked with in the past. Not wanting to turn down such a wonderful face, Malik begins to waiver to the request.

"Sure," Malik says softly, "I'll go to my sources to investigate these images. Your grandfather told me of some professors from overseas that studied the same artifacts. I can possibly meet up with these people."

Audrey smiles, then lets go of her grip. Afterwards, she finishes her coffee and gets up.

"Thank you for doing this. It really means a lot to me." she ended, "You have my number now. Please keep me updated."

Malik nods as Audrey walks out of the shop. Malik remains seated while looking over the book and pictures. "Wow… I know these relics are real because of my past ancestral experiences. *However, something doesn't seem right, so before I go, I need to verify something*." Afterwards, Malik finishes his tea, then leaves the shop as well.

Moments later, Malik makes it back to his luxury apartment. He gathers his suitcases and begins to pack for the journey. While gathering his things, he looks at the leather jacket that has served him in his early journey. The jacket itself commands an awe-inspiring attention that transmits through space and time. For a brief moment, Malik basks in the pool of self-revelation and how the journey of Shadowmoor has given him purpose as well as an identity.

"Hmph," he reminisces, "*It's been a long journey indeed. I can barely remember who I was before I put on this jacket: the overexposed, under-appreciated, and broken young boy. I associated myself as no longer exists in this body. However, despite this, my people still have the stench of hopelessness that has mutated their self-image and robbed them of their worth in this world.*"

Malik grabs the jacket, folds it neatly, and puts it carefully on the bottom of the suitcase. Soon as he finishes his preparations, Malik logs into his computer and orders his plane tickets.

"One of the men in the list Hauss gave me is a man named Winston Baker-Adebayo. He is a professor at Middlesex University." Malik plotted, "So I'll book a 1-way flight there for tomorrow. There's no way of telling how long I will be gone, so I better leave some layaway." As soon as he books his flight and hotel reservations, Malik takes his luggage out of the apartment, locks up, then makes his way to his Jeep.

Malik loads up the Jeep and then starts the engine. The roar of his Hemi soon settles to a level throttle as Malik reverses from his parking spot. Then, he leaves the garage and heads towards the highway to I-75.

The moment Malik merges into the interstate, he dials a number through his Bluetooth. As the phone rings, Malik contemplates about the mission he is about to enter. *"It's been a while since I've left the country,"* Malik reflects, *"It's a good thing my passport is still good for another year or so. But I still can't shake this feeling...like something is missing."*

After 3 rings, the phone picks up.

"Hello? Malik? What's going on?" Malik redirects his focus to the phone call. "Hey Emma, I'm on the road heading your way." "Here? Now?" Emma asks, "Why are you coming to Jacksonville?" "Well, for starters, I am about to go on a flight to London in the morning, and I don't want to leave the jeep at the Airport." "Ooooookay… still doesn't make a lot of sense. Why not take an Uber or a shuttle?" "Well sis because something else came up. I can't tell you now, but I need to show you and grandma." "Show me and grandma? I sense that there's something you're not telling me. What are you hiding?" "Emma, listen. It'll have to wait until I get there. However, I think this can help us learn more about our past as well as how to fix the future." "Sigh… Okay. I'll let grandma know you're coming. See you in a few hours." "Alright Emma. Later" CLICK. The phone hangs up, leaving Malik to dwell in his thoughts during the long drive.

5 hours later, Malik makes it to his grandparent's house. The lasting hours of daylight seem to set the sky on fire, as shades of red, orange, and yellow set on top of the house. Malik parks his Jeep in the driveway then makes his way towards the door.

Malik grabs his backpack, gets out of the jeep, walks towards the door, and before he could reach it, there's a creaking sound from the hinges.

"My Amir!" Geneva exclaims, "Welcome back." "Hi grandma," Malik responds while he gives her a big hug. "Malik, my boy. I am glad to see you." Kemba adds as they escort Malik inside.

When Malik walks in, Emma is standing with her arms folded, leaning, and with a sarcastic look on her face. Emma has changed a bit since the events a year ago. Her short curly hair has now grown to a longer, wavy afro, which she puts in a bun. She has gained more muscle mass yet maintaining her feminine figure. Also, her demeanor has become more balanced: confident, strong, but also perceptive and soft when needed.

"So, you are just going to stand there and pretend that I don't exist?" Emma sneers. "Well, it's hard to pretend when you clearly gained more than just more hair," Malik responded. "You know what?!" Emma smirks as she comes to embrace her older brother. "You lucky we are in this house." "Yes, we are." Malik winks as he hugs Emma real tight.

"Malik, are you hungry?" Geneva asks, "You look like a jackal on a diet." "Well, grandma, when I smell food, I must eat," Malik adds. "Well, you came just in time. Dinner will be ready in about 30 minutes." Geneva walks back to the kitchen to finish the preparations. Meanwhile, Emma interrogates her brother for the missing pieces of information.

"Okay Malik," Emma prompted, "Why are you here? Seriously?" Malik takes off his backpack, unzips the compartment, then grabs the photos. As soon as he recovers the contents, he shows them to Emma. Emma squints her eyes, over-focusing on the images as if to examine the authenticity.

"Where did you get these photos, Malik?" Emma asks while looking over the photos. "I received them from someone. I think it's a relic from one of our ancestors." "That's evident, especially with the carving of the Dracocernentia on the sword. But who gave it to you?" Emma insisted, "And please, don't make me pry it out of you. I'm more equipped to do so now." "I'd listen to your sister if I were you, my Amir," Geneva added while setting the table. "Ok grandma," Malik reluctantly conceded, "It was from a woman." "Oh boy…" Emma responded, "I knew it…" "No, just hear me out. She claimed to be… related to a friend that I lost. She needed my help to find some closure." "Closure huh? Are you this game goofy, or are you not allowing yourself to see within a person to find out their true intentions?" "Come on Emma, you know activating my eyes will expose my secret. You should know that there are other eyes out there trying to exploit that opportunity." "Yeah, I do." Emma stated, "Which is why I am suspicious." "Well, dinner is ready, and we can discuss this more." Kemba adds.

Moments later, the family gathers around the table to eat and discuss the photos. Geneva prepared Poulet Yassa, a Senegalese chicken with onions and lemon, with fresh fruits and vegetables.

"This is delicious grandma," Malik compliments as both Kemba and Geneva smile at their company. "Too bad I can't have this type of meal every day." "Well, my boy, you could always stay here as long as you like. We're family, and you two bring me such joy." Kemba responds. "Thank you, granddad. Which reminds me…"

Malik nods at Emma, prompting her to show Geneva the photos. "Do you recognize these pictures Grandma?" Geneva grabs the photo, looks at it, then her eyes widen like a present on Christmas Morning. Her gaze arouses concern at the dinner table, prompting Kemba to ask his wife.

"Geneva, what is it?" Kemba questioned. "What has startled you all of a sudden?" Geneva continues her moment of silence as she tries to gain control of her shock. "Grandma, are you okay?" Emma says, "It just looks like another sword made by our ancestors. What's the big deal?"

Then suddenly, Geneva whispers the words that generate odd looks on the siblings' faces.

"Harq Alqadr" she whispers. "Harq Alqadr," Malik asks, "Sounds Arabic. What does that mean?"

Geneva puts the photo down then gives Malik a serious look, a look so intense and focused that Malik begins to brace himself to the importance of this revelation.

"My Amir, this is the Harq Alqadr. The Burning Destiny," Geneva explains, "This sword is the symbol of Lordship. Only the Golden Dragon and the Dhahabi could possess this sword." "Dhahabi? Golden Dragon?" Emma asked, "I have never heard of these names, grandma." "We'll finish our dinner, my Ahfad (grandchildren). Then we will meditate. Only then can I fully explain the significance of this sword."

So, Malik and Emma look at each other, both feeling the gravity of the situation. Then they continue to finish their meal, as the table eats quietly.

# Chapter 3: Burning Destiny of the Moors

After a delicious dinner, Geneva washes the plates and cleans up the kitchen. While awaiting their grandmother, Malik and Emma wait in the living room. Emma is sitting down, with her arms and legs crossed; meanwhile, dangling her foot in anticipation for the revelation that is to come.

During this time, Malik is looking at the family photo of his grandparents and mother. The emotions surge through Malik as he begins to think about the road he's taken.

*"With all of this power, I wish I could talk to you mom."* Malik thought, *"That being said, I'm glad I'm given a chance to rekindle the relationship with our grandparents."*

Suddenly, Emma gets up and walks towards Malik. She pats him on the shoulder and consuls him.

"I do that too sometimes." "What?" Malik asked. "Mom… sometimes I'll just stand here and look at the picture. I wish I could talk to her too, but I haven't gotten that far in my training yet." Emma relayed as they both redirected their attention back to the photo. "Trust me sis; you'll have the power before you know it. If there's anything I've learned, it's that you have to allow yourself to open the valves that were closed off from outside influences."

Finishing the last of the dishes, Geneva looks on with love and a sense of hope. Her heart becomes warm and comforting at the sight of her long-lost grandchildren finally coming back to their roots. *"Alyssa, you have such beautiful children. I, too, wish you were here to witness this."* she thinks, *"Soon, they will be able to see you, but right now, there is something that must be completed."*

Afterwards, Geneva walks towards the siblings and directs them to the center of the den. "Come on you two," she commands, "we must seek the guidance of our ancestors if we are to uncover this mystery." Emma and Malik nod at each other before making their way towards the circle. There, they all sit down, hold hands, and close their eyes. Their breathing becomes rhythmic, their focus becomes precise, and their inner Fire Line once again becomes ignited.

Then suddenly, the lights of the house turn off. A gust of wind enters the house, and all of them activate their eyes. The glowing sensation of their fire allows them to project the images of their deities.

Swirling around like a mini tornado, the wind and smoke generate the silhouette of a Phoenix. This magnificent being has a bright blue plumage, with goldish, deep blue eyes, a feather crest, and fiery wings with every color of the rainbow. Geneva begins to chant after the form is completed.

"Illaaha, finiks almuqadas, wanahn naseaa hakmatak wamueriftak (Illaaha, the holy Phoenix, we seek your wisdom and knowledge)." The Phoenix illuminates her eyes then begins to respond.

"Speak your question, and it shall be revealed to you." "Nahn naseaa limaerifat masir alharqa. Nahn bihajat 'iilana maerifat makanah wakayfiat alhusul ealayh (We seek the knowledge of the Burning Destiny. We need to know where it is and how to obtain it.)." Geneva chanted.

The great bird begins to spread her wings then provides commentary for the images she displays. "The Harq Alqadr is a powerful sword that was wielded by many warriors. The first to obtain this blade is a commander by the name of Riaahn. 1100 Earth years ago, Riaahn traveled throughout Europe with his Dhahabi. Although powerful, Riaahn was also secretive, never allowing anyone to see his face or be recognized for his influences." "A man with such power yet doesn't have the ego to match?" Malik questions, *Now I'm starting to understand why such knowledge was concealed.* "It is more than just ego Dragon Moor," the great bird reiterates. *How did she… right,* please continue." Malik requested humbly.

Then Illaaha changes the images of a great Golden Dragon, then showcases its influences all over the world. "Riaahn was among the first to achieve the level of the Golden Dragon. The Golden Dragon becomes so powerful and revered that they mold the ideologies of the territories they inhabit. Nothing else was known from Riaahn, but I know that he hid the sword somewhere in Europe. Awaiting for the time a new Golden Dragon will claim it and reunite the power of the Moors."

During this trance, both Emma and Malik are dumb struck by the images and information given by the Phoenix. Then Geneva parts with one last question.

"Ayn ymkn 'an nabda fi albahth ean alsayf (Where can we begin to look to find the sword)?" "The Dragon Moor already has the starting point," Illaaha concludes, "but take heed to the wisdom of the Phoenix. Those who seek the sword do not have the power to possess it, so they will use one of our own to manipulate its use. Be careful."

As soon as the Phoenix appears, the great bird dissolves into the air, making her exit as the wind begins to calm down, ending the session.

After that, the lights in the house began to light up and the trio deactivated their eyes. Breathing really hard, both Emma and Malik struggle to catch their breath as Geneva gets up from her seated position. "You see, my Amir," Geneva warns, "we were once the most powerful force on this planet. Then we became arrogant, we lost our power, then were forced to hide in plain sight." Malik and Emma both get up to consort with their grandmother.

"So, this is why I stopped here first." Malik admitted, "I'm flying to London in the morning and I'm leaving the Jeep here. I need to find Hauss' colleagues and maybe locate this sword." "Malik, listen to me." Geneva pleaded. "Your granddad and I had to leave Mali to conceal our powers. I can't stop you from going, but please promise me that you will be careful." "Yes Grandma, I will." "Ok… my Amir. I'm about to go to bed. Your rooms are ready." Geneva says, then she hugs Malik while planting a kiss on his cheek, "I love you, my Amir." "Love you too, Grandma." Geneva walks towards the back of the house, while Malik stares at the window.

While Malik plots his moves, Emma walks next to Malik to offer him company. Both stay in silence for about a minute, as Emma takes her time to offer some words of wisdom to her single-minded brother.

"Malik, grandma is right." she states, "I don't have a good feeling about this. I mean, yes, the sword is an important part of our lineage; however, it was hidden for a reason." "Yes, Emma. Somehow, I believe it is my destiny to retrieve this sword." "And then what?!" Emma responds, while grabbing his attention, "I'm just going to say it. I don't trust this woman who gave you these images. Even if her story holds true, why would she go through the trouble to convince you to seek out this sword?" "For closure, Emma! Don't you understand what it means to miss something in your life? To wonder if you were meant for something important? Real? Worth wild?"

Emma sighs then look up at her older brother. "Malik, you already know the answer to that question. Before you freed me, I turned a blind eye to all of the shady things the Elite 8 did to get what they wanted. I'm with grandma here, and I truly believe this is more than just a sword." "Emma, I need to go." "Then I'm coming with…" "No Emma," Malik commanded, "You need to stay here and watch over our grandparents. If you travel with me, we will more likely be forced to reveal ourselves before the time is right." "Sigh… okay Malik. I'll drop you off at the airport in the morning, and I'll let you do this. I just need you to understand something; our ancestors were the most successful when they didn't overestimate their abilities. Ours have been and will continue to be our weakness. Be careful not to fall into that same perpetual trap." Malik smiles and nods before heading to the guest room.

While Malik lays in bed, he stares at the ceiling. Despite having the powers for almost 2 years, each new vision feels like he's only tapped a small portion of the potential of his ancestors. The words of the great Phoenix and that of his grandmother generate compounding questions that need to be answered.

*"At times like these, I would meditate and seek guidance from Amir. Yet, this new sword, this Harq Alqadr, seems to be a weapon as a need to know only the basics."* Malik gets up from his bed and sits for a while, continuing to dwell in his thoughts. *"I'm not usually this disturbed, but remaining a secret is proving difficult, especially with everything that is going on in the world."*

Then suddenly, a knock on the door disrupts Malik's thinking. "Hello, Malik… are you asleep son?" It was Kemba, checking up on Malik before going to bed. "No Granddad." "Mind if I come in?" "Sure."

So Kemba opens the door, seeing his grandson sitting at the edge of the bed. "What troubles you, Malik? You don't want to miss your flight." "Well Granddad… I don't know exactly. There used to be a moment where I completely understood who I am, but now I'm slowly realizing that my roots run deeper than I envisioned. I don't know what or how to feel about it." "I see… Well son, if you are up to it, I would like to show you something." Curious, Malik looks at his grandfather as he prompts him to follow.

Kemba takes Malik to a shed in the backyard of the house. After a few minutes of walking, Kemba unlocks the shed, opens the door, then invites Malik in.

"Granddad, what is this?" Malik asks. "Let me turn on the light." Kemba turns on the light to reveal a gallery of strange masks, statues, and pieces of clothing. Amazed, Malik is speechless, as he gazes upon such artifacts.

"Wow… what is all of this?" Malik questions while circling around. Kemba chuckles a bit, allowing Malik to take his time to soak in all of the wonderful pieces of culture. "This, my grandson, is from my tribe." "What tribe?" "Heh heh heh, I am originally Dogon, from my father's side." "Dogon…" Malik responded, "I'm afraid that I don't know much if anything about them." "It is quite alright, Malik." Kemba responded softly, "It is very important to know who you are and where you come from. Let me tell you a story that my father once told me." Both Malik and Kemba sit down in the middle of the shed.

"In old times, there was a woman who lived in a lush oasis in the middle of the desert. She was the most beautiful woman in all of the lands. Everybody wanted to take her as a wife. She was tall, dark, and wise. However, because of this, her father wanted to find a suitable partner for her." "So, what happened next?" Malik asks with the anticipation of a child. "Well, her father offered a challenge to anyone who could solve the mystery of the stars. What are they, where do they come from, and how to map them?" "That seems difficult. Even our own scientists can't always accurately pinpoint stars." Malik responded. "Indeed, Malik. No one could answer the man's questions. So, for years, she went unwed. So long that the woman thought it would be impossible to wed." "That seems really sad, Granddad." "Yes, very sad." Kemba stated, until he grabbed one of the masks, "However, all was not lost. One night, while the woman was walking, something in the sky drew her attention. It was very bright, so bright that it blinded her temporarily. For a few minutes, she could not see; however, she heard a voice that said to her, "I have searched the stars to find such beauty."" "Search the stars? So, he came from outer space?" "It is complicated to say. Our legend states that when she opened her eyes, the voice matched a man with dark, almost reptilian skin, black curly hair, and golden eyes. The woman was so perplexed by the appearance of this man yet was drawn to his energy." "*Reptilian skin, golden eyes... could it be?*" Malik thought as Kemba continued his story. "So, the woman led the strange being to her father. The father asks, "What do you know of the mysteries of the stars, traveler?". The man just stood there and smiled. Taking his time to answer. The father again asks, "What do you know of the mysteries of the stars?" The man continued to stand and smile. Finally, the frustration kicked in and the father began to turn the traveler away. Suddenly, the traveler speaks to the man." "So then, what did he say?" Malik asked.

Kemba picks up another mask. This mask had a long head with markings that looked like scales and eye openings. Kemba looks at it, smiles, then continue with the story.

"The traveler spoke and said this. "The stars are balls of condensed energy, contained by the substance known as the Black Power. This Black Power is so vast that there is no limit to its range. Only a few beings can contain such power. Those who do not, eventually perish because they can not control the power." Amazed, the father lowered his guard and asked one more question. He says, "Can you tell which stars from another?" The traveler turns around and faces the man and responds. The traveler smiles and says, "The only thing that moves is our thought on reality. The stars never move, only our will to reach them."" "Wow… that was powerful!" Malik responded. "So, the traveler was allowed to take the woman as his wife. Shortly after she bore a set of twins: 1 boy and 1 girl. The boy had the appearance of his father, with the bright gold eyes and skin like a crocodile, while the girl had her mother's beauty but with wings." "You've got to be kidding me!" Malik exclaimed. "So, how far down has this story been passed down?" "Heh, heh, heh, for as long as the Dogon have existed." Kemba concludes before prompting them to leave the shed.

Outside, Kemba gives Malik lasting words of wisdom. "Malik, you come from a family so vast, it rivals that of the stars. Remember my story to you, that the stars don't move, only your willingness to reach them. Do not fear the vastness of space because the power you have within you is enough to contain the stars. Remember that." "I will, Granddad. Thank you for showing me this." Kemba chuckles as he embraces Malik with a hug.

"Come now," Kemba commands, "You must rest so that you won't miss your flight tomorrow." Then the men head back to the house to go back to sleep.

# Chapter 4: New Journey, New Expectations

The phone generates a chime while vibrating against the dresser. This wakes Malik up from his deep and troubling sleep. Slowly, he looks at the time and begins to yawn. "3:00 am… ugh," Malik slurs as he gets up, "The flight leaves at 6:30, so it's time to get dressed."

Then, someone knocks on the door to his room." (KNOCK, KNOCK, KNOCK) Malik, are you up?" Emma whispered. "Yeah… argh… yeah, I'm up." Malik responds while stretching. "Ok well, I'll be waiting for you in the living room." "Sure."

Malik makes his bed and puts on his clothes: A blue Ralph Lauren Polo shirt with loose-fitting jeans and a pair of blue NMD Adidas sneakers. Afterwards, he makes his way to the bathroom, washing his face, brushing his teeth, grooming his goatee while brushing his taper fade; Malik finishes his morning routine by messaging his small, loosely twisted afro.

Malik then brings his luggage towards the living room, with Emma waiting for him in the living room. However, Emma is standing in front of the picture of their mother as well as their grandparents. "Emma… are you ok?" Malik asks. Startled, Emma quickly responds to Malik while helping him with one of his bags. "Yeah Malik, I'm just… (sigh) It's hard not to feel complete. You know." "Yeah, I do… Come on; we have to load up." Emma agrees as they make their way towards the door.

Before leaving, a voice stops Malik and Emma from exiting the door. "Let me get the door for you kids." Emma and Malik look back to see Kemba walk past them, opening the door and escorting them to the Grand Cherokee. As they walk, Kemba embarks a few more words to Malik for his journey. "Malik, my boy," Kemba continues, "Many things have happened to you and your sister. I just want you to know how much your grandmother and I love both of you as well as how proud we are." "Thanks Grandpa. I don't think this trip will take long." Malik responds while loading up the SUV. "Son, listen to me." Kemba grabs both Malik and Emma's attention as the crickets provide commentary during the otherwise quiet morning. "I have spent many years waiting for closure from your mother. There were days that I would blame others for my grief, even to some degree your father." Before Malik could speak, Kemba held up his hand and smiled, "However, seeing and meeting both of you made me realize that journeys are never meant to be short. Only the routes and trails that lead to the main road. After seeing you two, I've learned that your mother meeting your father was just a trail that led to the main road towards our journey." "Grandpa, what are you trying to say?" Malik asks. "What I am saying is do not rush the process, my boy. My tribe once said that no one knows if a bird in flight has an egg in its stomach. Be careful and learn from your travels." "I will Grandpa." Malik smiles as he hugs Kemba. "I love you too, and I'll see you again when the time is right." "Ok Malik, it's 3:30; I got to get you to the airport now." Emma reminded Malik.

So, Malik gets in the passenger seat of his SUV, straps in his seatbelt, and Emma drives him towards the airport. While driving through traffic, Malik asks Emma a question. "Are you still planning on doing the Big Sister program?" "Huh… oh yeah, about that." Emma responds, "I don't know if I want to do that. I mean, yeah, living with Grandma and Grandpa is great, but I'm not so good with people." "Hmph, you know sis, a wise (ass) woman once told me that I have to be comfortable with the people I am protecting. Otherwise, I will be seen as a stiff, if not a potential fraud." "Wise woman… what kinda sugar momma have you been messing with?" Emma questions. "No, it's not that (*or at least on my side*), but she had a point. Emma, you have to be able to understand and relate to the pain in others so that you can be effective enough to help them through it. You may find that helping the younger generation may give you more insight on how to heal, let alone better understand yourself." "Yeah perhaps, but what if the kid turns out to be weird: eating his boogers, having an imaginary friend, or talking to themselves?" "Then, you may have found another Moor sis." "Really Malik?!" "Seriously. If someone knew that we could talk with our ancestors, do you honestly think people would take us sane?" "...Good point." Emma relinquishes as she pulls up at the terminal.

A few moments later, Emma and Malik get out to unload the Grand Cherokee. Malik grabs his backpack, and his bag, and suitcase. "Well Malik, I wish I was going with you," Emma says. "I know, but I sense that you're needed here. I can't fully explain it but thinking about what Grandpa said makes me think that this is a small trail to a bigger path." "Yeah, you're right. Well…" Emma and Malik hug and kiss each other on the cheeks. "Alright little sis, it's that time." "Take care of yourself, asswipe." "You too shit stain." "You know what… I love you too" Emma responds, giving a middle finger as a parting gift. Malik smiles, grabs his belongings and heads to the checkout station. Emma immediately goes back to the SUV and drives back home.

While standing in line, Malik looks through his backpack to uncover the book given to him by Hauss and the picture. "*I wonder who took this picture and why Audrey wants to know the secrets behind it?*" Malik ponders, "*Hopefully, this Winston Baker-Adebayo can give me more information about it.*" Malik waits for about 5 minutes until he reaches the end of the line.

      "Can I help the next person please?" the receptionist asks. Malik walks up to the counter and addresses the nice woman. "Good morning, I am on British Airways flight 1357. My name is Malik Wilson." "Good morning to you sir, may I see your ticket number or driver's license?" "Here you go ma'am."

      So, the receptionist looks at the information associated with Malik's account and confirms his flight. "Alright Mr. Wilson, I see that you have first-class seats. Will you be checking in your bags?" "Yes ma'am. 2 of them." "Yes sir, and you do understand that there is an additional fee for luggage over 75 lbs?" "Yes, that would've been a problem if I were flying with my sister." Malik responds, prompting a small chuckle from the receptionist. "Ha, ha, ha. Fair enough Mr. Wilson. Please place the bags here."

      Malik places his bags on the platform next to the counter as the receptionist prints out two labels, tags the bags, then moves them to the docking rail behind her. "Alright, that's done. Here are your tickets Mr. Wilson; enjoy your flight." "Thank you, ma'am. Take care." After a small exchange, Malik makes his way through airport security.

      Malik reaches the security station and begins to prepare for the scanning. Due to his experiences traveling, he knows that he'll have to unload his laptop and belongings and put them in the tub. One of the security personnel reminds the passengers of the procedures. "Please take off your shoes, unload your belongings, including belts, jewelry, rings, and mobile devices, then put them on the tub." Malik makes sure his belt, shoes, backpack, and laptop are placed neatly on the tub. Malik waits in line as each personnel scans each passenger and their belongings.

      "Next." one of the guards' commands as Malik steps up. "Sir, I need you to place your feet on the marker and raise your hand please." Malik complies with the instructions and steps inside the scanner. He raises his hands while the machine scans for any irregularities. "Clear," the guard informs as Malik steps out of the scanner. However, while waiting for his backpack, the security grabs his things.

Malik grabs his shoes and belt, then is instructed to follow one of the guards. "Sir, can you come with me? We need to recheck your bag." Concerned, Malik follows the guard towards a corner section by the scanners. "Is there a problem? I took out my laptop, so there shouldn't be anything else electric in the bag." "Sir, it's just a random check. Standard procedure." "*If you say so…*" Malik complains as the guard checks his belongings.

As they inspect the backpack, the guard comes across the book and picture. "This is interesting. I have never seen a picture like this before." the guard says while looking through the bag. "Yes, it was… a gift. I'm into Medieval artifacts." Malik responds. "I see; I used to collect swords when I was younger. That's all."

After a few seconds, the guard gives Malik the thumbs up. "Ok sir, you're cleared. Have a good flight." Malik gathers his things, organizes his backpack and heads for his terminal. "*That was a weird encounter… Oh well, at least I will make my flight on time.*" As Malik walks away, the guard is contacted through his intercom. "He is checked in and heading towards the terminal," the guard states on his device. "Were you able to confirm that it is him?" the voice on the other end asks. "Yes, he has the picture of the sword. So, I suspect he will lead us to it." the guard confirms.  "Excellent, we'll keep an eye on him when he arrives in London." "We will always control the destiny of men, FOR WE ARE ELITE!" the guard whispers as he continues to scan the rest of the passengers.

It is 5:45 am, and Malik is sitting down reading the contents of the book Hauss gave him. In it, it has notes on his colleagues and their specialties. "It says here that Adebayo discovered the presence of Africans dating back to the 3rd or 4th century in Ireland." Malik summarizes, "Yet he claims that the notion of them using ships is partially accurate. States here that ancient ruins and sculptures depict the druids worshiping giant serpent-like creatures. *Well, if I haven't learned anything in this past year, I've learned that legends tend to be the truth diluted over time.*"

Suddenly, an announcement is made for the passengers for the flight. "Good morning, passengers, if you are scheduled to fly flight number 1357, we are now getting ready to board. Those who are in First Class, please line up and have your tickets ready. Thank you." Malik puts his book away, gets up, and patiently waits for his turn to load the plane.

While waiting in line, a woman in her late 50s looks at Malik with begrudging contempt. Masking her bigotry with concern, the woman addresses Malik by tapping him on the shoulder. "Excuse me sir, is this your first time flying?" "Excuse me? I don't understand." Malik responds. "Well, this line is for First class passengers. I was just wondering if you got up by mistake." Understanding the racist undertone of the questioning, Malik uses his wit to take control of the situation calmly. "Let's see here, (Malik grabs his ticket) It states here that I am in First Class, seat 5A." Malik responds slightly sarcastically, "But thank you for making sure I'm at the right place at the right time."

Before the woman could respond to the charming young man, the clerk awaits the passengers to show their tickets. She is a beautiful young woman: black with curly hair wrapped in a bun, slim figure with a lovely smile and small African earrings. She, too, notices the exchange between Malik and the woman. So, she proceeded professionally with quelling the bigotry.

"Good morning, may I see your ticket please?" She asks. Malik hands her the ticket while she inspects it. "Ok Mr. Wilson you are set. Just really quick though, you wouldn't happen to be Malik Wilson, owner and CEO of Pulseofthestreet.org would you?" she asks. "Indeed I am." Malik responds, quickly understanding the point of the matter. "Well, it is nice to have a celebrity flying with us." she says, while winking, "Have a good flight sir." The woman's contempt literally changes her face to red as she prepares to hand over her ticket. In a stroke of irony, the clerk scans the ticket and realizes there was a change in her seating. "Ma'am, I'm sorry to inform you that because you booked your ticket late, your seat has been moved towards the front of Group A." "WHAT DO YOU MEAN MY TICKET HAS BEEN CHANGED?!" she yells. Then a manager quickly comes over to calm the woman down. "Yes ma'am, it's true. Shows here that your initial payment declined and when you paid a few hours later, it modified your seating."

As Malik turns back to briefly look at the commotion, the clerk gives a brief look back while giving another wink. He smiles, as he makes his way towards his seat.

Malik sits down and puts his backpack on the ground while buckling his seatbelt. Time passes as the passengers make their way towards the seat. Among them, the woman who'd try to undermine him before walks by angrily as Malik smiles back. The Stewardess begin their instructions of the procedures of the plane, as well as exits, movie choices, and compartments in case of an emergency. "*Wow… I'm really going to England.*" Malik says, "*Well, since this is going to be a 1 stop, 10 hr. flight, I might as well catch up on some reading, good entertainment, and a glass of wine.*"

As the plane begins to take off, Malik senses the beginning of yet another enlightening and interesting journey.

# Chapter 5: The Autistic Loner

The morning sun is welcomed with the songs of songbirds of the neighborhood and the gulls off the coast. As the rays of the day warm the city, Geneva, Kemba, and Emma get ready for the day.

Emma puts on one of her favorite outfits: tight jeans with a thin layered pink blouse and thong sandals. She also fixes her hair, now as long, kinky, and high as the most elegant Acacia tree, into a single bun. She looks at the mirror at her natural beauty without the makeup she grew up hiding behind, then smirks as she better appreciates her beauty. "Oh, my Amira, you look beautiful." Geneva complements as she passes by. "Thank you, Grandma." Emma responds, "You know, I didn't use to feel that way. I can remember wearing a lot of makeup, putting harsh chemicals in my hair, and looking like a barbie doll." "Yes, I see." Geneva continues, "So how do you feel now?" "Well, surprised actually. Sometimes I feel weird. Like I'm learning how to be human for the first time." Geneva and Emma walk out of the bathroom and into the living room.

Both sit down on the couch as Geneva consoles Emma for her first day volunteering for the Big Sister program. "Sweet Emma. You are a powerful woman who has learned much, and well this past year or so. Remember that with training comes healing. You've learned to love yourself and rid yourself of the poison that contaminated your Fire Line. Now is the time to show that love for your people." Geneva reminds Emma. "(Sigh) I'm so nervous, Grandma. I mean, I didn't use to interact with people, let alone black people. It will not be easy." "The road less taken isn't supposed to be easy, but that's why it reaps the biggest rewards. Be yourself and be sensitive to your senses. You may find that it will steer you towards someone who collaborates with a Phoenix Moor."

Emma smiles with the words of comfort as she gets up, ready to go. "Alright, I'm leaving now." Kemba walks by and gives Emma a hug. "Have a good day Emma and remember what I told your brother this morning. It goes the same for you." "Yes, I know, no one knows if a bird in flight has an egg in its stomach. Love you both." "We love you too. Take care, child." Kemba responds as Emma walks out the door.

Emma gets in the Grand Cherokee and heads towards the local junior high. During the drive, Emma contemplates the array of scenarios that could present itself during the interaction. "I still feel a bit apprehensive about doing this." Emma continues, while weaving through the late morning rush. "I mean, I know almost nothing about kids, their needs, or how to help them. Still, as Malik said, I need to immerse myself in the masses to understand them. Alright, here goes nothing."

Several minutes later, Emma pulls up to the school and parks in the back of the building. She gets out of the jeep, lets out a sigh, then makes her way towards the office. Once she enters the building, she is greeted by the school secretary.

"Good morning; how can I help you?" she asked. "Hello, my name is Emma Ayokè. I am here to volunteer for the Big Sister organization." "Wonderful," the secretary responds, "My name is Ella Rios. The principal is in a meeting, but our counselor will escort you to meet your student." "I'm looking forward to it. When will I meet them?" Emma asks. "Well, lunch will begin in about 20 minutes, so our counselor will debrief you on your child." Emma nervously smiles with anticipation and a little anxiety.

Ms. Rios sends an intercom announcement for the counselor. Moments later, a woman shows up to greet Emma. She is a semi-tall woman: about 5'9'', red hair, glasses, and seasoned. "Hi, my name is Bethany Rollins. I'm one of the counselors at this school. We're super excited that you came here to volunteer." she introduces while shaking Emma's hand. "Nice to meet you. I'm Emma and I'm ready." "Wonderful, well, I will escort you to the classroom to meet your student." Emma and Mrs. Rollins walked out of the office and towards the classroom.

During the stroll, Mrs. Rollins relays some information about the student. "Well Emma, as you may know. Big Sisters provide mentors to troubled or kids with specific disabilities and needs." Mrs. Rollins states. "Yes ma'am. It's why I volunteered. I know the feeling of being alone and troubled." Emma responds. "Well, the young man that you will be mentoring is a very bright but quiet child. His name is Asir. He is on the spectrum, but he is very selective when it comes to opening up to certain people." Emma raises her eyebrow and pushes the counselor to elaborate. "What do you mean opening up to certain people?" "Well, he doesn't seem to trust most male figures. We suspect that he hasn't encountered many men in the household and sometimes, he will refuse to talk to people he doesn't like. There really isn't a consistent pattern to allow us to better serve his needs." "Uh huh…" Emma responds, "Is there anything else?" "As a matter of fact," Mrs. Rollins finishes, "He keeps to himself, but he draws all the time. Sometimes he will draw pictures instead of doing his work. Indeed, he is someone that will get bored easily." Emma keeps this intel to herself, meanwhile something sharp hits her head. *"What is this sharp pain?"* she wonders while messaging her scalp, *"I sense a power. Something similar to Malik's Fire Line. Ugh…"* Mrs. Rollins notices Emma and asks about her well-being. "Is everything ok?" "Oh yes… I had to drop my brother off at the airport this morning. I think my body is still adjusting." Emma responds while recollecting herself.

Mrs. Rollins and Emma make it to the classroom right before the bell rings for lunch. "Here we are," Mrs. Rollins says, "In about 30 seconds, the bell will ring. After that, we'll meet Asir, and you'll get a chance to get to know each other." "Great." Emma says.

BRING… the bell rings, many of the students wrestle their chairs, grab their bags, and head out the door. Mrs. Rollins and Emma maneuver through the stampede of preteens and teens as they enter the classroom. Once in the classroom, the teacher welcomes both Mrs. Rollins and Emma. "Hi, Bethany. This must be our Big Sister." the teacher recognizes. "Yes, she is, this is Emma and she's going to mentor Asir." "Yes. Well nice to meet you. I'm Mrs. Springle, his Language Arts teacher," she says, "Asir, your mentor is here." Emma looks at the end of the classroom to see a lone black child with glasses take his time getting his things. He's a normal-sized child, with a nice short haircut, a short-sleeved collared shirt, shorts, and a pair of Nike shoes. Despite hearing the teacher, he remains non-engaging.

Emma begins to sense something unusual about this child. "He really is a loner…" she concludes, "*Yet the sharp pain in my mind is somewhat amplified. What is it about him that stirs this feeling within me?*" As Emma directs her attention to Asir, Mrs. Springle alerts Mrs. Rollins about his progress. "He didn't want to do anything today." she relayed, "Today, all he did was draw these pictures in class. I'm getting concerned." Emma overhears the conversation and asks the teacher a question. "I'm sorry, but what did he draw?" Mrs. Spingle shows both Mrs. Rollins and Emma the pictures she's taken up from Asir for the past few months. "He has this fascination with 2 things: Dinosaurs and…" "*Dragons!*" Emma realizes as Mrs. Springle continues to debrief Mrs. Rollins. "Well, if I may," Mrs. Rollins asks, "I would like to have those pictures so that I can document a trail of behavior. It seems like it's the same with classes that he's not interested in." "Sure." Mrs. Springle complies, "Asir, it's time for lunch."

Asir slowly walks towards Mrs. Rollins and Emma as they prepare to go to lunch. "Ok Asir, we are going to do better tomorrow, right?" Asir looks at his teacher with contempt, then shrugs his shoulders. Mrs. Rollins escorts Asir towards the edge of the classroom while Emma asks Springle one more question. "Is there any way you can give me a sheet of paper and some crayons?" "Sure, why?" Mrs. Springle asks. "I think I know a way to break through to him." "Sure. I appreciate you volunteering." Emma receives several sheets of paper and crayons, then meets up with Mrs. Rollins and Asir.

As they walk towards the lunchroom, Mrs. Rollins introduces Asir to Emma. "Now Asir, we have someone special for you. I want you to meet Emma. She is going to be your mentor." Asir continues to show his noncompliant nature as he walks alongside them. Emma musters up the courage to speak to make her presence known. "Hi Asir, I'm glad to meet you." Asir looks at Emma: peering through her like a microscope, seemingly looking for any flaw or part that signals a reason to mistrust his new mentor. After looking at Emma for a few seconds, he looks forward and responds softly. "It's nice to meet you too," Asir says while avoiding eye contact. Taken back by this behavior, Mrs. Rollins tries to comprehend the new attitude from Asir. "Wow, he's usually non-verbal to new people. I think this may work out great."

The trio makes it to the lunchroom. Mrs. Rollins gives Asir final instructions. "Ok Asir, go ahead and grab your lunch. Emma will be right here so that you can eat together. Ok?" "Sure, whatever" Asir says while avoiding eye contact. Mrs. Rollins doesn't overstep her luck as Asir gets in line for lunch. "Thank you once again, and if you need anything let me know." Mrs. Rollins assures. "No problem." Emma responds.

As Mrs. Rollins walks away, Emma looks on to Asir while dwelling in the thought of the interaction. "*I see. This child has Autism.*" Emma reaffirms, "*However, he also has something else. Something that is not a coincidence. I think the ancestors are trying to tell me something. I think I have a way for him to open up.*" After Asir grabs his lunch, he walks towards Emma as she escorts him to the tables at the mentor section.

Both Emma and Asir sit down. Asir wastes little time eating his food as if he hadn't had a meal in years. He acts oblivious to the fact that Emma is sitting next to him. Emma cautiously waits until he's ready to speak. Not knowing what to say, she instead decides to put her plan into action. While Asir finishes his food, Emma takes out the paper and crayons, then draws a picture.

Moments later, Asir notices that Emma is drawing. Feeling uncomfortable with this strange yet familiar behavior, Asir musters up the courage to break his shell. "Um… Miss," Asir asks, "What are you drawing?" Emma smiles and shows Asir. "Oh this? This is a Phoenix. I like to draw too sometimes." "That's… very… pretty." Asir says slowly, "I like that color." "Oh, blue?" Emma asks. Then, Asir looks up with pure brown eyes hidden behind his thick glasses. Not wanting to open up too much, the very edges of his mouth curve up as he shakes his head up and down. "Blue is my favorite color." Asir says. "Me too." Emma says, "Do you want to draw with me?"

Asir couldn't hide his excitement as he smiled and shook his head yes. Then Emma gives him a sheet of paper while Asir grabs a crayon. "I want to show you something." Asir says as he quickly draws a picture. 2 minutes later, Asir shows Emma the picture. "Here you go… Miss." Asir says as his communication gets better. Emma examines the picture and is amazed at the artwork: a large red dragon with large horns, claws, wings, and it is spitting fire. "This is a great picture," Emma complimented, "You are a great artist." Asir proudly smiles, taking pride in his artwork.

Unfortunately, the bell is about to ring, and Mrs. Rollins comes in to inform Asir that lunch is almost over. "Ok Asir, lunch is almost over." Mrs. Rollins says, "Can you go throw your tray away?" Asir's demeanor quickly plummets, as if she was intruding in his space and good time. Asir gets up and throws his tray away. "So, how did it go between you too?" Mrs. Rollins asks. "Well, after we ate, we drew pictures." Emma responds, "He's very talented." "Yes, he is indeed." Mrs. Rollins adds.

Asir comes back and gets ready to go to his next class. As the bell rings, both Emma and Asir get up to address each other. "I really enjoyed our time together, Asir." Emma says. Asir takes his time to speak. "Are you coming back tomorrow?" Asir asks. "Well, Asir," Mrs. Rollins interjects, "Your mentor only meets once a week. You'll have to wait until then." Asir sulks as he refuses to make eye contact. Noticing this, Emma speaks. "Well, if it's alright with you. I wouldn't mind coming every day." Emma suggests, "It gives him something to look forward to." "Well, I'll have to call the agency to see if we can make an exception." Mrs. Rollins responds. As the last minutes transpire, Asir asks Emma one last question. "Miss… can I have your picture?" Emma looks at him and smiles, "Sure Asir. I'll sign my name so that you will always know who drew it." Emma signs her name and gives Asir the picture. He then puts it in his backpack, signs his name on his picture and gives it to Emma. "I want you to have this."

Emma takes the picture and thanks Asir. "Alright, well Asir, I'm going to escort you to your next class so that you won't be late." Mrs. Rollins directs. "Again Emma, thank you and someone will let you know if we can accommodate his request." Emma smiles and waves as Asir looks back, then walks towards his next class.

Emma gets in the Jeep, exhausted by the turn of events. She drives home and walks inside of the house. Geneva greets her granddaughter and asks about her day. "How did it go Amira?" "Well Grandma, today was interesting." Emma states as she slams her body on the couch, taking her sandals off and rubbing her feet. "Really, how so?" Geneva presses. "Well, this boy is Autistic, but I keep getting these sharp pains when I'm around him." "Mm Hm, go on child." "However, he has a talent. You won't believe what he drew me." "Let's see."

Emma takes out the picture and shows it to Geneva. Geneva smirks then look at Emma. "Do you see what I mean, Grandma?" Emma asks while trying to relax. "I think your senses are trying to tell you something. In due time, you will find that this boy has a lot more in common than you think." Geneva takes the picture and puts it on the refrigerator, sticking a magnet to keep it from falling. Afterwards, Emma sits down to rethink the interaction with Asir.

# Chapter 6: Parallel Routes

The plane is cruising at heights of over 30,000 ft in the air: floating effortlessly as the sound of air rushes through the jets and the calm prompts the passengers to relax for the long flight. Some order their service, while others take advantage of the new technology by plugging their headphones to watch media on the back of the seats.

Malik begins to feel sleepy after ordering a Meatloaf with mashed potatoes sauteed vegetables with a glass of red wine. *"Woo… this meal was delicious,"* he compliments, *"For a king. Sometimes you have to enjoy the small comforts in life."*

One of the Stewardess brings her tray, collecting trash, plates, or other undesirable items. Once she reaches Malik, she engages in a small conversation. "Sir are you finished with your plate?" she asked. Malik directs his attention to her and responds. "Yes ma'am." "Ok," she says, while collecting his plate and utensils, "How was your meal?" "It was very excellent. I haven't had a meal like that in a while." Malik addresses the employee. "Well sir, that is excellent to hear. I'm glad that you enjoyed the meal. If there is anything else we can do for you, let us know." Malik smiles and nods, prompting the Stewardess to continue with her route.

"I think I should take a nap," Malik suggests, "It's been a long morning and based on my timing, we still have about 3 hours to go before we reach London." So, Malik grabs a pillow and thin blanket from the compartment above his head. He adjusts his pillow by placing it behind his head. Afterwards, he wraps himself like a burrito while staring at the vastness of the cloudy skies. *"You know,"* he reflects, *"I can only… well understand the feeling my ancestors felt riding on the clouds like giant mattresses. The wind blowing in your face, the lack of limits to block your paths, and the feeling of reaching beyond is why I can imagine the resentment of someone not having that power."* As Malik closes his window, he concludes his thoughts. *"Well, one day, our people will be able to fly again, devoid of the restraints of gentrification, persecution, racism, and obliteration."*

Malik begins to close his eyes, allowing the musical harmony of jets crashing through the sky to perform the symphony of loud silence. Such sounds rock Malik to sleep like a baby, only taking as little as 5 minutes for him to be completely immersed in REM.

Several minutes later, images appear in Malik's self-conscious. There are several lights, ranging from neon yellow, green, orange, blue, and red. Swiftly, Malik finds himself flying through several realms and dimensions until he realizes that he is in a vision. *"Wow… I must either be dreaming or going through a vision,"* Malik reasons, *"However, this seems different."*

For several moments, Malik continues to journey through the road of lights until he reaches the epicenter of a larger sphere. When he stops, he is in awe of the corridor: the room has dark walls with several smaller lights that border seven doors, each door has several rows of light that stream up and down at the entrances, and at the ceiling, there is a continuous fire that burns brighter than the surface of the sun. "What is this place?" Malik asks as he continues to look around.

After several turns and looking around, smoke begins to form in the middle of the venue. Malik is drawn to the energy that forms the rigidness shape. Finally, out of the smoke, a pair of eyes form. These eyes mirror the Dracocernentia, but the features are less distinct, instead blended by two bright hues of gold on each side of the iris. Intrigued, Malik moves closer to get a better look.

"Welcome Dragon Moor." Surprised, Malik looks around, then looks at the eyes. *"Is it talking to me?"* he asks. "You are in the Clandestine Chamber. The epicenter of the Warriors of Time." *"Of course, he can read my mind,"* Malik realizes, "Who are you and what are you doing here?" "We are Hikma! The eyes of the Golden Dragon." it spoke, "We represent the Aleaqida of the Moors." "The Ale-what? First time I'm hearing this." "We will show you Dragon Moor."

The eyes illuminate, prompting Malik's Dracocernentia to activate without Malik's involvement. The eyes generate a giant projection, similar to a screen in a movie theater. As several images appear, Hikma narrates through the visions.

"Long ago, there was a being that traveled the stars, searching for a place to help contain the power it has contained. The being, known as the Ghyr Mahdud, was drawn to a blue planet with its vast resources and similar power in its body." "So, you're telling me he was an alien?" Malik asks. "Although limited in your understanding Dragon Moor, he did not originate from this world. However, this being comprises the dark matter that blankets all of existence." "I see; please continue."

Hikma now shows images of the being navigating to the dark continent. "About 6,000 of your years ago, the being landed in the Cradle of Life. The energy he felt was so strong it navigated his ship to pinpoint this seemingly isolated area in the vast world. When he landed, he searched the savannah to find the source of power. For days, he observed the beauty of the planet: from the mountains that seem impossible to form snow in such humid conditions to the magnetic and thermal impulses his sensitive feet can detect, to ultimately the vastness of the life that stretches to eternity." Hikma changes the images to show a beautiful woman staring at the stars.

"There was a woman, more beautiful than the combination of all of the flowers of the world, who would stare at the stars that rivaled her own complexion. She was always drawn to the vastness of the night sky, admiring its everlasting stretch. One day, her father was to find a suitable man to be her husband. However, no one could answer the question that has plagued his mind for many years." "WAIT, I KNOW THIS STORY!" Malik connects, "This is similar to the one that..." "Yes, Dragon Moor. As you know, the force that drew Ghyr Mahdud (The Unlimited) was the same woman who would peer through the stars. Although the story has been distorted through time, what is conclusive is that they did bore a set of twins." Then Hikma shows several images of the times as the family progresses through time.

"Now Dragon Moor, as the twins grew, the boy inherited the power of his father: tough skins, incredible strength, and eyes that glowed like fire. The girl inherited her mother's grace, wisdom, and beauty." "Wow… so my grandfather's tale…" Malik reflects as he continues to bear witness to this hidden history. "When the children grew up, both felt confined to the space of complacency and idleness. So, on their 21st spring, both journey down the mighty river to reach its mouth." "The river… *Could it be the Nile*?" "When the twins reached the mouth, they realized that they crossed a sea of desert that, despite the harsh conditions, bore treasure of opportunity, potential, and life. Each one had a different perspective on how to influence the world." "Influence the world? What do you mean?" Again, Hikma shows several images to convey his message.

"The woman believed that you could amplify the land by exploiting the most out of the resources in one land. By doing that, the world will see its glory and mirror the progress, emulating the epicenter like a galaxy. The man believed that you must spread your glory through travel and interaction; teaching as well as mentoring those who don't possess the knowledge." "So, what happened to them?" Malik asks, still ecstatic over the events of this vision. Images now show how the twins lived the rest of their lives. "The woman settled at the delta, expanding her empire along the coast and living out her ideologies by utilizing the limited resources to its full potential. She bore many children and passed down the wisdom she'd inherited from her parents. The man lived out his principles: spreading his beliefs of empowerment and resourcefulness, while absorbing the planet's energy through his dark skin. However, by absorbing the energy of the planet, he was able to expand his abilities, but when he bore children, they inherited something spectacular." "How so Hikma?"

As Hikma shows the last images, several visions of the man's descendants flood the visual plane. "One of his descendants was a man named Bodhi Dharma. He'd inherited the man's dark power, but he also had a strange ability. As he traveled through the forests, mountains, and grasslands, he observed the living organisms' movements, lifestyles, and life energy. Then, he decided to emulate the movements of those creatures, providing and documenting a vast amount of scrolls showcasing the techniques that will one day be called…" "Martial Arts!" Malik completes, "I think I know where you are going next." "Precisely Dragon Moor. This is the same man who was the only one capable, observing, then gaining the power of the most powerful animal in the land. This art was known as the most powerful, less perfected, and illusive of the arts. In time, the man's descendants, along with others, continued to travel around the world. Making their way to other continents, islands, and even remote areas in the farthest reaches of the Earth."

Hikma concludes his showing to impart lasting words of wisdom. "Dragon Moor, these forgotten warriors are the key to finding what you seek." "What I seek is the Harq Alqadr, a sword that can unite the people to fight against this oppression and end evil." "Be warned Dragon Moor; evil will never be eliminated. Like energy, everything is necessary for the balance of life. The object is important, but also understand that it is only a tool for a bigger machine. In time, you will understand."

Hikma's eyes dim, the smoke disappears, the voice reminds Malik of the meaning of the visions. "Remember Dragon Moor, the item you seek is only a small piece. Remember what you saw and take heed to what you have learned." Suddenly, Malik is transported to a tunnel of blinding lights, racing through the confines of his mind until he hears a sound.

"(DING)... Attention passengers, this is your captain speaking. We are about 20 minutes away from our destination. Please go back to your seats and buckle your safety belts. The Stewardess will walk around and assist you in any way. Please give them any trash or plates that you may have; we will be landing shortly, thank you." Malik wakes up to the announcement; meanwhile, he takes the time to regain his grasp on reality while preparing for the landing.

The fellow passengers take their last sips of wine and snacks as they approach the island. The roar of the engines signals the declination of altitude as Malik opens his window. Looking at the window, Malik sees the transition from the Atlantic Ocean to land, watching the plane flight through a scattered army of clouds. *"That was a wicked dream..."* he reflects, *"Rather a vision. What bothers me, is what Hikma mean by only a small piece to what I seek? Maybe this trip is more than just finding out the meaning of a picture. Still, I should be able to find some answers to this puzzle."*

Minutes later, the viewing of the bridge, tower, and the giant bell signal the arrival of one of the world's most recognizable and iconic cities. The captain begins to restate the protocol. "Ladies and Gentlemen, we will be landing in a few minutes. If you haven't done so, please ensure that you are in your seats with your belts on. Please do not get up until instructed to do so. Again, thank you for flying with us."

As the plane reaches the airspace, the pilot levels the plane, engaging the landing gear, and carefully eases the plane on the ground. The landing is bumpy like a rollercoaster ride, as the huge airplane slows down. Drowning the noise with the roar of the powerful jet engines, the flow of air rushes only moments later, seemingly following after chasing a vehicle traveling over 600 miles per hour. The plane then slows down and navigates towards one of the gates, being directed by a lone person with orange reflectors.

Once directed to the gate, the pilot then aligns the plane towards the parking area then makes a stop. After about a minute, the captain makes an announcement. "Ladies and Gentlemen, you may now gather your things as the plane has made a complete stop. Make sure nothing is left behind and that you have everything you need. Your luggage will be available to you once it's loaded in the terminal. Welcome to London, England and again, thank you for flying with us." Malik unbuckles his seatbelt, grabs his backpack, and gets up from his seat. After waiting a while, he walks out of the plane, smiles at the employees, then makes his first steps on the journey of new discovery.

# Chapter 7: Dark Presence

Malik makes his way towards the terminal to obtain his luggage. While walking around the airport, Malik takes his time to check out some of the local stands. He enters a newstand with several books, snacks, and other appliances. "Good day sir," the cashier welcomes, "may I interest you with something?" "Oh, I'm just looking for right now ma'am." "Jolly good, take your time."

Feeling a little famished, Malik looks for some items to snack on. While looking around, Malik is suddenly drawn to an unusual magazine. The cover of the magazine shows pictures of royal figures of the past. Normally, Malik would attribute such magazines as misinformed versions of history; however, this cover had black faces. "*Huh*," Malik thought, "*I don't normally see figures like this. Or at least not documented.*" Malik decides to pick up the magazine and flip through the pages. He is astonished to see several examples of black monarchs on the Island.

"It says here that many rulers of England, Scotland, and Ireland can trace their ancestors back to the dark continent." Malik reads, "For example, Charles II was known for his dark complexion and long kinky hair. Charlotte of Mecklenburg-Strelitz was known to be painted white to hide the features less admirable by the British courts. *I've heard of these figures but never imagined that they would be forthright with the information. I need to find Hauss' colleague.*"

Malik closes the magazine, grabs a bag of potato chips, a drink, then walks towards the cashier.

"Ah, fancy that book, do ya?" she asks while scanning the items. "Yes, I'm a bit of a history buff. I especially enjoyed the section about Charlotte of Mecklenburg." "Yes, indeed sir," she responded, "The queen was a charm: would add new plants to the garden, enjoyed the opera, and was proper until the very end." After scanning the items, she clarifies the price of the items. "I'll be 48 pounds sir." "Alright, here we go," Malik responds while handing her his black card.

After scanning the card, the cashier prints the receipt, puts the items in a plastic bag, then hands it to Malik. "Here you go sir, you have a merry one," she smiles. "You too ma'am."

As Malik walks out of the store and out of visibility, the cashier mysteriously takes out her cell phone to text. Few moments go by; the phone makes a sound in response as the cashier grins.

Malik then makes his way towards the Hertz counter. There, several long lines of people await their rentals despite being late in the day. To pass the time, Malik takes out his cell phone and begins to call Emma.

"Ring… Ring… Ring… Hey bro. How was your flight?" Emma answered. "Long. I don't care if you're riding 1st class or coach; sitting down for several hours is rough," Malik says, "However, the food was good." "Betcha boogie ass had lobster and wine." "Close… it was Meatloaf." "Meatloaf," Emma retorts, "(Sigh) I don't get you sometimes. I would've had lobster, a steak, or a Polar Bear rib in first class."

Feeling the conversation going nowhere, Malik quickly switches the topic. "Well anyway, how are things back home?" "Well, you know today was my first day volunteering for the school mentoring troubling kids." "Ah yeah," Malik remembers, "The Big Sister Foundation. So how did it go?" "Well," Emma reflects, "today was interesting. I was assigned to an unusual boy who, despite being bright, is introverted, emotionless, and content with little association." "Sounds like someone on the spectrum." "Yeah, but that's not all. I started getting these sharp pain headaches around him; it's like his energy is prompting me." "Sure, you're not just nervous," Malik assures, "I mean, I know what it feels like to try to reconnect with your people."

Then, Emma switched her tone to a serious one, emphasizing the coincidence that would raise suspicion.

"Malik, he had this thing for dragons. I mean, he would literally draw several pictures of dragons." "Ok," Malik responds unconvincingly, "A lot of kids have a thing for dragons and dinosaurs." "But none who could draw the same ones in our visions. I asked him to draw a dragon; it was red, had big horns and large wings. It was incredible." Malik pauses for a moment. When he takes into consideration that the Moors had the ability to absorb and detect energy, he no longer takes light of the encounter. So, he proceeds to give Emma some advice.

"Emma, listen to me. I think this boy may have similar ancestry as us." "How do you know bro?" Emma asks. "Trust me because it's not something that I can easily explain. Continue to mentor him and be there for him. I have a feeling that he may have the potential to possess something special." "Sure bro, well get some rest and call me later when you find out more from Dr. Adebayo." "Alright, Emma. Tell our grandparents hello and that I love all of you. Remember to be sensitive to what you don't see." "Likewise, asswipe. Later (Click)" Malik hangs up the phone as he gets closer to the counter. *"I have this uncomfortable feeling that I am being watched,"* Malik suspects, *"Yet, no one has made a move or stirred up trouble. Maybe it's my nerves trying to stay sharp from months without action. Still, I need to be careful."*

Malik is next in line at the counter. A young man, about the same age as Malik but clean-cut, short brown hair, and skinny calls out the next customer.

"Can I help the next gent in line, please?" he asks. Malik boldly walks towards the counter with his luggage and backpack. "Good evening, sir; welcome to Hertz International. How may I help you?" "Hey there," Malik responds, "My name is Malik Wilson and I have a reservation." "Alright sir, let me look at the list."

The young man types on his computer while searching through the manifest. "Ah hah," he states, "I have you right here Mr. Wilson. Seems that you are one of our Gold Members. Let me print you your receipt." "Thank you."

Malik patiently waits as the associate finalizes his contract while grabbing a set of keys. Moments later, the associate inserts the contract and keys in a brochure. "Alright then sir, seems that you are aware of the conditions of the rental?" "Yes sir." "Quite good. Now your vehicle will be parked in lot F10. It will be out the double doors towards your left." "Thanks, have a good one." "You too sir."

Malik grabs the keys, brings his luggage, then walks towards the double doors. Meanwhile, the young man takes out his cell phone and awaits for Malik to reach the doors. After reaching the doors, the man sends a mysterious text on the phone, waits for a sound to confirm the response, then grins suspiciously.

Walking into the cool, damp, and dark parking lot, Malik begins his long trek towards the assigned lot. "Whew," Malik exclaims, "this place is kind of creepy. *If I didn't have powers, I could see Dracula or the Werewolf jumping out right now.*" Again and again, Malik continues to walk down several isles until he reaches F. Then, he counts down to the 10th spot on the row.

Upon reaching his car, he is pleasantly surprised by the assignment. "Well Jason," he says, "It may not be a Hellcat, but she purrs just as loud." Malik gazes upon a brand new 2022 Dodge Charger R/T 392. The stunning black car shines in the damp lot as Malik begins to load his belongings in the trunk.

As soon as he's done, he gets in the car, steps on the brake, and pushes the start button. "It's starting to get late." he assesses, "I need to get to the hotel, rest up, and prowl the streets. I think Shadowmoor deserves to stretch his legs as well."

Then, with a heavy step, the powerful Hemi engine roars awake. Feeling the vibration of the powerful machine, Malik inserts the address of the hotel he made reservations for in his GPS. Then he plots his course as he makes his way out of the garage and into the busy, congested streets of London.

As he navigates through the busy streets, Malik is somewhat reminded of the life he left behind in the states. "In one way," he reflects, this is like Atlanta (which reminds me of why I avoid driving most of the time). *However, I feel a sense of overwhelming presence here, as if all the world's history congregates to this spot.*" Malik drives, as he sees the people walking around pubs and tea shops, tourists taking pictures of historical spots; then, when making his way towards the bridge, Malik can see the Tower as well as Parliament. "Well, the famous clock right before my eyes," Malik says, "I'll have to send Emma and Renee a shot before I leave."

Malik reaches the hotel at eight-thirty pm. The structure is somewhat grand: red brick coats the building with white shutters, white-walled windows, and cream-colored marble pillars. As Malik pulls up, he is greeted by valet. "Good evening, sir; welcome to our hotel. Our Valet service is customary to our guests." he says. "Sure, give me a second to unload the car." Malik instructs, while grabbing his backpack. Malik unlocks the trunk, unloads his baggage then addresses the valet attendant. "Here you go." Malik says, leaving the keys in the car. "Whenever you are ready, keep your reservation slip, then we will bring it out for you." Malik nods and smirks as he walks into the building.

Malik takes a moment to look around the f bh77oyer, appreciating the elegance of the tapestry, the rustic pictures on the wall, and the smell of rosemary and sage from the plants. "Well, it may not be the Marriott," Malik admits, "but it does feel like a home so far."

Malik begins to walk towards the counter. Then he is greeted by an unusual young woman: she is chocolate completed, with no make-up, deep brown eyes, and hair as thick as a bush put in a bun. Her smile is as welcoming as her words.

"Oh, hello there," she addresses, "welcome to our hotel. My name is Obioma. How can I help you?" "Yes," Malik responds, "My name is Malik Wilson. I have a reservation." "Certainly, let me pull you up in the system." Obioma begins to hum while she types on the computer, prompting Malik to spark up a conversation.

"Obioma is a pretty name." Malik compliments. Blushing, Obioma temporarily stumbles before catching herself. "Well thank you," she added, "My mother and father are Nigerian. They tell me that my name means kind-hearted." "Well, I think they picked a perfect name." Obioma continues to chuckle and blush, as she prints out Malik's reservation.

"Ok Mr. "Charmer", your room is 2510. It's upstairs to the right. You can't miss it." "Much obliged, Obioma. I hope to see you again and thank you." "My pleasure Mr. Charmer." "Please, call me Malik." She nods as Malik makes his way upstairs to his room.

After reaching his room, Malik grabs his keys and unlocks the door. As he enters the room, he takes in the feel of the otherwise antique style room: the drawers are polished with dark brown Mahogany wood, the bathroom has a small, white, ceramic tub, and the scent is flooded with potpourri of Plumeria, Lavender, and Vanilla. Immediately, Malik feels at home as he unloads his luggage and organizes his belongings.

Afterwards, Malik takes a quick shower to wash away the stench of travel while reaffirming his plan of action. "This journey does take quite a bit of energy", Malik reflects, "However, I sense something is off, like a dark cloud circling before a tornado. When the night takes over the sky, I think Shadowmoor should take a look around." The suds from his body wash collect the minute particles from his drenched skin as Malik washes his hair, face, and beard.

Malik steps out of the shower, dries himself off, then puts on his iconic jeans and sneakers. Before heading out on the streets, Malik decides to turn on the TV to watch some shows. While grabbing his leather jacket, Malik has a sudden sharp pain in his head. The intensity of the pain prompts him to sit down on the bed.

*"Man!"* Malik complains, *"This feeling hurts, what is going on?"* While he massages the right side of his head, his Dracocernentia activates, revealing several images of dark figures with glowing yellow, green, and blue eyes, a burning sword, and a silhouette of a giant Golden Dragon. The Dragon had eyes of fiery, reddish-orange eyes, teeth as shiny as ivory, 2 protruding horns, and a series of bumps aligning the spikes on its back. Inside of the dragon is a silhouette of a man with no features, lines, nor face to match. "Ugh, here we go again with these visions." Malik thinks as he gets himself together, *"Whenever I get these visions, it must mean that the energy in this area is a conduit to something hidden."*

As night plunges deeper into darkness, the city levels the noise; meanwhile, Malik puts on his iconic leather jacket then walks towards the window. Malik begins to put his hood on, then whispers his thoughts. "It's time for Shadowmoor to seek out the darkness, with the light."

With eyes glowing and teeth sharpened, Shadowmoor emerges from his hibernation to patrol the streets of London. Quickly, he climbs out of the window and up the hotel building. He surveys the city lights as he prepares to patrol the streets.

Swiftly, he maneuvers throughout the rustic buildings, utilizing his elevated speed and new mastery of his powers. Since the battle with the Elite 8 members, Shadowmoor can now amass energy by absorbing the sun's rays throughout the day while using the stored energy during engagements. His vision has also improved, enabling him to see some receptor fields even when the Dracocernentia isn't activated for a limited time. Lastly, Shadowmoor can adjust his body temperature, breathing, and energy consumption as a means to conserve stamina. Called reptile mode, Shadowmoor can rely solely on the sun if the battle or engagement occurs on days with the temperature being above 85° Fahrenheit.

Shadowmoor approaches the deep sections of the ghettos; then he senses a disturbance. A young woman walking home from her job is suddenly screaming. "I hear someone screaming in the distance", Shadowmoor deduces, "I need to hurry to help her." With an elevated sense of hearing, Shadowmoor races towards the source of the disturbance.

# Chapter 8: The Line of Protection

The alley is cool, dark, and damp. The flickering city lights do not reveal the horrors that await the young woman. She is another immigrant from Nigeria, walking home after a day of working and studying. The sweat from her scalp runs down her face like terror, her breathing is as inconsistent as rain in a desert, and the uncertainty of her attacker almost has her paralyzed.

Five men in black cloaks and masks surround the woman while two other men rush to restrain her. Shadowmoor catches up to the source and sees the young woman from a short distance. "*Wait a minute*," Shadowmoor states, "I recognize those receptors. *Seems that these guys run deep, even here.*" Shadowmoor sees the dark blue with some traces of red receptors filling the assailants' bodies.

Meanwhile, one of the goons grabs the woman and attempts to cover her mouth with his hand. The other attempt to tie the struggling victim down with rope while gagging her with a dirty piece of cloth.

Like lightning in a bottle, Shadowmoor crashes down to engage the men. From a short distance, the two men and the woman become shocked to see a man in a hood, with eyes glowing like a predator. The full majesty of the Dracocernentia and its wielder blind the men from their arrogance, replacing it with dismay and uncertainty.

"Who are you?" one of the assailants commands, "Stay back or by God, we will kill her." The victim tries to scream through the other's hand with muffled sounds and a wide-open gaze.

Before Shadowmoor could react, a sudden mist fills the alley. Thick with humidity and just as non-revealing as the night, certain sounds randomly spice the air with agonizing grunts followed by modulation of collapse. The movement and the commotion are so fast that Shadowmoor could only see the remnants of a strange trail left by the unknown being.

*"What in the world is going on here?"* Shadowmoor ponders, *"I don't see whoever is taking these guys out, but I can see a trail that looks like…"* Then, before he could piece together the events unfolding, the last goon is left standing with his petrified victim. The man begins to shake like a rattler's tail; meanwhile, the woman has become less frightened but more perplexed about what has happened in what seems to be seconds.

As soon as the mist gives way to the remaining party, a suspicious figure appears adjacent to the people left standing.

"You seem out of place, mate. Perhaps you should just quit while you're ahead." The goon looks feverishly around, drowning his hostage with sweat and angst. "What… who… are you…?" he questions while continuing to search around.

Shadowmoor calms himself down, realizing that this mysterious person has a familiar link to it. *"I can sense something analogous about this…these receptors…"* he ponders before getting interrupted by the same voice.

"You might want to let me take care of this, Yank." the voice requests, "The streets and the night are mine domain to protect."

Suddenly, Shadowmoor's Dracocernentia ignites, revealing the mystery man who took down the men in a flash. He appears right behind Shadowmoor as he walks towards the man and the immigrant.

He is an average height man: about 5'11'', with tan-colored skin, a defined strong posture, and thick long dreads down his back. His intimidating look is only overshadowed by his overt confidence; as he walks past Shadowmoor to confront the now, terrified man. *"I don't believe it,"* Shadowmoor confirms, *"He too processes the Dracocernentia… but how?"*

Sensing the influx of questions downing Shadowmoor's mind, the arrogant Moor addresses everyone in the vicinity.

"I suggest you stay put and enjoy the show. " He says, "And as for you chap, best you let her go before you burn as a parting gift to hell." "You...you don't scare me with your…"

Before the man could finish his threat, the strange man moves effortlessly next to the man. He grabs hold of his shoulder and begins to heat up his hand, causing the man to release the woman while yelling in anguish. "You see, had you bloody listened to me, your skin wouldn't smell like burning tar." The stench of skin could only be matched with the sight of a man literally burning to death. Shadowmoor could only stand in absolute astonishment as the other kidnapper ran in horror. The young woman looks intensely and shockingly at her rescuer.

"Go on then eh," the warrior conveys, "You're safe now. Run along."

Sparing no wasted time, the woman wipes the sweat from her brow, gets up from the dirty street, and runs towards the lighted streets of the city.

Before Shadowmoor could utter a word, the mysterious Moor quickly shifts his attention towards the bewildered hero. His overconfidence is only overshadowed by his long dreads blowing with the mild wind along with his definite stature. Finally, he whispers something, which elevates Shadowmoor's suspicion.

"We'll meet again, mate." he says calmly, "Until then, keep your eyes open and your mind vast...Shadowmoor..." "*Wait a minute*," Shadowmoor ponders, "*How did he...*"

Before Shadowmoor could complete his thought, the strange Moor blew out a thick blanket of smoke from his lips. The unusual smog clogged Shadowmoor's senses and surprisingly blocked his vision. "Ugh," he complains, "Normally I could see through most objects, but there's something about this smoke...and this guy."

As the smoke clears, Shadowmoor is left alone in the secluded alley. The music of distant cars and steps of unsuspecting people clear out the residue of the action that just occurred. Shadowmoor looks around to see if he could find any trace or receptors of the man he just encountered, only to find nothing but the surrounding signs of London's nightlife.

"Heh," he realizes, "I was foolish to think I was the only one, but he's right. I will see him again." Shadowmoor makes his way towards the top of the building. As he stealthily ascends to the skyline and briefly looks back with eyes of conviction with the feeling of acceptance. "something tells me that the world has become bigger...and darker. I need to rest so that I can find Adebayo in the morning." Afterwards, Shadowmoor concludes his patrol by slowly making his way back to his hotel room window. Making sure no one sees him; he enters the room and takes off his hood.

Malik slams his butt on the comfortable bed, gives a big huff, then recollects his thoughts.

"That guy clearly had the Dracocernentia and was wickedly powerful," he ponders, "Yet, he knows who I am and was able to create smoke that blocked my vision." Malik takes off his jacket, folds it up, then places it underneath some clothes in his suitcase. He paces back and forth slowly from wall to wall in his room; meanwhile, he pieces together some clues to help him better come up with a plan. "In the morning, I am going to make my way to Middlesex University to talk to Dr. Adebayo. It'll be difficult to convince him without revealing my powers. *For some reason, I still feel like I'm being watched.*" Malik walks towards the window to stare at the skyline one last time. He forces himself to put aside his anxieties to rest as he closes the window, turns off the lights, and covers himself in the sheets before falling asleep.

Several meters away from the hotel, the same woman who was evading capture makes herself to a dark section of the nearby ally. She catches her breath before reaching for her phone.

As she scrolls down through her listings, she punches a number and awaits a response while the phone rings.

"Yes dear," the voice says after picking up on the other line. "It was just as you said," she responds, "There was a man who rescued me and killed one of the attackers." "So, the Moor continues to protect the streets in the cover of night. Interesting…" The woman then begins to add more to the event to the unknown acquaintance.

"However, there was another in the scene. A man wearing a hood and mask." "What difference does it ma…" the caller sneers before being interrupted. "He too had the eyes, but he didn't seem to be working with the Moor. It was as if… I don't…"

Suddenly, the conversation switches to a more shrewd and calming tone. "My dear, this is a rather interesting development. Thank you for your help. I'll make sure that you get what's coming to you." the caller says before ending the conversation, "Now go home and leave this matter to us." "For you control the destiny of men, Daddy!" She concludes, then she hangs up before heading home.

Several blocks away, a charming man looks at his phone then begins to chuckle to himself. "Is everything ok, Daddy?" a voice asks. "Nothing dear, just one of my undercovers gathering intel. We must prepare for this new...Moor. I suspect he will lead us to the sword and, with it, complete dominance of this incompetent world."

The man takes a glass filled halfway with Crown Royal Cognac and sips it. Then he ends the night foreshadowing the events to come. "So, the adopted son of William Benson has taken the bait. It's a shame that such a decently adequate mind ended up on the wrong side," he pauses before taking one last sip, "Now, we'll sit back and wait for him to lead us to the greatest weapon the Moors ever constructed… and finally finish what we started 500 years ago."

Then the man puts his glass on the table and looks over the city as the sun prepares to arise from its slumber.

# Chapter 9: The English Moor

Such as it is in the world, the adventures, activity, and secrets of the night begin to migrate to their slumber as the night relinquishes its place for the morning sun. Still jet-lagged from the day before; Malik reluctantly looks at his cell phone.

"Ugh," he complains, "It's only a quarter til 6. I can't believe I got only a few hours' sleep at best." Sluggishly, Malik maneuvers his 6'2'' frame out of the sheets, then sits on the edge of the bed to contemplate the events that burn his mind like a match to old paper.

"That guy had the same eyes as I did. I can't stop thinking about that." Malik slowly gets up and walks towards the bathroom. *"Could it be...that there are more of me... us out there? I'll have to put that possibility aside for the moment. I need to get ready to go."*

Malik takes his clothes off, enters the tub, arranges the shower curtains, then turns on the nobs. As the water rushes down his leathery skin, the judicious hero stares at oblivion; meanwhile, his silence conveys the emotions and concerns of the inability to accurately predict the path of this new discovery. Washing away the dirt of cluelessness, Malik allows himself to commemorate the journey from social outcast to hero, smiling to himself to reassure that he is more than capable of any outcome. "Well, even if these eyes can't see the future, my desire to understand who we were is burning. I'm ready to see what the professor can tell me."

Seconds later, Malik turns off the faucets, steps out of the tub, then reaches for his towel. He then begins his morning routine: putting his boxer briefs on, lotioning his body, then putting on a pair of jeans while sliding his feet in his Adidas. Then, confidently, Malik brushes his teeth, washes his face, applies tree tea oil to his hair before brushing the sides of his recently cut fade. "Alright," Malik confirms, "I'll stop by the lobby to grab a bite to eat before I head out to Middlesex University." Afterwards, Malik puts on a neatly fitted white polo collared shirt, grabs his cellphone backpack, and heads out of his room.

Malik descends the stairs towards the lobby, where a cater of freshly prepared breakfast items grace his presence with the aroma of nutrition and good health. While grabbing pieces of apples, mandarins, grapes, kiwi, and mangoes while mixing them in a bowl, Malik completes his breakfast by selecting a cup of black tea. He sits down in the lobby enjoying his breakfast when something catches his eye.

Obioma makes her way towards the counter to see how the guests are doing. Seemingly ignoring everyone else, she nonchalantly walks around the lobby, ascertaining the few guests' mood getting accustomed to the morning mist.

"Good morning, sir, is everything alright?" she asks a man sipping his coffee while reading his newspaper. Although nodding, he avoids eye contact and resumes his reading.

Slowly she makes her way to Malik as he concludes his brief breakfast.

"And you, Mr. Malik," she flirtatiously speaks, "How was your night?" Malik wipes his mouth with a napkin then answers her with a calm and leveled tone. "Very good, thank you. The view is beautiful and peaceful. I think I'm going to like it here." "Well, London is very nice outside," she responds. "Well yes, but I wasn't talking about London, at least not entirely."

Obioma blushes for a bit, letting out a small squeak before covering her mouth with the tip of her fingertips. Malik gets up and disposes of his bowl in the trash. "Well, I have a busy day," Malik finishes, "Have a good one Obioma." "You too, Mr. Malik," Obioma responds, embarrassed by her lack of civility.

Malik walks down towards the valet, waiting for his rental to arrive. Still, the events of last night leave Malik pondering the possibilities of the information he may uncover.

*"I still can't get over the fact that there was someone else who processes the Dracocernentia,"* Malik contemplates, *"I don't know if Dr. Adebayo will comprehend, let alone speak to me about the Harq Alqadr."*

Suddenly, the rumble of the Hemi engine interrupts Malik's train of thought while disturbing the normal silence of the rustic block. The valet, a short man with light brown hair, clean-shaven face, and blue eyes, steps out of the car's driver side. "Here you go mate," he addresses Malik while exchanging his tip. "Enjoy your day sir," he finishes with his soft English accent. Malik nods as he enters the Charger.

While cruising around the aged streets, there is a level of history as well as a premonition that seems to be as subtle as the air. There are old buildings, pubs, and landmarks that blend in with the harbingers of modern society: such as Starbucks, McDonalds, and Nike stores. The route to Middlesex seems to show a colonial and empirical history timeline. "Wow," Malik observes, "growing up, we were always taught about the history of our country, as well as the ones that influence it. It's somewhat hard, yet not surprising, that this country contributed to so much modernization and death in the world." Malik continues as he quickly approaches the parking lot of Middlesex. He quickly concludes his thoughts before parking his car. "Well, *I'm here; it's time for me to look for the good Dr.*"

Malik gets out of the car and starts to walk towards the Antique structured buildings. Middlesex is like the university Malik attended back home: filled with students from many races, cultures, or religions, shrouded with buildings, some being more than 100 years old, and the social atmosphere different from the one he was accustomed to back in Georgia Tech. *"There is a lot of people here, just walking to their classes,"* Malik ponders, *"However, they seem to be oblivious to the stream of evil flowing around the globe."* Some students give him a friendly nod while others ignore Malik. Meanwhile, Malik pulls out his cell phone to quickly search the whereabouts of Dr. Adebayo.

Several minutes later, Malik comes across his profile on the university website. "Let's see. It says here that Dr. Adebayo is currently the head of the cultural research department." he states while scrolling, "I see that based on his schedule, he is finishing one of his lectures at the college building next to the Sheppard Library."

Carefully screening the scene, Malik slightly activates his right Dracocernentia to see the buildings. *"Ok, looks like the library is about 100 yards due north. So, chances are the building on the left must be where his lecture hall is located."* Malik releases his Dracocernentia then lets out a large exhale. "Well, here goes nothing." Malik proceeds to head in the direction of the building.

10 minutes later, Malik walks up the steps of the building. He enters through the large doors then meanders through the thin crowd. Suddenly, he hears a voice in the distance finishing his lecture. Like a moth to a flame, Malik curiously walks towards the source of the distinguished voice.

"Now, as we conclude the day, let us remember that not all...dark complexions only existed in Africa." the charismatic professor concludes. "Even in our own monarchy, there have been figures with African ancestry…" Malik stands in the doorway as he listens in, reminiscing his college times while awaiting his chance. A white female student with long highlighted blond hair and red plastic glasses raises her hand. "So, why then do we do not honor these so-called monarchs?" she asks.

Before the professor can answer, he looks at his watch to confirm that time is up. "Well, my dear, that will be a discussion for the next lecture." he responds, "Ok class is dismissed." All the students gather their belongings, wrestle their bags, then proceed to walk out of the lecture hall. Malik awaits as the last remnants of his class walk out of the lecture hall.

The professor is a very impassive man: standing at around 5'10 tall, with a grey cotton blazer, maroon pinstriped shirt, brown slacks and multi-colored necktie. As he collects his notes to insert them into his briefcase, he slightly notices Malik slowly walking towards him. The professor, not paying too much mind, responds in a stern tone.

"If you have any questions about the business of the class, we can address them during my office hours." Malik calmly addresses the professor with discernment and confidence. "No sir, I'm not one of your students. Are you Dr. Winston Baker-Adebayo?" The man looks up and gives Malik an inquisitive stare. His disposition reeks of annoyance while he tries to hold in his impatience. "What is your business with me?" he scolds boldly, "I am a busy man."

Malik opens his backpack and shows Dr. Adebayo the picture. The disgruntled professor briefly glances at the picture before stopping in his tracks. The once apathetic scholar begins to shake like a palm tree in a hurricane, trying desperately to maintain his composure before addressing the picture.

"I...I cannot help you young man" Adebayo yelps, desperately trying to gather his things. Persistent, Malik attempts to grab his arm to re-engage the request. "Dr. Adebayo, please?" Malik pleads, "This is very important. I need to…" Adebayo snatches his arm then responds harshly to Malik. "What you are asking is not worth seeking. I suggest you leave me be and go back to where you come from."

Refusing to give up, Malik continues by standing in front of Dr. Adebayo. Before Adebayo can force his way, Malik quickly grabs the distraught teacher and forces him to pay attention.

"Dr. Adebayo, I need your help and I am not going until you tell me about this photo!" Malik then activates his Dracocernentia, causing the professor to quiver with bemusement and intrigue. What seems like an eternity has turned the next full moments into clarity, in which Dr. Adebayo has allowed himself to calm down while realizing the glory of his eyes.

"My god…" he whispers, "So… you are a… descendant…" "My name is…" "Malik… Malik Wilson," Adebayo interrupts, "or should I say… Shadowmoor." Startled, Malik begins to turn his eyes back to his normal brown hue. Dr. Adebayo smirks nervously as he gathers his briefcase and instructs Malik. "Come with me, my boy. We need to talk about that photo."

Relieved, Malik follows Dr. Adebayo towards his office. During the walk, the professor becomes more forthcoming with some information explaining his knowledge of the young entrepreneur. "You were close friends with Professor Hauss, yes" Adebayo debriefs. "Yes… Yes sir. When did he tell me about me… and my, you know?" "Heh, heh, heh. Hauss and I have been colleagues for nearly 30 years. We first met when he was completing his doctorate thesis on the Moorish influence in post-Roman Europe." "I see" Malik responds, "So you were aware of his work?" "(Sigh). In some ways, I felt responsible for him losing his tenure. The artifacts that I've been able to recover proved the existence of more than just black people. I lost contact with him until about a year ago." "A year ago?" Malik asks in shock before making it to Adebayo's office.

Adebayo opens the door, puts his briefcase on his desk, then motions Malik to have a seat. While Malik sits down, Adebayo begins to grab several books, pictures, and other documents to present to his favorable guest.

"Here, Malik," the professor continues, "What you seek is the Burning Destiny. A legendary sword held by the greatest of your kind, the Golden Dragon Moors." "Golden Dragon Moors?" Malik probes. "Much like you but different. You see, only a few men from special lineages through anonymous generations had the ability to lead the people with this sword." Adebayo explains while showing the pictures of different ancient art. Each of the photos shows a legion of dark cloaked men led by a golden dragon holding a sword. Malik's curiosity creates a child-like atmosphere, peering into the photos like a lens through the lost pages of time.

“I can't believe that such documents still exist,” Malik continues, “So what is it about this sword that is so sought after? And why did Hauss keep this secret?” Adebayo lets off a long sigh. He sits down in his large, leather chair, staring at the wall filled with awards and degrees while searching for the words to say. Malik suddenly becomes concerned with the long, drawn-out silence. “Dr. Adebayo…” “Malik, the sword had the power to unify a mass of people. The great Moor Riaahn and his Dhahabi encountered a group of men. Unlike others who were inspired to learn from the advances of the Moors. These men wanted to use the knowledge to control and enslave men.” “Who are these men?” Malik asks. “They go by many names: Templars, Shining Knights, the Elites…” “The Elites,” Malik exclaimed, “*Is it possible…*” “Yes, young man,” Adebayo continues, “but their accepted name was known as the Dragon Slayers!”

Both men sit to digest the wealth of information being presented. Malik puts the pieces in his mind as Adebayo concludes his commentary.

“Rumor has it that the leader had to have a specific line to lead.” “A line...you mean lineage,” Malik inquires. “Yes, are you familiar with the Visigoths?” Malik squints his eyes and nods in confirmation. “Well, there was a ruler named Roderic. He ruled the area called Andalusia during the early 8th century. Then in the battle of Guadalete, he lost his life when he encountered your ancestors.” “That's right,” Malik remembers, “I remember seeing a few visions of the battle.” “Indeed, but he supposedly had a mistress that bore him a child. Malik, I cannot speak of such things beyond this point. These men have eyes and ears everywhere. Hauss knew this but refused to deny the truth. In the end, they ruined his career and…” “I know…” Malik remorsefully interrupts before getting up, “Thank you Dr. Adebayo, for the information.”

Dr. Adebayo gets up to escort Malik out of the office, then gives Malik one more piece of information. “What I can say is that the Moors mobilized their forces in northern Africa. It's also where the sword was forged. Find the source, then maybe you can find the location of the sword.” Malik smiles as he exits the office.

Filled with a new sense of hope and optimism, Malik strolls through the buildings towards the parking lot. As he reaches the parking lot, smoke from an undisclosed location comes towards Malik. Shocked and suspicious, Malik stops to see where the smoke is coming from.

*"This is weird. I don't see any fires, no alarms, Nothing."* Malik activates his Dracocernentia to scan the area. Somehow, the smoke blinds his vision like before. Suddenly, a familiar voice echoes across the lot with a cryptic message.

"So, this is the infamous Shadowmoor from America eh" it continues while remaining concealed, "yet still hasn't mastered his powers. You should've been able to pick up where I am." Concerned, Malik remains on guard while trying to figure out what's going on. "Are you following me? Who are you?" "Heh, heh, heh. You know it is really ironic what you are looking for..."

With a quick gust of wind, the smoke blows away and standing right in front of Malik is the same strange man he met the night before. Still arrogant and overconfident, the English Moor smiles and Malik is surprised that he is standing before him. "It's a good thing you're not the enemy, mate. Otherwise, it would've been a bit of a mop-up eh..." A single sweat goes down Malik's forehead and down his cheek. He nervously chuckles a bit before he re-engages the conversation.

"Wow," he reveals, "I didn't expect you to see you real soon. And how is it that you know my name?" "Well mate, it's about the same as you can identify the intentions of your enemies. However, you never allowed yourself to calm down long enough to see in my eyes." "In your eyes..." Malik retorts, *"wait a minute..."* Malik slowly closes his eyes to refocus his energy and the Moor continues to smile in anticipation. "Are you going to open your eyes, or should I read you a bedtime story?" he says sarcastically. Then Malik responds by opening his eyes, peering into the eyes of the imprudent companion. As their eyes link up, they have telepathically transported in the mental veils that project information like a movie. There, the Moor begins to communicate.

"The name's Bakala. London is my protectorate, and my Fire Line has been here for about 300 years." (Flashes continue as images of certain people flood the plane) Malik continues to look in aye as Bakala continues with his introduction. "My Line was the direct bodyguard to her majesty Charlotte of Mecklenburg, a descendant of the Royal Phoenix line from Portugal. Her mastery of the human body, medicine and botany made her a reliable asset to George III." "*Fascinating*," Malik tries to comprehend while witnessing the events unfold.

"However, when Queen Charlotte died, the involvement of the English Moors was relegated to obscurity in an attempt to diminish their contributions while distancing from their black royal lineage." The visions of Bakala continue while he concludes his introduction.

"Since then, we continue to work in the shadows, such as yourself, to fight for the freedom of our race."

As the vision concludes, both men disengage their Dracocernentia while debriefing the vision. "So, you see mate, as Moors, we have the ability to see into the past and present with our eyes. Apparently, you were not taught this from your parents." Malik lets off a small sigh while responding to Bakala. "Well, you see, I didn't… well" "That's right mate, I saw" Bakala interrupted with empathy, "I'm terribly sorry about that mate. I know that with our power, we are not immune to loss or the pain we endure from it."

Bakala walks with Malik towards his rental. "I must admit that I need your help, Yank." Malik refocuses his attention on his English counterpart. "There is a string of undercover kidnappings of immigrant women from Ghana and Nigeria." "Is it another sex ring?" Malik asks. "Not that I've noticed, Mate," Bakala continues, "Matter of fact, I don't know the motive or who's behind it."

Malik and Bakala stop at the muscle car. Malik, comforted by meeting an ally, responds with conviction and confidence. "How can I help?" The once cocky man shakes his dreads from his forehead, then lets off a smirk. "Meet me at the top of one of the columns of the bridge across the Thames tonight. A cloud of smoke will cover us; once we meet up, I will take you through several hotspots where these girls go missing." Malik gives a nod before he enters the cab of the car. "Oh, and yank," Bakala reminds, "it would be terrible manners to be late, you know what I mean?" "Hey, if you saw through my line, you know I'm a businessman, (mate)". "Right-o"

Malik shuts the door, turns on the ignition, then heads back to the hotel. As Bakala sees him off, he lets off a stream of dark smoke, blankets himself, then disappears into the wind.

# Chapter 10: Cementing Fragile Connections

The next morning in Jacksonville welcomes the day with a short breeze, the barrage on seagulls cawing for fish, and the traffic building up. At the Ayoké residence, Geneva is doing her normal routine as Emma slowly gets out of bed. Sluggish from her sleep, she quickly glances at her iPhone 12 to check for messages from Malik.

"(Ugh) That's strange. I haven't seen any texts from Malik (*I hope he's ok*)." KNOCK, KNOCK, KNOCK... Emma, are you up?" Geneva checks, "You should be getting ready to volunteer." "Yes ma'am," Emma responds as she slowly gets out of bed, "I'll be ready in a few minutes Grandma."

Emma looks through her closet to find an outfit to wear. Despite living in stress-free, her anxiety still mirrors that of women her age over the simplicity of life.

"Damn it!" she complains, "I don't know what to wear. This is irritating." "Is everything ok Amira?" Geneva consoles. "I just don't know what to wear, UGH!!! SOMETIMES I HATE BEING A GIRL!" Geneva chuckles at Emma's slight tantrum by complimenting her. "You are a beautiful woman who could probably pull off an outfit made from a dead baboon, heh heh heh heh." "Oh, that is not funny grandma," Emma retorts as she pulls out a short red dress with white stripe collars and white wedge flip flops. "I guess I'll wear this. Do you think this would be appropriate for school?"

Geneva examines the dress: midi length with cotton texture, plain colors, and comfort fitting. As she gives the dress to Emma, she turns away to give some privacy to her granddaughter, changing clothes.

"You know, Emma," Geneva states, "What you are doing is very good, both for you and the student you are reaching." "Well Grandma, I just...," Emma hesitates as she fixes her dress, "I'm still new at these types of relationships. Plus, there's... Asir." Geneva maneuvers herself and Emma on the bed. Geneva looks at Emma, as Emma attempts to fix her hair.

"(Sigh) Emma, Asir is lucky to have someone like you mentor him. Not many children have someone that cares for them, not even their parents." Emma refocuses her attention while Geneva imparts words of wisdom.  "My Amira, you cannot build a house in an hour, a day, or a week. Building a home takes longer, especially if it doesn't have a solid foundation to lean upon. Just remember, that fresh cement is wet for a reason, so that it can filter in potential cracks to sure up the foundation. Right now, what you are doing for him is like laying wet cement. Give it time for it to dry, Ok?" Emma smiles and Geneva gives her a hug and a kiss on the forehead. "Oh Grandma, I'm almost 25 years old..." "And still, my love, as well as your brother."

Moments later, Kemba is sitting in the living room plotting how to keep busy during his season of retirement—looking through the endless sea of channels while contemplating what books to order online. Emma decides to put on a short, blue denim jacket before addressing Kemba.

"Good morning, Grandpa, how are you?" Emma greets, getting her purse and keys ready in the process. "Well morning to you my dear, did you sleep well?" Kemba responds. Emma sits down on the couch next to him while Geneva cleans up in the kitchen. "Well, the bed is comfortable, but I don't think I'm sleeping well. It's as if... I don't know." "I see. Do you think you are thinking about that boy you are mentoring?" "You know Grandpa; I just have a strange feeling about him. Is it crazy to believe that he is the key to my destiny?" Kemba chuckles a bit before the embarrassment takes hold of Emma. Sensing this, Kemba quickly reassures his granddaughter before she heads out.

"Do not question your instincts child. My Hogon once said that sometimes the river creates its path or simply follows the path carved from the land. Your line flows from the flames of the phoenix; therefore, you have the insight to see this through. Trust yourself Emma." "Ok Grandpa, I have to get going. Love you." "Love you too, have a good day and remember who you are." Emma walks out of the door to get in the Jeep. After she shuts the door, Kemba asks Geneva a question.

"Are you going to inform her of who that child maybe?" "My dear Kemba, is it not best for a person to learn through time and experience?" "Perhaps you are right my love. Still, I wonder if she is ready for what can unfold." "Kemba, you know as well as I that the ancestors did not build the world without seeing what was out there first. She'll realize soon enough that what is troubling her will also fulfill her. Until then, we will support her." Kemba smiles as he nods in acknowledgement.

After 10 minutes of driving, Emma pulls into the school's parking lot. She gets out of the Jeep, treks across the lot then go through the double doors.

Once she enters the office, she is greeted once again by the school secretary. "Good morning, Mrs. Rios. How are you?" "Emma, good to see you again." "Is Mrs. Rollins going to escort me to Asir today?" "Mrs. Rollins is in an ARD meeting, so I'll have to take you." "Looking forward to it," Emma says cheerfully.

Mrs. Rios gets up from her chair as she escorts Emma out of the office. Mrs. Rios is a cheerful woman: short, heavyset, wears dark plastic glasses, with shoulder-length hair. Despite her overweight frame, her energy seems endless, especially when it comes to being the catalyst to keeping the school running.

"I am so glad that you take the time to volunteer for our students," she compliments, "It's not often we get someone as young as you helping out." "Well, I'm just glad I can make a difference." Emma responds. "So, tell me, what motivated you to join Big Sisters?" "Well, I know what it feels like to be abandoned. My mother died when I was a baby, so I wanted to share my time getting to know troubled kids. Speaking of which, how is Asir today?" "I'm not entirely sure. Unfortunately, I don't have the most intimate relationships with our students to know their moods. Still, I'm sure he's going to be excited to see you."

As they approach Asir's class, Emma and Mrs. Rios wait for the bell to ring. Moments later, the bell rings as the stampede of teenagers races to either the cafeteria or their other classes. When the duo walks into the classroom, they are greeted by Mrs. Springle. Before she could address Emma, Asir sees them as he is putting his things in his backpack. Emma smiles and waves as he waves back, showing little emotion yet pleasantly enthused about coming to her.

"Good morning, Emma. I see that Asir is ready to meet with you." "Well, I'm looking forward to our time together." "Um, Mrs. Rios, can you walk with Asir for just a few seconds? I want to relay something with Emma." "Sure. Come on sweetie."

Asir reluctantly walks with Mrs. Rios as if she was interfering with his moment of tranquil. Emma gives Asir another wave as they walk out.

"So, it seems that you've made an impact with Asir." Mrs. Springle informs, "Today, while we were working on creating short stories, I saw him drawing pictures." "Oh… was it dinosaurs or dragons again?" "Actually, it was a picture of him...and you." "Me?!" Emma shockingly responds, "So he didn't do his assignment?" "Well, actually he wrote a very interesting story. So, today's assignment was to create a short story. Now some of the kids wrote about simple things: video game characters, princesses, teenage drama, but not Asir." "Ok… so what did he write about." "Well, he wrote about a dream he had," Mrs. Springle explains while she shows Emma. Emma briefly reads it until something catches her eyes. "Wait a minute, Seminoles? Slave Rebellions? How, or what for that matter, would he know about such a complicated subject?" "I've noticed that his attention has dramatically shifted. I know I'm not supposed to disclose this type of information to someone other than his parents. For what it's worth, he is really responding to you." "Thank you for sharing; well, I have an impatience boy waiting for me." "Yes, of course. Thank you for what you are doing for Asir."

Emma nods as she walks out to greet Asir. Mrs. Rios shakes her head as Emma engages with Asir.

Showing some sign of progress, Asir attempts to engage Emma in eye contact while trying to engage the conversation. Emma takes the lead as they walk towards the cafeteria.

"Well good morning Asir; how are you today," Emma asks. "Mmm, ok I guess." Asir answers as he finds it difficult to maintain the social cues for normal conversation. "So, did you draw any pictures today?" "Mmm, yes I did. Do you want to see?" "Absolutely Asir; I can't wait to see what you created." Asir smiles like a kid on Christmas morning. He rushes to their table to set his backpack down. He grabs his lunch bag, sets it on the table, then searches his bag for his pictures. Poor Emma tries to catch up to the animated teenager, but her wedge flip-flops prove to be ineffective in keeping up.

A few seconds later, Emma is panting as she reaches down to sit. Her feet are sore from catching up, she is pleased to see Asir so excited. "Hey there speedy, just because I look young doesn't mean I can keep up." Emma says pleasantly. "Oh, I'm sorry Ms. Emma. I really want to show you these pictures."

Asir pulls out his pictures, three in total: one has Asir and Emma sitting on a table drawing, the second of a pair of eyes, and the last of a man and a woman. Emma takes the time to examine each one of the pictures as Asir eats his ham and cheese sandwich. "So Asir," Emma asks, "Can you tell me about these pictures?" "Sure, Ms. Emma" Asir proclaims while finishing his sandwich, "This one is us drawing pictures. You said that you like drawing pictures, so I drew a picture of you. But I didn't draw the right clothes, I'm sorry." "No, no, no, no, this is perfect...can I have it? I really like it." "Sure Ms. Emma." "Thank you Asir."

Then Emma takes a look at the second picture and makes some deductions. *"This one looks like the Dracocernentia, but the color is different."* The eye has the same sharp thin pupil, but the iris has a greenish-blue tent with three sets of golden claws surrounding the pupil. Intrigued, Emma prompts Asir to talk. "So Asir, what about this one?" Emma asks. At this time, Asir is eating a bag of rippled potato chips. Taking a look at the picture, he shifts his demeanor. Then he looks directly at Emma; his focus is clear as water, his attention straight forward, and he has the resolve of a conquering hero. "Ms., Ms. Emma, can I… can I tell you something?" Emma is suddenly nervous with this straightforward attitude. In order to mask her concerns and keep this newfound sense of trust, she responds accordingly. "Sure Asir. It will be between just the two of us. So, what do you want to tell me?" Asir lets off a sigh of assurance, sensing that he has finally found someone he could trust. Then he unloads his complex mind.

"I had a dream last night, but afterwards it kept me from going back to sleep." "What was the dream about, Asir?" Asir grabs the picture and begins to explain his dream. "The dream starts with this scary pair of eyes. I've never seen eyes like this before. They glow green in the dark." "Ok, go on." "Then," Asir grabs the last picture of the man and the woman. Asir drew the woman wearing a white top, a dark brown colored dress, and a rifle. The man had a feather in his ear, with a rifle in one hand and a tomahawk in another. "I see these two people fighting a group of men wearing blue suits. The man spoke in a way that I can't explain." Surprised by the detail of this dream, Emma presses him on. "Can you try to explain it?" "Well, it's like he was saying another language that I can understand. He kept saying Soletawake-yaka, somehow, I know it means Warhawk. I think he's..." *"Seminole?!"* Emma suggests.  Asir points to the woman, "She is fighting with him. She speaks like we do, but she seems different." "How so?" Emma continues with interest. "She had blue eyes."

The reveal is so shocking that a sharp pain hits Emma on the side of her head. She gently massages it until Asir begins to put his pictures away. Emma then re-engages the conversation towards Asir, knowing that the bell is about to ring. "So, after this dream, you couldn't go back to sleep?" "No. I couldn't go back to sleep." "Did you tell your mom this?" Asir takes his pictures and puts them in his binder. "Can I ask you one more thing Ms. Emma?" "Sure Asir, what is it?" "C-c-can you walk me to my next class?"

Emma is dumbfounded by the amount of trust this preteen has taken towards her. A day ago, he was skeptical, non-social, and wanted to keep to himself. Now, he is seeking companionship with a person he barely knows. Emma understands the significance of the moment, also remembering the words Kemba stated earlier. "Ok Asir," she answers, "I'll be more than happy to walk you to your next class."

Like clockwork, the bell rings, signaling the time to depart from the lunchroom. Emma gets up with Asir and allows him to lead her to his next class.

Despite the influx of students surrounding them, Asir feels a sense of newfound direction; meanwhile, Emma is flattered by the confidence she has given the once apathetic child. "So Asir, what class are you going to next?" "It's science, just a few doors down the hall." "Ok, Asir. Lead on."

At the door stands an older white man with thin glasses, bleach red hair with gray streaks, clean-shaven with a polo shirt, slacks, and brown loafers. As he sees Asir, he prepares to greet him just like his other students. "Well hello Asir, how are you sir?" "I'm good Mr. Reid," Asir says while avoiding eye contact. Then Asir turns around and smiles like a kid leaving an amusement park at Emma. "Bye Ms. Emma, see you tomorrow." Emma waves back as Asir goes to his seat. Before leaving, Mr. Reid addresses Emma, complimenting her with the interaction. "Well, I've never seen Asir so happy. You must really be good with kids." Emma tries to hide her blushing by keeping a straight face. "Well, we always seem to have fun," she retorts. "I see," he says before the bell rings, "I'm glad he has something to look forward to. It was nice knowing you."

She nods before she closes the door. Emma walks down the hallway before she is intercepted by Mrs. Rollins. "Emma Hi. I apologize for not being able to meet with you today." "Oh, no worries. Mrs. Rios took care of that." The two women continue their march towards the front of the school. "So, how was your time with Asir?" "Well, he was good. He started addressing me with some eye contact and he showed me more of his drawings." "Showed you, huh...Seems he's getting comfortable with you." "He also asked me to walk with him to class. I've never seen him so... relaxed."

Mrs. Rollins is shocked by the relationship Emma is quickly developing with Asir. "Well Emma, you sure have made an impact. I'm glad this is working out."

Both women reach the front of the building. Mrs. Rollins then parts Emma with last words before leaving.

"You know Emma, Asir has never been as comfortable with anyone so quickly as he is with you. What's your secret?" Emma carefully chooses her words, not wanting to disclose too much. "Well, I know what it feels like not knowing who or what family is. So, I guess he can sense that in me." "You have no idea..." Mrs. Rollins whispers. "I'm sorry," Emma responds. "Nothing. We'll see you tomorrow, right?" "Yes ma'am".

Emma exits the school then walks towards the parking lot. Something isn't sitting right with Emma and her mind clouds with thoughts. *"I'm getting those sharp pains again. Plus, he has images with a different color Dracocernentia,"* she debriefs, *"I don't know how to explain it yet, but I don't trust Mrs. Rollins. Something tells me she's hiding more than just student disclosures."*

Emma enters the Jeep then concludes her thoughts. "Maybe, tomorrow might clear some things up, but for right now, I'm ready to kick off these flip flops." She turns on the ignition, powers the SUV, then heads home.

# Chapter 11: Soul of a Seminole

Emma lets her mind wander as she meanders through the neighborhood towards her grandparent's house. The experiences dealing with Asir, as well as the revelations, leave the young woman inundated with duty, attachment, and the urge to explore the source of her sharp pains.

*"His dreams,"* she recollects, *"What are the chances that this boy has inherited the Fire Line as well. How could he? Who are those people in his dream? What is the connection?"* The floodgate of questions does little to quell the ability for Emma to answer.

She arrives at the house, still plagued with her newfound bond and trust from a child who once avoided social contact with most of his peers. This fact doesn't allude to Emma; still, she seeks guidance from someone who can empathize with her plight.

Instead of exiting the jeep, Emma pauses in her seat. Taking long, deep breaths, calms herself, then reaches in her small purse. After a few tussles, she reaches her iPhone, scrolls through her contacts, then presses a familiar number. Waiting with anticipation, the phone rings.

Ring...Ring...Ring…" CLICK Hey sis, what's up?" "Malik, Hi. How's London?" "Well, something interesting is happening here. Seems like we're not the only ones with powers."

Emma pauses in relief. Those words muster up the courage to confess her suspicions.
"Let me guess," Emma presses, "You found someone else who has the Dracocernentia." "Yes, I did," Malik replies emphatically, "he possesses powers that I never dreamed. The ability to create smoke to hide our receptors while spying on enemies." Malik catches himself as Emma responds to his claims. "Well bro, the world is big, and so are its secrets." "Yes," Malik finishes, "however, there is something else out here lurking in the shadows. I feel that it is somewhat connected to why the sword's existence is kept hidden. I plan to meet with the man in a few hours to explore the underbelly of this mystery."

Almost forgetting about her experience with Asir, Emma quickly turns the conversation back to her reason for calling.

"Malik, I think I found someone else who has the Dracocernentia here at home." "In Jacksonville? You mean…" "The boy I was assigned to, his name is Asir, and he has these dreams." Concerned, Malik presses on, "Go on." "Well today, he drew pictures of his dreams. One was of two people: a black woman in what looks like slave clothing and another, a Native American." "So, what about the other picture?" Malik asks. "The other was an exact replica of the Dracocernentia…"

The shock of the news hits Malik like a sucker punch. Both siblings stayed silent for a brief moment that seemed like it went on for eternity. After the awkward moment, Emma continues with the revelation.

"Every time I get these sharp pains in my head; I am with Asir." Emma pleads, "Malik, what if…" "Emma, I'm sure he has the Fire Line as well." Malik instructs, "If that is the case, then I fear that there are those who will try to exploit him." "*Just like what they did to me…*"

Malik concludes the conversation with lasting words of support and wisdom.

"Emma, as much as you get on my damn nerves at times, you are not the same person the Elite 8 tried to make you out to be. This boy is just like us at one time, oblivious to the power in his past. Keep in mind that he probably doesn't know his heritage and realize that his dreams are visual links of communication from his ancestors. I see now that this is your destiny as a Phoenix, to provide the bloodline to the Dragon awaiting inside Asir to awaken. Be who you are to me with him."

Emma smiles before answering her brother. "Alright Malik. Be careful out there and keep me posted." "Sure shit-stain. Love you." "Love you too, ass-wipe" Click.

Emma sits in the driveway for a while to recollect the thoughts of the conversation. Finally, her breathing slows down, her nerves calm down, and her resolve becomes concise and clear. "*You know, for someone who lacks tact at times, Malik can be profound. I think that tomorrow I will try to teach Asir about where he comes from without overwhelming him.*" Emma concludes her thoughts, exits out of the jeep, then enters the house.

Emma walks in the door. Geneva is in the kitchen preparing dinner while Kemba sits on the couch reading a book. Emma addresses them appropriately while she sits down next to Kemba.

"Ah Emma," Kemba says, "how was your day my child?" "Well Grandpa, I think I made some strides. The boy that I am mentoring is really growing attached to me. It… it…" While Emma stumbles to find the right words, Geneva walks in to join the conversation.

"I sense that this new feeling is unsettling, yes?" She inquires. "Something like that," Emma reacts, "I just got off the phone with Malik about my feelings. It's hard getting used to change." Kemba and Geneva smile as they respond to Emma's concerns.

"My Amira, change is always difficult when you lack the knowledge of its necessity." Geneva quotes. "My Emma," Kemba adds, "I believe that this is why your path led you to this boy. When you learn to care for others, you may find the strength that overpowers anything that gets in the way of reason and justice." "Seriously," Emma retorts, "how does protecting someone unlocks untapped power?"

Geneva steps into the conversation to calm Emma's inquisitive attitude. "My Amira, when your brother first sought us out, I could sense the turmoil in his soul before I even met him." Geneva sits next to Emma, rubbing her shoulders while comforting her like the supportive grandmother that she is. "I didn't want to believe that my daughter's children lived, because it was too painful to relive the death of your mother," Geneva concludes, "However, when I met your brother, he was so concerned for your well-being, despite not knowing who you are or where you are, I had to relinquish my fears to add to his Fire Line."

Emma nods her head, comprehending the underlying messaging while putting her concerns to rest. "I understand, by helping Malik, he was able to help himself, thus (Geneva kisses Emma on the cheek) …" Emma looks at Geneva and hugs her. Her emotions let loose a bit as she sheds a tear. This is one of the few times that she feels real love and support since her alliance with her brother. "Thank you both," Emma reminds as she gets ready for the night, "You helping Malik allowed him to help me." Kemba responds to Emma before the party migrates to the kitchen for supper. "Now, you care strongly enough to help another."

Moments later, they enjoy Geneva's dish. She prepared Malian Jollof Rice with sauteed spinach and seared goat chops. After the meal, Emma goes to her room, takes off her clothes, and lays in bed. Overconfident from her exchange with her family, Emma lays staring at the wall while contemplating the outcomes.

*"Clearly, Asir is descendant from a Dragon Moor. However, what troubles me is my role with his Fire Line? Does he truly understand who and what he is? I need to be very careful how I tread this path, because something tells me that the shadow of the Elite 8 still looms over the masses."* Emma shuts her eyes, breathes very slowly, and falls asleep.

The next morning, Emma wakes up and goes through her normal routine. She crawls out of bed while making grunts of displeasure. She attempts to pick out an outfit for the day, only to paralyze herself with uncertainty and frustration. "Ugh," she complains, "I never know what to wear." Geneva walks by to check on Emma. "Emma, are you ok?" She asks. "Grandma, I don't know what to wear...I'm just going to…" Geneva walks in and rubs her shoulders, "A wise woman once said that impatience makes wise people do foolish things." "What are you saying in plain English, grandma?" Geneva picks out a blue collared shirt and a pair of tight-fitting jeans. "I'm simply saying, a shirt and a pair of jeans will always do. They are clothing, are they not?"

Emma slaps her hands over her eyes in shame as Geneva chuckles out of the room and into the kitchen. Emma puts on the clothes and grabs a pair of black yoga mat sole flip-flops to wear. She brushes her teeth, washes her face, and brushes her thick, wavy, kinky hair into a bun.

Feeling refreshed and energized, Emma makes her way to the door while speaking to her Grandparents. "Bye everybody, I'm off to the school," Emma says. "Have a good day, Emma. And remember our conversation." Emma blows a kiss to Geneva before walking out of the door.

Emma gets in the Jeep, starts the ignition, and pulls out of the driveway. Emma is fueled with superb levels of hope, optimism, and eagerness. "I actually can't wait to see Asir," Emma ponders while driving, "I notice that the sharp pains have stopped. Maybe, I'm the one to help him. In that case, I think I should low-key teach him how to comprehend his dreams."

Emma pulls up in the parking lot. She exits out of the car, grabs her purse, and walks towards the school doors. She opens the doors and walks in towards the office. Mrs. Rios is organizing documents when she notices Emma. "Oh, hi Emma," Mrs. Rios exclaims, "I'm glad you are here. I just wanted to say that I notice that Asir has been more open to usual." "Well, I'm glad I can help," Emma responds with a smile.

Suddenly, the energy of the building shifts: the temperature drops, the air becomes thick, and a roar of students disturbs the positive vibes. Mrs. Rios immediately stops while she notices some students running towards something. "What in the world is going on?" Mrs. Rios asks as she and Emma locate the source of the commotion.

A large group of students are circling in the middle of the hallway. The congregation of teens and pre-teens hoop, holler, and chant as Emma tries to trek towards the middle of the spectacle.

As soon as she gets to the middle she is horrified by the sight of the event. Asir is getting bullied by 3 of his peers: one is white with short brown hair, dirty jeans and a t-shirt, another is Hispanic with jet black hair with a growing mustache, orange shirt, and jogger pants, the last is black with a short, nappy haircut, collar shirt, and shorts. The boys push Asir around, while one grabs his backpack to examine its contents. "Oh," the white boy teases as he takes out Asir's pictures, "let's see what Dino-Dork drew today." The other boys laugh as they try to contain a crying, scared kid. The boy throws his drawings into the floor until he comes across the picture he drew of Asir and Emma.

"Aw…" again the boy teases, "Dino-Dork has an imaginary girlfriend." "NO!" Asir screams, "Don't…" The Hispanic boy punches him in the face; then the black boy pushes him to the floor. Asir is drowned in tears as Emma tries to stop the boys. "Leave him alone!" Emma yells, trying so hard to contain her powers. Unfortunately, the boys pay Emma no mind as they continue with their bullying.

The boy then smooches the picture as the kids stand around laughing. "Well, I guess Asir's imaginary girlfriend won't save him, so…" RIP, the sound petrifies both Emma and Asir. The pieces of the picture fall like dry leaves on a fall day. For every piece of paper, a tear sheds down the traumatized boy's cheeks, as the boys continue to taunt and bully Asir. Emma is stunned by the horrific lack of empathy and compassion for Asir. Her gasp is only overshadowed by the sense of energy-generating from Asir.

Once the last shred of paper hits the ground, a glow covers Asir's body. Small flames begin to form, his tears evaporate in the intense heat, and his eyes begin to transform. Asir begins to chant in a language unknown to anybody in the vicinity.

"A…anowah Chittoluthphwa (I am Snake Eyes)" Asir whispers in a demented, vile voice. The other boys snicker as they circle around. Emma stands back, anticipating what may come to pass. "*I see*," she concludes, "*the bullying is triggering his ancestors.*" The main bully comes up to Asir while he is still on the ground. The once dormant magma of emotion has now triggered an eruption of rage. The flames manifest into a silhouette of a long-forgotten warrior in Asir's past. Emma watches along with a stunned, amazed, yet frightened student and teacher body. The assistant principal comes with 2 police officers as they witness the spectacle. "*I knew it…*" Emma realizes, "Asir is…"

All the boys struggle to gain distance, but Asir's angered state corners the white boy towards the wall. Petrified by his abandoned arrogance, and consumed with abhorrence, the boy pleads with the uncompromising entity that has possessed his classmate. "Co..co…come on Dino- D… I mean Asir! We were just…" he continues, "Somebody help me!"

Unfazed by the terror in his enemy, Asir's possession grants him the justice he so desired and deserved. "Hajo metachak-ulke… (crazy Englishman)" Asir holds up his hand and reaches the sky. The flames create a silhouette of a tomahawk in his palm, ready to strike the terrified bully.

As the crowd gasps and the police prepare to draw their guns, Emma yells to intervene before the situation escalates.

"STOP!" she commands, "ASIR DON'T!" Asir's Dracocernentia turns to investigate the source of the screams. The police attempt to move closer, but Emma stops them. "Wait," she pleads, "Let me talk to Asir!" Cautiously, Emma moves closer to the huge manifestation, over 7 feet tall, very hot, and fueled with rage as intense as the flames themselves. Emma understands how to approach the glory of Asir's Fire Line. She matches her energy while slightly transforming her pupils to deep blue. "I know who you are Asir," she whispers as she gains more ground. Finally, Asir calms down enough for Emma to draw closer. "Let me feel your pain," Emma states, then placing her hand on Asir's chest.

Afterwards, Emma is transported into the confines of Asir's sleeping mind. Emma notices a small figure sleeping in a corner inside the dark veil. As her consciousness walks closer, she sees a man standing near him. As she approaches the wall, the man turns around. He looks like the flame manifestation, but in his human form. As Emma's eyes meet the man's, his Dracocernentia allows them to speak to each other.

"You remind me of my mother… Loot-kah Lamhi (Fire Eagle)" the man says. Strangely, Emma understands the language and responds. "Fire Eagle, how was I able to...understand you?" Emma asks, "Who...exactly are you?"

The man smiles as he approaches Emma; he is a magnificent figure despite being the same height as Emma: 5'10'' tall, chocolate complexion, hair clearly mixed with kinky curls with some straight black streaks, wearing buckskin pants, sleeveless leather straps, a headband with triangular patterned colors of red and green, and green hue with his Dracocernentia.

"My name is Chittoluthphwa (Snake eyes), and I am Asir's ancestor. I can tell that you have my mother's power in you." "Your mother's power…" Emma responds, "So that means that she was a…"

Chittoluthphwa's eyes illuminate so that Emma can sync his eyes. "Allow me to tell you the story of my mother and why the lak-kits wyhome (big spirits) lead you to Asir." Then, a flash of white light transports Emma back in time in Asir's DNA.

# Chapter 12: Alliance of the Runaways

The flash of light pulses through like a train in a tunnel. As Emma is drawn towards its end, she is astonished by the pace of the vision. Chittoluthphwa narrates and guides through the maze in Asir's Fire Line to quell the uncertainty.

"Is this your first time traveling through the mind, Loot-kah Lamhi," he inquires. "I'm used to visions, Chittoluthphwa," Emma responds, "but I don't know exactly where we are going." "I am going to take you towards the memories of my mother and our lineage of defiance, freedom, as well as how my tribe fought back the same people who forced us into hiding. Learn from her; then you will be able to help Asir." Afterwards, Emma is transported into the mind of a slave woman running deep into the swamps.

The year is 1809, a slave woman wearing a wrinkled white top, brown skirt with patches, a head wrap covering her kinky medium length hair, and completely draped in sweat. She is panting hard as she crosses through thick brushes of limbs, bushes, and low-lying trees. Pursuing her is a small party consisting of horses, dogs, and 3 slave catchers. As the woman valiantly tries to escape, Emma is dumbstruck subconsciously as she is reliving the traumatic memories.

*"I can feel her anxiety,"* she continues, *"her heartbeat is pumping hard, her breath is short. It's as if…I am her. Somehow, I know what she… I need to continue to see where this goes."*

An hour goes by until the woman stumbles to a meadow in the middle of the forest. Worn out, feet bruised, and tired; the woman is cornered by her pursuers. One of the men, wearing a brown jacket, straw hat, and high boots, hurls bigotry commands at the slave.

"Alright nigger bitch," he yells, "You've run far enough! It's time to go back!" The young woman, despite her feeble condition, refuses to give up. "I refuse to go back! I deserve my freedom!"

The men all look at each other and laugh with disgust. The lead man gets off his horse, takes out his pistol, and approaches the cornered woman. "The only thing you deserve is to be back at the plantation," then he cocks his gun, "and if you are good…heh heh heh…I may privilege you with my company…in my bed."

As hope of her escaping blows away like the evaporation of her sweat, a yelp interrupts the apparent capture. An arrow silently struck one of the men in the chest. He lowers his head, loses control, and falls seamlessly off his horse. The remaining men look around to attempt to ascertain where the attack is coming from. Frightened, the woman comforts herself by wrapping her arms against her chest and crouching down to the ground.

"Who's out there?" the lead catcher demands, "Show yourself!"

Out of nowhere, a single shot from a rifle hits the other man right in the middle of his forehead, killing him instantly. At this point, the remaining horses scatter and leave the lonely catcher to his demise. A shiver of fear overwhelms the man as he steps away from the runaway to try to save himself. He continues to whimper to salvage what little courage he has lost in the past few moments.

"I...I… am warning you," he whimpered, "I'm armed!" He points his pistol erroneously in different directions. His imprudent judgement and reckless movements blind him to a Native man sneaking up behind him. The slave woman sees this and covers her mouth in an attempt not to alert her captor.

Slowly, like a panther stalking a deer, the Native man slithers through the brush with a knife in his hand. The catchers continue to point his gun in the other direction, distracted by the leaves rustling. He cocks his gun, ready to fire. Then in an instant, the native catches the catcher, covers his mouth with his left hand and slits his throat with his right hand. The catcher crashes to the ground holding his neck while he gargles the last gasps of life. He rolls around on the ground until he takes his last look at his killer. The native stands on top of him, devoid of emotion but full of conviction.

As the blood stains the meadow ground, the catcher's eyes roll towards the back of his head, and the last gasp of air disappears into the wind. Startled by the turn of events, the runaway slightly lowers her guard as 3 more natives expose themselves from the brush. The lead native puts his knife away and slowly approaches the woman. Not wanting to scare her, he simply asks a question before getting too close.

"Hie la! Ay-it-liepts-e-chez (Ah! How is your health?)" the native asks. The slave shakes her head, signaling that she doesn't understand by pointing to her mouth and ears. The Native smiles, understanding the gesture of communication, then switches his language.

"I will speak white man talk then," he declares, "how is your health?" The woman rises up from the ground then responds appropriately. "I am tired and hungry. Please...I need help." The Native then nods to his party to lower their weapons then addresses the slave again. "I will take you to our village. I will help you." The woman begins to shed tears of joy and looks up at the sky, "Thanks to Ogun!" as she allows herself to be led by her saviors. The Native smiles again then address his party, "A-la-kus-cheh (Come let us go)". The men then escort the slave woman out of the meadow and into the deep woods.

While walking down a hunting trail, the slave woman walks with the lead Native while the others watch the rear for intruders. Feeling comfortable to speak, the woman starts up a conversation.

"My name is Consuela, but some folks call me Cassie." she continues, "I was running away from the white men that kept me in the house of Massa." The Native looks at her with deep brown eyes, his face becomes soft and his lips curve upwards in response. "I am called Soletawake-yaka (Warhawk). We were forced to leave our lands to come here to start over." "I know that can be hard. I was kidnapped and brought to this country. I haven't seen my family since I was a little girl."

Soletawake-yaka nods his head while leading his party back to their village. Seconds later, they enter the outskirts of their village. Cassie is surprised by the diversity of men and women, Natives and former slaves working together like a utopian community. "You see Cassie; you are not the only one of your kind to settle here. We work together to keep the way of life of our Hitloschi Chilth-Keh (Cloud Fathers)." Soletawake-yaka continues, "Come. I will introduce you to our village at the Mico-etchay (Council House)."

Soletawake-yaka leads Cassie towards a group of former slaves as they intermingle and immerse themselves with the new guest.

Hours later, the residents meet at the Council House. The house, like the others, is built with sturdy hood foundations with multi-straw roofs. Inside the house has a banquet of goods from the harvest as well as an assortment of deer, hog, alligator, and rabbit meat. The village all partake in the feast as they all congregate in a circle, a stone pit with a fire at its epicenter to heat the cabin.

As everyone continues to nibble on their plates, Soletawake-yaka stands up to grab everyone's attention. "Hello, hello!" he roars, "We have a new guest. This feast of plenty is to celebrate our new ally. (He gestures to Cassie sitting next to him) Welcome...Cassie." Everyone smiles and cheers as Cassie embraces the warmth of the community. "Thank you all; I am glad to meet all of you."

A former slave man smiles, then incites another conversation. "What plantation did you run from miss?" he asks. Cassie looks at him while nibbling on a bone from a rabbit. "I was brought to New Orleans as a child. Before that, I came from an island that was at war with the white people." she continues while looking down, being fueled by the turbidity of emotions flooding her mind, "my master took me away from my mother and put me on a ship to New Orleans. There I was bought by a Spanish family that made me the house nigger."

The man, along with other members, nod their heads to give condolences to her struggle and story. Then the man answered back by recounting his life. "I's was working in the fields of North Carolina." he continues, "Massa used to beat us nearly to death if we didn't pray to him as the Lord Jesus. Even then, he'd have us beaten just so none of us would run away." Then the man takes another bite of his meat before finishing his story. "One day, I say I won't take another beating. I would rather die. So, I ran south until they found me...That was some time ago."

Cassie nods in acknowledgement as Soletawake-yaka adds to the conversation. "We are all runaways. My people were forced to leave the home of our fathers by white men who broke their treaties and took the land. They refuse to share and destroy what our mother provides." The village all acknowledge this as the Native continues his monologue. "Cassie, we live here in peace. We work together, live in peace, and live as a family. I hope that you will come to find us as your new family."

As Cassie nods, the village nods in agreement as singing and chants resonate throughout the cabin. Former slaves clap their hands and sing, with Cassie singing along as well as laughing; meanwhile, the Native begin to chant and hum to their ancestral tunes. The night ends like a concert on a summer night, playing for the stars up above.

As the memory fades, Emma regains her consciousness as the flash of white lights brings her back to the current plane.

"What's going on?" Emma inquires, "That was an extraordinary memory." "Yes indeed, Loot-kah Lamhi," Chittoluthphwa continues, "but these memories need to be taught to Asir. He needs to understand who he is before you can help him." "Me... but how? And why?" "Because, as my mother understood at the end of her life, each dragon, as you say, needs a firebird. You were chosen by the Hitloschi Chilth-Keh to guide Asir." Emma does not buckle by the weight of this responsibility. She instead understands that what Malik did for her, she must do for Asir. "Alright, Chittoluthphwa," she answers, "I will help your descendant discover his Fire Line." Chittoluthphwa smiles before his silhouette disappears, leaving a lasting message. "Hink-lah-mas-tshay. Lopko (It is well. Make haste)."

Emma is back in the present. Her palm is still on Asir's chest as the fiery silhouette simmers as the young man regains his consciousness. Woozy, Asir adjusts his vision to see Emma, smiling a little.

"Ms... Ms Emma?" "Yes, Asir." Emma answers, "It's me. Are you alright?" "I...I...don't feel good."

Then the assistant principal orders everyone to go back to their classes. The police then rush in to restrain Asir. Not wanting to make too much of a scene, Emma pleads with the officers.

"Asir didn't start the fight," she demands, "Why are you cuffing him?" "Look, Miss," the officer sneers, "I need you to step away and let us handle the situation." Emma looks at the assistant principal; he is a big, obese man with a short haircut and a full beard with gray streaks. He is also stern and uncompromising. "He posed a bigger threat to the students than the 3 boys." he exclaimed, "I need you to allow the officers to do their jobs."

Emma reluctantly moves back as the officers' handcuff and escort Asir out of the building. He looks back at Emma with sad, watery eyes, confused as to what happened as well as why he is being treated this way. Emma struggles to control her emotions, knowing that doing so will cause more damage than good. "*Your Great-great-great grandfather entrusted me with helping you discover your Fire Line,*" Emma surmises, "*And dammit, that's what I'm going to do.*"

Emma then looks on, fully aware of her new mission and solidifying her determination to restore Asir's Fire Line.

# Chapter 13: Fuel for the New Machine

As the brightness of the day ends, Malik sits on his bed pondering the possibilities of the night. He sorts through his suitcase and finds his hooded leather jacket. "*I'm perplexed by the nature of these disappearances,*" Malik continues, as he gets up to pace around his hotel room, "*back home, there was a motive. There was a pattern. However, there is no outrage, news, or any casualties.*"

Malik looks at the window. He witnesses yet another day surrendering to the night, signaling the urge to move out. Malik puts on the jacket, puts his hood over his head and prepares himself. "It's time for Shadowmoor to extinguish this atrocity."

Shadowmoor exits out of the window and climbs to the top of the building. He surveys the London skyline while ascertaining the quickest route to the bridge. "I can see the river about 4 blocks north of me. I'll head that way and wait for Bakala."

Shadowmoor moves like a ninja, running and jumping through the streets undetected. While maneuvering through London, he tries to pick up any receptors that prompt trauma, foul play, or concerning behavior. But strangely, nothing comes up as he approaches the bridge.

Upon arrival, Shadowmoor gets on top of a rail. Shadowmoor carefully and tactfully runs up the rail leading to the top of the cable using his unrivaled sense of balance. There, he majestically stands at the top while embracing the beauty of the city.

"Living my adult life in Atlanta, skyscrapers aren't new to me," Shadowmoor continues, "but this… This is absolutely stunning. I see why this is the new capital of fashion in the world." Shadowmoor takes a moment to appreciate the beauty of the city.

Moments later, a cloud of smoke appears around Shadowmoor. Not fazed by the smoke, Shadowmoor closes his eyes. He waits, he controls his breathing, and he settles down. SWOOSH! Smack! A fist meets the hand of Shadowmoor, as the receptors of his companion show colors of green and gold. Shadowmoor smiles as the smoke clears up, revealing Bakala in a tranquil state.

"Well done, chap," Bakala compliments while he removes his fist, "Seem you Yanks can learn." "Yes, I saw the smoke build-up and allowed my mind to clear," Shadowmoor chuckles, "As I could get in touch with my environment, I was able to see it with new eyes." Both men smirk at each other as they overlook the lights of the city.

"Alright Yank," Bakala continues, "We'll survey the city streets and trail the girls from the immigrant districts. I suspect that one will eventually get taken." "How will we know what we are looking for?" Shadowmoor asks. "As you know, we can see the receptors of living things and ascertain their behavior patterns, yeah?" Shadowmoor nods as Bakala further explains his thought process. "However, I've noticed for a while that these so-called disappearances do not match the actual feelings the victims exhibit."

While trying to comprehend the messaging, Shadowmoor continues to screen through the population of people minding their business in the streets. His imprudent demeanor and antsy body language generate a response from Bakala, who remains composed and confident.

"You're thinking a bit too much about it, Yank," Bakala states before prompting Shadowmoor to focus due west of their position, "Don't be daft Yank, and take a look." Shadowmoor intensifies his Dracocernentia to see the receptors of someone familiar to him. His eyes widened a bit and his pupil's dialect, revealing a person who didn't act like what they seemed.

"I know that woman," Shadowmoor reveals, "That's Obioma. The front desk clerk, but her receptors…" Shadowmoor looks back at Bakala. He responds with a smirk and a nonchalant stance. "Shall we follow her? Just to make sure she's not fagged?" Shadowmoor raises an eyebrow with a level of uncertainty. Bakala's nature is perplexing yet familiar to Shadowmoor; meanwhile, Bakala continues to smirk, anticipating the question he already knows the answer to.

"Yeah, this is your city," Shadowmoor relinquishes, "However, why are her receptors stagnant? You would think there would be some level of concern walking alone in the dark." Bakala doesn't answer Shadowmoor's question. He instead descends the bridge before inviting Shadowmoor. "So then Yank, should we bugger off then?" Not wanting to stall due to his indecisiveness, Shadowmoor follows the English Moor down the bridge.

Both men keep a safe distance as Obioma peregrinates through the dark alleys. For several blocks, Obioma walks with little or no concern for her safety, with the men following behind. Then, Obioma makes a right turn to a dark alley. Shadowmoor and Bakala crouch down to rest as well as maintain a close eye on the limited lighted environment.

As she reaches a dead end, she begins to shiver and quake. Meters behind, Bakala and Shadowmoor witness this, fueling Shadowmoor's eagerness to quell what lurks in the shadows. His fist becomes hot, his breathing gets heavier, and his eyes glow brighter.

"What a bit chap," Bakala cautions, "before you go all playing hero, pay attention to her receptors." Shadowmoor calms down enough to allow Bakala's warning sink in. His eyes slightly dim; he focuses his attention, then he is amazed at the results.

"Her receptors don't match her behavior," Shadowmoor understands, "Even people who act can't hide the chemical impulses of their body. It's as if she's…" "That's what I wanted you to see," Bakala adds on, while observing, "There's more to this than either one of us understand at this time. So, whatever happens next, we need to just be patient." Shadowmoor nods in agreement as they look on with attentive eyes.

Seconds later, 3 men creep out of the shadows to surround Obioma. Despite her receptors, she shivers and quakes in fear. Attempting to walk another in the other direction, one of the men grabs her and covers her mouth. She attempts to scream through the gloved hands while squirming to get free.

Shadowmoor's impulse to help has triggered emotions from his past; he still has trouble reconciling with the girls who were kidnapped, drugged, and raped. Knowing this through their interaction, Bakala firmly grabs Shadowmoor's arm to remind him to stay calm.

"Remember Yank; something isn't what it seems," Bakala reminds as the men subdue Obioma, putting her seemingly unconscious. Then the men grab her and disappear into the shadows of the streets. "Now is our time to follow," Bakala whispers, "Try not to spend too much energy with your eyes. It's a bit nippy out here, so recharging will take too much time." Shadowmoor once again nods. Gathering his confidence and ability, Shadowmoor and Bakala stand up and pursue the 3 men.

The men continue to move within the confines and crevices of the western blocks of the city. Their journey ends at an abandoned factory: with shattered glass, half-cracked wooden doors, and stones that have weathered down to dull browns and grays. The men take Obioma inside, not looking around or sensing that they have been followed.

Shadowmoor and Bakala reach the abandoned factory and plot their next move. The eerie silence and deathly shadows of the dissipated building do little to dissuade the Moors. Their eyes continue to glow, exposing the cracks that seem to showcase the weak foundations of the society.

"Alright chap, seems that this is their place of operation," Bakala senses, "Looks like we'll have to split up once we get in." "You're right," Shadowmoor responds, "We can out flank whatever is in there and support whoever engages the enemy first." "Right-o Yank." Both men silently nod at each other and go their separate ways.

Bakala decides to follow them in the main entrance by going through the front door. Shadowmoor approaches the western side of the building and enters through the second set of broken windows to maintain the high ground.

Shadowmoor quickly enters the building and scans the area for any signs of life. His Dracocernentia provides the only light in the room, only showing colors of temperature fluctuation and receptors of rats that made their home in the deteriorating, cracked walls. Shadowmoor quietly moves downstairs to find the fraudulent kidnappers.

Slowly, he walks downstairs to see the main floor stripped of the major machines that once operated the factory. Again, he scans the area looking for anything. Suddenly, he hears rumbling in the distance. Shadowmoor amplifies the powers of his eyes. The pupils' glow in the darkness like a beacon; meanwhile, his other senses become attuned to the minute sounds and vibrations.

The strange men escort Obioma downstairs. Shadowmoor keeps his distance while following them. When Shadowmoor reaches the bottom of the stairs, he is mildly amazed at what he sees. The basement is an underground laboratory: stainless steel tables covered with liquid flasks, several mini greenhouses with a large variety of plants, a 50 ft by 30 ft flat screen, a round table with 12 separate leather chairs, and a single row of cells housing 3 lethargic, motionless African immigrants.

"*What in the hell is this*," Shadowmoor rationalizes while remaining hidden. The memories of the kidnappings and his run-ins back home revise his consciousness. His anger quickly turns to discernment, the quivering stops to a calm flow, and Shadowmoor deduces the inevitability of the situation. "They're back...*so who now leads them?*"

Bakala perches on the rails above the secret room on the other side of the basement. He observes the men putting her in an empty cell. Despite the lack of struggle, Bakala still can't detect Obioma receptors.

"It's strange," he whispers, "She isn't showing any signs of duress or anxiety. *What are these men up to?*"

One of the men goes towards one of the greenhouses. He opens the compartment, takes several green leaves from a vine, puts them in a bowl, crushes the leaves, then mixes the residue with a chemical. Several seconds go by; then the man puts the mixture in a syringe. Meanwhile, the other man sits Obioma down and shackles her hands and feet on the wall. Shadowmoor is also observing the men performing the incision on her arm. Obioma becomes a motionless slave; her motionless body succumbs to the drugs as she slips into a peaceful-like slumber.

Afterwards, the man cleans the syringe with a clean, white towel while the other man makes his way towards a computer station next to a huge monitor. As Shadowmoor and Bakala, respectably, observe the strange routine, the man begins to key in some commands on the laptop.

A few strokes later, the screen pops up to reveal a man awaiting to engage with the men. He is a sophisticated man: sitting with his ankle on the opposite knee, wearing a pin strap jacket, white button-down shirt, fitted blue jeans and wearing brown loafers. He is also clean-shaven, with few indicators of a beard and brown hair combed to the left side of his head while the sides and back of his head are shaved. This immaculate gentleman is rotating his glass of cognac with 2 ice cubs as 2 women swarm over him.

In the background, Shadowmoor intensifies his eyes to identify the man. Despite the proficiency of his Dracocernentia, he is unable to pinpoint the receptors of the man in the screen. *"What is going on?"* Shadowmoor ponders, *"It's one thing to not see the fields in the girls being drugged, but I can't see anything at all. It's as if this man lacks..."* Before he can articulate his limited knowledge of the events, the men begin to speak.

"Mr. Goth," the man who initiated the video meeting starts, "we just secured another one of our girls. She is now in a deep sleep and probably won't wake up for a while." The man on the screen continues to woo the women, acting as if he has no concern in the world. The men look at each other with a bit of anxiety and nervousness. Again, the man tries to re-engage the report.

"Sir? About the…" The man on the screen raises his finger, prompting them to exhibit some patients. He then air smooches his 2 acquaintances while shooing them away. The women giggle and walk away, anticipating the moment they can intoxicate themselves with the man's presence.

The man on the monitor takes a sip from his glass slowly. He tastes the strong liquor, closes his eyes, then lets out a sigh of regret with the tedious task of business. Afterwards, he addresses his perplexed minions.

"Ah…" he starts, "Gentlemen, the pleasures in my life pale in comparison to the inevitability of life's consistent trends." "Sir," the other man says, "We don't quite under…" "Shhh" the man on the screen interrupts, as he gets up to give his full undivided attention, "Gentlemen, I'm talking about strength and weakness, those who hold power to those who thirst for it, and of course winning and losing. That's why we do this, yes?" "Of course, Mr. Goth" the other man answers. "Good," Goth answers, "So what information have we obtain from our latest…sssssssss…street secretary?" "Well, Mr. Goth, she works at the hotel where someone by the name of…Wilson shacks," the man remembers, "but I don't know why that's important."

Bakala squints his eyes and controls his breathing. *What is it about the Yank that you want?*"

Goth takes another sip from his glass; then semi-slams it down on a nearby table. The man lightly grits his teeth while wiping his forehead. Then he gathers himself and smiles towards the camera.

"It's not your job, nor your intellect to know why it's important," he reprimands, "All you need to know is that these girls, like our Mr… Wilson, are a means to an end to achieve our work's purpose, Gentlemen."

Both men quiver a bit as if they expected to be yelled at like children fighting over a small toy. Despite this, the men continue to relay information to Goth.

"We were not able to grab more subjects," the man near the computer station states, "Seems our efforts are being thwarted by…" "Yes, I'm aware" Goth interrupts, "Gentlemen, my ancestors fought these demons back in the Dark Ages. They fought valiantly, but unfortunately didn't have the resources nor the will to beat them."

As the conversation continues, Shadowmoor is deeply disturbed by the demeanor of both Goth and the men. His usual deductive demeanor suddenly falls into a pit of confusion and uncertainty, trying to make sense of the speech pattern while trying to discern the details of their plans.

"These men are showing yellow receptors," Shadowmoor ascertains, "but what is it about this guy? Why is he following me? And what exactly is referring to when he says his ancestors?"

The conversation enters the final stages as the men brace themselves for further instructions.

"Continue to follow Mr. Wilson" Goth commands, "Another girl should be out to collect data on the whereabouts of the Harq Alqadr. We need that sword to finalize our plans." "Yes sir," the man further back answers, "So what about the girls?" Goth chuckles seemingly astonished by what he perceives as an idiotic question. His temper was only checked by his professional aura. Then he gives a chilling response. "Look at my quarters, Gentlemen." he commands, as the men peer in the background, "Do you see any blemish, any spotty mess, any trash?" Both men look confusingly at each other, hesitant to answer. Goth's impatience grow as he reiterates the question. "WELL...do you see any impurities in my circle?" "Wwww...Well no" the men answer simultaneously. "Then damnit, why would I want trash? You idiots know what to do with trash, right? Is it so hard to understand?"

Both Shadowmoor and Bakala light up their eyes, awaiting their chance to spring into action. Shadowmoor senses a presence within Goth, something familiar yet new to him. *"There is something about this guy that triggers my response to fight. I don't know who this Goth is, but he is trouble...I can feel it."*

The men gulp before answering Goth, "Yes, we understand. We control the destiny of men…" Goth chuckles a bit while he grabs his glass. He swirls the melted ice in his glass while avoiding eye contact. His smile is sinister, and so is his closing remarks.

"We will remain elite…" as he mumbles, "And burn this world into purity." Goth looks up and closes the meeting. "Gentlemen, we shall meet again. Until then...WE ARE ELITE!"

The screen turns black. The men gather their nerves, then converse amongst themselves.

"That guy always creeps me out," one of the men says to the other, "but he is destined to rule." "Yes" the other man agrees, "So I would have to disappoint him." Then the men begin to grab their knives and guns. "Well, like he said. We have to dispose of the trash."

Then, Bakala comes out of hiding. Jumping from one of the rails, he faces the men as the startled men figure out what's going on. The English Moor makes a quirky statement before they can let out a word.

"Hello there, I'm here to remove you trash." Bakala says. "Remove, you trash?" one of the men asks, "you mean your right?" "No…" Bakala retorts, then illuminating his Dracocernentia, "like I said…You…trash!"

# Chapter 14: The Flow of the Universe

The men stare down the overconfident more with eyes of disgust, annoyance, and contempt. One of the men cocks his gun while the other issues a warning.

"I don't know who you are," he snears, "and quite frankly, I don't care chum. I suggest you surrender or meet your maker."

Bakala snickers and smiles. His defiance is only masked by the incoming smoke that begins to engulf the men. The men begin to panic and swerve their heads around as the smoke gets thicker and thicker. "*What is going on?*" one of the men questions. "*Where did this smoke come from?*" the other ponders while trying to keep Bakala in their sights.

Shadowmoor continues to blow dark grey smoke from his lips. Perfecting the technique that once alluded his understanding, Shadowmoor blankets the smoke large enough to eradicate the visibility of the whole basement.

Bakala smiles in admiration while waiting for the right time to strike. "So, the Yank can learn new tricks," he compliments, "*Well done...Shadowmoor!*"

When the smoke gets thick enough, the men begin to panic. His blindness petrifies the one with the gun while the other one creeps towards the exit. In an attempt to abandon his comrade, Shadowmoor moves with precision and stealth to outflank the men. Slowly he stalks his unsuspecting enemy as they continue to figure out their plight. The receptors glow with yellow and orange; meanwhile, Shadowmoor gets within striking distance to deliver a fatal blow. "*Now I know I was too lenient on you bastards back home,*" he concludes, "*This time...*"

Shadowmoor approaches the man towards his back. The horrified villain continues to wiggle his way back towards the arms of vengeance. Then, Shadowmoor grabs the man and covers his mouth.

The other man calls out his comrade. "Hey! HEY! Where are you?" he shouts as Bakala continues to smirk. His eyes continue to glow as he sees Shadowmoor subduing the other man.

As the other man continues unsuccessfully to get free, Shadowmoor whispers in his ear a cryptic message. "So, you didn't learn from your buddies in America," Shadowmoor murmurs, "So I think it's time to send this...Mr. Goth a message..."

The other man muffles and screams through Shadowmoor's hand. After a few wiggles, SNAP! The man's hands slink down his sides; his body becomes motionless and heavy, then a huge thud follows after he hits the ground.

After hearing the crunch of death, the other man becomes too entangled with angst to mourn his comrade. His courage leaves his body like heat in winter despite having a gun. Soon the smoke dissipates, showing the lifeless body on the ground with Shadowmoor staring back at him.

He focuses his attention back on Bakala's smug face. Bakala then gives the man an alternative.

"Well, o'boy, seems you are left with a bit of a sticky situation," he states while looking at Shadowmoor, "So here's the deal. You either go tell your boss what happened here, or you become a tinder for our Fire Line." The man shakes profusely while he takes a look at an irate Shadowmoor. Knowing the doom that may await him, the cowardly henchman drops his gun and runs out of the basement. Shadowmoor and Bakala watch him run as Shadowmoor addresses the composed hero.

"Getting soft (old) boy" Shadowmoor mimics the English accent. "Well...It is what it is!" Bakala responds in a deeper, more American slang.

Bakala then walks over towards the greenhouses to examine the plants. Shadowmoor drags the lifeless body towards the screen while looking at Bakala. Bakala reactivates his Dracocernentia to look within the bioelectrical pulses within the plants. He examines the plants and takes several leaves while Shadowmoor meets him.

"My Fire Line specializes in healing through botany," Bakala explains while Shadowmoor observes, "Her majesty Charlotte of Mecklenburg used to have a botanical garden to treat the King's historical mood swings." "So just how we can see the receptors in living things, you can take the same concepts to heal people?" Shadowmoor asks.

Bakala then takes several leaves of Ginseng, Guarana and Rhodiola plants and crushes them into a liquid pulp enough to fill 4 small cups. "Exactly Yank," Bakala explains as the two make their way to the girls, "It's like an equation really. Each person has a receptor sequence with timing. When I find the right ingredients, I can plug in the missing sequences, thus healing the body." Shadowmoor nods in acknowledgement, realizing that there are depths of his powers still to be explored.

Shadowmoor opens all of the cages that house the women, including Obioma. He then unlocks the shackles of each prisoner. He lays each of the women down carefully while Bakala continues preparing the antidotes.

Slowly, Bakala uses his herbal mix to inject them into the lethargic immigrants. One after the other, they slowly wake up woozy and confused. Finally, as the girls regain their consciousness, Shadowmoor feels a sigh of relief. His experiences in America have affected the way he sees his resolve while immersing himself into the role that defines his existence.

*"I'm glad the women are ok,"* he contemplates, "Seems like this journey is becoming a deeper rabbit hole than I expected."

Bakala walks towards the cage with Obioma, followed by Shadowmoor. Shadowmoor keeps his distance while Bakala inserts one last syringe in her upper right arm.

Shadowmoor looks on with anticipation. Confident in the English Moor, he anxiously waits for what seems like an eternity for Obioma to wake up.

As the other girls begin to stumble out of their cages, Obioma wakes up and tries to get up. When she stumbles and falls, Shadowmoor rushes in to catch her, allowing her to rest in his strong, sturdy arms.

"(Groans) RRR...ack... Wh... WH...Who are you?" Obioma slurs. Shadowmoor carefully masks his voice by lowering the pitch. "Don't worry," he responds, "You're safe and we're going to get you out of here." Obioma squints her eyes to look deep into Shadowmoor's Dracocernentia. She undergoes a state of euphoria while further stating her feelings. "Somehow...you seem familiar."

Bakala interrupts the conversation by instructing Shadowmoor to evacuate the building. "Sorry to stop your Soap Opera, Yank, but we need to get these ladies out of here." "Agreed," Shadowmoor confirms, "Let's go."

The Moors quickly lead the victims upstairs. Bakala takes the lead while Shadowmoor takes the rear. Then Shadowmoor begins to blow blue flames from his lips to destroy the basement. Bakala and the victims are briefly shocked but continue upwards towards the exit. "You could've warned us mate, that you were up for barbeque." Bakala complains. Shadowmoor doesn't allow himself to be deterred, as he continues to spit a continuous flow of heated flames to destroy the building.

Moments later, Shadowmoor, Bakala, and the rest of the women make it outside before the building is completely incinerated with flames. As the party looks on, the women shiver and rub themselves to shake the after-effects of the drugs. As Shadowmoor looks on, Bakala turns his head to the right to address the hero.

"Well done, Yank," Bakala says, "Although you seemed a bit daft about the situation. Was it killing that bloke, or..." Shadowmoor interrupts the questions by letting off a sigh. He briefly looks down, closes his eyes, then deactivates his Dracocernentia. Afterwards, he lifts his head and looks back at Bakala.

"Bakala, back home, I began my journey because the Elite 8 were murdering the boys and kidnapping the girls. I thought that I brought that to an end," Shadowmoor reflects, then looks at the burning building, "And now, these bastards are back. Makes me wonder if we are ever going to rid the world of these guys."

Bakala looks at Shadowmoor with a level of concern not shown up to this point. His eyes flicker with the stars of the night, his face is stiff, and his demeanor softens. Bakala puts his hands on Shadowmoor's shoulders then offers words of comfort.

"You know Yank, hard to believe that we are more alike than it seems. Yes, you wonder if the fight will ever end, or if you are like a dog chasing its own tail." Bakala removes his hand, as Shadowmoor reengages the conversation. "You did good back there, and the ladies are safe thanks to you and your "American" style. At least now we know what their motives are." "Ugh…" one of the victims mumbles, "my head still hurts." Bakala and Shadowmoor aid the woman while the others circle around.

"Take it easy there Love," Bakala instructs. "Mmmm...I know who you 2 are." "Save your strength. We'll get you back home."

The woman, dark-complected with microbraids, skinny frame, and dark natural lips, looks at Shadowmoor. Her determined state forces her to let loose the information-building pressure in her head.

"You are the Moors seeking the sword that will unite the people." she says while pointing at Shadowmoor, "I can't fully explain it, but I sense great power and energy in you. I think that you are the bridge of our generation." "The bridge," Shadowmoor questions, "What do you mean by that?" "Back in Mali, there is a place where those who seek such knowledge shall converse with the White Fox." "A White Fox?" "Yes, during the Sigi; a rite of passage held every 60 years."

Shadowmoor intensifies his eyes while taking in the influx of information. "How do you know about this?" The woman chuckles before concluding her advice. "I come from an ancient tribe that had a connection with the universe. It was said that we were descended from a being from beyond the stars. Our Hogon once said that if we encountered another from our tribe that has strayed from their path, we could sense their energy and direct them back."

Shocked, Shadowmoor stands in amazement as the woman finishes her thoughts. "Although I don't cling to the old ways like my ancestors, I know a presence when I sense it and you… you are destined to converse with the White Fox. I beg of you, go seek him and your journey will not be in vain." Afterwards, the young lady falls to the ground from exhaustion. Bakala and the other girls pick her up.

"So then Yank," Bakala asks, "Shall we be off before Scotland Yard shows up?" Without any hesitation, Shadowmoor, Bakala, Obioma and the rest of the girls leave the scene. Shadowmoor and Bakala personally escort each of the girls' home to make sure they are safe. During the run, Shadowmoor remains quiet in speech but fluid in thought. *"That woman's words sound somewhat like Granddad Kemba's words...Is it...possible?"* While dwelling within the mysteries circling in his mind, Shadowmoor and Bakala make it outside Obioma's apartment.

Reaching the apartment, Obioma slowly makes her way towards the steps. She looks back at the Moors then stops to give them her thanks.

"I… I really appreciate what you did for the girls and me." She says. "No worries Love," Bakala responds, "All in a night's work." "(Mmmm)" Obioma chuckles, "and you too." Obioma blows a kiss towards Shadowmoor before making her way into the apartment. Shadowmoor blushes, despite still having his hood and mask on. Underneath the clothes, he's still a bit shy when it comes to female interactions.

"I say Yank, you are a bit of a Ladies Man, no?" Bakala asks sarcastically. Shadowmoor looks at him with an annoyed yet calm gaze. Then Bakala finishes the conversation. "In all seriousness, it looks like you have another lead to the sword." "It would seem that's the case," Shadowmoor responds, "but how do I know if this does indeed lead to the sword."

Bakala once again places his hand on Shadowmoor's left shoulder. Then he gives parting words to the confused hero. "Yank...Shadowmoor," Bakala commands his attention, "not everything in this world is about going from point A to point B. Sometimes you'll have to detour to point F, then circle to point Q." Bakala let's go before finishing the conversation. "I believe that the girl sensed something in you to tell you this. I think you should go to Mali." "And what about you, Bakala?"

Bakala lets off a stream of smoke, then smiles. "It was fun fighting alongside you Shadowmoor. Just remember that the world is bigger than even us. We'll meet again someday: either in person, in spirit, this life, or in the afterlife. Until then…" "Bakala wait," Shadowmoor yells until the smoke completely covers the men. Seconds later, Bakala disappears along with the smoke. Shadowmoor stands in the middle of the walkway while redefining his resolve.

"I didn't expect the Elite 8 to be back. However, Bakala and the woman are correct. I, too, sense that finding this White Fox can help me find the sword," Shadowmoor concludes, *Looks like I'm going to Mali.*"

Shadowmoor activates his Dracocernentia, then faces towards the direction to his hotel building. Knowing that the night is almost over, Shadowmoor quickly scales the tops of London's buildings and makes his way back.

On the other side of the city, the other man escapes to a Condo off the Thames River. He quickly scales the stairways towards the 14th floor. Meeting the guards mounted outside the door, the man struggles to catch his breath while pleading with the guards.

"Huh...Hufff...huff...I...I... need to see him now!" the man yells while catching his breath. The guards remain unemotional and stoic, almost dismissing the distress in the man's voice. "Did you not hear me? I said that I need to speak with him." Again, the guards refuse to acknowledge the man's pleads.

On the other side of the doors, Goth is shrouded with affection from a beautiful white woman with blond hair, blue eyes, supermodel physique wearing a tight white dress with 5-inch pumps. Rubber her hands all over his body; Goth takes his time to look at the camera to see the man pleading with his guards. Suddenly his mood shifts to irritation, knowing that the man's presence reveals a problem. Goth then pushes a button on his chair to activate the intercom.

"Ugh...Let him in" Goth says in the intercom. The man looks up as one of the guards turns around to open the door to the suite. The man rushes in through the doors and stands in front of Goth before collapsing to his knees.

"Mr. Goth. We have a problem. It's the…" "Shhhh" Goth interrupts before prompting the woman to get up, "Hey sweetie, my friend here is thirsty. Can you walk your fine ass towards the bar and grab my special bottle please?" "Well, of course," she smiles back. "Excellent," he says, then smacking her butt while she walks to the bar.

Victor Goth is a sophisticated man: about 28 years old, 6'1 ½ '' tall, suave, charismatic, and accomplished. He walks towards the man as he regains his breath. His smile calms the man down as Goth puts his hand on the man's shoulder.

"So, what seems to be the problem?" "Well, Mr. Goth. After our meeting last night, we were attacked." "Attacked" Goth exclaimed while directing the main towards the bar, "Who would do such a thing?" "It…it was 2 men. One had dreadlocks and the other wore a hood." "2 men, you say? Please tell me more?" "Well, they seemed to be negroes. But both of them had these… crazy-looking eyes. One of them killed the…" "Shhh shhhh shhhhhh" Goth interrupts, "It's alright. It's quite alright."

Goth sits the man down while the woman brings out the special bottle. Then he pulls out a drawer, taking a picture out of it and showing it to the man. It is a picture of the Dracocernentia, carved in a stone tablet that was discovered years ago. He shows the man the picture. "Hey sweetie, can you pour our guest a glass from our special bottle please?" "Well, of course, Daddy, anything for you?" "That's my girl," Goth compliments, then turning his attention to the man, "Did these…attackers have eyes like this?" The man takes a good look at the photo and is petrified by its presence. The sweat from his forehead migrates towards his red cheeks, and the man musters up the courage to answer Goth. "Indeed, they did have the same eyes."

Goth stares at the man and smiles. He attempts to calm the man by showing levels of hospitality and humility. "Don't worry now," Goth says, "let's drink to calm your nerves."

Goth prompts the man to take the glass. The man calms down, smirks, and takes a sip from the glass. Goth again smiles and addresses his guests. "You see, everything is alright. We can fix this."

Moments later, the glass hits the ground and shatters. The room is filled with sounds of struggle and loss of breath. The man begins to gurgle spit, blood, and foam while grabbing his throat. Goth doesn't flinch, as he and the woman witness a loose end being cut. The man crawls on the floor, grasping the last few gruesome moments of his life. Then Goth whispers while taking a sip of his cup, "This world does not need inferior incompetence. Either you succeed or…" Goth walks towards the man as he dies with a pool of spit and blood flowing out of his mouth. He then smiles, then drains the last of his drink on the lifeless body. He looks up and addresses the woman.

"Have someone take this trash out of here, and please make it quick." "Of course," she says while walking towards the doors. Goth faces the window to greet the rising sun from the east. "So, it begins again," Goth recollects, "I knew they should've killed him in America. But no matter, he's going to lead me to the greatest weapon unknown to the majority. Only then will I dispose of him and have my revenge."

Afterwards, Goth greets the rising sun and the promise of a new day.

# Chapter 15: Diverted Destinies

It is nearly 5 am in London. The light glimmers of light appear on the eastern horizon, blocked only by the many buildings and structures of the city. Shadowmoor makes it to his hotel room and enters through the window. The night has drained the hero of almost all of his energy. Despite this, he removes his jacket, walks towards his backpack, and pulls out his laptop. Malik walks to a desk near the TV, pugs up the adapter and lifts the screen.

Malik is so tired that he sits down and lowers his head. His shoulders were barely able to support him while his fingers interlace themselves behind his neck. His breathing is slow and heavy, his mind is as unsettling as a brewing storm, and his original course of action is challenged by new compelling information.

"I thought that finding the Harq Aldaqr would be as simple as following the dots," he reflects, while rubbing his eyes in an attempt to get comfortable, "Yet, I sense that the shadows of the Elite 8 stick with me like the brown in my skin. *Should I contact Audrey and let her know?*

Malik sits in front of the laptop pondering in silence as he tries to recuperate from the night. Then, moments later, a familiar sound interrupts the peace.

RING...RING...RING... Malik gets up to locate his phone. After a brief look, he uses his thumb to swipe sideways before answering.

"Emma, it's late. What are you still doing up?"

There's an awkward quiet moment. Seconds seem like a millennium, and Malik grows more concerned.

"Is everything alright?" Malik probes, "Emma..." "Malik..." Emma struggles to speak, "Today wasn't a day that I was prepared for." "Prepared... What happened?"

Malik sits back down in front of the laptop while Emma is wrestling with the phone. He knows instinctively that Emma is in a rough patch in her journey and just needs a catalyst to let go.

"Malik, it's about Asir." "Asir, the kid you suspect may have the Fire Line?" "There's no suspicion. There's no mystery, matter of fact, there's no doubt." "Emma, what's going on?"

Emma braces herself while trying to get her erratic emotions under control. The shock of the events, as well as the purpose placed on her, gives her a level of anxiety she has never experienced before.

"So I go to the school, and when I get there, a couple of boys was bullying Asir. The kids just all circled around them, laughing, and taunting him as these boys grabbed his backpack." "Ugh, where were the other teachers?" "None of the teachers surprisingly tried to break it up, so I tried. But you know I couldn't do much because…" "Yeah, I know." "But that didn't matter…"

Malik squints his eyes, anticipating the revolution that has his sister shook to the core. "Emma…" "When one of the boys took out the picture, he drew of himself and me, he ripped it in half and threw it on the floor. Then that's when it happened." "What happened," Malik pushes, "Emma…" "Asir's voice changes. He started speaking Seminole, then bursts into flames."

Malik's eyes widened so much that the gasp could be heard from the other line. Malik remembers the moment his Fire Line was triggered and ignited. Knowing how unexpected and possessed such power can have, he continues to gather more information.

"The Inner Flame," Malik responds, "the moment when the dormant flame from within gets a spark. Tell me Emma, did it form a dragon?" "No, but it did form a silhouette of someone in his past. The flame created a tomahawk from his hand and almost struck the kid" "REALLY!!! So, it got that far?" "Malik, I had to approach Asir carefully to calm him down. The police showed up with the assistant principal, literally ready to shoot Asir. It was…" "So, the public knows. Damn…" "Malik, when I touched Asir, I was able to communicate with his ancestor. A Seminole Warrior who had the Dracocernentia that he inherited from his mother. He told me that it was my destiny to help Asir recognize his Fire Line."

Malik is rejuvenated from this news, despite the trauma of the events. It confirms what he has learned that more people from across the globe may have the same powers.

"Emma turns out we're not alone. Tonight, I thwarted a plan to use kidnapped immigrants as test subjects with the help of another person with the Dracocernentia. But, now that I think about it, the fact that more of us are discovering this power must mean something beyond our understanding is coming." "Bro, do you think that the public is afraid of this power? I mean, how do you cover this up?"

Malik logs on to his computer and gets on the internet. He begins to google search on the Dogon, the Sigi, and the other information he'd gathered. While doing so, he puts Emma on a speaker to conclude their debriefing.

"Emma, I now know that this is bigger than us. If more of our people are awaking their Fire Lines, then there's no secret why the Elite 8…" "Elite 8! I thought that…" "Emma, you should know as well as I do that all we did was cut off one head of a Hydra. There are many more heads and minions from behind the scenes. I know they too seek the sword to help aim their schemes to World oppression and domination." "So, what do we do?" "I got information from one of the victims that an old entity called the "White Fox" resides within the Dogon in Mali." "The Dogon, you mean Grandpa's…" "That's right; I need to book a flight asap to get there and find this White Fox." "Malik, you know that…" "Emma, I need you to listen to me. You've got to keep tabs on Asir. I suspect that they are going to hold him for God knows what. But try to do it discretely, see if you can get to know his family." "I gotcha bro, but what about you?" "Like I said, I have to go to Mali." "Well Malik, just be careful. If the Elite 8 are still out there, they have eyes and ears everywhere." "I will, meanwhile, you take care of yourself and protect Asir. I know that is your destiny." Emma nods before concluding the phone call.

"I love you shit-stain" Emma says. "Back at you ass-wipe. I'll call you when I make it there." Both brother and sister hang up the phone, putting Malik back in motion to plan his next move.

"It says here that the next flight to Mali won't be until tomorrow afternoon. Good, it'll give me some time to rest and pack for the journey. *I hope this won't waste time that we don't have…*"

Afterwards, Malik makes a few transitions, checks his accounts, and books a flight for Mali. The endeavor takes a mere 45 minutes to complete. Still drained from his lack of sleep and the exertion of power, Malik is literally walking on fumes. He gets up from his chair, shuts his laptop, and sluggishly walks towards the bed before crashing headfirst on the soft mattress. Without a moment's notice, Malik falls fast asleep to regain his lost energy.

The peaceful morning gives way to REM sleep. The weight of Malik's concerns is lifted like a boulder in a large body of water. His mind goes into a dream state deep within the confines of his consciousness. Like many visions before, he is drawn into a corridor of flashing green, orange, and yellow lights.

Not able to speak, the vision transports Malik into a void in space, surrounded by billions of stars. With it, there is a large circle of fire with 3 strange figures. One of the figures is a black deity with short kinky hair, a red cloth covering his loins, metal bracelets covering each wrist, while holding a machete. The figure also had glowing white and cloudy eyes.

The other figure, standing on the other side of the circle, is a being wearing a gold and white loincloth stretching towards its knees, a multicolored neck garment, brown skin, and the head of a falcon. Its eyes burned bright blue, matching the staff held by its right hand and the golden ankh held on its left.

The last figure, positioned in between them, is a giant white fox with golden, brown eyes. The fox had oversized ears that twitched in different directions, a narrow nose with few whiskers, and a toy dog's posture.

The deities all nodded their heads, communicating with one another without speaking or making a sound. For what seemed to be several minutes, each deity would animate their concerns with hand gestures, body movements, and head nods to convey some sort of point.

Suddenly, a rumble in the heavens shakes the sphere. Each member of this circle stops what they are doing, they give their undivided attention. Nothing shows up but a pair of huge, strong, rough hands. The other members of this coalition turn their heads to the hands as it projects images within the circle of fire.

The hands clap together and rise their palms, prompting the fire to show a burning image from within the circle. This image shows several atrocities placed upon black people: from the feeding of black children to dogs during the Spanish Inquisition to the kidnapping and deporting of slaves to the western hemisphere, to the beatings, raping, and killing of slaves, to reconstruction and the loss of property of prominent black families, to the injustices of the white supremacist machine.

As the flaming theatrics concludes, the deities look at each other, seemingly with concern and litigation; meanwhile, the pair of hands clap, creating a shockwave that spans the universe and the heavens to regain their attention.

Finally, the pair of hands raise the left palm several feet up to reveal three objects.

The first object is a burning curved sword with the carving of the Dracocernentia on the cross guard.

The second object manifests into a magnificent golden dragon. This beast has 2 long whiskers, followed by two protruding horns curving backwards, tough razor-like scales, claws as red as blood, wings as broad enough to engulf small nations, and surprisingly with its eyes closed.

Lastly, there is a pile of ashes. The other objects move away as the aches begin to ignite. After a short moment, the pile ignites into a flame covered by a barrage of colors: ranging from blue, red, green, orange, and yellow. As the flames continue to flow, the eyes of all the deities become fixated; anticipating the shape, the flame will take after it has settled down. Finally, as the smoke clears, a silhouette of a man forms. The man doesn't do anything. Shoulders and arms go up and down as if it were signaling breathing or panting.  The other deities look at each other with confusion and anxiety.

Suddenly, the hands clap again, generating a soundwave that shakes the space. Afterwards, the silhouette begins to open its eyes slowly. With each inch, a glimmer of light glows more bright and powerful. The silhouette takes time until it fully showcases eyes; however, theses eyes are different. These eyes are completely golden, with the pupil shaped like the curvature of a sword.

As the eyes glow, it illuminates the space, spreading the energy throughout the cosmos. As the deities stand firm, the silhouette grabs the sword, then mounts the dragon, which also opens its eyes to show the same pupils, linking them together.

As the dragon roars, the hands then point towards the direction behind the deities. Then, the deities follow their gaze as they all migrate their attention to follow the point.

After about 3 seconds, Malik wakes up sweating, breathing hard, and shocked by another profound vision. The drips of water percolate through the side of his face; his gaze is still in a state of shock, while his panting slowly gets under control.

"I don't know what I just witnessed," Malik recollects while grabbing his phone, "I kinda miss the days of having normal dreams. *What in the hell did that dream mean? And why did those hands point at me?*"

While looking at the phone, the time shows 3 pm. Malik had slept throughout the morning and the early afternoon. Despite this, Malik quickly realizes that his dreams are not coincidental but indicators of the direction of his path. He gets up out of bed and stretches. Then he begins to pack some of his clothes while reaffirming his dream.

"I bet that the sword is the Harq Alqadr," he concludes, "but that figure and the dragon represents something else. Could that be the Golden Dragon Moor? And I bet that White Fox is the one I need to seek in Mali."

Malik walks towards his laptop, opens it, then confirms the tickets for the next day's flight. He rubs his head and his beard while looking at his Shadowmoor jacket. The intensity of the journey has Malik questioning how far he is willing to go.

"This trip is turning into a deeper Rabbit hole than I thought," Malik looks out in the window before concluding his thoughts, "I now know how anyone would be intoxicated by all of this hidden history. I think I owe it to Hauss and his granddaughter to figure this out so that they can have closure."

Malik then continues to finish packing for the next phase of his journey.

# Chapter 16: Catching the W.A.V.E.

After Emma hangs up the phone with Malik, she sits quietly on the bed, reliving the events in her head. Her face softens, her eyebrows lower, and the weight of her hair in a bonnet seems to add to the strain in her neck. All she could think of is the fate of a child who had befriended her in such a short time.

Geneva senses the energy and checks on Emma. KNOCK KNOCK KNOCK, "Emma… Emma…" Geneva asks, "Are you ok child?" Geneva walks in to see Emma sitting down on her bed. Geneva's eyes tighten as she approaches Emma. Emma continues to look down, staring at the air in the room. Geneva then walks next to Emma, sits on the bed, and caresses her shoulders.

The moment of catering prompts Emma to lift her head. Emma's eyes begin to water, and a single tear falls down her cheek before she can wipe it away. Then Geneva starts the difficult conversation that has Emma feeling completely torn.

"My Amira, is it about the boy?" Emma takes her time to speak, drawing up the strength during her time of vulnerability. She looks directly at Geneva, trying her best not to break down. "Grandma, I don't know why I am so emotional. I mean, the way that they treated him…" "Yes, I overheard what you told your brother about what happened today. So, it seems that he does have the ancestry." "Not only that," Emma adds, "They were willing to shoot him, despite the fact that he was the one being bullied."

Emma wipes her eyes again then asks Geneva a profound question. "Why do I feel so weak when I care for someone else? I've never felt these kinds of feelings before." Geneva looks down and takes a breath. The weight of these questions requires a subtle, yet direct answer.

"You know, it is easy to have all the power in the world and abuse it if you have no attachments or people to love. However, it is the love of your people that we draw our strength from. My Amira, you spent the first 24 years of your life as nothing more than a weapon to be used to control and destroy. Now that you found love and a purpose, those driving forces have left, leaving a void." "But Grandma, I don't want to be that person anymore. I mean, yes I do miss the power, but I was also lost, angry, and soulless." "And now you have a new purpose."

Geneva refocuses her attention towards Emma while Emma tries to position herself to Geneva's words.

"Did you get in touch of this boy's Fire Line?" "Yes, it was his ancestor. A man with Native American and Slave blood. He said that it was my destiny to help Asir reconnect with his Fire Line." "Emma, as Phoenix Moors, we are attracted to others like magnets. This is how your mother found Malik's father, how Malik found you, and how you found Asir." "I suppose," Emma presses while letting go of her fears, "So then, will I find the source of my power by helping Asir?" "(Sigh), It is rarely as simple as that," Geneva encourages, "However, I think that helping Asir is a first step to helping yourself. We tend to see the reflection of ourselves through the eyes of those we interact with. Maybe you see something within yourself with him." "You know Grandma, when Malik sought me out, he mentioned that he grew up being ostracized and abused by his adoptive parents. So, when he pointed those things out in me, I didn't want to hear those words at first. I wanted to destroy him."

Then, in a shift of mood, Emma begins to smirk and shake her head. Then redirects her attention back to Geneva. "You know something Grandma, he was right. Once I realized that, I had to burn off the fallacies that kept me from reaching my potential. Maybe, just maybe the love and the determination to protect others is the way to reach my potential." Geneva smiles back then gives Emma a long, tight hug. "My dear Emma, an elder once told me that a dragon needs blood to fuel its muscles. We are the blood." "Thanks Grandma."

Geneva releases her grip, gets up from the bed. Emma gets her long legs underneath the comforter before turning in for the night. Then she stops her grandmother before she walks out of the room.

"I have a plan to reach Asir. Hopefully, the school will let me know if he doesn't show up tomorrow where he is." Geneva nods, then bid a good night. "My Amira, remember where your source of power comes from. Love you." "Love you too Grandma Geneva." Geneva closes the door while Emma turns off the lamp next to her bed. She closes her eyes, relaxes her breathing, then falls to sleep.

The next morning, Emma goes through her daily routine of taking the bonnet out, washing her face, brushing her teeth, and combing her hair into a kinky bun. Then, she looks through her closet to pick out another outfit. This time, she's more decisive: grabbing a short sleeve baby blue t-shirt, a jean skirt, and a pair of white sneakers. She also wraps a small, gold bracelet around her left ankle for an added touch.

"Good morning, Emma," Kemba says, "How are you feeling?" "I'm better." "Your Grandmother told me something about the conversation you had last night. I just hope you are ok." "Sure am," Emma responds while kissing Kemba on the cheek.

Geneva is in the kitchen preparing some food for lunch and dinner. Emma addresses her while meandering towards the front door. "I'll see you in a few hours, Grandma." "Wait a minute," Geneva scolds, "Shouldn't you eat something dear? You're already like a giraffe on a diet." "I'll grab something on the way." Emma leaves while Geneva puts her hands on her waist and shakes her head.

Emma gets in the Jeep and turns on the ignition. As soon as she pulls out of the driveway, she heads towards the direction of the school.

During the drive, Emma plays several scenarios in her head, trying to anticipate the reception she will receive from the school. "*It's hard to believe that they'll just allow him to come back to school after what happened yesterday,*" Emma thinks, "*So hopefully, I can figure out where he is and where to find him.*"

The drive is short and easy. Like before, Emma parks the Jeep in the parking lot, then grabs her purse before getting out of the SUV. She locks the door with the key button as she travels through the parking lot towards the front door.

Emma enters the school building and notices 2 women talking with Mrs. Rios. During the conversation, Mrs. Rios notices Emma and gives her a quick nod with her finger telling Emma to wait a bit. Emma smiles, sits down, and crosses her legs. Once Emma gets comfortable, Mrs. Rios redirects her focus back at the women.

"So, you see Mrs. Rios, we're here to help with yesterday's unfortunate events." one of the women says. "Well, Asir is a good boy who just happened to get bullied. I've already contacted his mother, but I was only able to brief her on what's going to happen to him," Mrs. Rios responds.

Emma overhears the conversation while pretending to scroll through her phone. She slightly dilates her pupil to blue while amplifying her senses of hearing.

"Mrs. Rios, I assure you. We at W.A.V.E are committed to limiting violence in schools among our children while giving them counseling for those who are victims of it. Asir will be with us for about a week or 2." "*A week or 2*," Emma pauses, "*What are they up to?*" "Well, as long as he gets the best care," Mrs. Rios reiterates, "We care for Asir and want the best for him."

Both women nod after ending the conversation. As they approach the front door, Emma reverts her eyes back to normal and gets up. Mrs. Rios then takes the opportunity to introduce Emma.

"Ladies, this is Emma Ayokè. She's the one who has mentored Asir from the Big Sister's foundation. Emma, these ladies are from W.A.V.E." The women briefly greet each other with handshakes and smiles. "W.A.V.E?" Emma asks, "What is it?" "Oh, well, we're Women Against Violence Empowerment. We counsel kids who are involved in violent situations while working towards limiting conflict amongst our students." "Right," Emma responds suspiciously, "Well, it was very nice to meet you." The women smile and wave before exiting the office.

Afterwards, Mrs. Rios lets off a huge sigh. Her shoulders drop, her hair follows, and she can remove the mask of pleasure while showing a face of pain. "Oh my God, what a day!" she complains while escorting Emma to her desk. "What seems to be the problem?" Emma inquires. "(Sigh) So the event that happened yesterday has gotten everybody going nuts. The police are trying to investigate what happened to Asir while covering it up, the Principal and Assistant Principal are trying to quell the complaints from the parents, and now W.A.V.E. wants Asir to be sent to an alternative facility." "But Mrs. Rios, Asir didn't start the…"

Mrs. Rios interrupts Emma by putting her hand up. Her usual bubbly has now shifted to a serious and controversial gaze. She prompts Emma to move in closer to intensify the message.

"Between you and me, those boys should've been punished, not Asir." she whispers, "I know that turning into a giant flaming warrior isn't normal, but he was clearly scared and frightened. Plus, I don't trust keeping a kid for more than a few days." "So, what is W.A.V.E going to do with Asir?" "I don't know. Now the Assistant Principal wanted to know if you'd be interested in mentoring another child?"

Emma pauses for a moment to understand the undertone as well as the complexity of the question. Her heart skips a beat, knowing that she'd made such a connection with a young man, only to lose him again. Then Emma regains her nerve to answer the question.

"Mrs. Rios, with all due respect, I truly care for Asir and want to help him." Mrs. Rios smirks as if she'd anticipated the answer before it was spoken. "I know I'm not supposed to tell you this, but his mother is a real piece of work. I legally can't tell you where he is or where he'll be held. You have to get the information from her." Mrs. Rios extends her hand and nods at Emma to shake it. Despite not having her Avemcernentia activated, Emma can see minor receptor fields of green pulsing through her body. Immediately, Emma follows the gestor by shaking Mrs. Rios' hand. Mrs. Rios' grip is firm and conveying. She smirks then looks down. Emma feels something crumbly and loose in her hand.

After they release the handshake, Emma looks in her hand to see a slip of paper. The contents have the name of Asir's mother, her phone number, and her address. Afterwards, Emma looks back at Mrs. Rios while she gets up.

"I know that you care for Asir." she concludes while keeping her voice low, "Go and make sure he's ok. I can't say much, but between you and me, I don't trust them." "I will and thank you Mrs. Rios."

Emma takes the crumbled piece of paper, nods and smiles back at Mrs. Rios before exiting the office.

When she exits out of the building, there is a sudden dread that overwhelms her. The intensity of the surge of negative energy is so dense that she nearly collapses in the middle of the parking lot.

*"Oh my God!"* she complains, *"What is this sharp pain? What is going on?"* Immediately, she is getting flash visions and images of Seminoles fighting, slaves revolting, and eyes gleaming. She is unable to focus long enough to ascertain the meaning of this pain. She struggles to make her way towards the Jeep. Each step is like walking in a pit of lava with plastic shoes carrying a mountain. Emma continues to fight on, contemplating giving in until she hears a voice.

"Press on Child," it echoes, "All will be explained. Press on." Not questioning the voice but understanding it, Emma continues her trek until she reaches the SUV. She struggles to get the keys from her purse. Then once grabbed, she pushes the button to unlock the Jeep. Afterwards, she opens the door to get in.

Once inside, Emma pants profusely: her breath is heavy and loud, her forehead is littered with beads of sweat, and her eyes bulge out of their sockets to release the pressure inside of her head. The young woman sits in the Jeep long enough to regain her senses. Then the voice triggers her eardrums with instructions.

"Go to the source," it whispers. "What source!" Emma yells as she tries to catch her breath. The voice doesn't respond. Emma waits for a minute; then she surveys the parking lot. Realizing that no one is around, Emma makes a risky move. "There's only one way to get some answers," Emma concludes.

Emma closes her eyes. She allows herself to control her breath. Her heartbeat becomes rhythmic and distinct, her resolve becomes stern, and her inner flame begins to build up. As soon as the blue light blankets her body, her Avemcernentia activates to transport inside of a veil.

Like most meditations, the veil is secluded deep within Emma's self-consciousness. The meeting may appear briefly in the physical plane, but the encounter can span from days, months, years, or centuries. The silhouette of Emma appears, and she begins to communicate her needs.

"I need your help!" She yells, "I am having pain and visions that I am not accustomed to having. What does all of this mean?" Emma circles around, waiting for someone, anyone, to appear. Her impatience grows within her, to the point that she begins to get frustrated.

Suddenly, something screeches like an eagle, and a flame silhouette of a White Phoenix appears in front of Emma. Enamored by the sight, Emma witnesses the Phoenix flapping it's wings to morph into a familiar face. A beautiful, dark woman with light blue eyes, a white hajib over her head. She is also wrapped in a light brown and white cloak with no shoes. She smiles as she greets Emma.

"We must work on your patience, my child," she says, "but then again, when you want to understand your journey, it is reasonable to want to know in a short time." "Great-great-great- grandmother Muqadas," Emma responds, "I am honored to see you again." Emma bows in reverence while Muqadas smirks and makes her way towards Emma. She gives Emma a big hug and a kiss on the forehead. "My child, I am your ancestor, not your dictator." she explains, "You honor me by continuing our legacy." "Yes, I understand. Still, it's good to be loved." Muqadas chuckles before letting go.

"So, you are wondering about the visions and pain you are experiencing, yes?" Muqadas briefs. "Yes, I came across a young boy who has the Fire Line. He comes from a lineage indicative of this land. My first question is, how is this possible?" Emma asks. "My child," Muqadas explains, "when our ancestors learn the secrets of both the Dracocernentia and the Avemcernentia, we traveled the world. We were not confined to just Africa, as was told to you, or even Andalusia. We wanted to make an impact in the whole world." "I see," Emma responds as Muqadas continues. "However, when we lost our power and control, some lineages had to hide their identities so that their lineage wouldn't be detected and destroyed. Sometimes these lineages would mix up with others who had remnants in their own family past. Take your brother, for instance; our lineage of Phoenix Moors happened to mix with a powerful lineage of Dragon Moors…" "Which explains why Malik was able to regain his power without prior training." "Precisely my child."

Emma takes the time to understand and to press on towards her new goal.

"So then what about Asir? Why am I so drawn to this child and why am I seeing visions of his past?" Muqadas switches her tone to seriousness and concern. She no longer smiles but speaks to Emma through her eyes. Emma picks up the gesture and prepares to listen intensely.

"I sense great evil brewing. During the times of unease and war for our survival, the Phoenix Moors would gravitate to the mightiest of the Dragon Moors to quell the threat. I suspect that not only is this boy from a powerful line but that the time is near to shore up our numbers for what's to come." "What's to come?" Emma asks, "I don't understand." "My child, when you were subjected to the enemy, they blinded you into their puppet of destruction. When you broke away, you only amplified the inevitable. There was once a war that started with the defeat of our people. I believe that this war is reaching a pivotal point of the ultimate solution." "So is my destiny with Asir tied to this so-called holy war?" "Just as your brother is on a quest to find the blade that will unite the people, yours is to awaken the power of the one who will help fight back."

Emma suddenly understands the gravity of the situation and comes up with a solution to Muqada's words.

"I need to find Asir and teach him how to reconnect with his ancestors. If I can do that, then maybe he'll be able to control his power." "Exactly my child," Muqadas concludes, "but be careful. This evil you have encountered before, but not their weaponry. Be on your guard and remember that you are more than just your eyes." Emma nods before Muqadas disappears into flames. Afterwards, Emma wakes up.

After only a few minutes have passed, Emma begins to wipe her forehead, turns on the Jeep, looks at the paper then makes her way towards the address. "Ok Asir, I'm coming."

# Chapter 17: Broken Homes, Broken Minds

Emma continues to make her way towards the address on the sheet of paper. The tension in her muscles grips the steering wheel so hard that it leaves temporary fingerprint impressions on the plastic. Her face is compressed and robotic. She shows little emotion; meanwhile, her inner thoughts become a conglomerate of feelings, insight, recollection, and resolve.

"The piece of paper says Asir lives in the housing projects off Southside Blvd," Emma states, "That's just 3 blocks from where I am now. I sure hope his mom isn't what Mrs. Rios says she is. (Sigh) *None of that matters. I need to get to the bottom of this.*"

Emma comes towards Southside Blvd and makes a right turn. As soon as she turns, she is mortified by the scene. Growing up in clandestine privilege, Emma has seen or experienced very little when coming across deplorable diving conditions. The housing projects have a light orange, yellow, and red brick work; however, the energy of hopelessness and poverty emulated from the few people roaming the streets like a stench of death. Emma looks for the office building and proceeds to park the Jeep in the parking area, making the SUV look less conspicuous.

Emma gets out of the car and takes another look at the crumbled sheet of paper. "Ok, it says here that she lives in #21, so I guess I'll have to walk until I find it."

Despite having powers, Emma maintains her composure and wits. She calmly walks around the buildings until she reaches a set across the street from the parking lot. Emma treks across the grass as some of the residence look suspiciously and curious. Some of the older residents sit outside of their porches basking in the Florida sun, while others sit around drinking bottles or generating small talk.

When Emma reaches the buildings, she begins to count the numbers on the doors to navigate to her destination.

"*Let's see*," she deduces, "15… 16… 17… 18… 19… 20…" Emma makes it towards the end of the building but hears roars of dialect from different voices. The back and forth amplifies as each perspective emphasizes a point.

"Girl! You know these people at the school are tripping," one voice continues, "You know they had the nerve to tell me that they can arrest my child!" "What? They can't do that! So, what did you do?" the other voice asks. "Girl, I cuss they asses out. Then had the nerve to tell me they'll get the police to escort me out. I said, I don't give a damn about you or the damn police. I'm trying to figure out why my child was the one getting bullied, but the kids who did it didn't get in trouble!"

Emma cautiously walks towards the door, anticipating a less than warm welcome. "*Wow*," she wonders, "*she does seem like a handful...Well Emma, here goes.*"

Emma takes a deep breath and briefly closes her eyes. She relaxes her shoulders and rotates her neck. After shaking off the anxiety, Emma walks towards the door.

Upon arrival, she notices that the screen door is open and filled with the aroma of something strange to Emma. The smoke fills the air like a cloud, the women continue their cackling like hyenas to a carcass, and the smell causes Emma to cough a little. Despite this, Emma presses on towards the screen door.

Knock, knock, knock, knock… "Who the hell is at my door?!" the woman yells. Emma chooses her words and, with prudence, confirms the name of the residence.

"Hello?" Emma responds, "Is this the Tameka Sims?" Irate, the woman puts down her blunt and walks towards the door. The woman is dark, about 5'5'', with long eye lashes, blond colored box braids, with dark rings in her eyes, dark red lip gloss, several tattoos on her chest and arms, with a medium gut protruding through her night gown. She opens the door then sizes Emma up. She raises one of her eyebrows then lifts her lip with discontent.

"And who are you?" she sneers. "Hi… um, my name is Emma Ayokè. I am Asir's mentor… through the Big Sister's program." Tameka gives Emma another smug look as she rolls her eyes with her hand on her left hip. "Um Hmm...so you're the "Miss Emma" he talks about in school," she responds sarcastically, "What do you want?" "Well…"

Emma is interrupted by another voice echoing through the back of the home. A frail, scratchy voice follows the squealing of wheels scrapping through the cold floor.

"Cough... cough... cough... Tameka, now I did told you about smoking that crap," she complains, "You know how it messes with my lungs." "Momma, you need to go back to bed!" Tameka commands while redirecting her focus back to Emma.

"Yeah, well as you can see, he ain't here. And quite frankly, I don't know why you are here or how you found this place!" "Um hmm" her companion adds in the background while putting out the blunt.

The old woman arouses her curiosity by slowly making her way towards the front door. She is an elderly and sickly woman, with a head nearly bald, with thick glasses, wearing a pink gown while holding on for dear life on her walker. Despite her condition, she exhibits a more hospitable attitude.

"Who are you talking to Tameka?" she ponders. "(Sigh) Momma, she's just that mentor that Asir talks about at school. She was just leaving."

Emma continues to keep her composure by smiling a little while observing the interaction of the women in the house. As the woman reaches the front door, she takes a good look at Emma and smiles.

"You sure are pretty... and tall too," the woman compliments. "Um hmm... whatever," Tameka sneers again. The woman gives Tameka a stern look. "Tameka, now you know better than to have her just standing in," she reprimands, "Baby come on in, please." "Now Momma!" Tameka objects. "Now nothing," she responds, then prompting Emma to come in by smiling at her. Tameka rolls her eyes then welcomes Emma in. "Thank you," Emma says while walking in.

The woman maneuvers her way to her love seat while Tameka sits next to her friend on the couch with her arms folded and legs crossed. Emma sits in a chair on the opposite side of the living room. Tameka's friend is just as suspicious: heavy-set woman with her hair poorly put in a ponytail, and a tattered A shit with grey leggings and black slides. Emma can feel the bad energy: the air is still thick with smoke residue and ash floats around the air like birds in the sky. Despite this, the old woman presses Emma.

"So, you're that woman that's been helping Asir?" she asks. "Yes ma'am," Emma responds, "I have been seeing him for the past few days. I wanted to check up to see if he's ok." "Well, they said that he was a danger to the school, so they sent him to some damn program." Tameka angrily adds while maintaining her noncompliant mannerisms. "Shhhhh Tameka, now this young lady was (cough, cough) nice enough to check up on Asir." "Yes…" Emma cautiously interjects, "I was the one who stopped the other boys from… going too far."

The old woman shakes her head. Her eyes droop while she struggles to maintain a smile. "I don't know why that school continues to mess with him." she complains, "Thank God for people like you." Emma smiles then continues to question the women.

"Do you know where Asir is being held? I want to visit him if it's possible." Tameka closes, then opens her eyes while smacking her lips. "I know he's being held in that W.A.V.E. building downtown. It's supposed to help kids who get bullied, but they won't let the kids go home." "They don't go home?" Emma asks. "Yeah. Shit, it might as well be jail," Tameka concludes, "I don't like it one bit." "Well, I want to visit Asir soon, just to make sure…"

Tameka gets up and walks towards Emma. "You are too gun-ho for me. I don't think you can do anything about Asir or where he is." Tameka then walks towards her mother, "I think it's time for you to go."

Emma knows that the tension in the room won't go away. So, she prepares to get up as Tameka walks down the hall. Her friend picks up the unfinished blunt and sparks it up. She continues to stare down Emma. "Momma, I need to remake your bed and wash your sheets!" Tameka yells. "Baby you're doing too much." her mother answers.

Emma finally gets up and smiles. "It was very nice to meet all of you." "You're such a sweet woman. I'm glad Asir has someone like you at that school. Come back now ya here." Emma nods then walks out of the house.

Emma treks across the housing projects towards the Jeep. Emma tries to reconcile her thoughts during the walk while putting the pieces together. *"I had no idea that Asir was living with such a volatile woman. It was hard to tell if she cared for him or didn't want to be outshined by my involvement."* Emma takes out her phone, scrolls to the internet and types in the address to W.A.V.E. While she gathers more information, she makes it to the parking lot where she parked the Jeep. She gets in the vehicle, buckles her seatbelt, and starts the ignition.

"Ok, so I'm able to find the W.A.V.E. building. Says here it's downtown." She pulls out of the parking lot and drives towards the direction of downtown. Emma becomes skeptical based on the limited information she'd just gathered. "I find it weird that they wouldn't allow Asir to go home. *Hopefully, once I make it there, I can get some answers."* Emma concludes while driving.

After 20 minutes of driving, Emma makes it to the W.A.V.E building. The structure is inconspicuous: bland grey color concrete walls, limited windows, about 2 stories high and 19,000 square feet. Emma drives around to find a parking spot on the west side of the building. After parking the Jeep and shutting it off, Emma gets out of the vehicle and makes her way to the front doors.

When Emma walks through, she is surprised by what she sees. The foyer is decorated with brown and tan marl stones on the floor, a wide-open venue right behind a front desk and a security officer. The eloquence of the floor is enough to wonder how such an organization is funded. Still, Emma walks towards the front desk to address the clerk sitting at the desk.

"Excuse me," Emma asks, "I am looking for someone who may be here." The clerk looks at her with a half-hearted smile. She is an average-looking white woman: with slightly longer shoulder-length brown hair, blue eyes, wearing a purple blouse, black tight-fitting jeans, and black flats. "Um, are you a parent or a teacher?" she asks. "I am part of the Big Sister's organization, and one of my students was admitted here." "Oh, I see," she responds, "however, we have strict rules against allowing visits without appointments." "I see. Is there any way I can see him?"

The clerk tries to hold in her irritation by giving a smirk while typing on her computer. Emma can sense the negative vibes from the woman but remains cool and collected while pressing the matter.

"I'm sure there is something that could be done," Emma continues. "Well, again… unless you have an appointment, we are very limited with our visitation. I'm…" Before the clerk could finish, another woman showed up to ascertain the situation. This woman has a commanding presence about her. She is just as tall as Emma: about 5'9'', heavily built yet muscular, with bold streaks in her dark brown hair, wearing a black and white long sleeve thin blouse, white leggings, and 3-inch peep hole Stiletto pumps. Unlike the clerk, this woman is welcoming and confident.

"Hi, my name is Sharon Bennett. I'm the manager, is there a problem?" "Oh, Hi," Emma responds while shaking Sharon's hand, "I'm Emma Ayokè. I was trying to see if a student that I mentor is here." "Oh, I see," she says, "can you look up the student's name?"

The clerk reluctantly logs on to an online database, then addresses Emma. "What's his name?" "Asir… Asir Sims." Sharon raises her eyebrow before speaking. "Oh, that young man. Yes, I know exactly where he is." "Is there any way I can see him?" Sharon crosses her arms and lets out a big sigh. "Well, we have protocol with our visitation, but I can escort you to see him." "Thank you very much," Emma says, "I just want to make sure he is ok." "I completely understand. So, if you'll follow me, I'll take you to the visiting room."

Emma walks with Sharon down the long hallway. The sound of heels clacking does little to dissuade Sharon from conversing with Emma. "So, you are his mentor, right?" she asks. "Yes, I started seeing him earlier this week," Emma responds, "So W.A.V.E., how exactly do you help the kids here?" "Well, we developed many techniques: including mental therapy, counseling, and herbal therapy." "Herbal therapy?" "Yes, we try not to rely on so call drugs here. Instead, we use natural remedies to help people cope properly in dealing with anything that generates violence." Emma nods as they reach the visiting room.

Sharon uses her id car to scan the electric door key. Once the light turns green, a single click allows the woman to open the door. "If you would wait here, I will have someone bring him here so that he can see you," Sharon informs, "However because this is unscheduled, you will only have 15 minutes to visit." "I understand," Emma says, "Thank you for your help, Sharon." "No problem, and it was nice meeting you." Sharon smiles as she goes towards the other doorway.

The room is completely white walled, with tinted windows, a camera in the ceiling, and a metal table with 2 chairs. Emma sits down on one chair, crosses her legs, then contemplates her experiences.

*"I sense that something is off here,"* Emma ponders, *"yet something in the air is messing up my judgement. I don't know, but I can't figure it out just yet. Regardless, I need to see how Asir is doing."* Suddenly, the doors open. Emma looks up and sees Asir being escorted by another female adult. His demeanor is broken; he looks down and walks towards the table like a prisoner marked for death. Emma squints her eyes but says nothing.

The woman walks Asir to the table then speaks. "Ok Asir," she says, "You have a visitor." As soon as they reach the table, Asir looks up. His eyes are glassy, his lips are parched and dry, yet despite this, his spirits are lifted briefly. "Mmmm… Ms. Emma…" he says softly. Emma smiles while holding back tears. "Hi Asir." she says. The woman looks at Emma and reminds her of the time limit. "I can only give you 15 minutes." she says. Emma nods then redirects her attention towards Asir. The woman then leaves Emma with Asir.

Once the door closes, Emma looks at Asir's pitiful state. The mixture of pain, anger, and sadness mode into one mixture that drives Emma to question his sanity. "Asir, are you ok here?" Asir looks down and frowns. The sadness flows like a flood, yet Asir doesn't easily express himself. Emma tries to find the words to comfort him.

"Asir, what happened at the school wasn't your fault. It's something that very special people deal with." Asir continues to look down while Emma addresses him one more time. "Do you understand what I am saying?" Then Asir begins to communicate what is tormenting him.

"I keep having these dreams Ms. Emma." he says while he tries desperately to look at her. "But everybody here thinks I'm crazy." Emma's left eye sheds a single tear before she could rub it from her face. She calmly proceeds with the conversation with prudence and love.

"Asir, you are part of something special. You have the power to see things that most people cannot understand." "Cccc...can I tell you this one dream that hurts my head?" Asir asks. "Sure Asir, take your time."

Asir sits up straight in his chair. He musters up all of the courage he has left and looks at Emma. "I lived with this weird family; they were white. It was a mommy and a daddy. There were also 3 boys." "I see. So, what were their names?" Emma presses, "It was Noah, Chris, and Ethan. Ethan was a baby." Emma nods as Asir continues. "We went to different places: the carnival, the mall, fun places. Then we would go home. I would go upstairs to Ethan's room. When I get there, I see some pictures." "Pictures of what Asir?" "It was a tiny black family. I don't know why, but the mommy came in really mad. She looked different. She had cut her hair. She put Ethan in his bed but looks at me really mean. Then the baby would throw things at me and scream at me."

Emma is in awe of the detail and the visuals of the dream. She knows from her experiences that these dreams are a way for the ancestors to communicate with the inheritors of the Fire Line. Then, Asir adds on with more details.

"So, then a storm comes in. It's thundering and lightning outside. I go outside of the house and see these clouds form into dragons. There were 2 big cloud dragons. The first one would roar, then disappear. The second one creates a tornado that comes towards me." "Were you scared, Asir?" Emma asks. "I was at first, but when it came to me, it destroyed the house but gave me power. After that, the skies became clear, the storm stopped, and a strange man with these markings on his body, pure white eyes, and sharp, big knives came down from the sky. Then... I wake up."

Emma is completely at a loss for words for a while. Noticing that time is almost over, she gives Asir instructions.

"Listen Asir, I need you to do something for me ok?" "Ok Ms. Emma." "Before you go to bed, I want you to sit on the floor Criss cross apple sauce. Do you remember how to sit like that?" "Yeah, like story time." Asir asks. "Right, like story time. After that, close your eyes and breath slowly. After that, something amazing will happen." "What Ms. Emma?"

Then, a buzzer goes off and the woman comes back to escort Asir. Asir starts to cry while pleading with Emma. "I don't like this place Ms. Emma." Emma smiles and shakes Asir's hand before letting go. "Don't worry Asir," she states, "Just do that thing we talked about. I'll see you again, Ok?" Asir nods before he gets up and walks with the woman.

Emma wipes her yes, gets up and makes her way back to the front of the building. As she walks, she begins to plot her next move. *Tonight, I'm going to come back and rescue Asir. He's not telling me everything that's going on here, but I know there's more to this W.A.V.E. than they're letting on.* Emma then walks past the front desk, looks back one last time. The same clerk as before begins to wrestle her things while awaiting her relief. Emma faces the setting sun of the day, then treks out of the front doors.

# Chapter 18: Child of a Half Breed

Asir walks down a dark corridor with the female escort. The woman is cold, uncompromising, and emotionless. She offers no comfort while looking forward. Asir is rubbing his arms and shivering. They reach his dorm. While he waits to enter, the woman grabs her key and swipes it on the electric key. The light turns green, and the door slides open. She looks at him with stoic eyes. "Time to go in for the night." Asir slowly walks into his dorm room. The area is like a prison: With a single mattress twin bed, a thin blanket and pillow, a small bathroom, and cold, grey concrete floors and walls. Asir looks back, only to see the woman shutting the door and walking away without a word.

Asir walks to his bed and begins to sulk. Tears flow down his face as he begins to complain. "I want to go home… I miss my mom… I miss grandma… I miss Ms. Emma…" Then Asir remembers what Emma told him to do. "Oh yeah, Ms. Emma wanted me to sit on the floor and close my eyes."

As the lights turn off for the night, Asir faces the wall away from the door. He sits on the cold floor and crosses his legs. "Ok, she says I should close my eyes and breathe slowly." Asir closes his eyes and rests his hands in front of him. He takes 3 deep breaths. His body is still. The bad energy is converted as Asir becomes a conduit to ignite his Fire Line. His body begins to glow bright orange. It illuminates his small space as Asir takes his final deep breath.

Suddenly, a gust of wind blows in the room and Asir begins to see flashing lights. Already in a trance, he begins to flow down a tunnel of lights. Not understanding that he is going through a vision, Asir stays still as he becomes a witness to images of a time long past, long forgotten, and embedded in his DNA.

The year is 1816. The village is thriving in the swamps of Florida. As the many species of birds flock to find their way, the waterways and marshes give the local wildlife sustenance, shelter as well as food and stability. A former slave walks out of her lodge with a pot. At the edge of the village is a small pond shielded by a man-made dam to prevent large alligators from surprising the citizens while getting water. She leans down on her knees and puts the pot in the water. As the water fills up the pot, a voice somewhat startles the woman.

"Momma… momma!" the child yells and runs towards the woman. She shakes her head, smiles, then picks up the pot filled with water and meets the young child halfway. Once the little boy sees the woman, he quickly recognizes the woman. "Momma… Momma…" he says. "Malee, I told you to stay in the lodge," she scolds, "Now come along, we have chores to do." She takes the boy's hand while carrying the pot with her right hand.

As they walk back to their lodge, they are greeted by other villagers performing their normal routines. "Mornin Cassie" a black man says while waving. "Mornin James." Cassie has fully emersed herself within the village. She now has a son: caramel complexion with jet black, curly hair, and a stout body. The boy resembles his father while retaining some of the kinky hair of his mother. Cassie continues the small talk with James.

"So Soletawake-yaka is out hunting again?" James asks. "Yes, he is, so I'm trying to prepare for his return. I tell you James; sometimes I feel like we work harder than when I was on those plantations." "Well, at least we work for ourselves and don't get beat in the process," James adds on, "Hi there Malee, how are you?" "Mornin Mr. James" Cassie smiles and shakes her head. "Now this one makes me work nonstop," Cassie complains, "but he's a blessing from Ogun." "Indeed, he is," James says, "Well, we'll see you for dinner tonight yer here?" Cassie nods while James waves at Malee. "You be good Malee yer here." "Yes Mr. James."

Cassie and Malee continue to walk towards their lodge. Malee looks up at Cassie and asks a question. "Momma, what's… Ogun?" "Ogun…," Cassie answers while returning to their lodge, "When I was your age, my momma told me to be of a lak-kits wyhome (big spirits) from our home. He had a large blade that could cut down anything. We would call on him when we were at war or to protect each other." Malee sits down then presses his mother to elaborate on her story. "Momma isn't this our home?" he asks. She maneuvers her skirt and sits down next to Malee. "Malee, I came from a land across the big water. My momma told me a story of how she was brought there as a little girl. When war broke out, my slave master took me away from her and brought me here." "Oh…" Malee says without understanding the complexity of the situation. "Know this my son, I will not allow you to go through the pain that I went through," she declares, "as long as I have Ogun, I will always have the will to fight." Malee smiles at his mother as she prepares a fire for dinner.

Moments later, Malee hears the ramblings of other children running around the village. Wanting to be a part, Malee tugs his mother's arm while she finalizes the preparations. "Can I go play please?" he asks emphatically. "Do not go bast the fields of corn and beans." "Yes Momma." Malee runs off to join the other children as Cassie looks on. *I hope my son will never know the pain I endured when I was his age…*" she reflects.

A gust of wind blows through the back of her neck like a doorbell. Cassie turns around, sensing something off. From a distance, Cassie and some of the villagers can hear the faint sounds of something neighing in the bush. She squints her eyes while grabbing a rifle from her home. Some of the other villagers begin to stop their morning routine to investigate the sounds. "I hear horses," one of the Seminoles stated. "I can hear it too," another black man added.

The thunder crashes into a nightmare, the sound of gun fire is followed by a thud in the ground. A Seminole woman was struck in the chest and fell like a chopped tree. The shot is followed by a series of yells and screams from incoming soldiers. There were a barrage of men wearing blue uniforms, tall hats with feathers mounted on top and armed with bayonets attached to rifles.

Some of the men begin to grab their weapons and fire back. Women and children begin to scream and run chaotically. Cassie is startled and immediately calls for her son.

"Malee! Malee! MAL-EE-TUL-KAH!" She yells. During the barrage of dust, noise, and death, Cassie was able to run towards the crop fields. At the corner of her eye, she sees Malee hiding in the corn stalks. Some of the soldiers breach the initial defenses, and one of them tackles Cassie from behind. Cassie struggles and yells to get free. "Let me go! I's said let me go!" The soldier begins to laugh maniacally until POW. The soldier is bloodied from a brunt force of a rifle. Cassie looks up and sees a friendly face.

"Cassie gets up and go to Malee!" James commands. Cassie nods her head, brushes herself off, grabs her rifle and continues to go for Malee. James loads his rifle and begins to provide cover fire for Cassie. Cassie continues to run towards the corn fields and hugs Malee tight when she reaches him.

Malee is drowned in tears of fear and surprise. The shivering of his body does little to quell even with the warm embrace of his mother. "It's ok Malee…" Cassie consoles while caressing him, looking on as the last remnants of the villagers mount a feeble defense. James is valiantly fighting the soldiers but is quickly overtaken. Suddenly, POW! POW! POW! James is shot by three different rifles. Cassie yells out while blowing her cover. "JAMES! NO!" Some of the soldiers hear her and begin to approach with the intent to either kill or kidnap. "Hey," one of them yells, "We can sell her if we catch her and the boy for a pretty price." "You're right; let's get her."

Understanding the severity of the situation, Cassie looks at Malee and instructs him. "Malee run...run…" Malee is still in a moment of shock. He shakes his head with tears flying. Cassie slaps Malee and yells at him. "Malee… I SAID RUN!" Malee wipes his eyes, feels his face, and starts to run away from his mother.

While the soldiers begin to close in, Cassie rises up and charges towards the intruders. With her rifle in hand, she begins to swipe the weapon with conviction and force. Again and again, she keeps the soldiers at bay, putting them at a standstill.

"You're coming back with us wench!" One of the soldiers says. "I will not go back or give up my freedom," Cassie declares, "Come if you dare." Foolishly, one of the soldiers' charges at Cassie. Cassie takes her gun and swings hard, striking the soldier with the butt of the gun, breaking it in the process while knocking her opponent to the ground. Afterwards, the other soldier grabs Cassie and takes her down to the ground. Cassie begins to yell, scream and struggle to gain her freedom. The soldier slaps Cassie across the face and begins to tear her clothes off.

With most of the villagers dead, 2 more soldiers come to assist in the apprehension of Cassie. The main soldier commands the soldier to chase after Malee, who is 40 meters away, witnessing his mother being ravaged. "Get that little nigger over there," he commands, "I got the wench." As the soldiers begin to home in at Malee, the main soldier licks his tobacco-stained tongue on the side of Cassie's face. He then whispers something sinister in her ear. "I'm going to make you pay," he continues, "and then I'm going to get your son."

At that moment, Cassie snaps. Something dormant within her begins to boil, she begins to grit her teeth, she begins to moan, and her body begins to heat up. Oblivious to the potential danger, the soldier continues to violate her, laughing during the tormenting event. Before he could pull down his pants, the Fire Line that was hibernating in Cassie erupted. She lets out a long screech, her body becomes full of blue flames, and her eyes transform into a pure blue hue. Before the soldier can react, the flames form a phoenix and burn the soldier completely within seconds. Before he turns to ash, his yells alert the other soldiers who were less than 20 yards from Malee. Malee looks on in amazement as he sees his mother transform. A whisper leaves his lips like air in a punctured balloon, "Loot-kah Lamhi (Fire Eagle)". The men turn around and begin to load their muskets.

Cassie becomes possessed by the entity: her eyes are as pure as snow water, her skin glows, and her body partially levitates. The other soldiers finish loading their muskets and prepare to fire. Cassie lets out another screech as she charges at the soldiers. The soldiers began to tremble with fear and surprise. Barely able to stand still enough to aim, both men point their rifles. As Cassie gets closer, the men aim. Afterwards, both pull the trigger and fire. The musket balls pierce through the air, following a puff of smoke. One of the balls melts with the heat while the other goes through Cassie's chest. Despite this, Cassie rampages towards the soldiers until her silhouette spreads its wings. The men try to escape, but the wings create a hot and intense fire wave that the men literally melt in place. When the wave reaches Malee, his eyes partially transform to the Dracocernentia, allowing him to absorb the heat.

Afterwards, Cassie takes several long, deep breaths as the waves of flames simmer down. Once the flames disappear, Cassie gulps, then spits out blood from her mouth. Her eyes are still blue, but she stares at the horizon. Malee runs towards his mother as she falls to her knees. Malee catches her and yells at her to get her attention.

"MOMMA! MOMMA! MOMMA!" Cassie remains unresponsive. The breathing suddenly stops, her heart refuses to beat, and Cassie begins to fall to the ground. The event is like slow motion to Malee. With each inch the body gets closer to the ground, the reality becomes thick until it hits as hard as his lifeless mother's body. Malee looks at the body with tears dripping from his partially green and yellow eyes. Then he looks around to see the bloodied bodies of his neighbors, children, and burning lodging. The wind blows as the eerie sound of silence overshadows the devastation. Malee could do nothing but sit next to his dead mother.

An hour later, a group of Seminoles rushes back to see their home partially burned to the ground. Several warriors begin to wale in anguish and yell in frustration as they see their loved ones covered with dirt, bullets, and blood.

Soletawake-yaka rushes through the bush, desperately runs towards his lodge to find his family. As he gets closer, he notices something small in the corner of his eye. He redirects his attention to the small object, panting hard with the gun at the ready.

When he reaches the object, what he sees brings him to tears. The lifeless body of Cassie generates a mosh pit of grief, anger, sadness, and shock. Then he notices a small child hovering over the body, sobbing and breathing hard. The child notices something and looks up. What he sees is not only a familiar face, but the face in return breathes a sigh of relief.

"Chacteka (Father)..." the child whimpers. "MAL-EE-TUL-KAH!" Soletawake-yaka whispers before rushing to hug his son. Malee cries for joy as he rests his head on his father's broad chest. "Mal-ee-tul-kah," Soletawake-yaka says softly, "my chakpootsi (son)." Father and son embrace as the dream fades to white.

As the image disappears, Asir finds himself in a veil covered in dark grey walls. His silhouette walks around to see if it leads to a door or another area. Asir is still confused about what he is experiencing. "*I'm scared,*" he thinks, "*That was a scary dream.*"

A voice out of nowhere begins to speak. Asir becomes even more anxious, questioning the realm between the dream or reality.

"It wasn't a dream; it was a memory." the voice says. Asir frantically looks around, trying to figure out who's speaking to him. "Who's talking to me?" he asks while continuing to look around.

After a few turnarounds, an image begins to manifest in front of Asir. Gold dust congregates together to form a person that is familiar yet strange to Asir. After a few moments, the voice's true form takes shape.

"Hey!" Asir says emphatically, "You're the guy that's been in my dreams!" "Yes, I am," he responds, "Asir, my name is Chittoluthphwa. What you saw was me when I was a child." Despite his limited communication skills, Asir is strangely motivated to understand what's going on. "Why do you keep showing up in my dreams?" "Because I am your father's father's father's father's father," Chittoluthphwa states. "I... I... don't know my dad. I don't..." "Don't worry Asir. You have channeled your Fire Line. Now I must show you who I am and who you are. Because you, Asir, have the Fire Line of warriors who refuse to be conquered. Come...Let me show you."

Asir slowly walks towards the intimidating man. However, because of the ancestors, Asir feels a sense of comfort and complies with Chittoluthphwa. Then Chittoluthphwa illuminates his eyes and flashes Asir towards another memory.

# Chapter 19: The Boy with the Snake Eyes

Chittoluthphwa transports Asir to years later. Before Asir can experience the crucial moment in his childhood, Chittoluthphwa gives Asir clear and concise instructions.

"Asir, you are about to learn more about where you come from and how to harness the same powers," he continues, "It will feel like a dream, but in real life." "I… I think I understand," Asir responds, "So I get to see how you grew up as a little boy?" "Yes, but you will discover something else as well. Allow yourself to listen, taste, feel and absorb the lesson." "I… I will try," Asir says inconvincibly. Chittoluthphwa smiles as the flash of light disappears after a moment of clarity.

The vision transports them back to the year 1822. Mal-ee-tul-kah is now 12 years old. He is roaming the swamps with his father on a hunting trip. It is summer and the infestation of mosquitoes, flies and gnats blanket the otherwise subtropical landscape. The ground is muddy and saturated with green plants, leaves, and water.

Soletawake-yaka surveys the land for potential food. With his rifle at the ready, Soletawake-yaka tunes his sharp senses to any unusual movement or sounds. Mal-ee-tul-kah nervously follows his father's side while trying to find relief from the questions that compound his young mind.

While walking down a ravine, Malee generates the courage to express his concerns. "Chacteka (Father), what type of game are we looking for?" he whispers. "Primarily echo-cluccko (deer), tcho-fee (rabbit), ko-wi-kee (quail), and penwaw (turkey)." Soletawake-yaka and Malee continue slowly through the woods, scanning like satellites to pick up any faint signs of food.

Suddenly, something is rustling 30 yards in front of Soletawake-yaka. He stops and starts to unlock his rifle. He quickly glanced behind him to see where his son was. Malee is about 10 yards behind his father, cautiously looking for prey. Not wanting to alert their position, Soletawake-yaka redirects his focus in front of him.

What emerges from the camouflage of willows, oaks, and ash trees is a male White Tail Deer. The young buck, with furry, underdeveloped 4-point antlers, cinnamon-colored coat, and its distinctive white underbelly with tail, looks at the direction of the wind to pick up any signs of danger. Soletawake-yaka lifts his finger to test the wind direction. The wind is blowing towards the hunter, giving him the confidence of knowing that he is downwind from the potential feast. He slowly crouches down on the tall grasses and bushes and prepares to fire.

Meanwhile, Malee is drawn to a yelp near a saturated marsh in the bushes. He notices his father crouching down. Not wanting to risk alerting what he sees, Malee slowly maneuvers his way to investigate the intriguing sounds. He brushes away the leaves and grass, using his hands, determined to find out what is making those sounds.

"Yelp...Yelp...Yelp" it gets louder and louder. As Malee draws closer, it leads him to a watery marsh with a large tree facing it. The black mangrove tree has shiny green leaves, dark brown to nearly black sturdy tree trunk, and roots that look like the fingers from an octopus. As Malee gets up, he hears the loud yelp sounds that catch his attention.

As Malee looks within the protruding roots, he is astonished by what he sees. His eyes widened, his breathing stopped, and his resolved questions. A black wolf puppy is whimpering around the depression of the tree. It continues to yelp, seemingly struggling to get out of its imprisonment. "I can't believe it," Malee whispers, "it's an eyaha (wolf)." The small creature looks at the boy with glossy eyes. Despite not trusting Malee, it seems more concerned with getting out than fearing the young boy. "You are trapped," Malee deduces, "I'm going to try to get you out."

Taking out his small knife, he cuts a thin root to make room for himself. He cuts and saws his way through the root as the puppy timidly walks back. The commotion makes rumbles that create ripples in the water behind them.

Several seconds later, Malee cuts through the piece of wood and tosses it in the water. Malee then pries himself in the section of the mangrove, but the puppy is still afraid. Malee slowly approaches the animal with caution and prudence.

"Shhhhh… don't be afraid eyaha (wolf). I will get you out." Slowly, Malee reaches for the traumatized puppy. The puppy barks back, showing its undersized, white teeth. Malee hesitates for a moment to allow the wolf to calm down. Malee closes his eyes, controls his breathing, and suddenly feels the gust of wind blowing against him. After a moment of clarity and peace, something overcomes the fear in both Malee and the puppy. His eyes begin to change color, changing his eyes from brown to almost green. Not fully transformed, Malee was able to look at the yellow and red receptors of the puppy. *"I don't understand what is happening to me,"* he questions, *"I see something different…"* Miraculously, the puppy gazes into Malee's eyes and its receptors change to green and sky blue. Slowly, the puppy walks towards Malee as he begins to reach his hands forward. With each step, the tension lessens as Malee patiently waits for the wolf to reach his hands. When the wolf reaches his hands, Malee grabs the puppy and slowly makes his way out of the tree.

When Malee gets up with the puppy in his hand, The puppy begins to sniff and wiggle for joy, reaching for Malee to lick his face. Malee beings to smile and chuckle while standing at the edge of the marsh. "You have a fire spirit little one," Malee compliments, "How did you get in there?" Suddenly, the puppy begins to bark loudly as something in the water begins to ripple. The cattails begin to move, the wind begins to blow, and a low frequency grumble follows an explosion of splashing and thrashing.

A large, 14 ft alligator sprints out of the water and charges towards Malee. Malee turns around and, with no time to react, runs with the puppy close to his chest. Malee runs as the Alligator sprints closer towards the boy. Malee huffs and puffs in a desperate attempt to evade the jaws of the reptile until he trips over a dead branch, dropping the puppy nearby. The puppy gets up and shakes the dirt off. The Alligator then tries to go after the puppy.

As the beast gets closer to the puppy, Malee reaches his hand out and yells. "NO!" he screams until the flames from within consume his body. His arms, legs, chest, and torso become covered in greenish orange flames, his hair begins to flow like the wind, and his eyes fully transform into the Dracocernentia with a unique color scheme of greenish blue and gold iris with a single sharp black pupil.

As the Alligator opens its gape, Malee moves like a flash fire and tackles the 1000 lb beast. He wrestles the animal as it performs a death spiral on the ground to free itself. The puppy looks at the fight by barking and moving to gain access to view the match. The Alligator rumbles and roars as Malee forces the jaws shut with his skinny but powerful fire engulfed arms. Malee continues to maneuver and wrestle the alligator until the eyes begin to illuminate. Malee's eyes glow so bright that it lights up the field for Soletawake-yaka to take notice. *"What is that light?"* he wonders, then he looks behind him, "Where is my son... MAL-EE-TUL-KAH! MAL-EE-TUL-KAH!"

Meanwhile, as the eyes of the alligator and Malee meet, a flash of bright white light transports Malee into a strange dimension. The veil looks like outer space, with monochromatic color scheme of black, purple, and blue with countless numbers of stars. Malee looks around with a confused and wondrous gaze. "Where am I? What is this place?"

SIZZZZZZZZZ. A sound erupts the quiet void as a cloud of smoke begins to form. Malee tries to look within the cloud of smoke with his eyes, only to see the same smoke that clouds his curiosity. As the cloud gets bigger, lightning and thunder begin to sprinkle throughout the mass of smoke as it gets bigger and bigger. Then, when the cloud gets big enough, it explodes by showering flashes of multicolored lights. Malee covers his eyes with his forearm until he gazes upon a magnificent sight.

As the explosion clears, a huge, monstrous, dragon with a black body, gargantuan black wings with blue, red, yellow, orange, and green feathers, a long red face with antler-like red horns, and a long snout with sharp teeth. As Malee looks upon the beast with reverence, the dragon's golden eyes meet the boy as it begins to speak.

"You have been chosen as a bridge to both of your people," the beast prophesied, "In time, you will be destined to help the people from many timelines yet to come to past." Malee slowly approaches the dragon as it musters up the courage to speak.

"Who, and what are you Hitloschi Chilth-Keh (Cloud Father)?" Malee cautiously asks. "Before the time of your father's father's father and your mother's mother's mother, I was known by many names. I have lived among the mortal men, searching for the one worthy of my secrets and power," it continues, "Years ago, your ancestors painted a picture in my honor and named me. You can call me Piasa, as your fathers did." "Piasa," Malee repeats, "Piasa, what has happened to me? Why do I have these powers?" Piasa blows a blanket of smoke from his jaws; then the smoke creates images that aid with his explanation.

"When you were younger, you witnessed your mother turn into Loot-kah Lamhi (Fire Eagle) in an attempt to save you. She comes from a line of people who refer to themselves as Moors. One represented the men, Dragon Moor while the other is referred as the women, Phoenix Moor. Your mother passed down the Fire Line to you despite having her lineage deluded through birth and time." "So, what you are telling me is I have the power of your kind Piasa?" Piasa smiles as he blows another cover of smoke to reveal another vision. The vision shows the ritual of fire that the Moors underwent, the formation of the Elite 8 as well as other white supremacist agencies, and images of Asir, Emma, Malik, and another mysterious man.

"In order to achieve our power, the people from your mother's side had to perform a ritual to consume themselves with the blood of the dragon and phoenix, then burn to purify their spirits. As time went on, they covered the world to keep it in balance as well as work with nature to thrive." Piasa continues while transitioning to the next images, "However, evil men have conspired to conquer, destroy, and rule the world through brutality and the color of their skin. These men are responsible for the wars, destruction, and disregard for life in this world. Soon they will come again to rage war, just like what they did when they raided your village." Malee gasps by the revelation of the images. His heart pounds out of his chest like a mallet, his breathing is sporadic, and his body is drenched with sweat. The burden of his newfound responsibility begins to take a toll on his psyche. "I am only a boy," Malee responds, "How can someone like me be the bridge to the salvation of my people?"

Undeterred, Piasa shows one last vision of his descendants and their allies. "Because if you don't, your children and their children will cease to exist. You doubt your abilities and your power. Your ancestors all found their destiny at the same age as you. You must understand who you are and accept the power that resides within you."

Malee begins to remember his mother's courage at the end of her life. He can still remember the power that brewed from within and the stories she told of her escape. As the blood in his body begins the flow fluidly, so does the Fire Line from within to solidify his resolve. Malee then looks at the vision with new eyes, understanding his Fire Line's plight and will.

"I see Piasa," Malee confirms, "These are the children that will come from my line, so I must fight to preserve it, just like my mother did. (Piasa smiles as Malee turns to him) Piasa, how will I fight these men?" "They are led by a man your people call Sharp Knife. You must defeat his forces and never allow your line to leave this land. Once you achieve this, you will allow the bridge for your children to continue the fight." "I… don't completely understand," Malee responds, "but I understand that I need to fight for my people." "Before you depart back, know this. Your life will change and so will your name. You will not find all the answers you seek nor understand the questions in this lifetime. But do not despair; when the time is right, you will be able to fulfill your destiny. Now go… and fulfil your destiny."

Piasa opens his mouth and spits a tsunami of fire so big and colorful, it completely engulfs Malee. As Malee is purified by the flames, the array of colors and lights allow his eyes to develop, creating a set of micro claws around the pupil. Malee then subconsciously understands and embraces the warmth of the flames, purging the self-doubt, uncertainty, and blockage that disabled his ability.

Moments later, Malee is flashed back to the present plane, placing himself between the alligator and the puppy. As Malee and the alligator gaze at each other, a single gunshot breaks the concentration. The alligator suddenly runs back to the watery marsh. Soletawake-yaka rushes towards Malee with his rifle in his hand.

"Are you alright?" he asks. "Yes, I had a vision while fighting the hulputta (alligator)." Malee responds. "That was very foolish, you could've been…" Suddenly Soletawake-yaka notices the flames disappearing from Malee's body while looking at his eyes. The sight of the Dracocernentia completely overtakes Soletawake-yaka as he is left paralyzed by his shock. "It… can not be…" he whispers in surprise. "I was shown a vision by a huge beast, with a large black body, wings with different color feathers, and a large red face. It breathes fire and speaks of the time before our father's father." "Piasa…" Soletawake-yaka whispers, "How could this…" "You know of Piasa?"

Soletawake-yaka puts his hand on Malee's shoulders and smiles. His pride lights up brighter than any fire created by man or beast. "You have been chosen, my son. And it is our custom to rename you to fit this new role." "What will my name be Chacteka (Father)?" "You have the eyes of Piasa. They are like the eyes of a snake, powerful, majestic… Your name will no longer be Mal-ee-tul-kah. From this day forward, you will be known as Chittoluthphwa (Snake Eyes), the warrior with snake eyes." "Chittoluthphwa, I like the name. What about the puppy, can I keep him?" Soletawake-yaka looks at the puppy and smiles. "Come, you two, let's go back to the village." Chittoluthphwa smiles back, picks up the puppy, then follows his father back to the village.

As the vision closes, Asir suddenly feels more comfortable and calmer by the array of visions. He then asks Chittoluthphwa a series of concise, coherent questions. "So now that I know I have these powers, what am I supposed to do?" "Now that you know more about me, and you," Chittoluthphwa explains, "Your mentor and father will need your help. The same people who killed your great-great grandmother and your people are the very people who are holding you here. You must help them rid the planet of this evil." "My mentor… You mean Ms. Emma and the other guy in the vision?" Chittoluthphwa nods in confirmation, then concludes his statement. "Be patient and build up your power. The winds are in motion and soon the time will come to fulfill our destinies."

Afterwards, Asir closes his eyes, and the vision ends. Asir finds himself on the floor, sitting still. As he understands the role he is to play, he continues to sit down and cultivate the Fire Line within until the moment is right.

# Chapter 20: The New Faces of an Old Enemy

The perpetual cycle of the day transforming into night resurfaces as the city is cloaked in darkness. 2 hours has passed since Emma left the W.A.V.E building and now surveys the building from a nearby building. Dressed in her blue hoodie, skinny blue jeans, and sneakers, Blue Phoenix is once again transformed.

*"There's still some lights on in the W.A.V.E. building,"* she plots, *"How am I going to get access without alerting anyone?"* Blue Phoenix activates her Avemcernentia to scout for receptors and any blind spots. While she moves her head, she notices a vent in the upper east side of the building. *"Hmmm... I can only detect 1 set of receptors on the top floor, so that must mean that Asir is being held somewhere below the building's main floors."* Blue Phoenix puts her hood over her head and makes her way towards the building.

She gracefully uses her agility to scroll down the buildings, not making a sound or alert the city of her presence. She maintains her calm state by controlling breathing and calculating her moves. She makes it to the vent of the building. It blows warm air with no signs of smoke or contaminants. Emma carefully removes the metal guards, sets them down, then enters the vent.

Blue Phoenix uses her eyes to pinpoint the best way to enter the building while remaining conscious about the only set of receptors she saw. Despite her tall physique, her small frame allows her to move within the tunnels with little trouble. However, something is plaguing Blue Phoenix as she becomes woozy and uncoordinated.

*"I don't feel good all of a sudden..."* she ponders, "I can't see or smell anything. *Is it something in the air?"* Not understanding the sudden reaction of her body, Emma decides to prematurely exit the vent way into a locked office.

Blue Phoenix looks for an opening and sees a storage closet with boxes, supplies, and enough room for her to land without making a sound. Emma removes the vent cover, lands on the floor, and carefully coughs out any impurities that caused her unusual condition. "That was close..." she whispers, "Now I need to make my way towards the lower floors."

Blue Phoenix begins to maneuver her way from the 8th floor of the building. Down the hall, she locates a door that leads to stairs. "I'll take the stairs; that way, I'm less likely to be detected." With conviction and confidence, Blue Phoenix keeps her head on a swivel to look for potential employees. With the coast clear, Blue Phoenix makes it to the door.

Blue Phoenix opens the door and proceeds to walk down the stairs. She cautiously walks down the flight of stairs. As she descends the building, thoughts consume her mind, and her body becomes numb with the possibilities that await her. "Something about this place makes no sense. Why would they keep the boys here overnight? Also, my body still feels strangely out of order...*Like my muscles are lethargic and stiff. I am also having a hard time breathing. I know I'm not afraid...*"

Blue Phoenix reaches the door that leads into the main lobby. She carefully opens the door and peaks outside. The main lobby is dark, with a few lights on the ceiling lit up. Blue Phoenix continues to walk slowly down the hall to get to the corridor that leads to Asir.

Blue Phoenix reaches the area where she met Asir. She gets to the door but remembers that a key is needed to open it. "Damn it..." she complains quietly, "I don't have a badge, and I don't want to punch through this glass without setting any alarms. (Sigh) What can I do?" As Blue Phoenix leans towards the door, it opens, much to her surprise. "What? The door is opened?"

Blue Phoenix grabs the handle and pushes the door open. Despite the fortune, Blue Phoenix maintains her wits, suspecting something is off with the situation. "*W.A.V.E. doesn't seem like the organization that would carelessly leave doors open,*" she recollects, " *I sense a trap...*" Suddenly, a loud sound is followed by lights throughout the room lighting up. Blue Phoenix is looking around, trying to figure out what's going on. Then a series of click-clack sounds notify Blue Phoenix of someone coming out of the shadows. Despite the Avemcernentia being activated, Blue Phoenix is unable to ascertain who is coming towards her. Moments later, the figure begins to speak.

"So, I see you walked blindly into my trap," it says, "I can't believe you were once revered as the perfect weapon." Blue Phoenix widens her eyes. She recognizes the voice but does not talk. "*SHARON BENNETT! What the…*" Out of the shadows, still wearing her long sleeve blouse, white leggings, and 3-inch pumps, Sharon struts out smiling with her arms crossed, face tanned, and a smirk.

"So, Emma comes back to rescue a sad little boy...or should I say Blue Phoenix!" "How did you…" "Oh honey," Sharon interrupts, "Let's not be coy or stupid. Matter of fact, how about you take off that ridiculous hood so that we can have a little chat. Just between us girls." "I'm sorry, but I'm afraid I'm going to have to refuse." Sharon shakes her head while she circles around the tables. She starts taking off her earrings and jewelry as she begins to speak.

"(Sigh) Suit yourself. You know Blue Phoenix; it is so touching how much you have changed. You actually care for these little monsters." "They're not monsters. What is your endgame, Sharon?" Sharon continues to circle around, chuckling with her condescending tone and apathetic approach to the questioning. "You know," Sharon stops, then points at Blue Phoenix, "I don't think I have to answer any of your questions. But (Hee hee hee), I'm in a playful mood, so I will oblige you. When you and that bastard, Shadowmoor, stop the ring, most of us had to figure out a way to fight you. You had regained the powers that dominated our race for almost a millennium." "Really? So, how's that going for you?" Blue Phoenix responded sarcastically.

Sharon shakes her head, puts her earrings and jewelry on a nearby table. Then she struts slowly towards Blue Phoenix. "You know…. Heh heh ah… you black people...don't deserve those powers you inherited. So, head up, there's no way we could defeat you." "So then, how about we make this easy and you release Asir." "Wait a minute, I said, head up, we can't defeat you. I didn't say you could never be defeated." Blue Phoenix squints her eyes and balls up her fists. "What are you getting at?"

With sophistication, grace, and overconfidence, Sharon takes off her pumps, grabs something from her back pocket, opens the golden containment and takes a big sniff from its contents. She then walks towards Blue Phoenix until they are about an arm length away from each other. "You know, a girl like me doesn't just get this glamorous just because. Let me in on a little secret, before I was the head of W.A.V.E., I was an accomplished martial artist, body builder, and all-around… well… you'll find out in just a second." Growing impatient, Emma begins to build up her Fire Line. "Enough of this, I'm just going to send you straight to Hell!" Blue Phoenix brightens her eyes, takes a deep breath, and blows. However, no flames come out of her mouth, just some sparks and smoke.

*What the hell is going on here?"* Emma thinks as Sharon begins to laugh. "Ha ha ha ha ha ha ha… oooohhhh… did someone lose their powers?" Sharon lifts her leg and implants her size 11 dirty soles in Blue Phoenix's stomach, kicking her several feet back. Blue Phoenix is temporarily stunned while trying to generate flames on her fist. As she looks up, she sees Sharon walk up towards her. "We control the destiny of men...I'm sorry, women too…" Blue Phoenix's eyes widen. "Noooo…." she whispers. "That's right; you now know" Sharon finishes while putting one hand on her hip. "You… bitch… you're part of the Elite 8. Now I'm going to kick your ass".

Emma yells and rushes towards Sharon. She throws a punch, but her fist doesn't ignite, so Sharon catches her fist. "Ugh...you almost made me break a nail. Guess I'll have to break you...Black bitch!" Sharon draws her in and head butts Blue Phoenix. Blue Phoenix is stunned, and Sharon then does a spinning roundhouse kick to Blue Phoenix's head. A splash of blood exits Blue Phoenix's mouth as she crashes down to the floor. The sadistic villainess looks at her foot. "Oh dear, I got blood on my perfect pedicure...Oh well."

Suddenly, alarms go off in the building. The sound of broken doors, broken glass, and boots alerts Sharon of intruders. "Shit… I need to take care of her before they get here." Blue Phoenix gets up to face Sharon. "I don't care what has happened to me; I'm going to take you down." "(Sigh) Really? You like ass whoopings this much? Oh well. Bring it!"

Blue Phoenix rushes towards Sharon and starts to throw punches. Sharon effortlessly dodges her attacks. She folds her arms as she taunts Blue Phoenix. Blue Phoenix attempts to kick Sharon, but Sharon raises her shin, then repeatedly kicks Blue Phoenix in her nose. Blue Phoenix can't dodge, thus taking the barrage of kicks until Sharon uses more force on the 5th kick, which she yells while sending Blue Phoenix back to the ground.

Meanwhile, Asir hears the alarms in his room and gets up to see what's going on. He hears windows breaking, doors opening, and the commotion of the events. He then runs towards the door and looks out at the windows. Having a better grasp of his powers, he activates his Dracocernentia. When his eyes transform, the color of the iris is greenish blue with a sharp, snake-like pupil. He is able to see the receptors of a squadron of men with guns freeing the other boys.

Suddenly, one man in black tactical gear, combat boots, a fitted gas mask and dark goggles comes towards Asir's door and communicates with him. "Get back son; we're going to get you out of there." Asir stumbles a bit before running towards the back of the room. The man then plants a clay-like explosive on the door. He then takes several steps away before detonating the door. With a loud pop, the handle explodes, and the man walks into the room. Asir stands as the man looks in his eyes. Surprisingly, the man is hesitant. Shocked that this boy possesses the Dracocernentia, something rare that the man didn't expect to see.

"Oh my God!" he whispers. "Who are you?" Asir asks. "I'm a friend; you need to come with me?" "I don't know you…" Running out of time, the man removes his googles and mask. Tears run down the man's face as he gazes upon Asir. Asir looks at the man and makes a startling observation. "Your eyes look like mine." The man nods his head yes and he gathers himself and redirects his focus. "Asir… son, we need to go now."

Asir recognizes the face in his image, so he grabs the man's hand after the man puts his mask and goggles on. Afterwards, the man lends out his hand to Asir. Asir grabs his hand then makes their way out of the room.

Despite the commotion, Blue Phoenix is desperately trying to hold her own. She is weak, bloodied, badly beaten, and tired. Sharon grows impatient, trying to state the inevitable. "Honestly, I'm messing up one of my best outfits. Why don't you just give up?" Blue Phoenix grits her bloodied teeth, lets out a roar, and carelessly charges at Sharon. Sharon lets out a sigh and a breath then rolls her eyes as she dodges Blue Phoenix's ill aimed punch.

Then Sharon kicks up a gear by punching Blue Phoenix in the gut. Then she jabs Blue Phoenix in the face, followed by a left hook. All Blue Phoenix could do was yelp and moan with each hit. Her left eye has been completely shut, her nose is broken, and so is her spirit. Sharon ends her combination with an uppercut, which causes Blue Phoenix to erupt a stream of blood in the air until collapsing to the ground.

Blue Phoenix slowly gets up, leaning her body on the tables and chairs. When she finally reaches Sharon, she leans on Sharon's left shoulder before losing consciousness. Unfettered, Sharon picks up Blue Phoenix and power presses her body over her head.

As the man and Asir make it towards the door, they see the women concluding their battle. The man holds Asir as he gets his weapon ready. He has something unexpected yet familiar to Asir. A tomahawk completely painted black with the initials OBR on it.

Unaware of anyone else, Sharon's body slams Blue Phoenix on the ground, causing a large thump and some broken tile. Blue Phoenix is left motionless on the cold floor. Sharon begins to pant hard while fixing her hair. Her skin is boiling red, with sweat and blood stains all over her body. After catching her breath, she crackles at her defeated opponent then considers the ultimate solution.

"Well, well well, I think our little bird is close to croaking. I think I should help you out with that." Sharon lifts her dirty sole, aims it at Blue Phoenix's throat, and gives her an air kiss.
When the man and Asir see what is going on, Asir realizes who is on the ground. His eyes begin to water, his lip begins to fluctuate, and he tries to control his sobbing. Then, his rage intensifies in a split second, and his body becomes warm. As Asir lets out a cry that sends chills down any stoic man's back, the man looks on in amazement.

"LEAVE MS. EMMA ALONE!" Sharon stops before stepping on Blue Phoenix, then is greeted with a huge Fire wave. Asir lets out a Wave so powerful it not only throws Sharon against the wall, temporarily knocking her out, but it shatters the glass barriers between him and Blue Phoenix.

After the display, Asir runs towards an unconscious Blue Phoenix. He notices that her receptors are gray and almost black around the chest area. Asir nudges Blue Phoenix in a feeble attempt to wake her up.

"Ms. Emma, MS. EMMA!" The man walks up behind Asir, as Asir turns towards the man. "We have to help her! PLEASE DON'T LEAVE HER HERE!" The man activates his Dracocernentia behind his goggles and sees the same receptor patterns. He also whispers to himself about the wounded warrior. "This is Blue Phoenix, the same one who stop the rings back in Atlanta and North Carolina." The man puts his tomahawk in his holster and picks up Blue Phoenix; then he puts her over his shoulder. "I got her. We have to get out of here now!" Asir gets up and follows the man as he uses the walkie-talkie on his right shoulder to shout out commands. "OBR, OBR, RETREAT! I REPEAT, RETREAT!"

The man, along with Blue Phoenix and Asir escape the W.A.V.E. building by jumping in the back of a large cargo truck. After entering through the back, the man radios the driver. "The precious is in, I repeat, the precious is in." "Copy that, prepare to move out." The truck then drives off away from the building and towards their secret hideout.

During the drive, the man removes his mask and goggles. Asir continues to look at Emma as she remains unconscious. As tears begin to run down his face, the man grabs a syringe and a liquid bottle. He carefully extracts the contents then looks at Asir.

"Don't worry; this will help her get better." Asir looks at the man as he looks for a suitable vein on Blue Phoenix's arm. After wrapping a band on her arm and finding a vein, the man injects the syringe into her vein and pumps the contents in her. Then he takes the syringe out and immediately bandages the wound. Almost immediately, Emma wakes up with one eye open and gasps for air.

"Ms. Emma! Ms. Emma!" Asir yells. "Err...eh...A... Asir," Emma stumbles, "but…" "Save your strength Blue Phoenix. We need to get you better, then we'll debrief you on what happened." Asir hugs Emma and the convoy drives off towards the undisclosed location.

# **Chapter 21: Rite of Passage**

The first sliver of sunrise penetrates the covered windows like a laser. The single beam of light aims at Malik's head, prompting him to get up from an eventful night. As he wipes his face with his hands and wiggles in between the sheets, the relenting light urges Malik to relinquish his slumber for the next chapter in his quest.

"Agh...Morning already?" Malik says while he grabs his phone, "The flight leaves at 10am. It's 6:30 now, so I need to finish my packing." Reluctantly, Malik gets out of bed and heads for the shower.

Like clockwork, Malik rinses the aroma of his adventure away with warm soapy water and a calmness that Malik rarely experiences. *"The other night, I killed a man..."* Malik ponders as he continues to lather his body, *"Yet I don't feel sorrow, remorse, or even sorry that I did it. So, the question I have is, am I getting so infatuated with the Elite 8 that I end up just like them? Do the ends justify the means?"* Malik turns off the facets and steps out of the shower. He dries himself off with a towel while concluding his thoughts. *"Well, I can't get too distracted with comparing myself with them. What's important is they too are seeking the sword, so I have to beat them to it."*

After grooming himself in the bathroom, Malik puts on his clothes: a Red V-neck T-shirt, a pair of light tan Cargo shorts, and a pair of Red, Black, and white Air Max 97 sneakers. After applying a spray of cologne, Malik grabs his bags and heads downstairs.

As Malik reaches the bottom of the stairs, he heads towards the breakfast buffet. Sitting at the front counter is Obioma. She pretends to overlook the manifest on the computer while Malik walks by with his bags. Her heart and breath begin to flutter, sensing the energy that Malik inconspicuously exerts. She briefly closes her eyes and puts her hand on her chest in an attempt to control her emotions. Meanwhile, Malik looks for a place to settle for his morning meal.

As he sets his things down at the nearby table, he heads over to the buffet to get a small bowl of mixed fruit, a toasted bagel, and a glass of orange juice. He begins to open his laptop and asses the logistics of his online company. Suddenly, a woman develops the nerve to accompany the oblivious bachelor.

"Good mornin' M'lik," Obioma nervously says as she approaches his table. Malik looks up, smiles, and closes his laptop. "Oh, Obioma! You are looking lovely, or am I being to, as we say in America, fresh?" Obioma chuckles a bit while crossing her hands behind her back. "Mind if I join you?" she asks in her thick English accent. Malik smiles and extends his hand, prompting her to sit down. Obioma sits down in front of Malik. Her timidness shifts to a more assertive, but feminine groove. Her courage compels her to muster up the words to a man who was once a stranger that she may not see again. Malik picks up on the minute mannerisms, so he leans back on his chair to get comfortable.

"So, are you here to see me off before my flight?" Malik asks. "In a matter of speaking," Obioma responds, "Although…(scoffs), I think I've gone plump crazy." "Crazy, how?" Obioma straightens herself up, clenching both of her hands together on the table, then reengages the conversation by giving Malik direct eye contact.

"You may not know this, but I was...involved...with some bad chums. I learn things, and I see things…" Obioma hesitates before forcing herself to reveal her truth, "I also feel things." "Feel things, like spiritual…" Malik ponders while rubbing his beard in interest. Obioma smiles a little and nods yes as she continues. "(Scoffs) Heh… You know, my mum's family… would worship Yoruba back in my country in Africa. She used to tell me stories of the gods and how they shaped us to be productive and powerful." "Yoruba heh," Malik responds, "I learned a little bit when I studied the Haitian Revolution some time back, but unfortunately, I don't know much about it." "Well, when I was a l'ttle gurl, I would pretend to be Oya. She was the god of the elements: wind, storms, death and rebirth." "Wow...she seems powerful." "Yes," Obioma nods, "But I learned that it's not the most powerful who can be the most important." "I'm sorry, I don't…" Obioma puts up her hand and interrupts. Malik squinches his eyes and gives her his undivided attention.

"I think I am Eshu, the messenger of the gods in this case," she continues, "I sense the spirit of Ogun in you Malik. Ogun was called upon by my people to give them the strength to liberate our people from any plight." Malik chooses his words wisely, understanding that she may be spying on him. "Well, Obioma. I'm flattered that you think so highly of a stranger from America," Malik looks at his watch, "Well, I must get ready for my flight." Before Malik gets up, Obioma grabs his hands. Then she closes his eyes and brings his hands to her forehead. Then she whispers a prayer. Immediately, Malik slightly transforms his pupil. He sees not only green and golden receptors, but he briefly sees a hand wielding sharp blades and a torso of a black man. Before Malik could react, Obioma concludes her prayer and lifts her head.

Malik transforms his eyes back before she can re-engage eye contact. Her deep brown eyes and dark complexion glow like a lighthouse. Malik is taken aback by this unusual level of support and confidence. "Be safe in your travels, M'lik Wilson… (She kisses his hands) and let Ogun protect you." Obioma lets go of Malik's hands and smiles. Malik stands in shock but musters up the sense to smile back. "I'll have the doorman help you with your luggage," she says before heading back to the counter. Malik nods in acknowledgement, then gathers his things from the breakfast lobby.

Malik awaits the valet in front of the Hotel Doors. The low rumble of the Charger slowly makes its appearance when the worker makes it out of the car. "Here you go sir," he says as he opens the trunk. Malik unloads his luggage and backpack in the trunk, then tips the Valet $5. "Thank you, sir, and safe travels." he says. Malik nods then get in the car to head towards the airport.

While driving through the busy streets, Malik reflects on the past 3 days. The thoughts in his mind swirl around like a tsunami, smashing through his consciousness while awaiting validation of the inevitable conclusion the journey may bring.

"What Obioma did wasn't an accident, nor was it planned. I knew that I had powers to see the feelings and emotions of people, but this… is the first time I glimpse anything reflecting spirituality," Malik continues as he enters the block towards the Hertz terminal. Malik pulls up in one of the return slots outside of the Hertz return building. He shuts off the car then sits for a while to conclude his immediate thoughts. "*I think this trip is more than just looking for the Harq Alqadr. So, what is this journey leading me to?*" Malik takes a deep breath, looks up, then pushes the button for the trunk. He gets out of the trunk, gathers his things, then walks towards the small building.

Malik walks in the door and drops the keys into the drop box. A receptionist notices the activity and addresses Malik.

"Hello there Sir," she says, "If you need a shuttle towards the terminal, it will be here outside. Just wait by the black bench past those doors." "Thank you," Malik replies as the woman points in the direction of the bench.

Malik continues his trek with his backpack and luggage. Once he exits the door, he stands on a metal pole next to the black bench. Suddenly, something vibrates in his right pocket. BZZZ BZZZ BZZZ, "*Huh? Who could be texting me?*" Malik wonders as he digs in his pocket for his phone. When he retrieves the phone, the messenger slightly surprises Malik. ***Hey Malik? How's it going?*** the message says. "*It's Audrey,*" Malik realizes, "*What should I text her…*" Malik hesitates for a minute to collect his thoughts. The breeze from the English skies offers little push or comfort to ease his stress.

Moments later, the shuttle arrives to escort Malik to his terminal. He temporarily procrastinates his response to load up. As he enters the shuttle, the driver addresses Malik.

"Where to Chum?" the driver inquires in his thick English accent. "My ticket says Terminal 4 Gate B32." "O'l right then, it's on the south runway. So, it'll be a bit of a drive mate." "That's fine; based on my watch, I still have about 2 hours until my flight." "That's fine. Lead away." "Right-o mate." The driver shuts the door, pushes down on the clutch, changes gears, then accelerates towards the other side of the airport.

Forced to confront the messaging, Malik pulls out his cell phone to address the text. ***Good evening, Audrey. Traveling is nerve wrecking. At the airport now.*** Malik sends the message while awaiting a response. Immediately, the phone buzzes again from the response. ***So, are you coming back? Did you find something about the pictures?*** Again, Malik is reluctant to say too much. So, he responds with something cryptic. ***The artifacts in the pictures are leading me to some ancient sights. I feel that I'm getting close to uncovering them.*** Again, Malik looks up as the driver maneuvers through heavy traffic. "*I still don't know that I can trust her. Still, I want her to have some peace of mind and close a chapter in her life (sigh).*" Another buzz indicates another message, this time compounding the bachelor with more emotions and consciousness. ***I really wish I could see the world with you. I feel like you are my hero. Safe travels xoxo*** 😊. Malik blushes at the sight of the message. The tenderness of the text hits him like a gut punch as he sits idly, forgetting about the here and now, past, and present, or life and death.

Suddenly, the shuttle stops and the opening of the door snaps Malik back to attention. "Here you go mate," the driver instructs. Malik gathers his belongings and walks towards the door. He gives the driver a nod while walking off. As Malik heads towards the doors, the driver takes out his phone and texts something. He gives a quick glance at Malik, then looks back at his phone. When the phone buzzes, he chuckles to himself, then whispers the message. "We control the destiny of men, for we are Elite". Afterwards, he drives off to pick up other travelers.

An hour later goes by, and Malik manages to check in his heavy luggage, go through security, and sit at the gate awaiting the plane. He opens his laptop to look at the activity on his website and app. Meanwhile, his head starts to hurt. Sharp pains on the left side of his head prompt him to message and rub it to alleviate the tension. Suddenly, something flashes through his eyes.

Malik is immediately drawn into another vision. This time, it shows blotted images of a White Fox, an old shaman, and a flaming sword. As quickly as the vision appears, it disappears as soon as the stewardess announces the instructions to load the plane. "Ladies and Gentlemen, the flight leaving for Bamako will begin to board 1st class passengers in the next 5 minutes. Please have your tickets ready and your luggage properly labelled."

Malik quickly shakes his head, puts his laptop back in his backpack and gets up to stretch. "(UGH) *What is going on?*" Malik wonders while waiting to board the plane, "*These visions are becoming more erratic. I haven't felt this way since I first discovered my powers.*" The doors behind the stewardess begin to open, prompting Malik to gather his things. As the other passengers begin to do the same, Malik begins to process a way to gain further understanding while not revealing his true identity. "*So once I board the plane and sit down, I'm going to meditate by pretending to sleep. I'll ask one of the attendants to give me a mask to cover my eyes. I have a feeling HE will know what's going on.*"

Minutes later, the stewardess gets on the microphone and announces the boarding. "Ladies and Gentlemen, we are now accepting 1st class passengers. Please line up in an orderly fashion and have your tickets ready. We are scheduled to take off in 30 minutes. Thank you for flying with Royal Air Maroc.

Malik gathers his things, takes his ticket out of his backpack pocket, keeps it in his right hand and walks up to the line. The line moves quickly as Malik makes it towards the front counter. "May I see your ticket please?" the stewardess asks. Malik takes his right hand and gives the ticket. The young woman: short, skinny, with dark brown hair and rosy cheeks, inspects the ticket, then reluctantly looks back at Malik. "Alright sir, you're all set. Right this way." Malik nods then walks down the walkway.

Malik reaches his seat on the plane and puts his backpack in the compartment above him. He patiently waits in his seat as the other passengers' board the plane. Despite his outward confidence, Malik is anxious inside. He would stop himself from grinding his teeth, constantly release his muscles, and would rub his thumb and finger together like a perpetual tug of war. Wanting to know the answers that come from new questions unravelling once again crowds his mind.

"*I wish they would hurry up*", Malik complains. Then as the last passenger boards the plane, Malik notices a customary bag in his seat. It provided some trinkets, a menu, brochures, and something unexpected. Malik could barely contain his excitement when he looked inside and grabbed an essential item. "Out of all the places, they actually have a head mask," Malik whispers while unwrapping the plastic surrounding the mask, "*Now, all I need to do is wait for them to take off.*" Malik puts on his seat belt, adjusts his seat, and gets comfortable as another stewardess gives instructions for the flight.

A few minutes later, the plane maneuvers around towards the runway. The roar of the engine creates an atmosphere of calm, putting Malik at ease. As he takes a last look at London, he smiles as he reflects on the experience the city has brought him. "*Who would've thought that I would learn more about myself than the location of the sword,*" he concludes, "*Seems the deeper I go, the more I want to seek out…*(sigh) Well, on to a new journey.*"

As the last plane takes off, the engines begin to spin quickly, generating more kinetic energy as the passengers begin to brace themselves. Then, like an Olympic sprinter, the plane quickly accelerates. Increasing in speed, the plane goes so fast that it outruns the wind itself; crashing towards the horizon with purpose, the plane builds up the speed necessary to take off. The nose of the plane leans upwards as the wheels gracefully move underneath the body. Despite the exertion of energy, the plane floats gracefully in the sky and above the clouds. Once the plane levels off at a consistent speed, the announcement rings through the intercom.

"Ladies and Gentlemen, you can now walk towards the bathroom or get up. In a few minutes, we will serve snacks and drinks. Alcohol will require an ID to purchase, and we do accept cash or credit card. The fight is scheduled to be 7 hours long so feel free to enjoy the flat screens and our movie choices. Again, thank you for flying with us at Royal Air Maroc."

After the cue, Malik grabs a blanket from underneath his seat and covers his body. Then he takes the mask and puts it over his eyes. He relaxes his breathing and muscles. He grasps his hands together, places them on his lap, and then leans back. After confirming that he has the look of a man not to be bothered, Malik activates his Dracocernentia.

Immediately, Malik is flashed into the confines of his mind. The conglomerate of lighting and coloring do little to ease the excitement Malik feels on uncovering more of the mystery about the sword. Moments later, Malik is drawn to a space that mirrors a desert. The sand is hard, dark brownish, and abrasive. The wind is fast and uncontrollable. And towards the end is a group of mountains surrounding a giant locked door.

Despite the conditions, Malik treks his way towards the door. When he reaches the door, he is amazed by its structure: about a story high, with an upside-down gold Ankh with a silver lining and a lock with the shape of a fox. "What is this door?" Malik wonders as he tries to open the door. "Dammit! It won't budge." Malik continues to struggle with a door until a voice chuckle in the mist.

"Heh heh heh heh" it laughs as the voice triggers Malik's curiosity. He turns around the blistering sandstorm while calling out. "Who's out there? And What's behind this door?" Again, the voice sounds off. "Not all doors are meant to be open, my heir." "*My heir…*" Malik ponders, "WAIT… COULD IT BE?"

As the winds slow down, a man begins to walk towards Malik. His magnificent presence is cloaked with a red garment, dark brown boots, sleeveless showing his well-defined biceps, and a beard so thick; it barely covers his smile. Despite this, Malik recognizes this king of the past.

"Amir?!" Malik addresses, "What is the… I am glad to see you." "I as well, Malik," Amir responds, patting him on his shoulder. "Amir, what is this door? And how come I can't open it." Amir chuckles, then removes his massive hand from his shoulders. "In all of us, 2 destinies converge into one. It's what makes us, but it's also can be hidden from us if we do not allow ourselves to be educated on where we come from," Amir counsels. "2 destinies," Malik repeats, "Wait a minute, like 2 parents." "Correct, my heir. You learned about destiny laid out for your father...my line." "But I know little about my mother… so this locked door, the white fox…" Amir crosses his arms, looks at Malik with a stern gaze, and demands his attention. "You went through not only my trials to the Invisible Ember but your own internal battles, yes?" Malik nods in acknowledgement. "Well, that is only 1 destiny from your lineage. The other is a mystery. Without the knowledge of who you are as a whole, you will not achieve full power and clarity. I have seen through your eyes what our ancestors are trying to lead you. It is not a coincidence that you seek the tribe that was ancient during my time, the same tribe whose blood also runs in your veins." "My veins… *my mother…*" "Just like you have to battle to find the key to your core, you have to unlock your mother's side. Only then will the door unlock." "I see…" Malik responds, then the winds pick up. He quickly turns around and sees Amir disappearing in the sandstorm.

"Amir wait!" Malik yells. "There is no need to fear, my heir. You have already demonstrated that you have the courage to face yourself. Now face it again, but in a new line…" Before vanishing in the wind, Malik can see the smile and the green receptors emitted from his ancestor. After the last remnants of his body blow away. The vision explodes into a bright light, leading Malik out of the profound moment of his meditation.

# Chapter 22: Back to the Motherland

The shock of the vision, combined with the intercom announcement, wakes Malik up. He wipes away the minute beads of sweat from his forehead while looking around the plane. "Ladies and Gentlemen, we are about to approach our destination in the next 20 minutes. If you haven't already, please have a seat and buckle your safety belts. When we land, please do not exit out of your seats until instructed to do so. Thank you again for flying for Royal Air Maroc."

Malik rubs his face, takes the blanket, folds it, and puts it underneath the seat. Meanwhile, a stewardess collecting trash and plates comes by to check on Malik. "You seemed to be out of it," she says, "You missed dinner and snacks. Would you like me to get you something?" "No thank you ma'am," Malik responds, "I tend to get sleepy when I fly. The sound of the engines calms me down." "Understood," she says pleasantly, "Let me know if you change your mind." "Thank you." The stewardess walks down the aisle to continue her duties as Malik grabs his cellphone. *"As soon as we land, I'll text Emma to see if she's ok,"* he plans as he looks at the window to see the city.

The city of Bamako is a spectacular sight from above: filled with houses surrounded by Palm and Acacia trees, the skyscrapers forming the nucleus of the city, surrounded by the large, meandering, mighty Niger River. Malik can fill the energy swelling within him. The feeling makes Malik attuned to his surroundings while putting his anxiety at ease. *"I can sense it,"* Malik realizes, *"This place feels familiar to me. As if my line was meant to come here. Despite this, I need to come up with a way to get to the White Fox, and that means finding the Dogon."*

Malik makes his way to baggage claim as he takes out his cell phone. With a flip of a thumb, he scrolls down to find a number, then presses it. Awaiting a dial tone, Malik puts the phone on his right ear as the ringing commences.

RING…RING…RING…RING…" Malik, my boy, how are you?" "Hey Granddad, I'm at baggage claim. How is everybody?" "Well, your grandmother is fine, but your sister didn't come home last night." "Last night!" Malik responded, "What's going on?" "Well, as far as I'm aware, she went to go investigate the young man she's been mentoring. Something happened at the school a few days ago…" "What do you mean, something happened?" "Did she tell you about the incident at the school?" Malik pauses while he sees his luggage.

Malik quickly grabs his luggage and goes to a seating area to re-engage the conversation. "Yes… she said that he…" "Yes, well she went to go investigate the group that has him. Some organization called W.A.V.E." "W.A.V.E… I'll have to dig into them when I have the time." "So, Malik, you said you're at baggage claim. Are you not in London?" "No, I got a lead on the whereabouts of the sword. Also, I keep getting visions of this strange entity." During the conversation, someone in the background is making noise, so Kemba puts the phone on speaker.

"My Amir, are you alright?" Geneva asks emphatically. "Yes Grandma, I just touch down. I was going to explain to Granddad about the vision I've been receiving and where I am." "Alright Malik. Tell us." "Well, I keep seeing this weird, glowing White Fox in both when I'm meditating and when I'm dreaming. That's why I flew to…"

Immediately the phone drops. The weight of the reveal takes the wielder by surprise. Malik grows increasingly concerned and calls out to his grandparents. "Hello. Hello…" Still no answer. Malik begins to clinch his phone tighter. His lips become still, and he gulps before answering again. "Hello…." "Malik…," Kemba responds softly and sternly, "Are you where I think you are?" "If you're talking about Bamako…" "MALIK!" Geneva responds surprisingly, "Do you have any idea where you are…"

Malik pauses in shock. Though he has fought many enemies and been in dangerous situations, the reaction of his grandparents has taken Malik out of focus. His forehead begins to sweat as an old man addresses Malik's visions. "It's the Sigi my boy." Kemba says, "Malik, what you are seeing is the White Fox of my people. You are being led to pass through the Rite of Passage to manhood." "You mean to tell me that the god of the Dogon is trying to speak to me? Why? And why does it know about the Harq Alqadr?" "It is said that the formation of the Moors originated exactly where you stand. There was a ritual for those who are chosen to get wisdom from the gods to lead the people in the next generation." "Lead the people?" Malik questions, "But why m…" "Because you have Dogon blood in you boy…" Kemba interrupts, "and because you will fulfill the prophecy that I was shown when I was your age!" "What?! Why didn't you tell me this?" "Because those with that foresight were already being hunted. Remember, your grandmother also had similar visions and at the time…" Malik shakes his head slightly. He now realizes that the events he's experienced isn't an accident. So, he takes the time to ease his grandparents' concerns and worry.

"I get it. I'm supposed to be the bridge for our people and generations. I was told this some time ago and now, I'm in your home country. Granddad...Grandma… How do I find your people?" "You must catch a short plane from there to a town called Bandiagara. There you must hike up to the hills, and there you will find your grandfather's people." "Gotcha." "My Amir, let me make a phone call. I will take care of it for you." "Thanks Grandma." "Malik, listen to me son," Kemba ends, "The Dogon are a strict and secretive people. They will not welcome you as easily as you may think. However, the wisest among them, the Hogon, will be able to validate your lineage through me." "How?" Malik asks. "You will see when you meet them. Be safe and be careful." "And wait for a text message tonight before you sleep. We love you, my Amir." "Love you too and keep an ear out for Emma. I'm sure she's fine."

Malik hangs up the phone and sits at the baggage claim for some time. The interaction with his grandparents makes him nervous not about the journey, but about the new information he has to process.

"Ever since I have taken this quest, I realize just how big the world is…" Malik compartmentalizes as he tries to relax his body, "*Not only am I meeting new people with powers like mine, but Emma has also back home, and random people seem to be sensitive to my energy. It's as if I'm… like a sun or a star…*(Malik gets up with his luggage and heads towards the exit); I just need to get to the hotel, rest and wait for grandma's text."

Malik carries his luggage out of the airport and takes a shuttle towards the hotel. There, a driver asks Malik of his destination. "Good afternoon," the man states, "Where can I take you?" "To the Azalai off… Avenue de Mali...2000, I think," Malik answers while struggling to ascertain the directions. "Ah yes, I know it well." the driver answers. Malik nods as he takes a seat behind the driver.

As soon as Malik takes a load off, the driver pushes on the accelerator and drives down the busy streets. Bamako is a place mixed with time, having modern affinities such as cars, skyscrapers, and restaurants while still retaining some cultural identity with holy mosques, markets, and people wearing traditional African garments. The presence of progressive black people has Malik in a state of awe, capturing the very essence of a thriving black community.

"This is kinda amazing," Malik whispers while looking out the window. The driver: a lanky medium-sized man with a patchy goatee, beady, kinky hair, and yellow eyes, strikes up a conversation with Malik. "So, where are you from, traveler?" he asks. "Oh...I'm from America. Atlanta, Georgia." "Oh, I see. You travelled far. What brings you here?" "Oh, just always wanted to see this part of Africa. I'm vacationing." Malik is hesitant to say too much, knowing that there was a reason his family fled this country. "Well, we welcome you here. Very nice places to visit here, especially the food." "Good to know," Malik responds.

The shuttle pulls up in front of the Azalai Hotel. This extravagant pinnacle of architecture has white cemented walls, several pools and rivals any hotel you can find in Las Vegas. Malik begins to step out and becomes amazed at the site.

"Here we are my friend; enjoy your stay." "Thank you," Malik responds, leaving a tip for the driver. Malik walks out of the shuttle and into the hotel lobby. As the automatic doors open, Malik takes a look around and sees similarities of his condo back home with the array of brown, velvet, orange, and red color schemes that blanket the walls, tables, chairs, and loveseats. Malik then walks up to the counter and is greeted by a young woman with brownish-orange skin, dark lips, golden brown eyes, wearing a matching headscarf and dress, loop earrings, and the country's biggest smile.

"Good afternoon, welcome to the Azalai Hotel. My name is Kadiatou. How may I help you?" "Hi. My name is Malik Wilson, and I booked a reservation for a room for 3 days." "Alright, let's see...hmm...Oh there you are. You seem like you are from far away." "Yes, America." "Ah… America…" Kadiatou responds, "Wait here while I give you your key."

Kadiatou sashayed down the hall like a model, twisting her hips through her loose-fitting dress, pretending to be oblivious to the attention she drew. Malik tries to control his wandering eyes while shaking his head. *"If Pat Pat were here right now… Hell, she'd probably go straight to the bar. Still, small pleasures will have to wait."* Kadiatou struts back with an envelope and key inside. Then she responds with a big smile. "Your room is on the 3-floor overlooking the pool. Enjoy your stay Mr. Wilson." "Thank you, Kadiatou." Malik responds as she gives him a flirtatious wave.

Malik makes it to the elevator and pushes the button. He patiently waits while looking at his envelope. "Says here that I'm in room 325. Ok." DING, after about 45 seconds of waiting, the doors open, and Malik drags his suitcase inside. Once the doors close, Malik pushes the #3 button to direct him to his room. The elevator quickly shifts gears, raising the traveler up 3 flights before releasing him to the 3rd floor. Malik steps into the hall and notices a sign pointing towards his right to his room. Coincidentally, his room appears to be only3 doors away. He casually approaches the door, takes out the key and places it next to the magnetic scanner. Once the green light shows, the click signals the door being unlocked, and Malik opens the door.

His hotel room is splendid: a queen size bed lined with maroon and white sheets, a hardwood coffee table with a port for internet, a clear glass shower with ivory toilet and sink, and as promised, a window overlooking the vast pool as well as a small view of the Niger River. Still feeling the effects of traveling halfway around the world, Malik decides to take off his clothes, take a shower and put on some comfortable clothes.

As usual, Malik allows the cool water to wash away the grit and grind of the day while dwelling in his thoughts. "*I wonder how the Dogon will react to me? I wonder what's going on with Emma? And I wonder when Grandma is going to text me?*"

After about 15 minutes of showering and changing clothes, Malik notices his phone vibrating on the small dresser by the bed. Malik walks over to the phone and looks at the message. ***My Amir, go to the Dianeguela district off the Niger first thing in the morning. There you will see a small airstrip and meet a man named Adama. He will be expecting you. Take care and be safe.*** Malik nods his head while looking at the window. The setting sky marks the end of one day and the beginning of another. "Alright, tomorrow I get to the bottom of this White Fox character. Then I can finally find the sword." Malik closes the sheets of the window. He turns off the lights then gets in the bed to rest for the night.

For the first time in days, Malik sleeps soundly throughout the night. The cool temperature of the room mixed with a comfortable bed and the African presence relaxes him to the point where he could truly relax his body. The seconds turn to minutes, and the minutes turn to hours until the glimmer of light once again penetrates through the sheets.

In the morning, Malik gets up from a well-rested sleep. His muscles no longer ache, and his mind is no longer cluttered. He walks up towards the window and gazes upon the land his ancestors once roamed.

"This sure is a pretty sight," Malik compliments, "When you live in the city, it's easy to take these things for granted. Now I need to get ready."

Malik walks in the bathroom brushes the fade in the sides of his hair while applying some oil in his short fro. Then he picks out an outfit to wear, along with making room in his backpack to store some extra clothes for the trip. He finds a blue V-neck T-shirt, a pair of boot cut, ashy blue jeans, and his blue NMD Adidas sneakers.

After putting his clothes on, he rechecks the supplies that he has in his backpack: 3 extra pairs of shirts, boxer briefs, 2 pairs of cargo shorts, his laptop, phone charger, deodorant, and the pictures along with the book given to him by Hauss. "Where I'm going, I'm probably not going to have access to electricity, so once I get to Bandiagara, I need to turn the phone off." Malik grabs his backpack, his hotel key and then walks out of the room.

Malik walks down to the hallway and the elevator. He pushes the button down and waits for the signal. After 15 seconds of waiting, the doors open, allowing Malik to walk in. As before, Malik pushes the 1 button before the doors shut. The elevator quickly moves down to the first floor until the doors open again.

When Malik reaches the first floor, he walks towards the lobby and past the front counter. Kadiatou is now wearing a bright red and green colored scarf and dress. She sees Malik, smiles, and immediately addresses him.

"Good morning; how was the room?" Malik looks at her, smiles and addresses her back. "The room was very comfortable and quiet. I haven't slept so long and peacefully in a while." "Very good." she smiled back, "Help yourself to our restaurant; we have very good cuisines." "Um, I just want fresh fruit. I'm in a hurry...to see the city." "Well sure, we have fresh fruit right over there. Help yourself and enjoy your day." "Thank you, ma'am."

Malik walks by a small kiosk with a small fruit stand. He grabs an apple, a banana, and a bottle of water. Then he walks out of the lobby, where there is a shuttle parked outside. Malik takes a moment to unpeel his banana and eat it while looking over the text message from his grandmother. "Ok, so I'm supposed to go to the Airstrip in the Dianeguela district to find a man named Adama. Alright, here goes..."

Malik throws the banana peel away in a nearby trash can, steps in the shuttle and addresses the driver. Luckily, he is the same driver from the day before, so there were no awkward reintroductions.

"AH, the American!" he spoke, "Where can I take you today?"
"Can you take me to an airstrip? In the Dianeguela district?"
"Hmmm...ah yes, by the river. Certainly." Malik sits behind the driver as he closes the door and drives off the parking lot.

The drive was moderately short but rigorous. The amount of traffic from people, cars, cattle, and commercialism is enough to remind Malik of home. "*Damn...*" he processes, "*Go through all of this traffic that reminds me of Atlanta. No wonder I don't like to drive.*" Before pulling up to the district, the driver strikes up another conversation. "So, what takes you to the airstrip?" "Oh, a man there from a mutual acquaintance is going to take me on a small safari," Malik embellishes to conceal his purpose. "Oh, I see. Well, this country has been through a lot in the last many years. We didn't use to have travelers from all over the world. Now, it seems like anyone wanting to visit or make money comes here." "I can imagine. I think I fit the category of the one who would want to visit." "Indeed," the driver concludes.

Moments later, the shuttle pulls up on a small shack with a runway and a small plane. The driver stops and announces the arrival.

"Here we are," the driver announces. Malik gets up from his seat, smiles at the driver, and gives him another tip. "Have a good time sir," the driver says as Malik waves back at him while exiting the shuttle.

Malik looks around the airstrip, trying to find someone to talk to. Scanning around the almost barren area, he is suddenly drawn to a garage with a white plane parked underneath it. Making a bold assumption, Malik makes his way towards the garage, thinking someone should be inside.

As Malik approaches the garage, he notices an older, black man performing small maintenance on the plane. He continues to tighten some bolts on the tail while not recognizing a visitor walking up. Malik lightly taps on the rim of the garage to grab the man's attention.

TAP TAP TAP. "Huh… who is there?" the man asks in his thick accent. "Hello sir, I am looking for a man named Adama." Malik responds. "Who is it that is speaking?" the man scorns, "Well, speak up." Before Malik responds, the man gets up and walks up to Malik. Then Malik speaks to the man. "My name is Malik and I'm looking for a man named…" "I heard you the first time," the man interrupts. However, his demeanor shifts when he gets a better look at Malik.

The man is about 5'9'' tall, wearing a button-up short sleeve shirt, cargo pants and boots. He has kinky greyish black hair, clean-shaven, and thick forearms. When he gazes at Malik, he arches the right side of his mouth. "Ah yes, Malik. I am the one you seek. I am Adama."

# Chapter 23: Descendant of the Dogon

Malik looks at the man as he looks around and inspects his 6'2'' physique. Malik doesn't know what to make of this interaction but plays it cool. "So…" Malik sounds off, "I was wondering if you could…" "Yes, I am aware," Adama interrupts, "You want to go to Bandiagara. I was told by… (Adama looks directly at Malik in the eye) someone special." "Yes, can you take me." "Of course, we leave as soon as we fuel up the plane. Now come with me."

Adama walks out of the garage while Malik follows. Near the broad side of the shack, there is about 10 gallons of gas. Adama goes towards the pile and looks back at Malik and speaks. "I could use a strong young man to help me with these." "Sure," Malik volunteers, "Where too?" "If you bring them back to the garage, I will fill the plane while you grab the gallons. The sooner we finish, the sooner we leave." Malik nods and begins to grab each gallon in each hand.

Several minutes pass by as Malik grabs the last of the gallons. Adama takes the last gallon, drains it in the gas containment, shuts and secures it. "Alright, my boy," Adama states, "Now we are ready to take off." "Alright, I'm ready."

Malik and Adama get inside of the plane: roughly 24 ft long, with a red stripe along the sides and a single propeller at the nose of the plane. Adama and Malik fasten their seatbelts as Adama starts the propeller. The blades begin to spin slowly, building up momentum as Malik braces himself for another ride.

"You nervous boy?" Adama asks. "It's just the first time being in a plane like this." Malik responds. "No worries, I promise you we won't crash. The flight will take about 2 hours." Then Adama directs the plane out of the garage and into the runway. Unlike the jets with their engines, the small plane exerts a loud and ratty sound, which annoys Malik. "*This plane sounds like a nagging wife.*" Malik complains. "Don't worry," Adama says, sensing Malik's annoyance, "Once you get in the air, you won't be as distracted. Shall we be off?" Malik nods nervously as Adama hits the runway.

Like a track star, the plane begins to accelerate. Building up speed, the propellers violently rotate over and over. The plane moves so fast that Malik is whip-lashed a bit, underestimating the speed of the small bush plane. After a few intense seconds, the plane takes off and heads west alongside the Niger River. The takeoff isn't as smooth as the commercial jets, but Malik is able to appreciate the spectacle of the meandering river over the landscape.

20 minutes later, Adama begins to spark up a conversation with Malik. "So now, you are here to seek something, yes?" "Oh, yes. A tribe that lives near that city." Malik says reluctantly. "Oh, you mean the Dogon?" "Well… er…" Malik stumbles before Adama chuckles. "Relax my boy; it is alright. Our mutual acquaintance also told me alittle about your journey. You see, my original tribe is the Bozo, and we have a history with the Dogon. As a matter of fact, I grew up in Bandiagara with my family and 3 sisters." "Oh really. Wow… so how do you know about the Dogon?" "Well, let me see…"

Adama takes his time to recollect his thoughts while shifting gears to follow the course. Meanwhile, Malik takes in the sights above the ground before engaging back in the conversation. "Well, my father told me a story that has been passed down to my people since the Earth began." "So, this story is that old?" "Indeed," Adama continues, "Long ago. The Dogon came from a land where the sun rises before anyplace else. They built vast cities along the mighty river. It is also said that they had a special connection to the animals on land, the mountains from the ground, and the stars in the skies." "Amazing." "Um Hmm… until one day, a group of invaders came with magic weapons and destroyed their cities. Most of them perished or were sold as slaves, but a few of them manage to escape westward." "So, who were these invaders?" Malik asks like a child. "Patience, patience… Some say these men were without morals or souls. Others say they didn't know how to speak, only kill. At any rate, they came across the mighty Nyame River. They had no way of crossing the river and none of the tribes would help them escape." "That's really sad. So, what happened next?" "There was one Bozo man who owned a large fishing boat. But he could not catch any fish. So, one of the men asked the fisherman if he would take them across the river. The fisherman says they have to pay him, for his family was hungry and could not return until he caught food. So, the man goes back to the tribe and converses with the other fleeing people. Moments later, the man goes back to the fisherman and proposes a compromise." "A compromise? Sounds civil," Malik responds as Adama adjusts the course.

Adama concludes his story after checking the fuel gages and elevation. The tank reads ¾ of a tank and the elevation is about 2,400 ft. "So, the man says if they build a fishing net and help the fisherman catch food for his family, would that be enough payment to cross the river. The fisherman thought about it for a minute. He thought no one had ever offered to help him before and he could not see his family starve, so he agreed. The tribe showed the fisherman how to make a net that has anchors in the edges to dive deeper into the river. Then they devise a wheel to pull the slack for bigger catches. So, 3 days later, the fisherman went into the heart of the river and used the net built by the escapees. He tosses it into the river and allows it to settle. After a few minutes, he ties it to the wheel and attempts to pull up the net. However, the fisherman didn't expect the load to be as heavy. Suddenly the boat tilted as the fisherman desperately attempted to pull his catch. After a few rows, he was able to bring in a full net of fish. So many fish that it covered the whole bowl of his boat." "Truly amazing," Malik responded. "Yes. The fisherman was so happy that he could feed his family and sell the remaining fish; he gladly took the few runaways across the river where they live today. And to this day, Bozo will always help Dogon." "Wow, that is an amazing story." "Yes, the Dogon always had ways that rivalled those around the other tribes. However, only a few cling to the traditional ways." Malik nods in acknowledgement as the plane continues to fly.

An hour later, Adama reaches the town of Bandiagara and looks for an airstrip to land the plane. Malik patiently awaits a landing spot as Adama gives Malik some instructions. "When we land the plane, you will head south towards the hills. It will take several hours to make the journey." "You don't think it will be dangerous?" Malik asks. "Well, for most people yes, but I have a feeling that you will far better." "If you say so," Malik responds. Adama circles around the town until he finds an airstrip in the outskirts of town. Adama re-assesses the gages and prepares the land.

The plane levels as Adama reduces the speed. Malik braces himself as the plane delegates towards the runway. The noise of the propellers drowns out any chance to communicate as the pilot masterfully lands the plane on the sand-covered asphalt. Quickly, the plane gains its control, allowing Adama to maneuver the plane to a spot near a building. After some bumpy spots and patchy roads, the plane makes a stop and Adama shuts down the engines. While waiting for the propellers to completely stop, Adama gives Malik a few words of advice.

"Well Malik, it was a pleasure to bring you here. I will be in town visiting family for about 3 days. Then I will head back to Bamako." "Thanks, Adama; it was a pleasure as well." Malik responds, then shakes Adama's hand.

The men get out of the plane and are greeted by a lanky, average height, greyish blond hair man with a mustache, some dark spots, and yellow teeth.  "Mon Ami, you drop by without a phone call or a message?" "Well, you know, sometimes the winds pick up on themselves." Both men shake hands and pat themselves on the shoulders. Malik stands by as the man redirects his focus. "Seems you had a passenger with you, no?" the man asks. "Yes, my name is Malik," Malik extends his hand. "Jean Pierre Rochambeau, at your service," he responds with a handshake. "Jean owns the airstrip and some of the businesses here in town. Malik wants to go visit the cliff buildings of the Dogon." "Oh. Magnifique! (Magnificent), well, you must be careful. They are very secretive and strict people. Getting there will not be easy." "Here Malik, (Adama gives Malik a small red pendant tied to a string) go to the river and find the fishing boat with this same symbol. They will take you across the river to your destination." "Thank you again Adama." Malik responds. "La vitesse de Dieu (God's speed), and it was a pleasure meeting you, Malik." Jean says. Malik nods and walks towards the town.

Malik treks down the dusty town. The streets are underdeveloped, and the people live simple lives. Malik sticks out in the crowd by his bright-colored clothes, height, and demeanor. *"The people here are not as bubbly as Bamako,"* Malik notices, *"I just need to get to the river and look for this boat."* Despite his hesitations, Malik continues to walk towards the river.

After an hour of walking through the streets, Malik makes it to the river's edge. The riverfront is busy, congested, and an epicenter for the town's economy. Several shops, tents, and shakes house people making purchases and deals. Meanwhile, several boats come and go to cash in on their day's catches. Malik takes his time to walk around the people while trying to look out for the boat.

"Wow, this place is crowded…" Malik says underneath his breath, "Ok, let's see here. (Looks briefly at the pendant) So I just need to find a boat with this symbol." So, Malik carefully meanders through the sea of people while looking for the boat.

Several minutes later, Malik gets tired and tries to find a spot to sit and rest. The sweat from his forehead does little to alleviate the constant beating of the African sun refracting from the water. Malik wipes the sweat with his forearm, takes the water bottle from his backpack, and takes some sips. "Ugh...Damn, it's hot out here. I don't know where I can find this boat." Malik complains, "This sun is going to be the death of me." Suddenly, Malik's head starts to hurt. He begins to see flashes of the White Fox appear. Malik immediately gets up, rubs his left side, then closes his eyes.

"(Ouch) This again! Why do I keep seeing these images? *Does this mean I'm close?*" Once Malik looks to his left, divine providence allows him to notice a strange, mud-brown-colored boat. Malik is strangely drawn to this boat: it is about 15 ft long with a low, red-colored roof and a single man sitting at the edge. "That must be it," Malik deduces as he walks towards the strange boat.

When Malik arrives at the boat, he inspects the outside. The boat doesn't look reliable: there are cracks in the side, some water is inside of the boat, and structurally doesn't look like it can carry much. Then, Malik notices a man sitting inside the boat's roof. He is a quiet man with a bald head, very skinny, old, wearing nothing but a mangy blue faded shirt and brown shorts. He looks at Malik but says nothing.

Malik attempts to communicate with the man by introducing himself. "Hi there. My name is Malik… and I was told you can take me across the river." The man says nothing and does nothing. Malik begins to raise his eyebrow and raise his shoulders in frustration. "My name is Malik. Do you understand me?" Again, the man says nothing and does nothing, he just looks at Malik.

Then Malik remembers the pendant Adama gave him. So, he takes it out of his pocket and shows the man. "Here is something I think you need." Malik addresses. Suddenly, the man gets up and walks towards Malik. While he says nothing, he looks at the pendant and nods. The man sticks out his hand. Malik notices the gesture, looks at the pendant, then gives it to the man. The man takes the pendant, moves it around, inspects it, then looks at Malik in the eye.

After being satisfied, the man nods and prompts Malik to climb on the boat by pointing to it. To reconfirm this gesture, Malik asks, "So you want me to climb in?" The man remains silent but nods. Then the man turns around and grabs the oher. Malik walks into the boat and sits in a dry spot. The man uses the oher to push the boat further into the river and leaves the bank.

Despite the width of the river, Malik tries to remain still as the heat continues to bear on him. The relenting African sun beats down on him like a drum. *Man, I thought Atlanta was hot, but this is a whole new level.* Malik complains, *"Well, at least I'm close to the village."* Meanwhile, the man remains stoic as he carefully and patiently steers the boat through the murky waters.

After 20 minutes, the boat lands on the other bank. Immediately, Malik stands up, dusts himself off, and walks towards the end of the boat. The old man simply sits down and looks straight ahead, staring at the horizon like a paradise. Still, he says nothing. Malik walks by and looks at the man one last time. Malik addresses the man with respect.

"Thank you for your help." The man says nothing yet again. Still, Malik attempts one last time to communicate. "I really appreciate it; do you need a tip?" Then the man looks at Malik. His gaze is intense and his pupils pure. The energy emitted from the look causes Malik's Dracocernentia to activate, showing him visions of a white fox on the man's face. Malik quickly closes his eyes while stepping off of the boat. "Ugh...What in the hell is going on?!" Malik yells, trying to grasp the situation, "How did he force me to awaken the power?" Malik runs his face, then opens his eyes.

When his lids open, the boat and the man disappear. Malik looked at the banks and across the river but could not find the man or the boat. "Either the heat is playing tricks on me, or I'm going insane," Malik remarks, "Well, at least no one is around. So, I can switch to Reptile mode to use the sun as an energy source." So, Malik reactivates his Dracocernentia and shifts his body to Reptile Mode by creating a small fire barrier around his body. This allows him to absorb the sun's energy without expending his own while protecting him from getting too hot. Malik then uses his eyes to pinpoint the area the Dogon may be residing. "I can see them about 2 miles away. I see the houses on the cliffs, so it shouldn't take me long to reach there." Afterwards, Malik readjusts his backpack and begins to journey across the barren landscape to the village.

After 30 minutes of walking, Malik makes it to the base of the cliff. With his eyes still activated, Malik scans the area to find any inhabitants. "So far, it seems like it's empty. *Maybe they're deep in their village. I need to be careful.*" So, Malik begins to climb the cliffs to reach the village.

As Malik climbs the ancient cliffs, he becomes in awe of the old structures that used to house the Dogon's ancient ancestors. Despite time turning them into ruins, there are still distinct rooms, drainage systems, and sections to grow food. "Wow," Malik exclaimed, "This is really cool. I can tell that I'm one of few people in the outside world that has seen such structures."

Then suddenly, when Malik reaches the base, his eyes pick up several receptors of yellow, gray, gold, and red. Several voices murmur in different dialects while others yell in excitement. Malik releases the Dracocernentia, but still puts up his guard as he approaches the outer rim of the village.

When Malik makes it to the top, he is greeted by several villagers: some with spears, others wearing masks, led by an older man and a middle-aged woman next to him. The man is dressed in a long, pink strawed garment and a headdress. The woman has rings on her neck, a multicolored dress with a headband.  "What are you doing here!" Malik stays calm, knowing that at this point, he could not afford to cause any more duress. "I mean no disrespect; I was sent here through a vision." Malik responds while holding up his hands. The woman next to the elder squints at Malik with intense eyes. The look on her face signifies to Malik that there is a familiarity not spoken or communicated. *"Why is she looking at me like this?"* Malik wonders while trying to calm the villagers down.

"Look, I just want to talk to the village elder and explain to him that I have to fulfill a vision." "Why should we trust you?" the elder said, "Leave at once, NOW!" Some of the villagers begin to point their spears. The tension is as thick as a fog and so quiet, you could hear a mouse breathe. Malik knows that he has to do something drastic or else his journey will be in vain. Not seeing any other choice, Malik reacts to the situation. "I can't go back; I have to see this vision come to pass, BY ANY MEANS!" Then Malik activates his Dracocernentia and uses the flames surrounding his body to create a dragon. The Dogon look in awe as some of them walk back. The Elder and woman look at each other as well as the spectacle with confusion, then realization. "It… It… can't be…" the elder whispered. The woman follows with a sentiment, "Father… it's the Dragon Dogon… I know it… the prophecy…" She then begins to walk towards Malik while the man yells out. "Djeneba NO!" he commands, "Stay back!" "No father, I know that he is one of us. He has returned. I, too, have seen it."

She then stands in front of Malik. She lowers herself to the ground and gives reverence. Malik lowers his flames and crouches down to the woman. She then looks up with a smile and tears in her eyes, speaking softly to him. "Welcome home… grandson of Kemba…"

# Chapter 24: The Sigi

Malik is taken aback by the unusual show of respect from the woman. His eyes transform back to their normal brown hue while she witnesses tears flowing from her dark-colored cheeks. "How do you know about my grandfather? Matter of fact, how do you know about…" "Arise," Djeneba states, "You must come with us to the village. All will be explained there." "Djeneba, how dare you speak of that deserter!" "Father, regardless of how you feel, he is still your…" "Enough of this!" the elder interrupts, "He is not part of this tribe. His grandfather abandoned his purpose, thus abandoning us. Therefore, he is not welcomed!"

Djeneba boldly stands up to confront her father. Malik is reluctant to reactivate his eyes while ascertaining and comprehending the vitriol thrown at him. *"Granddad… what did you do that you didn't tell me?"* Meanwhile, Djeneba stands in front of her father while he refuses to abide by her welcome of Malik. The other members of the tribe stand around, awaiting a conclusion to this conflict.

"Father, how can you not see that this is the prophecy shown by the Hogon? Can't you see that he is the Dragon Dogon?" Djeneba asks. "My stubborn daughter, our way of life has been dying. Each year, we lose more of our people to the wicked ways of the world and soon, I fear for our survival. He is from a line that refuses to execute his responsibilities." "But father, look at him...LOOK AT HIM! (She points at Malik, then continues her point) DOES HE NOT FAVOR MIGHTY MAMADOU, ELDER OF THE DOGON AND THE BROTHER OF KEMBA!"

Malik's eyes widened with the reveal of Djeneba's soliloquy. His shock of the news pales in comparison to the passion in Djeneba's words. "Father, we have no one to participate in the Sigi who is of age. Yes, this man is a bit old, but he's young enough to represent a part of his heritage in the Sigi. Will you show hatred to a man because of how you feel about his grandfather? Are you going to remain cursed in your stubbornness?"

Mamadou looks at the glisten in his daughter's eyes. She tightens her face and arches her brows downward, breathing hard and standing her ground. His reluctance to show favor shrivels like the dry leaves blowing in the harsh cliffs. He then walks around Djeneba and towards Malik. Despite only being 5'8'' tall, he still has an imposing stance and immovable energy about him. Even when he relinquishes his stern standards, he still maintains a level of decency and regal attitude.

"It will seem... that your cousin speaks highly of you." Mamadou states. "Sir... I don't mean to cause problems. I am just here for answers," Malik responds, "and I'm willing to do what it takes to get them." Mamadou sees the same level of determination in Malik's eyes. He struggles with maintaining the old ways while allowing himself to feel for the long-lost grandnephew that has returned. Then he addresses everyone in the vicinity. "We will take him before the Hogon at once. If he deems him worthy, this... young man... will participate in the Sigi... (then Mamadou looks directly in Malik's eyes); if you deem unworthy, then you must leave at once." Malik nods his head, prompting Mamadou to do the same. "Let us go back to the village and escort our guest."

The rest of the villagers congregate and head back to the village. Malik slowly follows behind but is quickly accompanied by Djeneba. While they walk, Malik converses with his long-lost relative. "I didn't get a chance to fully introduce myself. My name is Malik and... I guess you already know that Kemba is my grandfather." "Nice to meet you, Malik. You have the name of kings. I am your cousin, Djeneba, the daughter of the Elder, Mamadou, your uncle." "I see, so why does he... hate my grandfather?"

Djeneba sighs as they continue to walk. Her anxiousness doesn't stop her from relaying what she knows to Malik. "It was said… that when your grandfather and my father were young, they were chosen to participate in the Sigi. When the Hogon sent them on their journey, the boys were supposed to find the White Fox and communicate with it. The White Fox had the power to show visions of the future and the direction of our people. However, my father did not see the white fox and slept under the stars. His brother, however, kept looking and looking. All night long, he searched the landscape until he nearly gave up." Malik takes his time to process the story Djeneba tells him. He tries to select the right words to ask so that he or Djeneba get overwhelmed. Malik can relate to strange visions and meditations but does not know the level of understanding from Djeneba yet.

"So, what happened?" Malik asks. "Well, when your grandfather finally thought about giving up, he saw something running across the desert. It was medium-sized, white, and blended in with the stars. Your grandfather got up and followed it to the cliffs. For seemingly hours in the night, he continued to follow this odd white thing running up the rocks and through the caves. Then, your grandfather found himself lost in one of the caves. Completely dark, nowhere to see, or nowhere to go, your grandfather sat down." "Wow! So how did he end up surviving?" Djeneba chuckles a bit before finishing the story. "So, then a white light comes into the cave. It touches your grandfather and grabs his attention. Your grandfather didn't know what to make of the light until...POOF, A large, White Fox appeared to your grandfather and gave him a vision." "Appeared? Just like that huh?" Malik questions, "*No wonder he wasn't surprised by my powers or my visions.* So, what was the vision." "Well, it is hard to say. He supposedly told my father and the Hogon when they returned from Sigi. When he told everyone his vision, he and my father got into a huge fight about it. Then about a year later, he left."

Malik feels a level of regret that is indescribable. As Djeneba leads him deep in the village, his mind raced with the thought he imagined his grandfather must have felt. *"I wonder what kind of a vision would be so demonstrative that it would cause brothers to fight and run away from each other."* Then, Malik, Djeneba, and some of the tribe members make it to the hut of the Hogon. Djeneba pats her soft hands-on Malik's left shoulder. "I know that the power you possess makes you worthy, Malik. I am sure the Hogon will see it." Djeneba compliments. "I don't know if I want to display it in front of him. Won't that shock him?" Malik asks. Djeneba chuckles one last time. "Do not underestimate our understanding of the world, Malik. Yes, that is a great power, but it is not the kind I speak of. (She points to a direction in front of Malik) Now go, there is the tent of the Hogon."

The place where the Hogon resides is at the center of the village. It is built with mud-covered wood with a lifted black drape. Inside is a man in his early 90s, with little to no teeth, shriveled up, and with blackish-brown skin. His eyes have a blue ring around his dark brown iris with eyes so weathered they tell a story as long as a lifetime. The rest of the village gather around as Mamadou presents Malik to the holy leader.

"Mighty Hogon, I present this… stranger…" "Father!" Djeneba interrupts. "(Sigh) This young man, who wishes to participate in the Sigi. In your wisdom, we present him to you to weigh the worthiness of his heart." Mamadou looks at Malik and prompts him to step forward. "Step Forward and let the Hogon examine you."

Malik slowly walks up to the Hogon while the villagers look on. Malik feels the strain from the village. Some of them feel that he doesn't belong to the tribe, while others are curious about the stranger who covers his body with flames. Still, Malik takes a deep breath and steps to the Hogon before reaching within an arm's length to him.

The Hogon remains motionless for a minute. Despite the lack of movement, the wise old man peers deep into Malik, as if he was looking at his soul himself. Malik stood by idly while awaiting the decision from the shaman. *"I could activate my eyes and try to figure out what the man is thinking,"* Malik contemplates, *"However, if I am to gain the trust of the tribe, I don't want to rely on my power to force it. I want to earn their trust and respect."* The rest of the tribe looks on in bewilderment. Mamadou gives a stern look as Djeneba anxiously stands by her father. "Father," she whispers, "Why doesn't the Hogon do or say anything?" "SHHHH child, Quiet!" Mamadou scorns, "The ways of the Hogon should not be questioned. This is one of our most holy of traditions." Djeneba gulps and shivers as she redirects her attention towards Malik.

Shockingly, the Hogon gets up from his seated porch inside the shaded shack. His frail body gives way as he slowly walks towards Malik. There is a gasp in the air as each of the villagers looks amongst themselves in shock and disbelief. Djeneba starts to walk towards to get a better vantage until Mamadou puts his hand out. "NO!" he commands, "You must not interfere. Just watch." Malik stands by as the Hogon approaches him. The Hogon put his wrinkled, weathered hands-on Malik's torso. Malik does his best to stand still as the man continues to examine him.

After a few seconds of feeling on Malik's body, the Hogon reaches for Malik's head. He places his hands on Malik's face while reaching for Malik's eyes with his thumbs. Seeing this, Malik instinctively closes his eyes and allows the Hogon to feel upon him. Once Malik's eyes close, a sudden calm overwhelms Malik. The flow of energy illuminates his mind as the wonders of the stars blanket his mind. The images of black people all over the world and throughout history start to decorate using the patterns of the stars. *"This is incredible,"* Malik thought while in this trans-state. Then, a flash of light brightens the skies. Something rises up towards the heavens. As it gets closer, and closer, something magnificent appears at the base. A golden sword appears curved, the edge so sharp it cuts through the air, the grip with the Dracocernentia carved in its base, and the grip aligned with rows of silver and gold. Once the light reaches the sword, a pair of brightly golden eyes open behind it. When the eyes open, the blade ignites completely in flames in different colors. At that moment, Malik's Dracocernentia opens; meanwhile, the Hogon begins to chant in an ancient dialect while looking at the sky.

Then both Malik and the Hogon look up as their eyes link up. Malik creates a massive silhouette of a dragon, engulfing both him and the Hogon in flames. The spectacle completely stuns and overwhelms the whole village. Each man, woman, child, elder, priest, maiden, and even some of the dogs kneel on the ground, all except for Mamadou. Djeneba, however, begins to shed tears of joy. She grasps her hands together and kneels, whispering her confirmation and appreciation of the event. "The prophecy is real. Malik… is… one… of… us!" "Impossible…" Mamadou whispers as he too looks on in utter disbelief.

After a few minutes, the silhouette disappears. Malik closes his eyes again and the Hogon releases his grasp. He steps back and utters the words in English. "The return… of the… Golden… Dragon…" Malik takes a step back with the reveal. "Golden Dragon? What does that mean." The Hogon continues to look at Malik and mumbles in the ancient Dogon language. Malik's head begins to hurt while trying to figure out what is being said. Seeing this, Djeneba runs towards Malik.

"Are you hurt Malik?" Djeneba asks. "A part of my mind is trying to ascertain his speech, but it feels like my head isn't ready for it yet." Malik responds, "What is he saying?" Djeneba smiles as she translates Hogan's words. "You have been chosen to participate in the Sigi. Your journey will start tonight." "Ugh… well, that's good news. What is it?" "All will be explained, but for right now, we must get you ready to seek the White Fox."

All of the villagers get up and the Hogon walks back to his enclosure. Djeneba escorts Malik to her living quarters. While walking, Malik asks more about the Sigi. "So, Djeneba, how does this work? The Sigi." "It is a Rite of Passage for all Dogon boys to achieve manhood. They must go into the wilderness and survive the night. You must seek out the White Fox. If you find the White Fox, then it will give you a vision." "What kind of vision are we talking about?" "The White Fox will give you a vision of the future for the people and the world. However, if you don't find the White Fox, you are destined to be forever shamed." "Well, that sucks!" Malik responds as they approach the hut. Djeneba chuckles until she redirects Malik into the hut. "With eyes like yours, I think that a different destiny awaits you...Malik."

Malik sits down in an easy pose while women from the tribe come in with paint and other tools. "What is all of this?" Malik asks while being prompted to take off his shirt. "In order to participate, you have to bear the mark of the tribe in order to perform the Sigi. These women will pain and tattoo your body before you perform. Until then, I will see you later." Djeneba leaves the hut as the women continue to pain and put temporary tattoos on Malik. The experience is awkward for Malik. One woman raises his right arm and applies red paint in his armpits. The other woman tickles Malik's spine with bristles, all while trying desperately to stand still. *"Talk about feeling exposed,"* Malik complains, *"But then again, I could also be butt-ass naked. So might as well hold this* WHOOO…" Another woman dangerously places her hands near one of Malik's most private treasures.

After a few hours of preparation, the Dogon performs a ceremonial dance around the fire. Each dancer wears long masks with exhorted effort and pride. The masks all have distinctive facial expressions, color schemes, and in some cases, depictions of deities. As the dancing continues, Mamadou stands at the pillar overlooking the fire. He begins to raise his hands as the drummers up the tempo, causing the dancers to pick up the pace. Faster and faster, they danced around the fire. The villagers began to chant and shout. As soon as Mamadou raises both hands in the sky, the dancing and the drums abruptly stop. Everyone is dead silent. The crackling of the burning wood is all that remains of the sound as the lone participant of the Sigi walks towards the elder.

Malik slowly walks without his shirt on and an array of red paint in his armpits, orange dots in his back, and yellow ovals on each pectoral muscle. Mamadou looks at Malik with disguised disdain and contempt. His brows lower immensely and his lips curl. Malik notices the gesture but remains calm and collected. He knows that by capitulating to the ceremony will give him the answers he needs.

"Tonight, this… boy will become a man!" Mamadou announces, "For he has been chosen by the Hogon, to seek the counsel of the White Fox. He will wander into the wilderness all night and return… to share with us the vision." HOOT HOOT HOOT. The villagers all chant and yell as the chill in Malik's spine migrates up towards the back of the head while simultaneously causing him to gulp. Mamadou raises his hand, prompting the village to be quiet as he concludes his speech. "However, if he does not return with a vision from the White Fox and bears its paw print, he will be forever shamed and outcast." Mamadou steps in front of Malik. His antipathy towards Malik shakes the very essence of his soul. His breathing becomes intense, and his eyes transform from white to red from the strain of hiding his disapproval. Then he briefly closes his eyes, contains himself, then says one last thing to Malik. "Are you ready to do the will of the people?" Mamadou asks. Malik nods without making a sound. "Then, go! Seek the White Fox and fulfill your manhood!" Afterwards, the village chants and hollers as Malik starts running into the African bush. Some of the villagers return to dancing while Mamadou walks towards the outer reaches of the village.

Mamadou stands in a secluded spot towards the edge of the village. Then, a mysterious voice appears out of the darkness.

"Is he the one?" the voice asks. "Yes. He possesses the eyes of the fire beast. He will return in the morning...as agreed." Mamadou responds. Then the voice chuckles before concluding the short conversation. "Excellent. Nous contrôlons le destin des hommes, car nous sommes l'élite (We control the destiny of men, for we are Elite)."

Chapter 25: Engaging the Four Chambers

Emma wakes up from a bed in a secluded room. The pain thrusts her body into overtime, as the simple act of breathing is difficult. Emma attempts to lay motionless while staring at the wall. A simple tear runs down her left side as she contemplates the moments that led her here.

"I… I… couldn't defeat that cunt," she reflects. "What… What is wrong with me?" Before she could dwell in her thoughts, a series of knocks interrupts her processing.

KNOCK KNOCK KNOCK KNOCK KNOCK. The door squeaks open slowly. A man walks through: he is wearing tactical gear, a bulletproof vest, dark cargo pants tucked in combat boots, and a holster with a completely black painted tomahawk. He is relatively tall, about 6'0'' with a short taper fade, thin mustache and beard, and light brown eyes. He pulls up a chair and sits a few feet from Emma.

"Morning," he says. "I know this is uncomfortable for you. Our medical officers say that you suffered a minor concussion, bruised ribs, and a blood clot in your eye socket."
Emma struggles to sit up, but the man gets up to manage her attempt. "You're in no condition to get up, not yet anyway." "What… What about Asir?" she responds.
"He's safe," the man assures. "Right now, he's sleeping."
Emma avoids eye contact while continuing the conversation. "Thank you for helping me… and Asir. But… who are you? What are we doing here? And what happened to me?" The man takes something from his pocket and gives it to Emma. It is a bottle with a strange, green liquid. Emma looks at the man peculiarly. She squints her eyes by trying to activate the Avemcernentia, but her lack of power prevents her from fully transforming her eyes. "Ugh…" she complains.

"You see," the man responds, "that's why I'm giving you this. Drink this, then I'll heal you completely. After that, I'll answer your questions."
Reluctantly, Emma takes the bottle, opens the cap, and drinks the liquid.
"EWWW... This taste like lawnmower clippings!" She gags.
"Yeah, but it's all natural. And now, the finale." Emma looks at the man again.
      The man begins to transform his eyes. Emma becomes shocked by the reveal. The man also possesses the Dracocernentia, but his color scheme is bluish green iris with three sets of micro claws surrounding the sharp-shaped pupil. "I can't... believe..."
"Hold on," the man interrupts as he amplifies his body with a small, bluish yellow heat wave. As the room gets warmer, Emma's wounds begin to heal, her eyes begin to fully transform, her breathing gets better, and her strength is rejuvenated.
"Oh my god," she whispers, "you have it too. You are a descendant." The man lowers his power, deactivates his eyes, then sits back down. Emma maneuvers her legs out of the bed and sits on the edge.
      "My name is D'Shawn Bowden. My code name is Snake Sight. I am the local leader of OBR."
"OBR?"
"Yes, the Order of the Black Resistance. We are a militia group dedicated to protecting the lives and rights of Black people. We work in secret to prevent further oppression on our people." D'Shawn slightly looks away. "Sadly, our efforts are not enough to protect everyone, and we do not have enough in our ranks to solidify our operations in this whole country."
"So, if that's the case, why did you come here to Jacksonville?"
"Our intel confirmed that the organization you know of as the..."
"Elite 8... Yeah, I remember now," Emma interrupts. "W.A.V.E. is just a cover up."
"Exactly. Instead of prostituting young girls and sending them to sex trafficking spots, they are now using young boys as experiments for body enhancements while robbing them of their ability to cognitively think, reproduce, and react appropriately."

Emma raises her head and eyes wide open. The revelation of the information allows her to remember certain aspects of her last fight. "That's right!" she yells. "Right before that fight, I remember feeling something in the air while sneaking in the building. Then, before I fought Sharon, she pulled out something strange and began to sniff it."

"Was it a powder substance in a gold container?"

"Yes, it was. After that I couldn't… couldn't..."

"The smoke in the air is Reintergon, a compound that dulls the senses and renders them about 50% of their normal strength. That's why you felt sloppy," D'Shawn explains. "The powder substance that you saw the director take is called Maniacine."

"Maniacine?"

"It's a chemical that is extracted from ashwagandha, Guarana berries, and opioids. It's actually some of the ingredients in your bottle, minus the opioids. It brings out the primal impulses, strength, and endurance; however, it can also cause hallucinations, poisons your blood stream, and taken excessively, can cause death."

Emma sulks as her head slinks down towards her chest. Her shoulders drop and her hands are relaxed on her knees.

"There… there was nothing that you could do. The chemicals were too much for your body to fight off. That's why we wear these masks when we deal with anyone dealing with the Elite 8." Suddenly, a burst of tears and wailing alerts D'Shawn of a different dilemma. Although, strong, assertive, and empathetic, he could do little to soothe the pain that a once proud woman is flooded with. Emma begins to cry copiously: her face becomes red, snot runs down from her nose while draining along her face, and her mouth is filled with sticky saliva. Emma could no longer hide her embarrassment and vulnerability. D'Shawn goes to a cabinet, grabs a towel, and extends it to Emma. She briefly looks up and sees the towel. D'Shawn's face becomes soft and welcoming as he nods. Emma takes the towel and buries her face in the cloth.

"It's OK," D'Shawn consoles. "Even I couldn't beat her with all of those chemicals working against me."

"YOU DON'T UNDERSTAND!" Emma scolds as D'Shawn puts up his hands and backs up a bit. Emma tries desperately to calm down to recollect her thoughts. "I'm… I'm…"

"Hey, I understand. You are…"

"No, D'Shawn. I was once the most powerful weapon in the Elite 8. There was a time where I could kill who I thought was my own father without a single hesitation. People used to be afraid of me. I could generate my power easier than I could breathe. But now...I struggle. I feel like I don't belong, even to my own people. I have a hard time with relationships, and I don't feel powerful anymore." Emma chuckles while wiping her eyes from excessive tearing. "I can't believe a kid like Asir believes in someone like me, a woman without a sense of self or purpose anymore."

"Now, that's where I disagree with you… Blue Phoenix." Emma quickly looks up at a smirking OBR leader. "Yes, I am aware of who you used to be. I was destined to take you down when the time arrived. But then, you changed. You and Shadowmoor helped take down one of the most powerful men in the Elite 8 about a year ago. And… you mentored someone special to me, someone who didn't know who I was, despite the fact we share the same blood."

"Same bl… You mean that Asir…"

"Yes, Asir is my son," D'Shawn admits.

Emma takes a moment to process the information as D'Shawn leans forward, grasping his hands and looking down in shame. Emma finishes wiping away her tears, then sits quietly as the weight of emotion seems to overwhelm the room. Before Emma can generate contempt, she wants to give a fair assessment to D'Shawn's estranged involvement.

"So, is that the real reason why OBR is here in Jacksonville? Because you knew your son was here?"

"Yes." D'Shawn whimpers as he clinches his mouth closed. A single tear rolls down his face until Emma, slowly and with prudence, places a hand on his left shoulder. D'Shawn lifts up his head and nods, then sniffs his nose while wiping his eyes. "When I was 18, I was involved with his mom. Then I found out that she was cheating on me and somehow got pregnant. I didn't believe that the baby was mine, so I started to commit crimes off the street. Then I was arrested and sent to a facility where men would conduct experiments on me. They tortured me, drew my blood, and forced me to fight animals to see if I could survive."

"That is awful," Emma sympathizes. "How did you escape?"

"Well, turns out that because of my abilities, the government purposely deleted any records of me ever existing. However, another group knew about my abilities: OBR. OBR broke me out of the facility, which I later realized was funded by the Elite 8. They trained me to reconnect with my Black and Seminole ancestor, and now I am promoted as one of the leaders." Emma nods her head in acknowledgement and quickly realizes the connections between herself, D'Shawn, and Asir.

"I get it now. The tomahawk you carry, the code name you have, your ancestor, Chittoluthphwa. It means Snake Eyes in Seminole. He told me that I was to help Asir connect with his past because…"

"A Dragon Moor needs a Phoenix to complement him," D'Shawn finishes.

"So now you understand, but better yet, now that you are here, I think it's you that should train."

"Train? But how?"

"Tell me, has your brother ever told you how he was able to achieve the Invisible Ember?"

"The what? And how did you know that Shadowmoor is my brother?" D'Shawn chuckles a bit as he explains. "Let's just say that one of my mentors has met you before. Also, when a Moor reaches a level of enlightenment, they have to go through the 10 trials to the Invisible Ember, a place within themselves to draw out their power."

"Vaguely. He would talk about his visions and interactions with our ancestors, but not in great detail."

"Well, I think you should reconnect with yours. I'm not sure what the Phoenix has to go through, but I'm sure that your ancestor will enlighten you with that."

"I see. I think I just need a moment alone to meditate to find the answers," Emma says while crossing her legs on the bed.

"I figured as much," D'Shawn says before getting up. "I'm going to leave you to that. In the meantime, make yourself at home. I'm only down the hall, and the door will remain locked from the outside. I know that this can't be rushed, nor disturbed."

"Thank you, D'Shawn. And by the way, my name is…"

"I know, Emma. Asir can't stop talking about you."

"Then perhaps while I do this, you reconnect with your son. He's a wonderful kid." D'Shawn smiles, then exits the door.

Emma sits on the bed with a new sense of awareness and clemency. Her humility allows her to shed off all of the burden she has carried since joining Shadowmoor; she is now ready to take the next step. She closes her eyes and controls her breathing. The room becomes still and quiet. Her muscles become relaxed and fluid, like water. Then when the power of the universe is synced, her eyes activate and transport her within a sacred section within her self-conscience.

The room is light grey with a circular lair. There are four locked chambers with different colors: a brown, green, blue, and yellow door. Above Emma is a giant door shaped like the head of a Phoenix. "Where am I? And what is all of this?" Emma circles around while trying to figure out the layout.

Suddenly, something white manifests in front of Emma. The figure stands before Emma before materializing into a familiar form. Emma's eyes open and she smiles by the reveal. "Welcome back, child," the woman says. Emma rushes towards the manifestation and hugs her. She sheds tears of joy and sorrow as the woman strokes her thick hair. "Muqadas, I am so happy to see you!" Emma snivels. "I am so lost, so broken, so…"

"There, there child. I know, and the young man you talked to is right." Emma looks up while wiping away a tear.

"You… you know?"

"While, yes, Emma. I can see the conversation within you, and he is right. Your brother had to go through his own pain and suffering in order to achieve the Invisible Ember. My blood flows in him as well, so as your elder, I must provide you a chance to reclaim your glory."

"So, am I going to have to do 10 trials?" Emma asks.

Muqadas redirects Emma's attention in the room. "Emma, do you see this room?"

"Yes, but I don't know what this has to do with the trials."

"My dear, this is our version of the trials. But unlike the Dragon Moors, ours is more subtle but direct. Tell me, what do you do for your brother?" Emma thinks for a while, then responds inconvincibly.

"Well, I back him up. I give him support."

"Indeed… just like how the heart pumps blood to the muscles. The Dragon is the muscle. It can seek, it can destroy, it can conquer, but it can also protect." Muqadas raises her hand around the chambers. "As you know, the heart has four chambers, but there is a fifth chamber that all Phoenix Moors have to face. This is why we call our trials the Khms Ghuraf (Five Chambers). Each door represents a chamber that makes up our heart. We are the heart for the dragon, but the dragon cannot survive without a heart. This is why we are essential."

"I see…" Emma agrees before asking more questions. "So, is that why I feel like I don't have power? Is that why there are four different doors in this room?"

Muqadas shifts her tone a bit. She is still loving and warm, but she also becomes stern and serious, looking at Emma directly in her eyes.

"Emma, you can no longer rely on pure power if you don't know the root of your essence. Yes, each door represents each chamber that all Phoenix Moors must master. However, I cannot tell you exactly what they are. You have to identify them and cultivate them in your own experience." Emma looks away briefly. Her shame disables her to fully grasp the concept Muqadas is explaining to her. Her eyes tell a story that Muqadas quickly deciphers. Her response reinvigorates Emma to overcome her defeat.

"Emma, what you will experience is a memory. My memory of how I was able to unlock all four chambers in a single mission. You will feel, think, move, and experience everything as if you were living it as well. I promise you, that at the end of this you will understand."

"And what if I don't?" Muqadas looks at Emma and smiles. She provides an answer so simple; it redirects the emphasis on Emma.

"What do you do when you fail? Hmm?" Muqadas looks at Emma with a stoic face. She peers into Emma like a bird to a bug, awaiting Emma to respond. Emma attempts to look in another direction while avoiding eye contact.

"Why won't she stop looking at me?" Emma wonders, while Muqadas continues to chuckle.

Suddenly, Emma develops the nerve to end this dragging stare contest. She responds with fortitude, confidence, and conviction. "I'm not going to fail! PERIOD!" Emma yells. "NOW… will you stop staring at me? You already creep me out because I never see you angry."

"Oh, trust me, child," Muqadas warns, "after this vision, you will know all of what we are capable of."
Afterwards, a flash of white light brightens the room and sends Emma back within her DNA of a time in her past.

# Chapter 26: Syncing the Link Part 1

The memory flashes back to the past. Long before modern technology, long before the noise of cars, traffic, cell phones, or easy interaction for people all over the world. It was a time of the beginning of a turning tide; a time where the ideologies of the current infrastructure were at their infancy.

The year is 1183, a woman stands at the edge of a cliff overseeing the forest. Her brownish white robes and hijab flow with the wind as the seasons turn. She had been traveling the world, searching for meaning and enlightenment. As Emma begins to sync with her past, she ponders on the mindset of such a woman.

"Is… this… you, Muqadas?" Emma asks subconsciously. "Indeed, it is, my child. As you will see, this mission will change mine, and your life, forever. Give in to our Fire Line. Embrace it, and understand how the pain, suffering, sorrow, and enlightenment become the source of our power."

The woman activates her Avemcernentia to survey the land. She scans for any signs of life within the dense forests. Her keen eyes pick up a faint series of receptors due south of her position. Suddenly, a screech interrupts her concentration. A giant bird with brown plumage, white breast, black spots, blue claws, and booted feet flies in next to her. "Qua-rwh (Power-spirit in Arabic), good to see you, old friend," Muqadas welcomes. "Do you see it too?" The bird caresses her head on Muqadas' left cheek, then lets off another screech. Muqadas then pets the bird's crown while refocusing her attention to the source of their sight. "I think it is time to investigate, yes? Clearly we can learn from such people." So Muqadas mounts the giant bird, both synchronizing their eyes until the blue flashes the horizon, then fly towards the spot.

Upon arrival, Muqadas and Qua-rwh land on a tree a few yards away from the group of receptors of green, gold, and pink. Several men and women gather around a circle in prayer. They all bow their heads to the ground, chanting, and praising in their native language. Muqadas watches very closely as they continue their ritual for several minutes. Afterwards, a single man grabs a small drum with a stick and begins to play in rhythm.

After a few seconds of rhythmic drumming, two men from the tribe begin to enter the circle. The rest of the congregation begin to get up and chant, clapping their hands and singing in rhythm with the drum as the two men circle around dancing with elaborate kicks, flips, or dodges. "Intriguing," Muqadas witnesses. "I must get a closer look. Qua-rwh, stay here until you are needed." Qua-rwh lets off a low frequency growl and Muqadas jumps down graciously from the tree.

Despite not wearing any shoes, Muqadas lands on branches with little to no pain in the soles of her feet. Her sense of balance and the alignment with nature allows her to reach the bottom of the forest with no effect. She slowly walks towards the celebration, becoming more entranced by the music and movement of the men. When she is within feet of the circle, a new set of men perform a front flip to enter the ring while the original men slide out of the ring. Again, the songs and chants sync with the rhythm of the dance. One man throws a punch while another goes to the ground by thrusting a kick. Afterwards, the man counters with a front roll. Muqadas smiles behind her hijab while a man walks towards her from her left side. He is a middle-aged man with modest clothing, very short hair with a patchy goatee. Noticing the tall heavily covered woman, he sparks up a simple conversation with the woman.

"You enjoy what you see, yes?"
"Oh, yes. I didn't mean to disturb. I came from far away and just happened to see this," Muqadas answers.
"No need to be polite, Phoenix Moor." Muqadas looks towards her left to find the man unphased by the revelation of the claim.
"How did you…"
"My father is the chief of our village. He has traveled far and wide. Seeking knowledge and wisdom so that he can lead his people well. As a boy, he told me stories of our people having the ability to control and adopt the power of great beasts. You wear the cloak of the group of women known as Phoenix Moors."
"I see," Muqadas responds graciously as both look at the circle.

A new set of men go in the circle and continue the ritual. Muqadas becomes so fascinated that she removes her hijab, revealing the face of a young, chocolate colored, kinky, but shiny haired woman. The man smiles as he sparks up another conversation.

"What is your name, Phoenix Moor?"
"Oh… I am called Muqadas."
"Holy in the sight of Allah, as my father taught me," he responds. "I am called Sherard."
 "Obliged by your acquaintance, Sherard. What is this ritual?"
"Heh heh, we call this Engolo. Passed down many generations by celebrating the stars of Kalunga."
"The stars of Kalunga?"
"Many years ago, our people witness vibrant colors in the sky. So many stars spark the night that many believe they can gain powers from beyond this world. So, in honor of the stars, we form a circle and dance to seek further understanding."
"I see," Muqadas continues. "We are taught that we are the lifeline of our nation. To supply the blood so that our land can flourish and grow. But lately… well…"
"It would seem that you have lost your way, Moor. Are you not certain of your purpose?"
 "I… just feel like…"
	Sherard smiles as Muqadas is at a loss for words. She is not used to being this vulnerable to a stranger, let alone a man that doesn't possess the power she has. However, he prompts her to step out of her realm of understanding with a new experience. He begins to yell a loud command in his native language. The people cheer and amplify their pace as Muqadas widens her eyes in shock.
	"What are you doing?!" Muqadas demands.
"I am helping you, Moor. You will be next in the circle."
"ME?!" Muqadas pleads. "But I am a warrior, not a dancer. I don't have the grace, the experience…"
"Yet you have the elegance of the bird you ride, no? You also scale mountains and cliffs. You run, jump, and embrace the ground with rough feet. Yet you still command presence." Muqadas calms down a bit while acknowledging the words.
"Your word speaks true, son of the Chief."
"Then, it seems that you no longer have the excuse. Allow Kalunga to guide you, as your masters guided your training."

As the beat intensifies, another man steps in the ring as the villagers' egg Muqadas on. Her anxiety increases, her heartbeat becomes so loud that it blocks out the noise, and her breath is slow and heavy. However, her code of conduct refuses to allow her to back down. So, with heavy feet, she plunges forward into the rings.

The other man in the ring smiles and bows his head in reverence. Muqadas does the same while they both move in rhythm. The man throws a kick, but Muqadas dodges it by leaning back. She can hear some of the crowd scream in confidence, compassion, and encouragement. Then she jumps up and thrust both of her feet in the air. The man dodges it by spinning his body in the air. As both land on their feet and smile, Muqadas suddenly loses the rocks that bound her feet on the ground. Sherard smiles as they both continue the dance.

After a few minutes, Muqadas does a sweeping kick. The man does a back flip. Distracted by the feat of athleticism, the man lands on his feet then throws a kick straight at Muqadas' face. The crowd begins to gasp as Muqadas anticipates the blunt force. However, there is a brief moment of silence. The man holds his foot in front of Muqadas. Muqadas shows restraint as the sweat drips down her face. Afterwards, the people cheer as the man puts his foot down, bows to Muqadas, then makes way for the new participants. Muqadas returns the gesture, then exits the circle.

Muqadas catches her breath and smiles as Sherard joins her. "How do you feel, Muqadas?"

"HUH...HUH...Huh… I feel… light… calm… strangely… enlightened," Muqadas answers. "It was as if my body was learning to move without the power I was born with."

"Or rather, the power you always had inside, but failed to train it. I have learned from my father that the path of true power can leave you blinded if you don't understand balance. When you saw the back flip, you were amazed but distracted, which left yourself open to attack. However, your partner saw the beauty of another life and held back. There will be a time when your flames die out before they reach the enemy. What then will you do… Phoenix Moor?" Muqadas sits quietly as she heeds the wisdom of Sherard. Her perception up to that point has been relatively one sided because of the power of the Avemcernentia.

"Sherard, I humbly thank you for the lesson you have taught me," she compliments. "I am currently on a mission to seek enlightenment and purpose. My sense of the world tells me to head east. So, I must be off."

"I understand. Take heed of what you have learned here today. When you are lost, look at the stars of Kalunga and you will find your answer." Suddenly, Qua-rwh flies in, awaiting Muqadas to join her. Muqadas smiles, closes her eyes, puts her hijab back on, then bows to Sherard. "May Allah give you everlasting life, Sherard."

"Likewise, Phoenix Moor," Sherard responds as Muqadas runs back to Qua-rwh. Qua-rwh lets off a soft screech, spreads her forty-foot wingspan, and climbs out of the forest floor towards the sky. Sherard sees them off as they disappear into the sky, then he resumes his participation to his people.

As Qua-rwh flies towards the east, Muqadas reflects the experience she just had and the effects; it has changed her perspective. "While I was dancing, I could move to my own internal rhythm. Yet, when distracted, I could have been kicked, or killed by a worthy opponent." Muqadas notices that the sun is beginning to set, so she searches for a place to rest. "This Engolo could be a valuable tool. How do you harness it, wield it, make it stronger?" Feeling the strength of her companion waning, Muqadas sees a crevice at the top of a ravine overseeing the Savannah. "Qua-rwh, let us rest there for the night." The bird screeches as she musters the last of her strength to fly towards the rocky outcrop.

Moments later, Qua-rwh begins to lay her head on the rock. She begins to relax on the hardened sandstones as Muqadas begins to stroke her feathers backwards. "Rest, Qua-rwh, rest. You have flown far, yet we still have far to go." Slowly, the bird's eyes begin to close as she dwells deep into the vast void of sleep. Still restless from the events and clouds in her mind, Muqadas decides to look at the stars for inspiration. Her worn feet grip the firm sand as she looks at the transformation of the skies. She then sits on the hard ground to await the ritual from day to night.

As the skies become darker, the illumination of the stars displays a concert of colors, transforming the sky into a pinkish blue. The sheer beauty of the skies causes Muqadas' eyes to transform into the Avemcernentia. With her eyes, Muqadas can see the movement of the galaxy run like the rhythm the villagers were trying to emulate. Suddenly, something compels her to get up. "I don't know what is going on, but I just… feel.. like…"

Muqadas begins to swing her arms from side to side. Despite not having anything but the crickets and minute sounds of other insects as her base, she begins to move to mirror the rhythmic of the stars. Then she throws a side kick. She pretends somebody is kicking her, so she dodges by doing a front roll. Then she does a cartwheel, then throws another kick. She loses balance, then falls, temporarily hurting her ankle. "Graceful I am not," she says. "At least not yet. I think I have an idea as to how to perfect this, Engolo."

After rubbing her ankle, she makes it back towards the crevice to lay next to Qua-rwh, then closes her eyes. Muqadas falls asleep for several hours.

The rising sun brings light to the Savannah. The songs of the birds flapping towards the river give way as herds of animals awaken to resume the daily task of eating and migrating. Muqadas and Qua-rwh wake up and greet the morning. "Good morning, friend, did you rest well?" Muqadas asks. Qua-rwh stretches her beak and wings as she gets ready for the flight. Muqadas then mounts her friend as the bird lets out a soft screech before plunging towards the air. She violently flaps her wings to elevate their altitude.

The skies are warm and clear. The multitude of wildlife is so vast that Qua-rwh soars just so Muqadas can take in the spectacular view of the activity. "Wow!" she yells. "This is a wonderful view. Look at all of the animals that inhabit this area. So diverse, yet beautiful." For minutes, they soar through the sea of grass, acacia trees, and bushes as Muqadas makes way towards their destination.

While flying, Muqadas notices a kindred spirit stalking the grasslands. It is a bird with a sharp beak, long legs, white with gray plumage, and a black crown. Muqadas smiles as she looks at the bird gracefully walking along the tall grass. "Such an elegant creature with grace and beauty," Muqadas compliments. "However," Muqadas activates her Avemcernentia and notices what the bird is closing in towards. A brown colored cobra is coiling in a desperate attempt to avoid detection. Unfortunately for the snake, the sharp-eyed secretary bird sees the snake, and it is hungry. "This cobra is similar to the ones we have back home," Muqadas analyzes. "The venom can kill several men. So how will this bird fair?"

As the bird closes in, the snake violently hisses. It gives warning strikes, faster than the naked eye to dissuade the bird's advances. However, the bird does something peculiar that grabs Muqadas' attention. The bird begins to overwhelm the snake with a barrage of kicks. The poor snake could not target the legs because it could not focus on a single object. "This is a strange way to deal with such a formidable snake," Muqadas wonders. "How is this effective?"

Again and again, the bird continues to kick. The snake becomes tired and lets down its guard. At this moment, the bird makes a quick, precise, and deadly strike to the snake's head. The poor serpent's body becomes paralyzed, and the bird begins to swallow it whole. Muqadas becomes enamored by the visuals of the hunt. "I see. The bird used its kicks to overpower the snake and render it unable to move. Without venom or a special weapon, it just used the tools the bird was born with. Thus, winning its prize." After seeing the spectacle, Muqadas continues east as she flies over the savannah.

Suddenly, something triggers Muqadas. Her senses pick up a potential disturbance at the base of the mighty river. She quickly activates her Avemcernentia and scans the area. "Something is troubling here, but I do not know where it is coming from." She moves her head side to side, desperately trying to find the disturbance that has Muqadas out of balance.

When she makes one last look, she notices a grayish red receptor hiding in the grass about fifty yards away from a huge herd of zebras. Muqadas squints her eyes while contemplating the implausible. "Is this the disturbance that has triggered my sight?" she wonders. "It is just a lioness hunting. What could be troublesome about the circle of life?" Determined to understand the reasoning, Qua-rwh circles around without making a sound as Muqadas pays attention to the events unfolding.

The lioness continues to stalk the herd low to the ground without making a sound. The zebra continues to graze, inconspicuous of the danger that they are about to encounter. With one more step, the lioness hesitates. She leans her head forward, only popping her head out of the tall grass. Then a small gust of wind blows behind the lion towards the herd. A single individual catches the breeze and starts to bray. The braying starts a stampede. Her cover blown; the lioness starts to run in an attempt to catch one by surprise.

Witnessing this, Muqadas understands the significance of this event. "I get it. The wind blew from the lion's back and the herd caught the scent. But I sense there is more to this, so I will continue to watch."

When the lioness catches a zebra, the zebra performs an evasive maneuver. When the lioness attempts to pounce on the rear of the zebra, the zebra dodges in the other direction. At that moment, Muqadas understood. "Just like I was distracted during the dance, the lioness used only raw power but refused to anticipate the elusiveness of her prey." Afterwards the zebra kicks the lioness, knocking her off balance, thus losing her footing and her prey.

At this moment, Muqadas contemplates the visuals of the secretary bird and the zebra. By understanding the movements of animals, Muqadas believes she may have uncovered something profound and ultimately, useful. "The next time I practice Engolo, I will incorporate these tactics and perfect this new form." Muqadas and Qua-rwh continue up the river to reach the destination of their mission.

# Chapter 27: Syncing the Link Part 2

After days of flying up the Nile River and the Sinai Peninsula, Muqadas and Qua-rwh make it to the port city of Gaza. Feeling weary of the long journey, Muqadas prompts the bird to rest in an outcrop overlooking the city. Swiftly, the bird extends her talons to gain its footing as it lands on the rocky cliff. Muqadas quickly dismounts the bird as she overlooks the city.

"My journey to the Holy Land is nearly complete," she states. "You stay here, my friend, while I scout out the city." Qua-rwh screeches in compliance while Muqadas makes her way down the rocky slide.

The journey down is swift and nimble. Muqadas uses her agility and skill to navigate through the cliff side. Then she makes her way towards the crowded post. With her hijab on, the only thing exposed is her eyes, ready to activate in the slightest signal of distress or attention.

The port is buzzing with activity and commerce. Many stands showcase goods and resources for the locals to purchase, some men pray and give thanks to their gods, while men in chain armor walk in formation. Towards the west side of the city, many ships crowd the limited port space, as all comers from the reaches of the known world seek their individual interests.

"The city is filled with a mixture of different belief systems and mindsets," Muqadas states. "But something is disturbing my being… I can feel it coming from that direction." Muqadas walks towards the center of the city in the middle of the crowd to follow the strange feeling that is leading her. Cautiously and stealthily, she meanders through the population while feeling out the disturbance in her psyche. Because of her training as a Phoenix Moor, she can detect minute impulses by the pinch points that excite pain points in her head. The more intense the pain, the closer she is to what's causing it. "I cannot allow myself to be distracted right now. I'll activate my eyes as soon as I get close."

When she reaches the east gate of the city, she comes across a squadron of armored knights from a few yards away. Unlike the rest of the knights who inhabit the city, these knights have helmets that completely cover their head and faces, white cloth over their chain armor bearing a single red cross. Muqadas activates her Avemcernentia to see the source of her disturbance. Her eyes illuminate into bright blue while she deciphers the intent of these strange men.

"Hmmm… I notice colors of deceit, corruption, and blood thirst in these men. I think I need to follow them. I need to signal Qua-rwh as soon as the men leave. As the men begin to mobilize, they reform their ranks outside of the gates.

Mounted on their horses, the men fortify their formations while Muqadas keeps her distance. She hides behind a group of palm trees and bushes until the men run towards their destination.

Once fifty yards away, Muqadas comes out of hiding and lets off a low frequency whistle. The long tune alerts Qua-rwh to levitate from her perch to fly towards Muqadas. After waiting for about two minutes, a low screech alerts Muqadas of her companion's presence. The bird lands on the soft sand next to Muqadas as she pets the bird. "You rested well I take it," she says as she massages her feathers. "Come now, we must go and follow these strange men." With a soft crackle, Qua-rwh lowers her body to allow Muqadas to climb on top. After sitting comfortably, Muqadas and Qua-rwh fly off to seek out the men.

Qua-rwh soars nearly as high as the sun, as Muqadas uses the linked Avemcernentia to search the desert for any signs of the men.

Meanwhile, Muqadas contemplates the meaning of her journey while reflecting back to her mission.

"I should be completing my mission, not following strange men," Muqadas complains. "However, I sense a sinister, almost demonic presence within these men that I cannot ignore." Qua-rwh continues to flap her magnificent wings across the sandy ocean as Muqadas continues to scan the horizon.

An hour later, a sharp pain erupts on Muqadas' right side of her head. She quickly succumbs to the pain; massaging the area while closing her eyes to identify the source of the disturbance. "UGH… something is wrong," she concludes. "I… can… almost…" Then, her eyes widen like the vastness of the desert. Her heart begins to sink, and her breath becomes nearly nonexistent. Her once vibrant attitude is quickly becoming overwhelmed with dread and despair. Then she reactivates her Avemcernentia with Qua-rwh. "Qua-rwh, WE MUST HURRY DUE NORTHEAST! JAEAL ALTASARUE (MAKE HASTE)!" With the command of her master, Qua-rwh flies with the speed of the wind towards the direction of the source of the disturbance.

Moments later, Muqadas picks up the receptors of grey, yellow, and black. She also sees a color, not of a receptor, but of a discharge from the body synonymous with pain, war, and death. The party come across a desecrated field of Saracen men, women, children, and some livestock lying face down on the parched sand. When Qua-rwh lands, Muqadas quickly gets off to see if she could find any survivors.

Moving through the field of dead bodies, something heats up inside of Muqadas. Her eyes bloom blue, her breath turns to smoke, and her body ignites into a fiery rage. She lets out a scream so big and low, her body becomes engulfed in flames. Qua-rwh maneuvers her head from side to side, then flaps her wings to relieve the stress of the area. Tears begin to flow down Muqadas' face, as the weight of her guilt is as heavy as the blood-drenched sand beneath her feet.

Suddenly, she hears a whimper a few yards away. Muqadas lifts her head, wipes her eyes, then surveys the area. "I thought I heard something," she deduces as she gets up. "I think it came from that direction." Northwest of her position, she sees a dead camel with torn pieces of tapestry, clothing, and scattered goods. Muqadas maintains her guard as she slowly walks towards the sound.

Louder and louder, the whimpering continues. Muqadas reaches the dead camel and discovers something tucked next to the bloody corpse. Something is shaking underneath a thick cover of blankets and clothing. Muqadas slowly unravels the layers and discovers the source of the whimpering. A small girl, no more than about 9 or 10 years old is uncovered from the ashes of death and destruction. Muqadas is shocked by the revelation. Her heart drops, her face softens, and her eyes transform back to their normal, deep brown hue.

Meanwhile, the little girl remains so frightened that she continues to shake uncontrollably. Slowly, Muqadas places her hand on the girl's shoulder and removes her hijab. The distraught heroine does her best to crack a small smile while easing the burden of the child.

"Alaikum Salaam tifl (child), you are now safe," Muqadas speaks softly. The girl stops shivering and stutters in response.

"SSSS...Salaam Alaikum..."

"I know that you must be frightened. You must come with me, eat and rest." The little girl wipes all the sand from her face. She has a caramel complexion, dark kinky hair, and light brown eyes. She has rosy cheeks, pink lips, and a gap in between her front two teeth. She stands up and shakes her head.

"We were traveling to Jerusalem to pray and... then to Damascus, and then..." The girl's head begins to slink down. The trauma she experienced was too much to debrief at the time.

Muqadas looks at the child, crouches down, and massages her left cheek. The girl looks up at a smiling Moor as Muqadas introduces herself. "It's ok. My name is Muqadas. What is your name?"

"Pariah," the girl responds. "My name is Pariah."

"Such a beautiful name for such a beautiful tifl (child). I will take you as far as you need to go."

"I believe I have family in Damascus. I have an uncle there who serves under our Sultan."

"Then Damascus we shall go, after you fulfill your obligations to your Hajj (Pilgrimage)." The girl smiles as Muqadas escorts the girl. "Come, let us go."

"But... how will we get there?" Pariah asks.

Then, a giant bird swoops in while letting off a small screech. Pariah's eyes look overwhelmed and excited. She looks at Qua-rwh, then back at Muqadas. "That is a big bird," Pariah examines. "That must be… UHHH…" Immediately, Pariah goes to the ground and bows in reverence. Muqadas chuckles and crouches down to the ground.

"HA HA HA… my sweet Pariah," she assures, "there is no need to perform so appropriately." Pariah looks up at Muqadas and responds. "But my mother and father have told me many stories. You're a Phoenix Moor, and that is a…"

"She is a ride, and I am your escort, tifl."

"I am truly humbled and honored to be in your presence, Phoenix M…"

"Muqadas will do, Pariah. Come, I sense another sandstorm brewing. We must get going." So Muqadas gets up, takes Pariah to Qua-rwh, picks her up, and mounts her on the back of the bird. Afterwards, Muqadas sits behind Pariah and instructs Qua-rwh to take off. Muqadas activates her Avemcernentia, syncs with Qua-rwh, and surveys the land. "My eyes pick up the storm heading from the east," Muqadas concludes. "However, I can see the city about an hour flight north of us. Let's go so that we can shelter from the storm." Qua-rwh lets off a strong screech, then extends her long broad wings before flapping furiously off the ground.

Qua-rwh uses the solar thermals to soar above the blistering desert air. While the brown plumage protects the bird, Muqadas's wardrobe shields herself and her passenger from the deadly, Israeli sun. "Don't worry, sweet Pariah," Muqadas comforts. "Jerusalem is just a few moments away. Once we land, Qua-rwh must hide as to not draw attention from unwanted soldiers."

"I understand, Muqadas," Pariah responds. Qua-rwh continues to fly until she reaches within sight of the large white walls.

A few moments later, Qua-rwh reaches a rocky outcrop about five miles from the city. The view is spectacular: large, 100-foot walls surround the city, and ancient buildings of sand, marble, and concrete fill the city's epicenter. Muqadas and Pariah get off Qua-rwh as she sits down and rests.

"It is a long walk, my tifl," Muqadas warns. "Are you able to walk?"

"Yes, I am," Pariah responds.

"Good. We will stay here for the night. Then, before dawn, I will carry you down the small cliff, and then we will walk into the city. I don't think we will draw too much attention."

"No," Pariah adds, "I have heard that the king of Jerusalem is fair and just. He allows the Muslims in the area to come and go as they please."

"I see. Then, shall we?" Pariah smiles as Muqadas puts on her hijab, then picks her up with her arms.

Hours later, Muqadas carefully and quietly wakes Pariah up. After they stand up, Muqadas picks up Pariah, then heads towards the cliff. Still barefooted, Muqadas carefully and stealthily scales down the rock face. With each step, few pebbles migrate down the foot of the cliff, as Muqadas does her best not to draw too much attention, even from the potential eyes of observers on patrol.

Once they make it to the base of the cliff, Muqadas lets Pariah go, then treks along the desert towards the ancient city of David. While walking, Muqadas undergoes the difficult task of debriefing Pariah's ordeal.

"So, Pariah, what happened to your convoy?" Pariah slinks her head down, trying to avoid answering the question. Determined to find out, Muqadas uses a sterner tone to generate a response. "Pariah, I cannot help you, nor avenge the death of your parents if you do not tell me who did this to you." Pariah begins to stutter, giving incomplete and scattered accounts to the events.

"It… it… happened so fast, Muqadas. All I remembered was my mother and father telling me to hide with our camel. Then these men… with shields and swords…" Knowing that she is still scared from the events, Muqadas buys her time by not pressing her any further. Instead, she lays out the plan for the next few days.

"Like I told you before. We will obligate your Hajj by saying your prayers to Allah. Then we will find a convoy that will take you to Damascus." Pariah looks up at Muqadas as both enter within a few yards of the city. "I will make sure nothing happens to you, on my honor as a Phoenix Moor!" Pariah smiles at Muqadas as they enter the city.

The streets are busy, despite the breaking of dawn with activity, commercialism, and traffic. People ranging from Jews, Muslims, Christians, Knights, and a few Saracen soldiers crowd the busy streets. As Muqadas weaves through the city, she looks down at Pariah while holding her hand. "Stay close to me, while I search where you should go to pray." Pariah nods in agreement as Muqadas, hijab covering all but her eyes, activates the Avemcernentia to locate any Muslims that may be congregating to pray. For a while, she takes her time weaving through the many receptors that cloud her view of vision. "Even with these eyes, it is hard to find others with the same agenda as Pariah. Still, I have to keep looking… for her sake… and for mine."

Suddenly, a pair of green and blue receptors glow with a group of Muslims trekking towards the east gate. Muqadas notices that their pace is consistent and unwavering. "Something tells me to follow them," Muqadas deduces. "It is almost dawn, and the sun is about to rise soon." After following the group, Muqadas and Pariah notice that there is a space that oversees the rising sun at the east side of the city. Many of them get in position and fall onto their knees. Understanding the gesture, Muqadas, along with Pariah, find a patch of ground, then fall on their knees.

The rising sun of the east begins to reveal itself, bringing light to darkness. Immediately, one man begins to chant in Arabic as everyone greets the sun with silence and appreciation. After the chanting is complete, each whisper a prayer as they cover their heads down. As the man once again chants in Arabic, Muqadas looks up with eyes gleaming blue to greet the sun. Something within her begins to understand the journey she was sent to undergo. Meeting the village prince in Nigeria, learning Engolo, finding this child, and meditation through prayer cultivates to a level of understanding without the use of words.

After hours of prayer and meditation at the east gate, Muqadas and Pariah walk through the streets of Jerusalem with a new sense of ease and peace. While striding along the city, Pariah is suddenly stricken by fear. She becomes paralyzed by the sight of something that immediately alerts Muqadas.

"Pariah, what is the matter?" Pariah stands motionless, staring at the source of her trauma. Muqadas looks in the same direction and sees soldiers with familiar markings. The same knights with white cloth and red crosses begin to formulate at the same entrance they came in earlier in the morning.

"So that's… Pariah, is that who killed your family and convoy?" Pariah nods in silence, confirming Muqadas's suspicions. "Quickly, we must fly to Damascus now." Pariah looks at Muqadas, then asks a question. "How will we get there before…"

"Qua-rwh is faster than you know, trust me." Pariah nods as they both make haste to exit the city. Once they are outside of the city gates, Muqadas lets off a low frequency screech. Seconds later, Qua-rwh clinches her wings and dives down towards the duo. Muqadas activates her Avemcernentia, picks up Pariah, then jumps on Qua-rwh's back as she picks up speed back in the air.

Qua-rwh flies with the intensity and speed of a jet. Focusing in on reaching the direction of Damascus. Meanwhile, Muqadas gives instructions to Pariah to shield her from the adverse effects of her power. "Pariah, I need you to hold still while I infuse you with some of my fire."

"Why?" Pariah asks.

"Because I sense that these men will attack another convoy along the way." Pariah nods as she clings to Qua-rwh's feathers.

Muqadas closes her eyes and focuses her energy to sync with Qua-rwh and Pariah. As she concentrates, the heat from their cores begin to emulate and coat their bodies. As it intensifies, Qua-rwh screeches loudly, as Muqadas opens her eyes. The Avemcernentia not only syncs with Qua-rwh, but Pariah as well. The eyes glow blue, as Qua-rwh's feathers transform from brown to flames of red, orange, and yellow. Pariah is overwhelmed by the surge of power and the ability to see beyond the range of normal eyes.

"Wow… this is the power of the Phoenix Moor." Muqadas meanwhile sees something a few yards ahead of her that signals another potential catastrophe. Then she instructs Pariah one last time.

"Pariah, I need you to stay with Qua-rwh."

"Why?"

"Because those same men are targeting another convoy heading for Damascus. You'll be safe with her. As long as you stay on her, the flames will protect you." Pariah gulps as they charge towards battle. Yards away, the group of soldiers spot a convoy heading north. The soldiers begin to unsheathe their swords and yell in a barbaric rage. As they form their ranks, the calvary begin to charge at the convoy. The unsuspecting group of Muslims see the danger as they come charging thirty yards away. Not having enough time to mount a defense, some of the women and children begin to scream in panic as the few men try desperately to hold their ground.

Then, when all hope is nearly lost, a volley of flames stops the men in their tracks, as Qua-rwh spits out a huge line of fire. The horses all begin to neigh uncontrollably while trying to avoid the flames. Muqadas jumps off Qua-rwh and instructs one of the Saracens. "See to the women and children!" Muqadas yells. "I will hold off these cowards." The man is in awe of her presence but understands that time is of the essence.

"So be it, Phoenix Moor," he responds. "Qital tawilaan wabishrf (Fight long and with honor)." Muqadas nods as the man retreats with the convoy.

One of the soldiers tries to outflank Muqadas and swings his sword. She dodges it and spits fire at the man. The flames cause him to dismount the horse and crash to the ground. Four other soldiers get off their horses and charge towards Muqadas. However, despite not having a weapon, the men underestimate Muqadas and take off their helmets. They all chuckle and laugh before charging with their swords.

Muqadas closes her eyes and controls her breathing. She remembers the lessons from Engolo and begins to move to her own rhythm. Suddenly, WHOOSH. A soldier swings his sword and misses. Another one swings his sword and misses, as Muqadas dodges her attackers. Then she spins and generates flames off her foot as she kicks one of the men in the face, burning his cheek in the process. The other soldier tries to attack by swinging his sword aimlessly at Muqadas. She dodges by performing a backflip, then spreads her legs wide like a break dancer to sweep the soldier off his feet by kicking him in his armored shin.

The remaining soldiers begin to hesitate until a Saracen calvary begins to reinforce the convoy. The cowardly soldiers then retreat back to their horses as Muqadas pants from exhaustion. Qua-rwh and Pariah circle around until they meet Muqadas. Muqadas starts to topple to the ground until Pariah unmounts the phoenix and catches up with Muqadas.
"Are you alright, Muqadas?" Pariah asks.
"I am fine, but I thought I told you to stay on Qua-rwh?"
"The Sultan's soldiers came in and chased the bad men away."
"I see." Muqadas gasps. Afterwards, the captain of the Saracen force walks in with his horse.
"You fought well, Phoenix Moor," he compliments. "My master would be pleased with your efforts."
"Thank you, sir," Muqadas responds. Then, Pariah begins to squint her eyes. She looks up at the magnificent, armored captain, recognizing his voice.
"A.. A… Akhw al'umi (Uncle) Faisal?" The man looks down at the little girl. His stoic face softens into tears as he recognizes the little girl.
"Pariah! Pariah!"
The man quickly unmounts his horse and rushes towards Pariah. Pariah in return runs towards the man as they both embrace in a long hug. The man is filled with emotion and some tears as he holds Pariah tightly.
"Oh Pariah! What are you doing out here?!" Faisal asks.
"Those men killed Mamma and Papa. Then… she saved me and brought me here." Faisal looks at Muqadas again with tear-filled eyes of joy.
"Once again, Phoenix Moor, I thank you for bringing her to me. I will take care of her from now on."
"Yes, I believe you will," Muqadas responds. "Who were those men? And why did they attack our people?"
"They are called Templars. My Lord Saladin will know of their treachery, but he will also know of your loyalty as well. You have completed your mission."
"Mission!" Muqadas yells. "What do you know of my…"
"I know why you were sent here. My Lord sent word to your king to have you survey the land of the threat yet to come to our people. You were to see how they operate while learning the lay of the land."
"I have seen the levels of their barbarism," Muqadas responds, "and I fear…"

"I know," Faisal interrupts. "But for now, I must tell the Sultan of what has happened."
As the memory fades away, Muqadas stares at the dust generated from the fleeing men, thinking about the words, and the imminent future that awaits her people.

# Chapter 28: Mending the Wounds

Emma is transported back to the dark corridor of her mind after the memory. She still notices that the five chambers are still locked. Then a silhouette of Muqadas forms in front of her. "I.. I... don't understand," Emma says. "We went through all of that experience, but the doors didn't unlock. What is going on?"

"My Emma, yes, we did relive my past life that allowed me to unlock the Khms Ghuraf, but I had to recognize it within me. I cannot tell you what each door represents, only you can unlock the chambers."

"But Muqadas, how will I know what each chamber represents?"

"You must face your most deadly enemy. That is the first chamber that can be unlocked."

"Which one?"

Muqadas points to the chamber in the ceiling of the veil. The chamber door is dark, grimly, decrepit, and oozing with black flames. It continues to bang and bang. Emma becomes terrified by the look and feel of the chamber. She begins to gulp in anxiety, then looks back at Muqadas. As she waits for the answers, Muqadas only responds with cryptic messaging.

"What you see behind that chamber is the greatest enemy that you still possess. You and you alone must defeat the entity that resides behind that chamber. But you cannot defeat it without unlocking the other chambers." Emma looks at Muqadas with confused and unsure eyes. Then Emma realizes that she's in a point of no return. She knows that, despite the look of the door, it is the key to unblock the pathway towards unleashing her full potential of her Fire Line. Before Emma can fully understand the ramifications, Muqadas begins to disappear.

"Muqadas, WAIT!" Emma yells.

"Don't worry, child," Muqadas responds before fading. "You have everything you need to achieve the Khms Ghuraf. You just need to be willing to face it. Remember, you must look within yourself to purge the impurity that is blocking your Fire Line. I love and believe in you. In time... you will know."

After those words, Muqadas disappears, and Emma immediately wakes up from her meditation. She is breathing hard, sweating heavily, and trying desperately to regain her sense of reality. The intensity of the memory puts a temporary strain on Emma's physical and mental state. As she catches her breath, she recollects on the memories and the words from her ancestor.

"What does she mean by facing your greatest enemy?" Emma wonders as she sits on the edge of the bed. "I've fought Sharron, but I don't think she's my greatest enemy...I don't know. She said look within myself (SIGH)."

Emma sits on the bed and looks at the ceiling with imprudence and frustration. The wheels in her head continue to spin and spin. The paradox of what she perceived herself to be and what she is now has put her in a mental state of suspended animation. All Emma can do is stay still to calm the pounding in her head.

After a few moments of doing and saying nothing, something inside of Emma sparks. She scrunches her eyebrows and begins to replay the meditation like a movie. She nitpicks every detail of the interaction, the moments of the memory, and the words being spoken. Then Emma reaches an epiphany. Her eyes widen, she grasps for air, then slaps herself on the forehead.

"Of course, that's what she meant," Emma concludes. "I may not know what the chambers are, but I think I know how to draw them out. I need to train...NOW!" Emma jumps out of bed, washes her face with a towel, and looks in the mirror with determined and resolved eyes. "I'm ready." Afterwards, Emma storms out of her room and races down the hallways to look for someone to help her.

D'Shawn walks down the hallway to a secret bedroom. His shoulders are still, his stride is slow and calculating, and thoughts flood his mind. "I wasn't there for Asir. I abandoned him and his mother before I even got the chance to confirm he's mine." The closer he gets to the door, the farther each step seems. The walls seem to close in around him, the breath from his mouth becomes so loud it blocks out everything around him, and small beads of sweat perspire down his shaven beard.

Then, the environment around him turns to normal. He reaches down towards the handle. He turns it slowly and creeps as quietly as he can to tiptoe in the room. Afterwards he looks at Asir, still sleeping in the early morning. D'Shawn puts on a halfway smile while he pulls up a chair.

As he watches Asir sleep, D'Shawn allows himself to fill his empty reservoir with the emotions only a father has: inspecting every closed eye, lip, ear, and hair while comparing it to his own physical attributes, the calmness and sense of security of a child not burdened with duress, and the moments only silence can orchestrate as the still moments offer an influx of clarity. For thirty minutes, D'Shawn looks at Asir sleeping peacefully while waiting to mend the pain, hurt, and confusion for a child finding his other half for the first time.

As the sun begins to rise, Asir begins to squirm, toss, and turn. D'Shawn continues to sit down quietly so that he won't startle Asir. After a minute, Asir's body gives way as the preteen rises his head from the pillow. He then begins to yawn, stretch out his arms, and rub his eyes. After waking up, Asir looks to his right and sees a familiar man sitting a few feet away from him.

Asir quickly looks at the man, then he looks down. There is an eerie silence between them, and for twenty seconds, neither speak nor have direct eye contact. Then, D'Shawn generates the nerve to break the silence and commence with the process.

"Good morning, Asir," he welcomes. "How did you sleep?" Asir takes his time. He gulps, then begins to studder.
"I'm…. mmm… I'm good." D'Shawn bits his lips and nods. Then he grasps his hands together as he leans towards Asir.
"Do you know who I am, Asir?" Asir continues to look away. He once again takes his time to answer, as if he too is trying not to deal with the strain of the situation. However, miraculously, Asir looks D'Shawn in the eyes. His eyes are wet and full, despite not shedding tears. He looks at D'Shawn as if he trusts a man he has never seen before yet trusts him to quell his fears. Then Asir begins to speak so coherent, that it shocks D'Shawn.

"I know from my visions of you who you are," Asir continues, "but when I see you… your face… your beard… your eyes… even the way you look at me, I know deep in my heart, that you're my dad." D'Shawn, again, bites his lips and nods. However, his emotions get the best of him as he sheds a tear. He quickly gathers himself by wiping his eyes and smiling.

"Yes," D'Shawn nods with a smile, "I am your daddy."

The two of them take their time to debrief their minds and hearts with the conversation. With each passing moment, Asir gains more confidence to express himself to D'Shawn.

"Mom never talks about you," Asir says. "I remember when I was younger. The other kids would talk about their daddies. What they did. What they got from them. But when I talked to Mom about it, she would yell at me by saying I didn't need a daddy, that I got her. It used to make me sad." Again, D'Shawn nods his head in acknowledgement. He chooses his next words wisely while slowly trying to earn Asir's trust.

"I bet it did feel bad not having a daddy, Asir. You know, I didn't grow up with my dad either. It wasn't until I was older that I realized how much it hurt me. You know, sometimes we adults can make mistakes and not admit them. Do you understand what I'm saying to you?" Asir avoids eye contact while he nods. "(SIGH)... Asir, can you tell me about yourself? What do you like to do? How do you like school?"

Asir closes his eyes. Then he starts to speak again, this time looking at D'Shawn.

"I don't like school as much. Sometimes my teachers don't get me. Other times they just pretend they care about me. But sometimes I can tell when they don't want me around. I don't have a lot of friends." Asir cracks a little smile. "I like to draw. I am really good at it."

"Really?" D'Shawn responds emphatically. "What do you like to draw?"

"I like to draw dinosaurs, but my favorite is dragons and phoenixes."

"Remarkable, so something inside of him drew him to his heritage before he even realized it," D'Shawn deduces. "I would really like it if you drew me a picture." Asir smiles a little as he responds.

"Yeah, me and Miss Emma would do it during our time together."

Then, Asir gets triggered. His hands grasp the bed sheets, his eyebrows face down, and his teeth begin to clinch. Before his eyes can transform, D'Shawn gets up from his chair and grabs Asir by the shoulder to calm him down.

"Asir, what's the matter?"

"I remember… Miss Emma… Is she…"?

"She's fine, Asir," D'Shawn assures. "She's resting. We gave her some medicine so that she can get better." Asir calms down. His shoulders drop, the muscles around his eyes relax, and his voice becomes soft again.

"I really hope she gets better. She's… a… good… person." D'Shawn nods his head and responds.

"Don't worry, Asir. She'll get better, and I agree with you. More than you ever know." Both continue their interaction while trying to build a bond that will take a lifetime to break.

Suddenly, the moment is interrupted by a series of loud knocks. POUND POUND POUND POUND POUND. Asir and D'Shawn look up at the door wondering who could cause such a racket.

"Who's at the door?" Asir asks.

"I don't know, but I'll check it out."

D'Shawn gets up and walks towards the door. He shouts back in response to the knocking. "Who is it?!" D'Shawn demands.

"Is it you, D'Shawn? Let me in," the voice answers. D'Shawn immediately recognizes the voice and answers the door.

After opening the door, Emma storms in before D'Shawn catches her.

"Whoa whoa whoa there," D'Shawn says. "You should still be in bed resting. Your injuries took a while for me to heal." Asir looks up and begins to smile. He jumps out of bed and rushes towards Emma.

"Miss Emma! Miss Emma!" Asir yells before hugging Emma tightly. Emma loses her breath quickly, but then recovers by hugging Asir back. D'Shawn steps back to give them some space. Emma kneels down to address Asir after the exchange.

"Hey Asir," Emma says softly. "Are you ok?"

"Yes, we're here. Oh, and guess what. I met my dad," he responds while pointing to D'Shawn. Emma looks at him, smiles, and winks at him as D'Shawn responds with a smile. Emma gets up and addresses D'Shawn.

"Do you have a training facility here?" Emma asks.
"Yes, we have a combat area about the size of a basketball gym just on the other side of this facility, why?"
"Because I finally figured out what I need to do in order to achieve the Khms Ghuraf."
"The K… Kims…" Asir stutters.
"The 5 Chambers, right?" D'Shawn confirms. "It's kinda like the 10 trials the ancient Moors had to perform before achieving the Invisible Ember, right? That's what you need help with?"
Emma nods as she awaits D'Shawn's answer. D'Shawn lowers his head and paces around the room. Asir and Emma look on with concern and perplexed eyes. D'Shawn briefly closes his eyes, takes a deep breath, and then voices the potential outcomes.

"What you're asking WILL be dangerous. You realize that you'll have to confront the most corrupted components of your being, right?" D'Shawn states while looking seriously at Emma. Emma lowers her eyebrows and faces D'Shawn. Asir looks at Emma, then asks D'Shawn a question.
"What do you mean? Miss Emma is nice and good." Asir pleads. "I don't think that she has bad in her."
"Asir, you have to understand how powerful WE are," D'Shawn asserts his voice as he continues to explain. "Do you remember when you were bullied? What happened?" Asir looks down and doesn't respond. The event is still fresh in his mind, and he remembers the outcome that came from that. Emma too pays close attention to what D'Shawn is forecasting.

"Blue Phoenix… Emma…" D'Shawn precedes, "when you were with the Elite 8, we trained and confiscated the same drugs and chemicals just in case you went on a rampage against our people. If you do this, there's a possibility that…"
"THAT'S WHY I HAVE TO DO THIS, D'SHAWN!" Emma yells with passion and conviction. The room stays silent with the rush of emotion and panic. D'Shawn's arms remains crossed as Asir sits down, knowing that this conversation is beyond his full comprehension.

"D'Shawn, I can sense the power within you. You're not that far from my brother, so I know that you'll do what needs to be done if I fail," Emma pleads. "But if I don't do this, I can't help Asir, the other boys, my people… and most importantly, I can't help myself." D'Shawn sighs as he continues to look down and think, while massaging his beard. Emma reengages the conversation by stating her final words on the matter. "D'Shawn, you know this is the only way to confront all of the horrible things I did in the past, because I was poisoned by the same people who, right now, pull the strings to maintain systematic white supremacy. D'Shawn, please…" Emma whimpers.

D'Shawn looks into Emma's light brown eyes, so deep with resolve, ambition, and desperation. Asir gets up and stands next to Emma. He too looks deep into D'Shawn's calculating eyes. D'Shawn is taken aback by the overwhelming show of support for Asir as he too pleads with him.

"We have to help her," Asir says. "Please… Dad." The word he rarely used growing up. The same word he never thought he would be called until a few days ago, now spur some emotion into the heart of a reformed man and warrior.

D'Shawn leans down to Asir and smiles.

"Yes, Asir, we will help her. And I think it's time that you learn to cultivate your own powers." Asir smiles as D'Shawn stands up to face Emma. "I need to prepare the men with the Reintergon guns."

"But won't that hurt you and Asir?"

"Listen, Emma," D'Shawn interrupts, "what you are going to have to do is go all out, even at the brink of death to achieve what you need to achieve. If things go bad, my men are prepared. Give me an hour to mobilize at the gym."

"Thank you." Emma smiles.

"Yeah!" Asir yells. "Let's become DRAGONS! And PHOENIX!"

D'Shawn smiles while he remains calm.

"Alright, Asir, Emma can stay here with you while I go make the preparations."

Both Emma and Asir nod while D'Shawn walks out of the room. Once D'Shawn steps out of the room he sees a mysterious man leaning against the wall. His arms are folded, he leans his head down, and he remains unphased by his discovery.

"How long have you been standing there?" D'Shawn asks. "Long enough to hear what you are planning to do," the man responds. "So do you disapprove, knowing that we have to maintain what little strength we have?" The man and D'Shawn begin to walk down the hall. His voice is calm, leveled, and commanding.
"Understand something, Snake Sight, I've seen her power a few months back, and that was when she barely understood what the Elite 8 did to her." D'Shawn looks at him with concerned eyes, almost as if he is showing a level of admiration not usually exhibited. "Snake Sight… D'Shawn… if we help her, she will return to being a weapon. But not for the Elite 8, for OBR… but more importantly for our race, thus helping her achieve what she has sought her whole life."
"Understood," D'Shawn responds. "As you said, get the men ready and mobilize. Once this works (D'Shawn again looks but doesn't interrupt), and I know it will, I will debrief her and then we can start Operation 1804."

D'Shawn nods then walks down the hall, leaving the strange man behind. The man crosses his arms, smiles, and whispers to himself. "It's time for Blue Phoenix… to finally spread her wings."

# Chapter 29: Embracing the Darkness to Bring Out the Light

Emma and Asir walk down the halls of the hideaway. The pace is steady and consistent; meanwhile Asir looks up at Emma. Her attitude is stable, her resolve is defined, and even Asir can sense a level of confidence that he can't fully describe.

"Why was my dad so worried about you, Miss Emma?" Asir asks. Emma sighs, not knowing what or how Asir will take her words. Her hesitation is only outmatched by Asir's anticipation. With a heavy heart, Emma slowly capitulates to Asir's curiosity by confronting her dark past.

"Asir, When I was… younger… I was adopted. Do you know what that means?"

"I want to say that it's when someone's parents die, and someone else takes care of them."

"Exactly," Emma confirms. "Well, because of that, I did… horrible things… things that…" Emma's lips begin to quiver. Her past weighs more than the conversation expected. However, she refuses to give in to her fears. She takes a deep breath, closes her eyes, then looks at Asir as they are walking.

"Asir, I need you to understand that I saw children as young as you being kidnapped and did horrible things. Things I can't tell you. Do you understand?"

"I think so. Is that why my dad said what he said? Was he really going to…"?

"(Sigh)... Asir, I need you to be like a dragon. Can you tell me what makes a dragon a dragon?" Asir takes his time to think. Meanwhile, Emma braces herself as she draws closer to her destiny. The closer the distance, the farther it seems, as if Emma can count in milliseconds how long it takes between each step. Minute pulses and twitches in her muscles que Emma that she is about to embark on a task she isn't fully confident she's ready for. Asir continues to walk by Emma, still waiting for her to express her true feelings.

After walking down several hallways in the facility, Asir and Emma make it to the doors which lead to the outside compound. The area is vast and militant. It is hidden in the middle of nowhere, about sixty to eighty miles southwest of Jacksonville in the middle of a heavily forested swamp. The huge gym size building is where D'Shawn told Emma to meet him.

"Wow… That is a big building," Asir says.
"Yeah, it is. You ready, kid?" Asir nods as they push through the doors and walk towards the structure.

Once the duo enters through the doors, they are amazed at how spacious the inside is. On one corner houses several military style hummers and trucks. On the other side of the area are several lockers and gates that house armaments, equipment, and other tools for protection. Then, at the epicenter is a squadron of soldiers surrounding the perimeter.

As Asir and Emma walk towards the middle, several members of OBR stop what they are doing and watch them carefully. Some of the faces on the men remain impassive while others peer through them like lasers, looking for any sign, pimple, or hair that could compromise their safety.

"Everybody in here is suspicious of me," Emma notices. "I don't blame them. Hell, I'm wondering about myself." Before reaching the area set aside for the arena, D'Shawn walks up to Emma and Asir to explain the layout.

"Alright, you made it," D'Shawn mentions. "As you can see, some of our best fighters are here to prevent you from being taken over."
"Are you sure they are prepared for what I may end up doing?"
"Trust me," D'Shawn assures, "they've seen what I can do, and I haven't even gone all out yet. They are also aware of you as well. Each of them will be armed with special guns that will shoot out the Reintergon. The chemical will paralyze you and everyone without the masks." "I see," Emma responds. "So, what now?"
"Now… you face yourself."
"What?!"

D'Shawn takes Asir and walks Emma towards the large field. He further explains his messaging and tips on how to help Emma. "You see, Emma, if you haven't figured it out, one of the chambers that I am certain of, is the darkness within yourself." Emma quickly realizes the truth in this, then proceeds to listen. "Everyone has something within that blocks them from their Fire Line. Only you can face it and unclog it. However, I don't know the depths of your hidden power, so beware." "Understood," Emma responds. "Well then… (sighs) let's get started."

D'Shawn nods as he takes position on the far side of the arena. Asir stands near his father as he looks on, anticipating what or who may come out of this event.

Emma begins to close her eyes. She breathes slowly, raising her stiff shoulders in rhythm. As she draws in more power with each inhale, the surrounding lights begin to dim. The surrounding soldiers struggle to maintain their control as some of them begin to quiver anxiously. Asir too begins to sweat and squint his eyes. "She'll be fine, Asir," D'Shawn reassures. "When the time comes, you'll know what to do. Just keep your eyes on her." Asir nods at his father as D'Shawn gets his tomahawk ready.

When Emma's lungs begin to expand, her eyes immediately transform to the Avemcernentia. Her body becomes engulfed in grayish, white, and blue flames. The flames manifest into a shape of a phoenix, ten feet tall. The whole area is illuminated by the silhouette the heat and light produce. For a few seconds, the flaming phoenix flaps its wings. Emma becomes fully entranced by the flowing power of her Fire Line.

As the flames continue to burn, her consciousness begins the process of unlocking the chambers within while allowing herself to let go. "Well, this is it," Emma reminds herself. "There's no turning back now." Her mind once again transports her to the veil in her mind that houses the chambers. As Emma looks up, she sees the dark, grimy chamber door that instills fear and anxiety in her. The flames continue to pore through the small openings of the door. The influx of dark energy is as heavy as fog on a cold day, stuffing the air with its putrid vibe.

Emma shivers as she draws closer to the door. "I don't know what's behind this door." Emma refocuses as she places her hand on the lever. "I must… have… the courage… to…" Without any further hesitation, she opens the chamber door.

Immediately, a surge of black flames floods out of the door, consuming Emma and covering the veil. Meanwhile, Emma's body begins to turn dark. The coloring in her eyes begin to turn black, and the blue flames begin to turn purple and black. The soldiers all tremble and Asir begins to shake like a rattlesnake's tail.

"Easy, Asir," D'Shawn commands. "She is facing the darkness within her."

"I don't understand…"

"Do you remember those visions you had, Asir?!" D'Shawn interrupts, yelling to cope with the influx of energy that is causing a small wind gust storm inside of the facility.

"Yes, I remember!" Asir yells back while covering his face with his forearm from the gust.

"Then, it is time… remember to breathe calmly, close your eyes, and draw from the power from within you."

While Emma's body is spitting out the dark flames that are quickly consuming her body, Asir begins to close his eyes. He briefly stops his shaking and begins to focus from within. As he begins to see the flame glowing within himself, a small layer of heat begins to generate around his body. D'Shawn sees the energy generate within Asir and smiles as he continues to brace himself. "That's it, son. Now it's time to…"

Moments later, Asir's eyes explode open so fast, he can hardly contain the power it exhibits. His eyes quickly change color from brown to greenish gold. The pupil changes into a nearly sharp line. The iris completely covers his eyes, and a set of micro claws form in the center of the eye, surrounding the reptilian-looking pupil. D'Shawn, who transformed his eyes as well, witnesses the transformation of his son embracing who he is.

Asir's eyes transform into the Dracocernentia. The receptors he sees shows a series of red and yellow lines, while he sees a more, in depth entity coming out of Emma. "I can see!" Asir yells. "Something bad is coming out of Miss Emma! What is that?!"

"It's what we all have inside of us," D'Shawn responds. "To put it simply, sometimes there's a bad person trying to tell us what to do. This is what Emma must face and defeat on her own!"

As Emma finishes throwing up the black flames, she crashes towards the ground. She lands on her knees and pants, as the black flames condense and take the form of something deviant, demonic, and familiar. As the smoke clears and the flames calm down, the figure forms and begins to strut arrogantly towards the middle of the platform. The figure is a direct clone of Emma, but she has purplish blue eyes, long black hair, a skin-tight t-shirt, and jeans. Her body is smoky in color, and her gaze is possessed with evil intent. The figure begins to laugh maniacally as the whole facility stand in horror of this being.

"GwaHAHAHAHAHAHAHAHAHA…you foolish little men," the demonic clone reprimands. "You dare release me from my inclusion, and for what… to help a loser who got her ass kicked by a normal woman?" Emma continues to pant while she gets up. As she looks at the clone of herself, she slowly begins to understand why the chamber gave her apprehension and fear.

"You… you look like…" Emma stutters. "You are…"
"Oh…right," the evil clone says, "I didn't see you there. No matter…" Suddenly, the clone moves like the wind, seemingly transporting as she hits Emma in her stomach, then kicks her in her face. The force of the blow sends Emma flying back fast. "GWAHAHAHAHAHAHAHA! Oh…. did the disgraceful bitch get an owie? Awh…"

As Emma struggles to regain her footing, some of the soldiers get in position to fire. Asir begins to get angry, thus creating fire surrounding his body. D'Shawn, meanwhile, keeps a level head and addresses his troops.
"Remain in position, men, and do not allow anyone in this arena to escape! Her power is great. Emma has to trust herself to fight this demon."
"Ugh… This clone is tough," Emma complains as she gets up, "but there must be a way to beat her."

Asir's anger prompts him to lash out at the clone. "Leave Miss Emma ALONE!" Asir's eyes begin to glow, he clenches both fists, then swings his arms backwards, creating a heat wave. The wave reaches the clone, but the clone chuckles as she absorbs the waves. Asir becomes startled, as D'Shawn and Emma confirm the reality of the situation.

"Only Emma can beat her, Asir," D'Shawn says. "Continue to watch, and let Emma fight her battle. We'll be there to help her."

"He's right, Asir," Emma says. She then looks at him and smiles. "I know you have my back, now let Miss Emma fight her battles."
"Fight your battles," the evil clone sneers. "Honey, you can't even fight who you are and what you've done. Hell, at least I am proud of what you were. I wonder if that bastard would like you if you admitted what you've done."

Emma's eyes squint, as she rushes towards the evil clone. The demonic villainess puckers her lips and blows black flames towards Emma. Emma allows herself to be engulfed in order to absorb the heat. However, something unexpected happens and Emma begins to scream in agony.

As the flames generate a ball, Asir and D'Shawn stand by as they know there is nothing they can do. Asir can see inside of the ball and tries to relay the information to D'Shawn. "I can still see Miss Emma," Asir yells, "but… it's hard to… I don't know how to…"
"I see it too," D'Shawn responds. "She's dwelling in her sorrow...this is not good."

Inside the flaming globe, Emma crouches down to the ground while holding her head. Her eyes nearly pop out of their sockets, veins pop out of her forehead, and her screams do little to showcase the amount of torture she is enduring. Inside of her head, she is shown visions of her previous life. How she would hurt and threaten, and a specific, horrific event that has scarred her up into this point.

"Hee hee hee hee hee…" the voice chuckles, "Do you remember… Do you remember the time you embraced your dark side?"
"No… NO!!!!" Emma yells. "I WAS A DIFFERENT PERSON THEN!"
"No, you are not… you will never change. Embrace who you truly are… a monster."

Multiple visions show the same memory all throughout the flame walls. The image shows a frightened teenager: very dark brown skin, with brown eyes, box braids, and torn clothes. Emma slowly reflects on the images, driving her to the brink of insanity.

"I… I remember…" Emma continues, while shaking her head. "Her… name… was Tiana. She was one of the first teenagers I helped kidnap. I… I… can still… see the tears of horror flow down her face."

"That's right," the voice adds. "Yes, it was you, who beat that poor girl nearly to death. Why was that I wonder? What was it about her?" Emma continues to cry, trying not to remember the traumatic event. Still, she continues with the memory.

"She… pleaded with me. Begging me to let her go."
"And what did you do?" the voice continues. "HUH? I SAID WHAT DID YOU DO?! You ignored her pleas, didn't you… DIDN'T YOU?!"
"(Sobbing)... I was told… that I was helping her, by extracting the genes needed to help them… and my…" Emma cries as she leans her head down.
"YOU KNEW THAT THEY WERE GOING TO KILL HER… AND WHAT HAPPENED AFTER THAT? WHAT HAPPENED?!"

All Emma could do was cry. Her eyes begin to turn black around the edges. The hope that once resigned in her body slowly migrates, as her sense of identity slips away. As the eyes nearly turn black, a small glimmer of hope desperately tries to blast through the wall.

"Miss Emma… don't give up!" Asir yells.
"Asir!" D'Shawn yells as he witnesses Asir blowing fireballs at the black flames.
"Miss Emma, you told me I needed to be a dragon… you cared for me… MISS EMMA!" Suddenly, Asir roars as the flames surrounding his body transform into a dragon: the flames are red, with wings resembling feathers, and a head as red as blood. The huge flaming beast glows its eyes, syncing it with Asir as he takes a huge breath. D'Shawn sees the power manifest in Asir. He sheds a small tear before wiping it off, cracks a smile, and whispers, "I guess I need to step it up as well. I'm… so… proud… of… you… Asir." D'Shawn then brightens his eyes and generates flames to cover his body. Then Asir and D'Shawn blow a barrage of flames into the black ball.

As the heat from the duo begins to penetrate the ball, Emma begins to regain her senses and come to terms with what happened. "Yes… I admit it. One of the clients ended up raping and killing her. Because she was from a single parent household, and her mom was strung up with drugs, no one inquired about her. I also beat her because she reminded me of...me. I hated her black skin, her black lips, because it reminded me of… what I could never escape. The melanin within my own skin, hair, and what I see in the mirror every day." Then, Emma's consciousness reverts to the veil of chambers. A brown chamber lights up. As Emma approaches it, she is shown a vision from when she first met Malik. "Yes, this was the first time I met Malik. I… could've killed him that day."

"But you didn't," a familiar voice echo. Emma looks around the veil to find the source of the voice. However, nothing manifests, but it doesn't deter Emma from asking.

"Muqadas, is that you?"

"My child, that day you fought your brother but didn't kill him. That was your dark side. So, tell me, what happened afterwards?"

"Well… we fought again… and when I allowed myself to burn, I met you. Then I came to his aid when he was going to die."

"So not only did you spare his life, but you also saved his life again. Tell me, what allowed you to do both?"

Emma looks at the door as it continues to shine a brown light. Then she looks at her bruised hands, her brown skin, and makes a revelation. "My skin… my beautiful brown skin… my body. This beautiful brown body that houses my…" Finally, Emma's eyes widen like a child on Christmas day. She wipes her face from sweat and tears, smiles, then grabs the handle of the chamber. She pulls and pulls and pulls. Afterwards, she yells the meaning of her revelation. "IT'S MY BODY AND EMBRACING THAT ALLOWS ME TO DRAW...STRENGTH!" At that moment, the door opens, releasing a flow of brown flames that consumes Emma. The flow of energy allows Emma to get up and flex her arms. With a loud screech, Emma loses the black in her eyes and then roars, creating a huge fire wave that destroys the black flame.

As the flames blow away, Asir and D'Shawn look on as Emma has small brown flames flowing from her body. The evil clone looks on in shock as she tries to belittle her foe. "It doesn't matter that you got out of that, you're still a monster like me...ARGH!"

The clone charges at Emma. Emma continues to stand still despite the impending danger. Asir yells to warn Emma. "Miss Emma, LOOK OUT!" As the clone's fire punch gets closer, Emma's eyes remain closed.

Suddenly, Emma dodges the punch while moving in rhythm. When she leans towards the right, she smirks as the clone continues to attack her. As the clone continues to kick and throw punches, Emma evades with the grace of an eagle catching a snake: weaving, flipping, and crouching as another chamber door lights up.

This chamber door this time lights up yellow. Emma tries to deduce why this door lights up. "I noticed that instead of trying to fight back, I'm dodging, just like when Muqadas was learning Engolo...WAIT A MINUTE." Emma realizes, "The fight with Sharon went bad because I didn't understand that there were factors against me: the chemicals, her enhancements, and my lack of understanding of my...I needed to know my limits." As soon as Emma realizes this, she grabs the chamber handle and pulls, releasing a flow of yellow flames that blend in with the brown flames around her body.

After a series of barrages of kicks and punches, Emma sweeps her leg, then does a spinning, reverse jump kick that sends the clone flying backwards. The clone gets enraged and yells back. "HOW DARE YOU TRY TO DENY WHO YOU ARE!" she yells as Emma smirks. The clone charges again, then throws another punch. Emma grabs her fist and applies a judo move to throw her to the ground. After the move, another chamber lights up.

As Emma once again sees the chamber light up in her mind, the color of green gives her an idea of what it represents. "You still don't get it," Emma scolds. "Throwing punches and kicks erratically is like a bird flying without direction. You have to navigate your battles through preparation, attention to detail, and... (I get it) application." Again, the chamber opens, allowing green flames to flow out and mix in with the rest of the flames surrounding Emma's body.

The clone, losing ground and her sense of victory, tries to scamper away while whining in her last attempt to dissuade Emma of her epiphany. "You… you… can never forget what you are. Who you are… face it… you are a monster." Emma slowly walks towards the evil clone. The clone, feeling trapped and out of options, lashes out at Emma in a last attempt to win. However, instead of hitting the clone, Emma grabs the clone, holds her, and then gives her a hug.

"I now understand," Emma sobs. "You are right...that I will never deny who I am. And what I am…" Before Emma could finish, the final chamber opens within her mind. The flow of blue flames is so powerful that it engulfs the radius of five feet around Emma and the clone. Emma embraces the floodgates of energy she once thought she'd never obtain again as she absorbs the evil clone. "No matter what you think or say, the darkness is a part of me… but so is the light. Now, join me, as we purify...as one." Emma once again allows herself to burn, but this time the combination of colors create a phoenix with blue plumage, with wings, with brown, green, yellow, and black feathers. Asir and D'Shawn lower their flames and look in awe as well as amazement. Asir looks at his father, then back at Emma smiling and cheering.

"Way to go, Miss Emma… Blue Phoenix!" D'Shawn gives the signal to his men to stand down as he looks on with a smile.

"You did it, Emma," he whispers.

"As I knew she would!" a man shouts from across the vicinity. Emma looks on and remembers the face she hasn't seen in so long.

"Wait a minute, I remember you… from North Carolina and…" Emma says.

"It's good to see you again, Blue Phoenix," the man interrupts. Then Emma smiles as she powers down, then looks on as the man approaches her. Emma concludes the conversation. "It's good to see you again… Mason Richardson."

# Chapter 30: The White Fox

The night sky fills up with an array of stars, colors, and clouds. Despite the absence of the sun, the heat from the continent still warrants perspiration from Malik's body. Malik treks across the barren landscape; wandering around seeking a deity that is just as elusive as a flower in a snowy day. To conserve energy, Malik chooses not to use his Dracocernentia but rely on a lighted torch and the full moon of the African scrubland.

"Woo…" Malik reflects, "I thought Atlanta was hot. This is a whole new level of disrespect. Hell, I don't know where to look or even what to look for." Malik continues to walk around the landscape.

After an hour of hiking, the torch is losing fuel to keep lit and exhaustion is beginning to take its toll on Malik. Malik sees an outcrop about thirty yards away. "I could use reptile mode and save energy," Malik contemplates, "but the Dracocernentia will drain faster if I use too much of its power on improving my night vision. I need to rest and come up with another plan, but first I need to make it to that rocky hill." Malik musters up his remaining strength to walk towards the rocky hills.

Malik makes his way towards the base of the mountain. He looks up at the cliff face and calculates his chances of climbing to a depression about forty feet up. "It doesn't look steep," Malik plots, "so at least I don't have to sacrifice putting the torch out." Malik gradually scales up the outcrop by finding soft spots to walk on. Slowly and methodically, Malik paces himself while finding soft spots to grip the sandy and rocky faces.

After a slow and cautious trek, Malik makes it to the depression of the cliff. The erosion has created a space large enough for Malik to almost stand-up straight in. With some medium-sized rocks around, Malik takes the time to gather a few so that he can prop the torch up, preventing it from touching the ground. Afterwards, he sits down and allows the cool air to circulate within the small cave. Now in a relaxed state, Malik can properly reevaluate his plans and course of action while overseeing the horizon.

"Even at night, this place is a spectacular site to behold," Malik marvels while he continues to bask in the shade. "So now I need to figure out where I can find this fox. Based on the testimonies, it flickers like a small bright light and shows up randomly, (sighs) so walking around is useless." Frustrated, Malik briefly closes his eyes and rests some more until he can figure out a legitimate plan of action.

About thirty minutes go by, and the torch is flickering at its last reserves of fuel. Malik briefly dozes off to recharge his energy. Suddenly, a huge gust of wind blows in the depression. The influx of air blows the remaining flame to the horizon while Malik shockingly wakes up. "What was that?" Malik whispered. "Whatever it is, it just knocked out the last of the torch." Slowly, Malik gets up and looks around to see where the wind is coming from. As he crawls towards the flameless torch, something glimmers in the corner of his eye.

When Malik turns to validate the source of his attention, two small, shiny lights hover over nothing but sand and air. At first, Malik attributes the lights to being some sort of insect. However, the lights do not move nor make a sound. Another rush of air blows from their position, knocking Malik back a few inches.

"What in the hell? What kind of strange lights just stand there?" Afterwards, a low howling sound circles around the small enclosure. Malik immediately gets on guard as the lights, despite the array of activity, stand out like stones. Growing concerned and anxious, Malik decides to activate his Dracocernentia despite the risks of losing energy.

When his eyes transform, Malik is shocked at what his eyes perceive. His response is slow, but his intrigue and curiosity amplify while trying to comprehend the strange sight.

"All I can see is smoke surrounding those weird lights," Malik reasons, "but I can also see a mixture of color receptors. There's no linear path or pattern, just a jumbled mess of energy." As Malik tries to comprehend the sight, the lights begin to move out of the depression. Another low howl is followed by a gust of wind that circles around and pushes Malik forward. When Malik is knocked slightly forward, the lights begin to move.

"I don't know why, but I have a strange feeling that I should follow this strange source of energy." Soon after Malik comprehends his thoughts, the lights immediately leave. "What the… WAIT!" Malik screams as he crawls out of the depression. The lights move quickly down the slope of the cliff face. Malik uses his eyes to keep track visually while he uses his energy to move with ease to keep up with the mass of energy.

The energy moves down the base of the cliff and heads east towards the barren scrubland. Malik desperately pursues the energy while maintaining visual contact. "Wow," Malik comments. "For a mass of energy, it's sure giving me a workout. I don't think it can get any stranger."

Suddenly, the mass of energy starts to generate four long structures that protrude from his smoky mass. As it moves, the structures form into legs. As the legs manifest, it begins to zigzag on the scrublands, making it more difficult to follow. Malik shakes his head and smirks. "Well, not only am I wrong," Malik remarks sarcastically, "I am a man, with the eyes of dragons, chasing a puff of smoke that sprouts legs. When you say it out loud, there isn't enough liquor on Earth to make this make sense (Sigh)."

Malik picks up his pace, as the mass of smoke then forms a tail. Now with four legs and a tail, the mass makes its way towards another rock outcrop. This time, it scales the cliffs so fast that Malik begins to feel his lungs overexert its capacity to supply the warrior with oxygen. Malik pants hard while he finds the words to motivate himself to continue the pursuit. "HUFF HUFF HUFF… If only the area was hot enough for me to switch modes. That being said, a puff of smoke that sprouts legs and a tail isn't something normal. I gotta keep going."

The smoke scales the top of the small mountain with little ease. The closer it reaches the top of the mountain, the more the smoke takes more of a shape. A long mass forms another oval with two smaller nobs protruding from each side. Malik struggles to keep up as he jumps and climbs from pieces of rock to keep up. As he reaches the top, he notices the mass of energy form. Curious, he tries to put together the events unfolding.

"So now this mass of energy is forming… what looks like…" Malik stutters as he struggles to maintain his breathing. Before the mass of energy reaches the top of the mountain, it stops abruptly. The mass of energy then turns its newly formed head, and the two lights look directly at Malik. Malik is taken aback by this unusual behavior and slowly climbs up toward the strange entity.

"Why is it just standing there? And for that matter, where is it leading me? When Malik gets within twenty yards to the mass, a gust of wind blows again, stopping him in his tracks. As he shields his eyes from the sand and debris, the mass then scales the top of the mountain and disappears. Feeling frustrated at losing the mass, Malik contemplates his next course of action.

"Damn it!" Malik scorns. "I can't believe I lost it. I don't know why these random gusts of wind keep blowing seemingly out of nowhere." Malik continues to wipe his face and eyes to remove the last remnants of sand. However, something in his mind clicks as Malik rethinks his course of action. "Wait a minute, that mass of energy was trying to reach the top of this mountain. Maybe if I go up there, I might be able to see the meaning behind all of this."

Malik closes his eyes and catches his breath. He allows his body to regenerate and takes the heat of the night to rejuvenate his body. After a minute to collect his energy, he reactivates his Dracocernentia and powers on towards the top of the mountain.

With each step, Malik grows more determined and resolved. His shoes are dirty and somewhat worn. His torso and chest are amalgamated with sweat, sand, musk, and remnants of paint for the Sigi. Each step towards the top of the mountain requires more energy than the last. Malik crunches his face and squints his eyes as he draws closer and closer to the top of the mountain. When Malik gets within six feet of the top, he can feel his power slipping and energy leaking out of his body. He grunts as he is literally down to his knees in pain, agony, and exhaustion. "I don't know why… but this mountain is harder than anything that I have scaled," Malik reflects as he is trekking slowly up the top. "However, I came too far to give up… or to fail. I will… (Grunt… Huff… Huff) make it to the top." Afterwards, Malik uses his right hand to reach as far as he can to a crevice just below the top of the mountain. With all the strength that he has, Malik pulls his long, lanky body up and forces himself to the top of the mountain.

After a show of resilience and fortitude, Malik strains himself to get to the top of the mountain. His eyes close and he lays his back on the flat part of the top of the small mountain. His body faces the star-filled sky, and his arms sprawl out like a fan to catch the few streams of air to breeze over his exhausted body. "I made it," Malik says to himself while breathing hard. "I… I… need rest… my body…"

Suddenly, a huge gust of wind blows on Malik. He quickly looks up and sees the mass of energy that eluded him for so long. Despite the strain he has put on himself, Malik manages to get up to get a better look at this strange form of energy.

As the two lights illuminate, the mass of energy gathers storm clouds and encases itself, forming a small cyclone. The gusts of wind are so powerful that Malik struggles to cement his feet on the ground to prevent them from falling down the mountain. The clouds continue to circle and create pockets of lightning and thunder.

After several seconds of circular motion, a large, white blast explodes in front of Malik, temporarily blinding him. Malik covers his eyes to prevent the bright lights of hurting even his powerful eyes. "What is this crazy energy?" Malik wonders. "I wish I could say I was dreaming… but that would be too much of a cop out." Then out of nowhere, a calming but majestic voice speaks loud enough for Malik to take notice.

"Your concerns are warranted. You are indeed dreaming, but in reality, you have sought me out." Malik uncovers his eyes and begins to look around. The ball of energy temporarily disappears, leaving Malik alone on top of the mountain.

"Where did that voice come from?" Malik ponders as he continues to swivel his head from side to side. Then, in the sky, the clouds suddenly appear and begin to form. The lights formulate the clouds into a shape. The deity is indeed snowy white, with large ears, a pointed snout, large yellow eyes, and pure teeth as polished as ivory.

The mass looks directly at Malik. Malik is paralyzed with intrigue, shock, and reverence. He chooses his words wisely, only speaking at a direct and respectful pace. "You… are… the White Fox," Malik stutters. "I am honored to be in your presence." The White Fox continues to peer through Malik's heart and soul. Its eyes squint and intensify, taking its time to examine the hero while it too chooses its words to say.

"Ah… the Moor," the White Fox starts, its voice is so conglomerated that it sounds like three or four different male and female voices in sync with the words it speaks, "who grew up in the land beyond the sea… in the house of the enemy… who has discovered his purpose… who has traveled far… and has fulfilled the prophecy given to his grandfather." Malik cautiously responds, not knowing the level or temperament of the Fox's power.

"So, you remember my grandfather?"

"You are the descendant of Kemba, a Dogon who sought me when he was slightly younger than you are now. Son of and once heir to the Hogon."

"Hogon," Malik exclaimed. "You mean that the elder is my…"

"I have looked within you, Moor. I have seen your destinies converge into you. You have the blood of leaders and warriors. I once told your grandfather that he will be the bridge to bring forth justice, not as the Hogon."

"White Fox," Malik says, "I humbly do not understand. What was it about the prophecy that led my grandfather to flee from his position?" The White Fox lights up his eyes and generates gale-size wind while the clouds form visions. As the images begin to form, the powerful deity narrates to ease the confusion of Malik.

"Young Moor, I told your grandfather that when his people were at the decline of their power, a certain group of people would rise from the colds and the caves to reap terror and horror to the world. These people do not possess the same love and appreciation for life, nor the land that we inherit." The White Fox continues to show images of the exile of the Dogon, then continues with its commentary. "When your ancestors finally made it to this land, I had entrusted them to bring forth those who were worthy to seek my wisdom and guidance."

"I… understand. "The Sigi…"

"Yes, Moor. When I told your grandfather he will bring forth the seed of change, I also told him that he will fall for a woman of the Bozo, who will help converge his destiny." Malik looks down and scrunches his eyes, trying to comprehend the words of the deity. After a few seconds, his eyes widen, and he refocuses his attention back at the White Fox. "So, the woman of the Bozo tribe was… is… Grandma Geneva."

"Yes, Moor," the White Fox confirms. "But do not be alarmed. I am well aware of your thoughts and your purpose."

The White Fox forms another set of visions and images that become familiar to Malik. Malik begins to understand the complexity of the conversation as the White Fox continues.

"As I am aware, you are seeking the Burning Destiny, the Harq Alqadr. I am also aware of the clandestine group of men who pillage, rape, destroy, and distort reality to substitute for their lack of internal validation and appreciation for their existence." Malik balls up his fist and thinks to himself.

"The… Elite 8."

"Young Moor, you will continue on your journey, but the outcome will not be as you will expect."

"Expect?" Malik questions. "Great Fox, I do not understand."

"Dragon Moor, what you seek isn't confined to just a physical tool. In order to wield it, you must understand the meaning of your Fire Line and how it will light up in the dormant state of your people. Only then will you take your rightful place… as the Golden Dragon."

"Golden Dragon...What does that mean?" Malik wonders. "And the dormant state of the people...are you talking about just the Dogon?"

"As I have explained to your grandfather, the people are not limited to
the name of the tribe, the land that they live, or the barriers that separate
them. They are linked together in the substance that covers time and
space, the same substance that can absorb and redirect energy. The same
substance that the men behind the destruction of this planet and the
original people occupy."

"Substance… not confined by tribe, land, or barriers? I don't
understand. How do I find the sword?"

The White Fox then transforms into a smaller version of itself
from the sky. It forms into a form about the size of a wolf. It then walks
in front of Malik before concluding its words of wisdom.

"What you seek can be seen and unseen by your mighty eyes,
Moor. You may find failure before you can find that what you seek is…
and has always resided in you. Malik still looks confused before the
White Fox begins to disappear in the wind. "Go to the land your
ancestors began their reign and conquest. You will meet another who
dwells in the shadows."

The last remnants of the Fox begin to disappear into the wind.
Some of the white essence swirls around Malik's body while Malik
looks on with awe and unease. Malik then shouts out in confusion before
the last forms completely evaporate in the air. "WAIT! Then what?!"
Malik yells while extending his arm. Slowly, the voice echoes into the
wind before reaching the stars.

"Remember, Moor, the Burning Destiny isn't just a sword, but a
power that has always resided in those worthy of wielding it. You must
journey to understand this first, only then will my words come true. Go
to the land of your other ancestors…"

As the voice disappears in the wind, the sun shows signs of
rising from the horizon. Malik stands on the top of the mountain to
compound the amount of information that Sigi has thrusted into him.
"Now I understand the weight of responsibility Granddad Kemba
experienced," Malik reflects. "Now I have some idea, but it doesn't
explain why they would leave this country."

Malik activates his Dracocernentia and powers up his body. He faces the direction of the village, then looks down at the mountain cliffside. His eyes intensified, his muscles pumped up, and his mind made up. "I have some questions to ask my dear uncle Mamadou. Something tells me he too has been hiding something." After bracing himself, Malik makes the long but manageable journey down the mountain, and towards the village before sunrise.

# Chapter 31: Demented Decisions through Deviant Deception

The sun is beginning to rise, showing the reflection of light from the Thames River. A crude, clean cut man, already awake, fully clothed, and standing greets the sun while sipping a cup of coffee. He smirks with an arrogant gaze while nodding his head. Then, something rattles in his pocket and lets off a chime. With his right hand, he grabs his phone, uses his thumb to swipe the phone on, and begins to converse.

"Bonjour Jean," he says.

"Bonjour Monsieur Goth. I have news of the Faiseur de troubles (Troublemaker). He was selected to participate in the Sigi. My contact will inform me of when he will return."

"Don't wait on your contact, Jean," Goth commands. "Gather your mercenary force and proceed with the plan. We must figure out the whereabouts of the sword. Remember, its power is rumored to have no limits."

"And the village?"

"What about the well-being of a dying culture," Goth responds.

"Jean, let's be reasonably honest. Why would the world waste precious resources on a group of people clinging to outdated and useless ways? For the sake of our domination, they are nothing more than dead leaves on a lawn waiting to be picked up and thrown away."

"Entendu (Understood), I will mobilize our men and surround the village."

"And Jean, make sure he is brought back alive. Only a Moor with the right blood and heritage can access the sword. Only then will I cut off his head… (chuckles) with the same blade his ancestors made no less."

"Indeed… Car nous contrôlons le destin des hommes (For we control the destiny of men)."

"Car nous sommes l'élite (For we are Elite). Au revoir my friend, and I await your call when the job is done."

CLICK. Goth hangs up the phone then continues to stare at the horizon. A beautiful, blond-haired, blue-eyed woman walks in. She is wearing a thick strapped white, blue, and green dress, with blue three-inch pumps. She walks behind Goth, rubbing his back and shoulders while Goth gives little notice of her presence.

"Good morning, Victor," she says. "I have your breakfast ready and your day's schedule ready for review." Goth takes another sip of his coffee and continues to look on at the horizon. The woman continues to smile nervously, awaiting a response from his cold and calculating vibe.

Ten seconds later, Goth closes his eyes, moves his head down, and smiles. Then he looks and smiles at the nervous woman. "Thank you, gorgeous," Goth responds, making the woman slightly uncomfortable with his unpredictable behavior. "Look at the window. What do you see?" The woman slowly moves her head out of the window. She squints her eyes, then looks back at Goth. Goth prompts her to redirect her focus at the window by moving the hand holding the coffee forward. She then moves her head back at the window. She rubs her hands up and down her arms to generate warmth and comfort. Goth chuckles and smiles at the gesture before engaging the conversation.

"What do you see out there, Sara?" Sara looks at Goth with confused and unconfident eyes. She quivers her lips, then smiles to pull herself together.

"Well, Victor, I see the sun rising on the river. I also see the city that you live in."

"Live in?" Victor chuckles, "Hmmm…"

Victor then turns around and walks towards his table facing a large screen. On the table are several documents, pictures, and transactions surrounding a large picture of the globe. He looks at the globe and re-engages the conversation.

"Do you know what your ancestors did? What my ancestors did?"

"Meaning what?" Sara asks as Goth looks at the globe.

"After the Spanish Inquisition, Spain traveled to the new world by stealing the maps and notes from the baboons they rid their country of."

"Steal? Notes? But Christopher Columbus found the new world," Sara retorted.

Goth chuckles as he walks around the table. Sara is once again nervous by the inconsistent pattern of behavior Goth is exhibiting, as he continues to make his points. "My dear Sara, nothing in this world is true, unless told by the winners of history. You see, what you call Black people, have been traveling to this "new world" decades, if not centuries before our people regrettably could read or clean ourselves from the filth we lay on." Goth goes to the bar near the table, grabs a glass and pours some rum. He then swirls the glass and takes a sip, afterwards he clears his throat.

"Good stuff… now where was I?" Goth continues. "Ah yes, the Spanish. Because of Columbus, the Spanish were able to rebuild their country and resources through the gold, silver, and precious metals taken from the people who saw little to no value in it themselves."

"I… I… see," Sara nervously responds.

"Um hmm." Goth smiles. "You see, after 100 years of… this sudden prosperity, their arrogance grew. So, they decided to invade this country with 130 large vessels in an attempt to solidify their dominance. But do you know what happened to this tiny island?"

"Ah yes, we won."

"Indeed, but do you know how we won, or the lesson in the victory?" Sara shakes her head while clasping her hands together. "Off course not," Goth scoffs as he takes another sip from his glass. "You see, the Spanish thought that power had to be big, boisterous, and overconfident, and yes, in some cases it is true. However, if you cannot move, weave, and manipulate your surroundings to bend to your will, then you become a stone in the path of a river. You see, Sara, England is a small island, but their aspirations extended beyond the borders of our oceans. After sailing around the world, they didn't just see it as a place that we LIVE IN. (Sips his rum) No, no, no, they realized that to dominate the world, you had to manipulate it to bend it to their will."

"So, are you saying that England conquered the world not by force but by manipulating the world of their power?"

Goth smirks again, viewing the comprehension of his companion remedial and basic. However, he also understands that not everyone is equipped to handle the intricacies of power. "You see, Sara, power cannot be simply defined in simple terms… or by simple people. Power only belongs to those who take it, by any means necessary. What you should've learned from the Spanish failed invasion is that just because you don't have a large force or large numbers doesn't mean that you must settle for your position. We do not make up much of the population, but we do make up most of the wealth and resources. Therefore, a small minority can control the vast majority."

Suddenly, an alarm beeps, prompting Goth to put his glass down and look at the clock. He then smiles and addresses Sara. "You can go now, Sara."

"Oh.. Ok… d… did I do something wrong?" Goth walks over to Sara. He slaps her very hard on the right cheek. Then he grabs her chin and kisses her on the left cheek. Sara's face and eyes turn red. She holds her right cheek and tries desperately to hold in her tears. Goth then smiles before answering. "A woman who doesn't think on my level… doesn't deserve to be by my side."

Sara then takes her que to walk past Victor and out of the door. While walking, she looks down in shame and her strut becomes slow, clumsy, and awkward. Goth fixes his hair and gathers himself. He fixes his collar on his shirt, presses a button, and watches as part of his wall opens, showing a secret compartment for ten large monitors. Goth boots up his CPU, clicks on a link to a conference meeting, then waits for the screen to pop up.

After several seconds of loading, shadowy figures, only showing their torso and shoulders, appear on each screen. Goth leans on his desk while addressing the mysterious men on the screens.

"Good morning, council members." The men on the screen take their time to respond to Goth. Goth clears his throat while trying desperately to remain calm in the face of shrewd men.

"Goth," the main council member states, "As you are aware, we've been taking a few steps backwards due to the mishap in America some time ago. It is critical that you proceed as planned."

"Council member, I fail to see how I have strayed from the plan. Here in London, our operations remain stable and our contacts in America continue to supply us with the data necessary to continue our work."

"Goth, you brought unnecessary attention with the loss of one of our secret laboratories. However, you were also excessive in the way you handled the...loose ends," another council member adds.

Goth walks towards the bar while maintaining his view to the council members. He pours another glass while he further assesses the meaning of the meeting.

"So, council members, is this the meaning of this meeting? To scold an up and coming, young and attractive member of this court?"

"Do not presume too much, Goth," another member reprimands. "One member is not more important than the next, especially when it comes to our work."

"Precisely," the main council member continues. "Your research on chemical enhancements and warfare will prove useful, but only when the time is right. We cannot afford to jeopardize generations of work before we have fully assessed all the risks and benefits. Do you understand?"

Goth takes another sip from his freshly poured glass. He closes his eyes, leans his head down, then nods. Afterwards, he responds his concerns to the council.

"There is… a certain matter that needs our attention," Goth brings up.

"We are aware of the meddling Black man who is known as the Shadowmoor. We will deal with him, but only in due time."

"Due time… DUE TIME!" Goth exclaims. "We need to get rid of him now! It's bad enough we have one of those animals snooping around my girls here. If we let him continue, he'll…"

"Do not make any rash decisions, Goth!" the main council member commands. "The adopted son will soon be dealt with, but not with our own hands. Allow the plans to come to fruition, and then the society will hunt him down themselves, ridding ourselves to get involved."

"Grrr… as you wish, council members," Goth relinquishes.

"We look forward to your reports on the progress of the chemicals. Goth, you must remain patient and clandestine. Understood?" Goth reluctantly nods while sipping his alcohol.

"Good, now this meeting is adjourned. For we control the destiny of men…"

"For we are Elite!" Goth says in unison with the other council members. Afterwards, each of the screens log off.

Once the screens turn off, Goth paces back and forth while sipping the rest of his alcohol. As the sweat from his brow continues to flow down his pale skin, his eyes scrunch downward, his mouth clinches, and his face turns slightly red. Then out of nowhere, Goth lets off a roar, throws his glass towards the same wall as the screens, shattering it in the process. Then Goth goes into a blood thirsty rant.

"Those smug, condescending, BASTARDS!" Goth yells. "Well… (clears his throat), the time is almost near when I won't have to concede to those outdated procedures. If only I have the sword, I can muster the loyalty and power needed to rule this world. Then those assholes would bow to me."

Goth regathers himself yet again. He grabs a towel, wipes his face and neck, then tosses it on a nearby basket. Goth then walks towards the window overseeing the river that divides London while he once again dreams of his eventual rise to power. "Soon, all of this, the money, the power, and the world, will be mine."

Suddenly, something vibrates in Goth's pocket, interrupting his brooding. He places his right hand in his pocket to grab his cell phone. He glances at the name of the phone, uses his thumb to swipe, then places it on his right ear.

"Bonjour Jean. How is the operation going in Mali?"

"Everything is going according to plan. The contact just contacted me about the course of action regarding the meddling nègre. I don't see why we just don't rid the planet of his existence."

"I share your zeal, Jean. However, we need him to show us the location of the sword. Then, we'll use that same blade to end his life and control the destiny of men… as we were always meant to."

"Entendu (Understood), so what should I do to persuade him to cooperate?"

"You are a brilliant man, Jean. I trust that you'll use some… French tactics to achieve your goal."

"And the tribe? What of them?"

"What about them? They've outlived their usefulness, yet cling to their outdated traditions, do what you must. When it comes to absolute power, no one is spared in achieving our goal."

"Well put, Goth. I will contact you once I've confirmed the location of the sword. Until then, Nous contrôlons le destin des hommes (We control the destiny of men) ..."

"For we are Elite," Goth answers. "Take care my friend."

Goth hangs up the phone and smiles. He continues to face the horizon as the morning sun continues to warm the city streets. "Soon, I will overthrow those unsuspecting council members and create a new order within the Elite 8. Heh heh heh."

A few moments later, a door opens. Goth doesn't move nor turn around to see who it is. However, the sweet smell of perfume alerts him of the presence of another woman.

"Hey daddy," the sweet voice says. "How is your day?"

"Well, my Caramel Candy, the sweet smell and feel of your warm embrace once again puts a smile on my face."

"Mmmmhmmm… I love it when you talk sweet to me."

"Indeed. So, have you spoken to our… mutual friend?"

"Not since he left London. He's persistent in finding the sword, but he's not talking to me as much as I expected he would."

"My dear, all you have to do is trigger him. Sometimes it takes deceptive femininity to move a man to conquer the world. It's only a matter of time."

The woman smiles, then walks behind Goth. She lays her head on his back while rubbing her hands on his chest. Goth continues to look out his window while finishing his glass of liquor. "You feel so good, daddy. How does a girl get so lucky?" Goth smiles as he continues with the foreplay. He turns around and sees the beautiful Black woman who graces his presence.

"Luck, my dear… favors the privilege and the strong… and…" Goth grabs the chin of the woman and draws her close. He then presses his lips against hers as they both share a passionate kiss. Afterwards, he looks in her glossy brown eyes and smiles. "Soon, you will be fulfilled. After the sword is found, you will find closure and peace."

"You are so amazing, Victor." Goth chuckles as he kisses the woman one more time. "You are still sweet as candy, and fine as wine, Audrey."

Afterwards, both begin to massage each other, make out, and then maneuver themselves towards the nearby couch to engage in adulterous, deviant, and passionate engagement.

# Chapter 32: Restraint of the Blood Thirst

The crickets and other insects begin to conclude their nightly symphony. The first slivers of light begin to migrate above the horizon. Worn out, nearly dehydrated, and still overwhelmed with the stimuli from amassing a gargantuan amount of information, Malik treks back towards the village. Despite his current condition, Malik allows himself to pinpoint key elements of his talk with the White Fox while acknowledging how far his journey has taken him.

"Who would've thought that locating the sword would take me this far," Malik reflects as he continues to walk. "The words from the White Fox did little to quell any notions or thoughts that allude my understanding. Still, something it said still bothers me… Go to the land of my other ancestors… but which one?"

As Malik continues to think, he draws closer and closer to the village. At this time, dawn is drawing near as the skies begin to change to a teal and greenish color. Malik sees the village about 150 yards away and begins to feel a sense of relief and accomplishment. The sweat from his body drenches his skin, yet there is a small smirk that rises the closer he gets. "Finally… I can go back to the village and get this part over with," Malik states as he draws what little strength he has to move faster. His legs become heavy with lactic acid and soreness, his breath is heavy but silent, and his eyes begin to strain as the view of the village gets bigger and bigger.

Suddenly, a sharp vibration in his head triggers Malik to stop fifty yards away from the village. Malik stops by a nearby rock outcrop while sitting down and massaging the right side of his head. The pain is excruciating, but Malik takes the time to self-evaluate what his senses are trying to tell him.

"What on Earth is wrong with me," Malik complains while attempting to ease the pain. Then, Malik stops and closes his eyes. He controls his breathing, lowers his shoulders, and relaxes. He calmly comes up with a plan to investigate the meaning of the feeling.

"When I get these feelings, I sense that something is wrong," Malik whispers. "I need to take a look around to see if there is anything out there or if it's just the exhaustion taking its toll on my body."

After Malik takes his time to calm down, he opens his eyes and activates the Dracocernentia. Malik peeks his head over the boulder and scans the perimeter of the village. He soon understands why his senses pick up the anomalies of the area. Several receptors of different men with guns patrol the outer rim while a group of men led by one hold Mamadou, Djeneba, and several Dogon people in the middle of the village. One man in particular shows several receptors of red, violet, and blue.

"What the hell…" Malik says. "That's the guy I met yesterday… Rochambeau! Why is he here, and why are all of these guys surrounding the village?" Malik crouches back behind the outcrop and sits for a while. He looks towards the east as the sun is beginning to rise, marking the beginning of a new day. "I can't confront these guys in this state," Malik admits. "So, it looks like I'm going to have to wait until the sun rises. Then I'll allow the sun to heat up my body and replenish my energy. That's the only way I can help them now." So, Malik crosses his ankles, places his hands on his knees, and closes his eyes. He allows himself to sit perfectly still while allowing the sun to heat up his body and the landscape.

While Malik is warming up, Rochambeau interrogates Mamadou and the other villagers. His patience weighs thin, and his demeanor fluctuates from condescension to irritability.
"Now Mamadou, I thought we had an accord," Rochambeau pressed. "You would give me the whereabouts of the man who possesses il de dragon (dragon eye) and I ensure that your tribe remains where they are."
"Please, Jean, it is barely dawn," Mamadou pleads. "I'm sure with his unique… skills, he will return."
Rochambeau slowly paces back and forth with his hands on his hips. He smirks and shakes his head while Mamadou looks on with confusion. Rochambeau then walks towards Mamadou. He puts his hand on Mamadou's shoulder and chuckles for a few seconds.

"Heh heh heh, you know mon ami, I have many qualities that make me a… valuable friend," Rochambeau says as he squeezes his hand on Mamadou. Mamadou feels the tension on his shoulder but tries desperately to maintain his stature and demeanor. Then Rochambeau erupts in a fit of rage. He loosens his grip and back slaps Mamadou to the ground so hard, the old man spits drops of blood on the parched dirt. Djeneba rushes towards Mamadou as a few mercenaries aim their guns at her and the rest of the villagers. Rochambeau paces back and forth, breathing hard and sweating profusely.

"Do you think I GIVE A DAMN ABOUT YOU AND THIS GOD FORSAKEN VILLAGE," Rochambeau roars as he gets himself together. "I have many good qualities, BUT PATIENCE ISN'T ONE OF THEM! So, either you deliver what you promised me or…" (Click, Click, Click as the mercenaries arm their guns) or today will be the day your people are wiped out forever."

Djeneba tries to help her father while giving Rochambeau a vile look. Her rage is controlled by her lack of leverage or power to overturn her predicament. "Sigh, you have one more hour to deliver him to me," Rochambeau reminds, "so do not make me wait long."

Thirty minutes later, Malik allows the sun's rays to rejuvenate his body. The radiation replenishes his strength and levels his mind. Malik takes the time to reactivate the Dracocernentia and to scan the perimeter once again.

"Ok, so I see that there are ten men surrounding the village," Malik plots. "Then there's five men corralling the people, with that dick Rochambeau leading them. So, I need to take out the outsiders first, then make my way to the middle." Malik stands up and faces the village. He clenches his fists while he takes slow, deep breaths. His eyes glow bright and the heat from his body creates a small heat wave. Once he reserves himself to engage the men, Malik methodically moves closer to take out the guards nearest to him.

Three of the mercenaries space each other by six feet apart while covering each of their blind sides. Each man scans the horizon for any intruders while the sun beats down on their exposed, pale skins.

As one of the mercenaries' steps away from the visual range of the other two, Malik slowly sneaks through the surrounding brush, rocks, and trees. His eyes reveal the blue and violet receptors that flow through his body as he continues to plot his course of action.

"This mercenary is impatient and wants to get out of the heat," he notices. "As soon as he turns around, I'll knock him out and go after the other two." Malik patiently waits for his moment to strike.

The mercenary looks around to see any potential danger. He's armed with a rifle attached with a strap, a field knife, and other tactical gear. However, the African sun cooks his nerves to the boiling point of his frustration and fatigue. He then grits his teeth, takes off his hat, and wipes his forehead with his right hand. "C'est de la merde (This is Bull Shit!)," he complains underneath his breath while putting his hat back on. "Well, I need to go back to my post. Nothing to see here." The thirsty man takes a canteen from his left pant pocket, takes a swig while pouring some on his neck and shoulders. Then he places the canteen back in his pocket, secures his gun, and turns around.

When the mercenary walks the other direction, Malik sees his opportunity and closes in on him. As the merc blindly walks back to his original position, Malik closes in with lightning speed and endurance.

Malik gains enough ground to jump up and cock his right fist and arm. Feeling a slight gust of wind and an unusual sound, the mercenary turns around to investigate. Unfortunately for the man, what he finds is a flame-heated fist landing on his face. The blow, too fast to react, knocks him backwards and unconscious which causes enough of a thump to be heard by the other two watchmen.

The other two mercenaries' sense something is wrong and call out to their comrade. "Hey, Demont! Demont!" one of them calls. No response as the they look at each other and nod. Both cock their guns and release the safety as they slowly creep towards the source of the commotion.

As the men approach, Malik drags the body towards the bushes while luring the men further away from the village. "I should be able to sneak around them and take them out through the surrounding brush," Malik schemes. "Afterwards, I'll handle the rest of the men."

As the men draw closer to the edge, they notice a pair of dirty combat boots lying on the dirt. The lead merc points his gun at the scene and slowly moves towards the boots while the other covers his 6 o'clock. Both men are nervous, tense, and confused on what to expect as they get closer and closer.

Finally, when they see the wearer of the boots, the men see their comrade knocked out and laid out on the red sands. "Incroyable (Unbelievable), Demont, you bâtard paresseux (lazy bastard), get up!" the man snarls. As he leans down, the other mercenary notices something odd about their fellow man. He has a red, slightly burned mark on his face that generates suspicion.

"Hey Remy, I don't think Demont is taking a nap. Look closely at his face." The first merc takes another glance at his face and begins to hesitate. His eyes widen, his breath stops for a bit, and he gulps before raising up.

"Que diable se passe-t-il ici (What the hell is going on around here)?" he asks while both shake with their guns.

"Me!" a voice shouts. Then suddenly, Malik surprises both with flame-engulfed fists. With the force of his might, Malik punches simultaneously in their faces, knocking them out before they had time to react.

As Malik disarms them and sets them out of sight, something puzzles Malik. "How did I know what those guys were saying?" Malik wonders. "I know that they were speaking French… It doesn't matter now. I need to rescue the villagers."

Twenty minutes later, Rochambeau looks at his watch while the rest of the villagers anxiously await their fate. Most of them are on their knees with guns pointed at them. Meanwhile, Djeneba tries to console her father by rubbing his right shoulder. Mamadou slinks his head downward in shame. The muscles of his face drop, his shoulders lose grip from the weight of sorrow, and his eyes begin to water as he lets off a subtle shake of his head from side to side. Afterwards he puts his hand over his face. Djeneba whispers in his ear to lift his spirits.

"Father don't worry. I know that he will…" CLICK. Rochambeau loads his pistol and immediately grabs Djeneba's attention.

"I don't like secrets, mon cherie," Rochambeau sarcastically sneers. "Well, time is almost up, and I think I have extended the limits of… my patience."

"You… are a coward!" Djeneba reacts, then spits on the ground next to Rochambeau's boots.

"Pathétique (Pathetic)," Rochambeau says while shaking his head. "Such a waste of… such a beauty." Rochambeau aims the gun at Djeneba and Mamadou. The rest of the mercenaries follow suit by aiming at the remaining villagers. "Your daughter's insolence will be the reason your tribe is wiped out from existence," Rochambeau says. "So, mon ami, all I can say is au revoir and…"

As the final tense moments play out like slow motion, a sudden heat wave emulates around the village. The area is so hot, that only Rochambeau and the mercenaries can feel the intense heat. The men all look around and try to ascertain where the sudden heat is coming from. Rochambeau loses sight of his target and turns around. Before he could fully grasp what is going on, a huge fire storm approaches him like a runaway train. With microseconds to react, he immediately hits the ground as the flood of reddish orange fire stampedes across the field.

The firestorm goes through the village, burning nearly half of the mercenaries while shielding the village and people. Djeneba and Mamadou are stunned as he wipes his eyes and look up at the source of such power. Three of the mercenaries try desperately to douse the flames on their clothes while Rochambeau looks up. What he sees sends a slight tingle down his spine, a bead of sweat down his face, and a thrust in his heart.

Malik stands in front of the village covered in reddish orange flames. His canine teeth slightly enlarge and sharpen, his muscles bulk up, and his gaze becomes intense, filled with rage, intimidating everyone that is witnessing this spectacle. Malik's eyes change from his usual golden-brown color to blood red. The micro claws drown in the ocean of indignation; only the elongated, sharp, and black pupil remains.

Once the mercenaries put out their fires, they begin to charge at Malik. They aim their guns at Malik while Rochambeau gets up, grabs, and strips Djeneba away from Mamadou while kicking the old man away, then retreats to the back of the village.

"FATHER! MALIK!" she yells to get Malik's attention.

"SHUT UP YOU LITTLE PUTAIN (WHORE)!"

"AHHHHHHH!!!!" Djeneba continues to yell as the mercenaries begin to fire their guns at Malik.

As the machine guns unleash their bullets, they are met and immediately melted in the fire shield Malik puts up. His sense of humanity slips as his animalistic urges to see justice mute his otherwise cynical outlook. As the sounds of clicks signal their empty clips, Malik turns his head slightly to the left, stares at the shaken men, then pauses.

After a tense moment of silence, Malik moves like a burst, and flame punches one of the mercenaries in the gut. The flames erupt through the man and expel out of his back. The flames are so hot, that the blood that squirts out of his mouth immediately incinerate in the air. As the man's eyes roll towards the back of his head, he begins to slowly transition towards the ground. Malik then looks at another mercenary. His receptor fields flow so much yellow, that the fear inspires even sympathy from the villagers witnessing this spectacle. Undeterred, Malik swoops in, ignites his right leg, and kicks the man so fast and hard, that he is flown twenty yards across the village, smashing against one of the mud-built huts. After the contact, all that is left is a smoking husk of a corpse; the skin burned to charcoal, only showing the man's skull and partially melted eyes.

As Malik slowly loses his senses, a large click grabs his attention. He turns to his left and sees that Rochambeau has a gun to Djeneba's head. Both he and Djeneba sweat profusely as Rochambeau catches his breath.

"Magnifique," he compliments, "you are truly a monstre, like your ancestors before you. Unfortunately, you will lose because you don't have what it takes to go beyond your honor, just to win." Slowly, Malik calms himself down. He closes his eyes, takes a few breaths, then opens his eyes. The color in his eyes return to the golden-brown color and his micro claws once again circle his sharp pupil. He regains enough sense and composure to attempt to reason with Rochambeau.

"Alright man, look," Malik pleads, "enough is enough. None of these people needed to get hurt, and there is already blood spilled. What is it that you want?" Rochambeau laughs as he continues to hold Djeneba hostage.

"You silly boy, what I want is what you already have. What you waste helping the people who deserve to die." Malik looks on with concerned and confused eyes. Rochambeau responds by nodding his head and chuckling. "Oui, that's right. Just remember one thing, boy, Nous contrôlons le destin des hommes, car nous sommes une (We control the destiny of men, for we are...) Malik's eyes widen and his gasp opens. Then his eyebrows turn downward as his resolve concludes the realization.

"You are part of the Elite 8... you bastard."

"Heh heh, you're one to talk... Malik Wilson... or should I say Marshall Benson... or that ridiculous name of Shadowmoor." Rochambeau pushes Djeneba down to the ground ahead of him. He aims his gun at Djeneba and reloads his gun. Mamadou struggles to get up and runs as fast as he can. Djeneba begins to shed tears as she shivers, shaking her head no as Rochambeau points his gun. As Rochambeau squeezes the trigger, he whispers underneath his breath, "Au Revoir..."

The bullet shoots out of the chamber. Everything moves in slow motion, and Djeneba begins to yell. Then suddenly, a body jumps in front of the bullet, then collapses on the ground. The shock of the moment brings out an eruption from Malik's body. However, instead of flames, a white mist brightens the sky and a howl echoes across the village.

The spirit of the White Fox emerges and focuses his sights on Rochambeau. While Rochambeau tries to fire at the Fox, the bullets fly right through the entity. Malik collapses to the ground while witnessing the White Fox corner the Frenchman while Djeneba desperately tries to stop the bleeding.

"Father. FATHER! PLEASE DON'T DIE!" Djeneba screams as Mamadou goes in and out of consciousness. Rochambeau tries to run, but the mist of the White Fox corners the man. Rochambeau is shaken and pleads with the spirit.

"Please, PLEASE! LET ME GO!" Undeterred and uncompromising, the White Fox darkens its eyes, opens its mouth, and shows its teeth. Malik runs to aid Djeneba as they all watch from a few yards away. The Fox lunges forward at a yelling Rochambeau, engulfs him, then silences the yells with a few crunches. Mamadou leans up and smiles. Then he whispers, "It… (cough, cough) is true… The White Fox has chosen…"

The White Fox then looks at the trio. The godly entity lets off a howl with a stream of white energy, then allows it to flow through Mamadou. The stream removes the bullet, cleans the bleeding, and heals his wound. Afterwards, the Fox disappears into the air, letting off one final howl.

Djeneba and Malik look at Mamadou as he slowly regains his strength. Djeneba sheds tears of joy and hugs her father. Then she looks at Malik, sniffs her nose, and smiles.

"I.... thank you, cousin from across the sea."

"No…" Mamadou interrupts weakly. He grabs Malik's arm, looks at Malik, and smiles. "We thank you, my nephew. Tell your grandfather… that I am sorry… and I wish to see him again." Malik nods, sheds a tear, and smiles as the rest of the village gathers around to show their gratitude to the Dogon who came home.

# Chapter 33: Full Circle

The next morning, Malik packs his backpack, puts on his spare clothes, and walks out of his hut. The sun is shining, the birds are chirping, and the villagers begin their usual rituals for the day. Malik takes another look around the village as peace has been restored and the Dogon continues to contribute to the stream of time. Malik smiles, turns around, and heads towards the edge of the village.

Before he passes through the last hut, a familiar voice echoes from the back of his head towards the cliffs. "You are not going to leave without saying goodbye, are you, Malik Wilson?" Malik turns around and smiles. Djeneba clasps her hands together and stares.
"How is he?" Malik asks.
"Despite the healing, father is still resting. The experience took a toll on him."
"I see. (Sigh) I… really don't know what to say."
"You don't have to save anything, Malik. You have saved us, our way of life, and my father. You have also received grace from the White Fox. Truly, you have fulfilled the prophecy given to your grandfather."
"Not yet, I still need to figure out one more thing. It told me to go to the land of my other ancestors. I have so many and yet I still don't know what the Fox means."

Djeneba looks away for a moment to think. Malik squints his eyes with anticipation as Djeneba takes a breath. "Long ago, some of our people joined several tribes to seek out a land that is always green, but it was across a narrow seaway. However, once they crossed, they would have to fight strange men in order to live in peace."
"What is this land?"
"The elders called it the land of Vandals."
"Vandals…" Malik takes a moment to ponder. When he realizes where he needs to go, his eyes widen, and he looks at Djeneba. "I know where I need to go," Malik yells. "I have to go." Djeneba walks up to Malik and points behind him. Malik turns around and sees another familiar face. Malik shakes his head and smiles as the man addresses him.

"I told you, Bozo will always help a Dogon," Adama says.
"Well, you sure are helping me make this trip quicker. Thank you."

"Well, what are you waiting for! Give the girl a hug then get on the plane!"

Malik looks at Djeneba's wet, soft eyes. A single tear rushes down her cheek as she embraces Malik in a long, tight hug. "We will never forget you, Malik Wilson," she says. "Do not forget about us. Where you come from, and how you face the future."
"Never," Malik says softly. "You're family, and for the first time in my life, I fill whole." After the hug, Malik walks with Adama towards a rough patch in the outskirts of the village. Malik and Adama board the plane as Djeneba watch them. Once Malik and Adama buckle up, Malik once again gets nervous.

"Are you sure that we have enough runaway to take off?"
"You worry too much, my boy," Adama responds sarcastically. "You Americans can be so unsure of yourselves."

Adama turns on the engines and allows the plane to roar. Malik puts on his headphones, glances out the window and looks at Djeneba. He gives out one last wave while Djeneba gives a teary farewell. After the tense moment of departure, Adama moves the plane eastward, gains airspeed, and takes off.

After a few minutes of reaching cruising altitude, Malik leans back and rests on his laurels. The past two days has pushed him even farther than the 10 trials to gain the Invisible Ember. Still, Adama briefly glances at him and smiles.

"Seems like your experience made you speechless," Adama starts. "What happened?"
Malik sits up on his chair and engages the conversation.
"So much has happened. I'm not sure that you can handle all of that."
Adama begins to chuckle as he steers his plane. "Ha ha ha… handle what? The fact that you visit the old fox god? Or that Jean is dead?"
Malik squints his eyes, turns his head towards Adama, then raises his left eyebrow. "Or… what about the fact you are trying to unravel the trail left by your powerful ancestors?"

Malik hesitates for a moment. He is faced with unleashing his knowledge of the events with a stranger while acknowledging that this man may be a friend. In the end, the willingness to unload the burden was too much to resist, and Malik complies with his heart.

"(Sigh) Who are you… exactly? Malik inquires. My grandmother vouches for you. How much do you really know?"
"Heh heh heh, have you learned nothing? The world is bigger than you, boy. As I told you before, Bozo will always help a Dogon. So, the fact that your uncle, cousin, and even the Hogon being your… you are Dogon as well."
"Yes, I am tracing my mother's lineage."
"That is good to know where you come from to know where to go."
"Yes, and as soon as I get back to the hotel, I need to book a flight for the morning," Malik concludes. "Still, the fact that Jean almost…"
"Jean has always been a shady man, and such men you have to keep your distance. I purposely came once the Sigi would be over so that I could help you conserve your strength for the journey to come."
"Well, I thank you again, Adama." Adama nods as he continues to navigate back to Bamako.
A few hours later, Adama reaches his airstrip and lands the plane. Despite being early afternoon, the journey felt like an eternity as Malik waited for the engines to completely shut off. Meanwhile, something buzzes and vibrates in his pocket. Malik reaches for his pocket and looks at his phone. Now having service, he sees several messages and missed calls. Adama looks at Malik, chuckles, and smiles. "You would be wise to call that person back, and please don't be shy. Put it on speaker," Adama advises.
"Ooooookay…" Malik responds suspiciously. Malik dials the number, puts the phone on speaker, and holds it in his left hand. RING RING RI…
"Malik, Malik!"
"Hey grandma, I'm back."
"Are you alright, my Amir? I was so worried," Geneva responds.
"Don't worry, your grandson is a strong, intelligent, and fine young man," Adama interjects while he blinks at a still suspicious Malik.
"Ugh, you can be such a nonchalant little brother!"
"Little brother! Adama!" Malik yells in shock.
"Well, of course," Adama responds. "I told you I grew up with three sisters. Geneva just happens to be one of my sisters." Malik slaps his right hand to his face, leans down, and shakes his head in utter embarrassment.

"I should've known… the special contact, wanting the phone to be on speaker…"

Suddenly, another voice from the phone's background enters the conversation.

"Malik, my boy, are you alright?"

"Yes, Granddad, and there is something I wanted to tell you."

"What is it, Malik?" Kemba asks.

"I… I met your brother… and your dad. They were… hard on me at first, especially your brother. He thought that you ran away from your responsibilities."

Kemba hesitates. He takes a deep breath and sighs before answering.

"Malik… I… it is really complicated."

"I know, granddad. I was chosen to participate in the Sigi."

"How… did you…"

"I met the Hogon," Malik interrupts. "Your dad, my great grandfather. And I also met the White Fox. He told me about the vision he gave you, as well as giving me a vision. It wasn't just for the fate of the tribe, but for our people in general."

"(Sigh) We're so sorry, Malik," Geneva chimes in. "We left Mali not only because of your grandfather's vision, but my…"

"I know that grandma. Matter of fact, the White Fox took care of the guy who was hunting you down. Which reminds me, tell Granddad that Mamadou says he's sorry and… he wants to see him soon."

Everyone remains silent for a few, tense moments to allow the conversation to resonate within each party. Adama looks at Malik, gives a small smirk and nods. Malik looks at his phone and awaits a response from his grandparents while his grandparents remain silent. Then Adama breaks the monotony by opening his mouth.

"You should be proud, Kemba and Geneva," Adama compliments. "I have lived a long time. I have seen the good. I have seen the bad. But for the first time in my life, I can see hope and I can see the future. Truly, our ancestors have blessed you with the man I am sitting right next to." Malik shockingly looks up and faces Adama. Adama squints his eyes, nods, and smiles.

"Thank you, Adama," Geneva says. "As for you, Malik, I still haven't heard from your sister yet. So, do not worry us by not checking in, OK? I sense that your journey isn't quite done yet."

"No grandma, it isn't."

"Where are you planning on going next?" Kemba asks.

"The White Fox told me go to the place where my other ancestors reside. Your niece also told me of a story that helped me figure out where to go. In the next day or so, I'm going to Spain."

"I see," Kemba responds. "We love you, Malik. Please keep us informed."

"I will, and I love you too."

Malik hangs up the phone and takes a deep breath. Then he begins to gather his things and gets out of the plane. Adama gets out as well and escorts Malik out of the airstrip. "So, (Uncle) Adama, I guess this is where we part ways," Malik says.

"Nonsense, my boy," Adama responds. "I will drive you to the hotel. It is good to spend as much time with family as we are still here."

"Again, I want to thank you for your help."

"Come," Adama instructs, "let me take you to my car." Afterwards, Malik and Adama walk towards the parking lot to find Adama's car.

In London, another woman walks through the door. She is wearing a black dress with red 4-inch pumps and a red sash. She sees Goth sitting on a chair overseeing the Thames River. He is smoking a large cigar while twirling his glass of liquor. She slowly walks to him and stands on his right.

For a few seconds, Goth continues to smoke his cigar and sip his drink. After making the young lady patiently wait, he breaks the silence with his low tone voice.

"What do you have to report?"

"There's a man on the line. He has a French accent and sounds frantic," she responds. Goth remains sophisticated and stoic. He doesn't show any physical signs of stress, anger, or concern. He simply smiles, takes one more puff of smoke, then looks at the woman.

"Would you be so kind as to bring me the cordless phone, please?"

"Yes, sir."

"That's my girl."

The woman walks towards his desk to grab the phone. Meanwhile, Goth continues to look at the window. A few moments later, the woman hands Goth the phone. "Here you go, Mr. Goth."

"Thank you, sweetheart. Now go on and scurry your fine ass out of here," Goth commands. The woman gives a half-hearted, nervous smile, nods her head, and heads out of the office.

Goth crosses his legs and puts his drink down on the armrest cup holder. He grabs the phone and puts it against his ear. "So, tell me, what is the meaning of this call?"

"Monsieur Goth, the Black man was too powerful. He took out almost our whole unit," a man answers.

"And Jean? What happened to him?"

"Well, he died. Or rather I think that's what happened."

Goth suddenly stands up from his chair and begins to walk around. He puts the cigar on an ashtray and runs his hand through his hair. Then he takes a deep breath and re-engages the conversation. "I see. Well, that's unfortunate. Do you know where he was planning on going next?"

"Before I snuck away, I overheard him saying the White Fox told him to go to the place of his other ancestors. Then a local conveyed a story about crossing a narrow sea to a land of green, inhabited by…Vandals."

"Hmmm…Poetic Irony. So, he's heading back to where it all started. Ok, thank you for your report. I will keep in contact."

"Yes, sir. Au revoir Monsieur Goth." Goth hangs up the phone, then walks towards his desk. He slams the phone down and looks down. He tries to keep his composure while plotting his next move.

A few moments later, a man wearing a black suit, white shirt, and black-tie knocks on the door. KNOCK KNOCK KNOCK. Goth quickly fixes himself up, clears his throat, and waves his hand, prompting the man to enter. "Mr. Goth," the man addresses.

"Call our contacts in Mali and take care of our loose end."

"I don't understand, sir."

"I don't like losers, and I despise cowards even worse. The idiot who just infected my phone with his incompetence needs to learn how making me upset has consequences."

 "Understood, sir."

"And one last thing."

"Yes, sir."

"I'm feeling Flamenco music and a bullfight. Prepare to book a flight."

"At once, sir."

The man nods and walks out of the office. Goth walks back to his burning ashtray and drinks. He continues to watch the window, as the sun begins to set on the river. "All of the pieces are in place, despite these setbacks," Goth concludes while taking another sip of his liquor. "Now Shadowmoor, let's see if years of planning will lead you to my sword… heh heh heh…" Afterwards, Goth embraces the transition to another night and the end of another day.

# Chapter 34: Spirit of Rebellion

Emma wakes up in her bed. She looks at the ceiling for a while, clasping her hands together as she experiences a new sense of wholeness. After a few moments of embracing the level of peace, she maneuvers her body to sit on the edge. "I have never felt this level of peace before," Emma contemplates. "It's like I can light up in a split second, but it's no longer fueled with rage and discontent…"

Suddenly, a knock interrupts her thought process. "Hello. Can I come in?" the voice asks.

"Go ahead. I think it's open." With a couple of twists, the door opens, revealing a surprising yet welcomed guest. The man pulls up a chair and sits right in front of Emma. Emma looks up and begins to smile a little as the man returns the gesture.

"Good morning, Mason," Emma welcomes.

"Hey Emma. I just wanted to check up on you to see how you are feeling."

"Well, I actually feel at peace. I mean, it's kinda hard to explain."

"No worries, young lady," Mason reassures. "You did well facing your inner demons. Most people don't achieve what you achieved. I'm proud of you."

Emma rubs her left arm and blushes. Then she turns her attention back to Mason.

"Thank you," she says, "that means a lot. Speaking of which, what are you doing here? I thought you were with the FBI?"

"Yeah, about that…" Mason responds while adjusting his chair and shifting his body directly towards Emma. "Emma, I was close to retirement when I first met your brother. However, that night you two stopped the Elite 8's operation, I knew that my time in the FBI was over."

"Over?" Emma exclaims. "But how did we…"

"Understand something. What you did was remarkable. However, I knew that my ties to the government would not allow me to be a better service to my people. As you may already know, there is only so much the government will overlook until they took certain events seriously. Had I stayed, I would be hunting you and your brother."

"But I don't get it. We stopped the kidnappings. We saved those girls lives. We…"

"Stopped a lot of people, corrupt people even working in our government from profiting from the illegal activities," Mason interrupts. "The reason I took the case was because I wanted to see how deep the corruption went, even in the Atlanta Law Enforcement. Then when the reports of the Shadowmoor kept arising, it led me to some deep, disturbing things; however, it also led me to your brother. To you."

Emma sits and looks down for a while to take in the amount of information presented. Her shoulders relax and her mind becomes colluded with questions. Finally, Emma allows herself to speak her mind.

"Mason, is that why you got with OBR? Are you really that committed to helping our people?"

Mason pauses for a minute. He then sighs, crosses his arms, then closes his eyes. His body becomes tense, his demeanor changes, and his voice gets deeper. "Emma, I was born in Chicago. My father and mother were members of the Black Panther Party, and even though I was young, I can still remember the lessons my father taught me about the love of the people as well as the love of yourself. However, in 1969, one of my father's best friends and regional leader was assassinated by the police. He retaliated and was put in prison for life for fighting the police. Afterwards, my mother took me and my sister, moved us to New Mexico to get off the radar of the government."

"Wow. So… why did you get into the same organization that put your dad in prison."

"(Sigh) When I was about 17 years old, my father mysteriously died in prison and my mother fell into a deep depression. I wanted to change the system and I thought that if I went to school, earn my bachelor's and master's, then I could make a difference within the system. (Mason shakes his head and smiles) How naive was I…"

Emma sits up straight and crosses her legs and ankles to get comfortable on the bed. Despite not having her eyes activated, she can sense the level of shame and regret in Mason's voice, posture, and breathing. Emma thinks with prudence before asking the next question.

"Mason, why are you so sad? I mean, I think you are an honest and honorable man."

Mason sniffs his nose, nods, and smiles. "Emma, when you graduate from college, mind you the first in your family, there is a level of capitulation that you have to exhibit to get to where you want to go. For me, there were times I had to persecute and oppress my own people in order to serve the United States. To come from a lineage of Black Panthers to serving the bureau that illegally dismantled them really ate away at my initial goals and ambitions."

Afterwards, Mason gets up, pats Emma on the shoulder, then begins to walk out of the room. Before Mason reaches the door, Emma calls out to Mason.

"Hey Mason, what made you change your mind? What gave you hope again to join OBR?"

Mason lowers his head a bit, and without hesitation turns his head around. "Your brother… and you. Believe it or not, when I first begin to investigate your brother's activities, I was prompted to stop him. However, when I saw how many girls he'd saved and the events of that night, it reminded me of myself at your age. At that moment I knew it was my responsibility to pass the torch of resistance to the younger generation." Emma smiles without showing her teeth and nods. Mason nods back, then exits the room.

Meanwhile, in the other side of the base, D'Shawn is sharping his tomahawk and cleaning his equipment. Then a small series of knocks interrupt his activity. D'Shawn looks back and answers the knocks.

"Come on in, the door is open." he commands. Asir walks through the door. He's more comfortable, more resolved, and more confident. He approaches his father and stands in front of him. "Asir, how was your night? Did you sleep well?"

"Yeah, I'm starting to like it here. It's better than school, but…" Asir hesitates for a second before finishing his thought. "I… I miss Mom and Grammy. Will I see them again?"

D'Shawn puts his tomahawk down and focuses his attention to Asir. He puts his hand on Asir's left shoulder and smiles. "I know you miss your mom and grandmother. I promise you; I will take you home when the time is right."

"What is it that you do here?" Asir abruptly asks. "Why do you fight? Why do we fight? Why do we have these powers?"

D'Shawn lowers his head for a moment to think. He lets go of Asir's shoulder and crosses his arms. Asir looks at his father with concern and anticipation. His eyes are focused, his face is still, and his body tightens up. Eventually after a few tense seconds, D'Shawn lets off a sigh and looks back at Asir.

"Son, I need you to follow me. I'll have to show you before I can tell you." Asir says nothing as D'Shawn directs his hand towards the middle of the room. Asir looks at D'Shawn as he nods and smiles. Asir reciprocates by arching the left side of his lip, then walks towards the middle of the room. "Ok, Asir, now sit down right here." Still confused, Asir reluctantly and slowly sits on the floor. He crosses his ankles and legs as D'Shawn sits down in front of him.

"Asir, do you remember how you connected with our ancestors?" "Yeah, I had to sit down like this, close my eyes, breathe, then activate my glowing eyes. Then I started seeing these visions."
"Right. You asked me why I fight. I am going to put up my hand. I need you to place your hand on mine, OK?"
"What will that do?"
"You will have to trust me, son."

Asir begins to shake. He is apprehensive in coming out of his comfort zone. D'Shawn senses this but says nothing. He puts his hand out and waits for Asir to follow his instructions. Asir looks down for a second to gather the nerve. Slowly, he raises his right hand. D'Shawn smiles and nods, encouraging Asir to touch his hand. With each push, each inch, each moment his hand gets closer, Asir shakes more and more. His eyes become glossy, his breath becomes still, and his whole body becomes unstable.

However, once Asir's hand meets his dad's, he is overcome with calm and peace. The shaking stops, he is still, and his eyes close. D'Shawn then instructs Asir to follow his lead.

"That's it," he says softly. "Now take a breath the same time as me. Feel my rhythm and keep your eyes closed." Both father and son synchronize their heartbeat and breath. As they come as one, the room becomes dark, a gust of wind swarms around them, and the beat from their bodies begins to light up.

After two minutes, a circle of flames form around them. Their bodies absorb the flames, and both eyes activate the Dracocernentia. Asir begins to get overwhelmed with the surge of power and starts to get up. D'Shawn stops him by continuing to instruct him. "Don't get up! Allow the power to flow within you. Let the members of your Fire Line answer the questions you seek, Asir." Asir musters up the courage to sit down and take in the power. Then, as the flames around them form an array of rainbow colors of fire, Asir lets off a yell as the Dracocernentia send Asir within the confines of his own mind and lineage. Asir sees flashes of light and energy. Although he is aware of the transition, he is unable to speak or comprehend the events unfolding. Then he hears the voices while his eyes continue to see deep in his past.

"Do not be afraid," the voices echo. "We are those who came before you. We will take you back to the boy you know. The boy you have experienced…"

"Ch... Ch... Chittoluthphwa," Asir concludes.

"He is now a young man. You will see a point in history where a choice was made, to fight or to die," the voices conclude. "Then, you will understand why the questions that now plague your mind, are engrained in your blood and Fire Line." After the eerie voices disappear, so do the flashing lights. Then Asir can see from the eyes of his long-deceased ancestor.

The year is 1835. Chittoluthphwa is standing on a tree overseeing the swampy horizon. His eyes, fully activated with two sets of micro claws around his sharp pupil, see the array of lights, colors, and receptors of living things. His eyes scrunch and his demeanor changes. A flock of birds begin to fly west as a familiar snarl temporarily breaks his concentration. Below him is a black wolf, weighing about ninety pounds with a grey patch underneath his right eye. He looks up calling out to Chittoluthphwa with a series of snarls and pseudo-barks. Chittoluthphwa jumps down from the branch of the tree and lands right in front of the wolf. The wolf embraces his comrade, licks him, then redirects his focus north with the same snarls. Chittoluthphwa looks at the same direction while trying to make sense of the disturbance.

"You sense it too, don't you, Huncelahtotika (Hard Fire)?" Chittoluthphwa says. "A disturbance with our mother (And the people). Come, let us return to the village." Chittoluthphwa pets Huncelahtotika and prompts the wolf to follow him back to village. "Come, boy. I'll race you." The stunning black wolf looks at Chittoluthphwa as he smiles. After a moment of silence, Chittoluthphwa yells, "GO!"

Both accelerate through the brush. Chittoluthphwa jumps and skips through branches as elusive as a squirrel. Meanwhile, Huncelahtotika races through the forest floor like an obstacle course. Each running so fast and so elusive that by the time they reach the edge of the village, both make it at the same time.

Chittoluthphwa crouches down to one knee while catching his breath. Huncelahtotika looks at him and starts to pant. Chittoluthphwa smiles while rubbing the wolf's head. "You are a quick and bold one, the fire on dry grass," he compliments before looking the other direction. Chittoluthphwa looks up as a group of Seminole Chiefs chorale around a white man. "Something does not seem right," Chittoluthphwa suspects. "Stay here, my friend. I will return." Chittoluthphwa makes his way to the leaders while Huncelahtotika lays down on the wet ground.

The leaders of the tribes surround this white man: about 5'9" tall, with a blue hat, brown mustache, and a white horse. He is a crafty but shrewd man who lays out the proposals of the United States. "Here me now, ol' great chiefs. Our president has issued a decree that you must leave these lands at once," he says, "and in exchange, you will be awarded lands west of the Mississippi." Many of the chiefs' grumble and converse amongst themselves until one in particular addresses the man. He is a fair, light brown skinned man with jet black hair but with a commanding loud voice.

"How can you tell a people who make this land their home to leave? You cannot make the trees move, nor the gators in the water or the bird in the sky. Your words, Wiley Thompson, poison my words with sadness, hunger, and death."
"Osceola, please," another Seminole interjects, "we must do what is right for the people!"
"Charlie is right," Wiley adds. "This is in the best interest for you people. Please take this opportunity."

Wiley mounts his horse as some of the other chiefs continue to contemplate the terms. Osceola burns with irritation. His eyes become red and his fists ball. As Charlie tries to console Osceola, Osceola shrugs his shoulder and walks away.

Chittoluthphwa sees Osceola walk away and slowly tries to intersect the disgruntled man. Feeling the anger and frustration, he cautiously asks the man the issue.

"What is going on?" Chittoluthphwa asks.

"This white man wants us to leave our home, so that his kind can take over the land we love. I do not trust these white men or their empty lies."

"I understand," Chittoluthphwa responds. "When I was a boy, my mother would tell me stories of how the white men would place people in chains, whip them, and take away their freedom. Then I saw these same white men murder my mother when she wouldn't go back to slavery and wipe out my village." Osceola calms down to take in the gravity of Chittoluthphwa's confession. Osceola places his hand on Chittoluthphwa's shoulder. His face softens, his eyes become wet with empathy, and his attitude changes.

"What is your name, friend?" Osceola asks.

"Chittoluthphwa."

"Hmmm...I hope to see you again, Chittoluthphwa. It seems that your mother gave you the wisdom to appreciate freedom. I sense in you a fire that cannot be put out." Chittoluthphwa nods as Osceola walks away. Chittoluthphwa watches Osceola walk away while he thinks to himself. "That is the kind the man I would follow to the end of the land for." Afterwards, Chittoluthphwa notices that only one Seminole is left with Wiley Thompson. "Why is he still with that white man?" Chittoluthphwa wonders.

Wiley and the Seminole walk at the edge of the village into a thicket of shrubs, trees, and bushes. Chittoluthphwa follows them quietly, making sure they don't see him. As he hides in the bushes, he activates his Dracocernentia, attunes his senses, and overhears the conversation between Wiley and the lone Seminole. Wiley gets off his horse, ties it to a low hanging branch, and focuses his attention to the Seminole.

      "Charlie, I am trying to help your people," Wiley pleads. "But Osceola will stir a rebellion you will not win."

"Wiley Thompson, Osceola loves his people."

"As do you, my friend, but surely you must know how this will end if you don't move."

"Yes, but I don't want to move either." Wiley puts his hands on his waist. He takes off his hat, wipes his forehead, and struggles to find the words necessary to convince Charlie. Meanwhile, Chittoluthphwa notices the receptors in both Wiley and Charlie.

"I see deceit and false words in Wiley Thompson," Chittoluthphwa deduces. "However, Charlie seems like all he wants is peace. I must continue to watch."

      Afterwards, Wiley Thompson goes to a pocket in the horse's saddle. He pulls out a large wad of money and presents it Charlie. "Charlie, I want you to have this," Wiley says. "If you leave now, you will be able to own land of your own, make money, and be accepted into our society. If you don't, you will die with the rest of those who won't. Also, take this money to convince the other chiefs to leave without bloodshed." Charlie stands in front of Wiley as he hands out the money. He begins to reach his hand then hesitates. He closes his eyes, sheds a tear, then wipes it away with his other hand. Wiley continues to prompt Charlie to take the money. After a few seconds of internal battling, Charlie extends his arm, reaches for the money, and slowly takes it. Wiley smiles and gets back on his horse. "Trust me, my friend, this is the only way." Wiley Thompson unties his horse, mounts it, then rides back to the fort. Charlie is left standing there trying to make sense of his shame. While he looks at the money, he puts it in one of his small bags then walks back to the village. Chittoluthphwa remains hidden until Charlie walks by.

"Osceola must be told." Afterwards, Chittoluthphwa emerges from the thicket and makes his way to the village.

# Chapter 35: The Price of Freedom

The night is filled with complete darkness, covered by the swamps and trees that blanket the land. The only light is emulated by a fire in the center of a circle. A group of Seminoles and Black freedmen congregate together while a fiery Osceola states his grievances.

"The white men are here to take our homes, wives, and children," Osceola roars. "He also says that our brothers should return to their masters, for they are not with us!" Many people roar and yell in discontent, especially the Black people, many of them were never enslaved but know how they could easily be taken back. One Black man arose and spoke.

"My pa told me how they used to whip him until his back became red and wet. I will not go, and I will stand and fight!"

"We will not allow the white man to take you, my friend," Osceola responds. "AND WE WILL NOT LEAVE OUR LANDS!"

The people begin to chant and roar by the fire. Each member becomes fueled with the seeds of rebellion and the will to fight. Then, Chittoluthphwa walks in with Huncelahtotika as Osceola turns around. Boldly, Chittoluthphwa walks towards Osceola and tells him the news.

"There is a chief who means to sell us to the white man with his money," Chittoluthphwa proclaims. "If we don't, the white men will come in and kill us for our land." The people stop chanting and begin to murmur amongst themselves. Osceola tilts his head and looks at Chittoluthphwa with concern as well as suspicion.

"What is this you speak of," Osceola questions. "The one who means to sell us?"

"It is the one you call Charlie, great Osceola." Osceola looks down, avoiding contact while trying to grasp the weight of this reveal. Then Osceola redirects his eyes back to Chittoluthphwa.

"How can you be certain of this? Charlie is my friend, as are you."

"My name…"

"Yes, the one who sees like a snake."

"I have the power to see within a man without him speaking or acting."

"Are you some man sent by the Hitloschi Chilth-Keh? How do you know this?"

Chittoluthphwa closes his eyes and begins to slowly breathe. Everyone, including Osceola looks on, anticipating what he is going to do. The council fire dies down to a simmer. A tense moment of silence fills the air, until a gust of wind blows. As Chittoluthphwa takes one last breath, he opens his eyes, activates the Dracocernentia, and the fire in the pit flames up into bluish green flames. His eyes illuminate so brightly, there is a collective gasp around the fire. Osceola stands in amazement and gives a slight smile.

"As your name's sake, you speak true," Osceola compliments. "I will round up the warriors to make it right for our people." Osceola slowly walks towards Chittoluthphwa and places his hand on Chittoluthphwa while he deactivates the Dracocernentia. The flames turn back to their orange color, and the rest of the people gather around to mobilize for the rebellion. "I will be honored if you were at my side for this fight," Osceola extends. Chittoluthphwa nods as the men in the council, Seminole and Black alike, grab their guns.

It is the morning of October 26. It has been two weeks since the meeting with the agent and the council. Osceola hides a group of fifty individuals in the brush. Meanwhile, Chittoluthphwa is mounted on a high tree branch as he uses the Dracocernentia to look over the horizon. Despite the thickness of the swamp, the power of the Dracocernentia and the warm weather allow Chittoluthphwa to magnify his vision: able to detect a grain of sand from the back of an ant to seeing receptors of any approaching person.

Moments later, Chittoluthphwa raises his left arm, signaling Osceola and his men that someone is coming. A lone Seminole is riding a small carriage, heading north along the road. He is inconspicuous to the Seminoles that surround him. The receptor fields flow with purple, yellow, and green, as Chittoluthphwa recognizes the identity of the Seminole. It is a heartfelt moment; he closes his eyes, nods his head, then faces Osceola.

Osceola nods back in response, signals his party, and waits for the Seminole to come into range. The Seminole continues to trek along the road, coming closer and closer to Osceola.

Suddenly, Osceola rises from the sea of grass. He clicks his rifle and makes eye contact with the Seminole. Before the Seminole can react, he faces the man he once called friend. In a split second, both shed a small tear, as the pop of the musket ball explodes out of the chamber. The shot hits the Seminole in the head, and he falls off the carriage, spooking the horse to run out of the way. Chittoluthphwa scales down the tree and walks towards the lifeless corpse. Osceola and his warriors go towards the body. The Seminole is carrying a bag around his neck. When Osceola removes his bag and examines it, the worse was confirmed. Chittoluthphwa walks next to Osceola as he sobs.

"Your words, and your eyes are true," Osceola whimpers as he dumps the money on the dead body. "Charlie was indeed my friend. But I will not sacrifice my people for the life of one man."

"I'm… I'm… sorry," Chittoluthphwa says.

Osceola smiles and pats Chittoluthphwa on the shoulder. "You were true to your word. Those who would betray our people will suffer many deaths. But there is more to come." The rest of the party begin to move out while Chittoluthphwa looks at the dead body covered with worthless paper. Then Chittoluthphwa addresses Osceola one last time before Osceola walks too far.

"Is this why we fight, my leader?" Chittoluthphwa asks, prompting Osceola to stop and address Chittoluthphwa. Osceola's face is focused, smooth, and uncompromising. He walks back to Chittoluthphwa and speaks with a heavy heart.

"I know many stories like you, Snake Eyes. The white men would kill our men, women, children… or sell them to slavery," Osceola says as he looks down at Charlie. "When you take gifts from wicked men, you become corrupt and live in the white man's lies." Chittoluthphwa takes one last look at the body, then takes a deep breath. Osceola concludes with lasting words. "We fight for our truth. The truth is we belong here, not the white man. We will fight and die for our people, our women, our children...our freedom. That is the only way to live… warrior with snake eyes." Osceola smiles, then walks to catch up with his war party. Chittoluthphwa looks on with a new sense of realization and purpose. Afterwards, several flashing lights take Asir and D'Shawn away from the genetic memories as they wake up in the present plane.

Asir slowly removes his hand from his dad. Asir is sweating hard and breathing like he had been holding his breath for a century. D'Shawn slowly gets up while wiping his forehead.

"The people who did that to your great-great-great-great-grandfather, Asir," D'Shawn says as Asir looks up to him, "are the same people who kidnapped you and put you in that cell. They are the same people who poison the water in Black communities, rob them of jobs and opportunities, and then incarcerate you for failing the same system they built specifically to break Black people."

Asir looks down while his father continues to look on with sad eyes. Then Asir slowly gets up and addresses his father. "I think I understand now. We fight for our right to live in our truth," Asir responds, "and our truth is, we don't deserve to be treated like animals."

D'Shawn smiles and pats Asir on the shoulder. No, we do not."

Suddenly, there is a knock on the door. D'Shawn looks up and addresses the knocking. "It's open!" The door slowly opens and a man wearing BDU pants, a black bulletproof vest, and black gloves informs D'Shawn.

"Excuse me, Snake Sight, the mentor is preparing our next operation. You're needed in the conference room."

"I'll be right there," D'Shawn responds. "Asir, I need you to stay in here. I'll be right back."

"Sure, do you want me to draw you a picture?"

"That would be wonderful. I'll be right back." D'Shawn walks out of the room while Asir looks for a sheet of paper and pencil to draw.

Moments later, D'Shawn walks in the conference room with Emma and Mason. Two squad members of OBR, consisting of ten young, energetic, and frustrated men, also join in the conference, led by their squad leaders Black Mamba and King Cobra. Black Mamba is slender, tall with a short afro, glasses, and a thin beard. King Cobra is shorter, with a wavy taper fade, and looks young for his age. However, his demeanor is as stout as a grizzly bear, and he has the eyes of a ferocious lion looking to make a name for himself. Both order their squads to salute while D'Shawn returns the gesture.

Emma addresses D'Shawn after he acknowledges his men. "How's Asir?"

"Well, we just… had some quality father and son time," D'Shawn answers before hearing Mason clear his throat. Emma and D'Shawn focus their attention to Mason as he points out plans on the desk.

"We already know that W.A.V.E. is planning on moving their operations to another part of town to better secure their facilities. They will assist the need of police, about twenty officers, potentially SWAT," Mason presses. "However, the boys that they kidnapped are still inside the building and need to be free. So, in order to prevent friendly fire on them, we need to engage the police surrounding the building."

"How are we going to take care of the police without shooting them?" one of the men asks.

D'Shawn clears his throat and explains the plan. "I will lead the assault by creating a fire wave. It will be strong enough not to burn the police, but the intense heat will dehydrate them enough to temporarily knock them unconscious. A squadron of men under my command will wear their FRCs and masks as they follow me through the door. Based on the intel that we gathered we will distract the Elite 8 mercenaries that are temporarily immune to the Reintergon and the Maniacine. These people will be super strong but will not have the stamina for a long fight."

Emma interjects while she moves towards the table. "Even with all of that, you can't be sure that they won't use some back entrance to move the boys!"

"You're right," Mason agrees. "That's where you come in. I know that Sharon will, in some way, direct the evacuation. You need to go in and engage her."

"Oh good, I'm ready for a rematch with that bitch!"

"I understand," D'Shawn says. "But remember that the boys are our number one priority. Don't lose sight of that."

Then a crackling, maturing voice yells as he busts through the closed door. "I want to fight too!" D'Shawn, Emma, and Mason turn around to see Asir holding a piece of paper.

"Asir, I told you to stay in the room," D'Shawn scolds. "This mission is too dangerous to…"

"I said I WANT TO FIGHT!" Asir yells as his Dracocernentia activates. His eyes generate two sets of micro claws around his pupil. D'Shawn immediately knows that with the formation of the micro claws, Asir's level of control is not accidental. Emma tries to talk Asir down to convince him of the severity of the mission.

"Asir, your father is right," Emma counsels. "You are still a boy. I know how powerful you are, but this is something that is not a game. You need to listen to us and stay here." Asir looks down and clenches both fists. He briefly closes his eyes, then opens them and looks directly in the eyes of D'Shawn, Mason, and Emma as he speaks.

"I can remember… being scared to go to school, making friends, and even bullies. Then, I got to meet you, Ms. Emma. I got to meet my dad. And I got to meet my ancestors. I saw that he saw his mother shot in front of him. When he was 12 like me, he fought an alligator and gained the power of the eyes. I'm not a little boy anymore. I know who I am." Asir looks at D'Shawn and continues. "I am his son." D'Shawn tries to maintain his composure and emotions as Asir continues to speak. "You were the first mentor I appreciated, Ms. Emma." Asir faces Mason. "I am the descendant of warriors who fought in battles when they were younger than I am. I am no longer a scared kid. I am the son of Chittoluthphwa. I am the son of Snake Sight." Asir's eyes glow so bright, they resemble fire. "I am a Dragon."

Asir slams his picture on the table for Mason to see. Mason, stunned by the resolve and conviction this boy has, slowly picks up the picture and looks at it. The picture has an artistic, detailed illustration of Asir, Emma, D'Shawn with a Red Fire Dragon, and a Blue Phoenix in the background. Then Mason looks at Asir. He looks at D'Shawn, then Emma, then the other members of OBR who are not only moved by Asir's words but gravitate around him. Mason closes his eyes and smiles, then he looks back at Asir.

"Imagine if old farts like me had the same kind of courage you have when I was your age, young man," Mason compliments. "As much as common sense dictates you stay behind, my common sense knows better than to cage a dragon. Sometimes, unleashing it is how we win."

A few members nod their heads while the remainder clap in response. "Alright, alright, gather around," Mason states. "Asir, you have an important job to do. Do you think you can do it?" Asir lights up his eyes and throws his fist in the air. Mason nods in response. "Alright," Mason reiterates, "this will be a difficult mission. After this mission, the BEA will certainly pass throughout the country and we as a race will be targeted. So, gather around… as we get ready for… Operation 1804!"

# Chapter 36: The Phoenix behind the Shadows

Malik wakes up early in his hotel room. The softness of the bed, the fresh smell of the sheets, and the cool room temperature provides an aphrodisiac that relieves the pain he endured during the Sigi. He quickly climbs out of bed and looks at his cell phone to confirm the time. Afterwards, he goes into the bathroom, brushes his teeth, and greases his hair. Then he takes out a blue t-shirt, boot cut jeans, and his Adidas NMDs.

While he gets dressed, he ponders on the journey and the enemy that has resurfaced. "So, it seems that the Elite 8 is back. I should've known such an organization wouldn't be down for long. It also seems that they could be after the sword as well. Which means I need to find it first." After a few minutes of freshening up, Malik packs the rest of his utensils and clothes in his suitcase, grabs his key and backpack, then walks out of the hotel room.

Once he shuts the door, he carries his belongings to the elevator. Malik pushes the down button and waits for the doors to open. While standing in front of the elevator, Malik checks his passport, tickets on his phone, and his account. "Ok, so my flight leaves at 11 A.M.," Malik whispers. "So, I have plenty of time to make it to the airport. I hope this will be my final stop. I'm starting to miss home."

Suddenly, the bell rings, the elevator door opens, and Malik brings his belongings with him. He pushes the button to go to the first floor, closes the door, and patiently waits to reach the bottom.

Once the elevator reaches the first floor, the door opens, and Malik makes his way towards the front desk. Kadiatou is performing her normal morning routine. However, she is wearing a different outfit: a black headscarf, white collar shirt, black skirt, and black flats. As usual, she smiles at Malik as he approaches the front desk.

"Morning," she greets. "Are you checking out?"
"Yes ma'am, I am," Malik responds as he hands her the key.
"Did you enjoy your stay?" she asks as she prints out the receipt.
"It's a trip that I will never forget. Bamako is a beautiful city."

"That it is," Kadiatou responds, then gives Malik a paper receipt. "Thank you for staying here and enjoy your flight back." Malik nods and smiles after he receives the receipt. He then turns around and heads out of the door.

Once he walks outside, he sees the same shuttle that brought him to the hotel just days before. The driver is still lively and talkative. When Malik loads his belongings in the shuttle, the driver sparks up another conversation.

"Good morning, American man," he greets. "Are we going to the airport?"

"Yes, sir," Malik says as he's sitting down.

"Very good." The driver shuts the door, shifts gears, and accelerates through the streets. As the man is driving, he continues to talk to Malik. "Did you enjoy the city?"

"Yes, I did, and now I'm ready to go home."

"Ah, home. I can understand that. Well, one day I would like to travel to America."

"Well, if you do, I promise you it will not be as hot as it is here," Malik says. The man chuckles as he continues to maneuver through the calm streets.

Fifteen minutes later, Malik makes it to the airport. He gets up, reaches for his wallet, and pulls out a franc. "Here you go," Malik says as he tips the driver.

"Thank you very much. Safe travels back home." Malik nods, then walks out of the shuttle. Malik slowly walks to the terminal as he keeps an eye on the shuttle. The driver puts the franc in his pocket, then drives off.

"I couldn't take any chances telling him too much," Malik thinks. "Now that I know the Elite 8 have bodies, I have to be more prudent in what I say."

Malik makes it to the counter of Royal Maroc and meets the receptionist. She is a white woman with blond hair, blue eyes, and a French accent. "Bonjour, how can I help you?"

"Yes, I have a flight, here is my confirmation," Malik says as he shows the number of his phone and his passport. She simultaneously looks at the confirmation while typing on the computer.

"Ah, Monsieur Malik Wilson, flight to Madrid. Oui, let me print out your ticket and grab your bag." Malik hands her his suitcase while keeping his backpack. "Merveilleuse (Wonderful), enjoy your flight," she says while handing him his ticket.
"Merci." Malik walks towards the security station.

After Malik goes through security, he walks to the section where he is scheduled to board his plane. He finds a seat, sits down, and takes his laptop out of his backpack. Once he logs in, he looks over the numbers and revenue from his online business. As he is looking, he notices the activity in PulseoftheStreet.org that is stirring concern.

"Seems the people are complaining about the uptick in police activity back home," Malik whispers. "This is odd. I wish I was back home to investigate it. However, I can't be in two places at once." While awaiting his flight, Malik continues to email and communicate with his moderators. He tries to distract himself with work to quench his impatience.

An hour later, a flight attendant makes an announcement that catches Malik's attention. "Good morning, passengers. The 11:00 flight to Madrid will soon be seating our travelers. Please have your tickets ready. Thank you." Malik takes the time to shut his laptop, put it in the back compartment of his backpack, zip it up, and stand up with his ticket. His eagerness to complete his journey is only amplified by a buzz in his pocket.

Many of the passengers begin to line up as Malik reaches inside of his pocket. He pushes the on button on his phone and examines the message.

*"Been thinking about you. Hope all is well 😨 "*
"It's Audrey," Malik realizes. "What should I text back?" As Malik gets closer towards the beginning of the line, he quickly responds with a short and direct message.

*"Thanks for checking up with me. I'm very close to finding the meaning of the picture. Will talk to you soon."* Malik looks up as the number of passengers ahead of him diminish. Each of them going through the motions of showing their boarding passes and passports. After a short while, another response buzzes through to Malik's cell phone. He quickly checks his messages.

"***Travel Safe XOXO***" Malik smirks a little as he places his phone back in his pocket.

Malik reaches the entrance of the boarding hall.

"Boarding pass please," the attendant requests. Malik cheerfully gives the woman the boarding pass. She examines it, then smiles back. "Enjoy your flight, sir." Malik nods then walks down the hallway towards the plane.

Malik quickly finds his seat next to the window. As usual, Malik stares at the horizon as he once again reflects on the journey that has brought him so far. "It was good to come here. To close the door of my mom's lineage, and to meet some of her relatives. However, Rochambeau's presence also means that the Elite 8 are still out there. I need to be more careful, especially once I land."

Like clockwork, another announcement interrupts Malik's concentration as the stewardess gives instructions to the passengers.

"Good morning, passengers, we thank you for flying with us today. We are nearly complete with our boarding and should be taking off pretty soon. The flight will be approximately eight hours. Please make sure your seatbelts are fastened and do not leave your seats until instructed to. There are four emergency doors pointed by each of the designated seats. The bathrooms are located at the back of the plane, and we will be offering snacks, drinks, and meals once we are safely in cruising altitudes. If you have any other questions, please let one of us know. Again, thank you for flying with us."

Malik takes his cue to shut the window, grab a blanket, and get comfortable. "Well, I know this will be a long flight. Might as well get a nap in." As Malik bundles himself, the surrounding doors begin to shut, the roar of the engines begin to rumble, and the plane begins to embark on another journey. Slowly, the plane reverses from its docking station and maneuvers towards the runway. A group of planes file in a single line as each waits for the other to take off. Malik continues to look on as his plane awaits its turn to take off. The subtle calm soothes the passengers while the pilot steers the plane towards the runway. Waiting for the last plane to fly out of reach, the pilot patiently waits for the plane to have a clear pathway.

After waiting for ninety seconds, the engines begin to amplify their sound. The crashing noise fills the plane, and the pilot quickly accelerates to flight speed. The plane races through the runway and begins to tilt upwards. Little by little, the angle reaches higher and higher, until the plane is completely off the ground and flying through the air. After fifteen minutes of gaining air speed and leveling off, the plane reaches cruising speed. At this point, Malik allows himself to lower his eyes, control his breathing, and fall asleep.

During his deep sleep, images begin to flood Malik's mind. A silhouette of Malik forms in the middle of a lighted stage. Malik looks around and tries to ascertain the meaning of the vision.

"This is strange," Malik whispers. "Normally something… or someone appears. But so far, it is nothing." Malik continues to walk around in the surrounding darkness, unable to pinpoint the meaning of this vision.

Suddenly, a burning sensation catches Malik's attention. He is drawn to it like a moth to a flame; slowly walking towards it without any regard to where or how he is getting there. As soon as he gets a closer look, the burning light takes the form of something Malik has been searching for: a large, golden Scimitar with the carving of the Dracocernentia on its base. Malik's eyes light up as he is paralyzed in awe of the spectacle.

"The Harq Alqadr!" Malik exclaims. "But how? Why?" Then, a vision appears, as a hand takes the sword and puts it in a castle. The hand disappears, but something comes out of the shadows. Malik squints his eyes as he tries to get a closer look. A series of beings begin to fly out and surround the castle. When Malik tries to move closer, one shadowy figure flies out of formation and towards Malik. The figure gets bigger and bigger and bigger. Standing his ground and expecting the worst, Malik activates his Dracocernentia. When the eyes illuminate, the shadowy figure responds by showcasing its dark, blue, fiery plumage, intimidating wings, and clear blue eyes. The magnificent bird continues to flap its wings and maintain eye contact with Malik. Malik soon realizes what the shadowy figures are that surround the castle. "It's a flock of phoenix," Malik deduces. "I bet that they are the ones who guard the sword and vet whoever tries to obtain it." After making the connection, the phoenix then lets off a huge screech. The noise is so distinct, so powerful, so regal, that Malik wakes up from his vision.

When Malik opens his eyes, he quickly looks at his phone and notices the time. He realizes that he has slept through the entire flight, as the stewardess makes another announcement. "Ladies and gentlemen, we are about to land in the next twenty minutes. If you have any trash or plates, please assist us in throwing it away as the stewardess will come by with a can. If you need to use the restroom, now is the time to do so. Afterwards, the lights will come on. Once the lights come on, seatbelts need to be fastened and no one is to get up. Again, thank you for flying with us." Malik yawns, stretches his arms, and folds his blanket. Afterwards, he puts the blanket underneath the seat, then he fastens his seatbelt.

The plane reaches the runway and lands. As the sea of air catches up to the plane, the pilot slows down after gaining traction and begins to steer the plane to the docking station. Malik patiently waits until the plane comes to a complete stop. Despite his sleep, he is still weary of all the travel and looks forward to completing his quest. "I'm ready to go home and sleep in my own bed. Well, it's almost over. I just need to follow the clues and find it."

After a few minutes, the plane stops and another announcement rings. "Ladies and gentlemen, you can now exit your seats and leave the plane. Make sure you take all your items out of the plane. We thank you once again for flying with us. Bienvenido a Madrid."

Malik grabs his backpack, gets up from his seat, and walks out of the plane. The trek down the exit is a long and gratifying one. The stiff muscles in his back and legs rejuvenate as he makes one long stride after another. Once he enters the airport, the traffic is just as busy as the one back home. Malik takes a deep breath, looks for the signs, and makes his way towards baggage claim.

Moments later, Malik makes it to baggage claim and waits for his suitcase. Meanwhile, Malik ponders on his course of action by rethinking his plans while in Madrid. "Because the Elite 8 may have operatives in disguise, I don't need to rent a car. Instead, I'll take a shuttle to the hotel. Afterwards, I'll stretch my legs and get a view of the city." Malik doesn't have to wait long until his suitcase comes up the belt and circles around towards him. Malik quickly grabs the suitcase and makes his way out of the hotel.

Malik walks out of the terminal and looks for a shuttle. Limited in his Spanish, he carefully looks for the shuttle that has the name of the hotel he has booked. Malik awkwardly walks down the line of shuttles, desperately looking for a way to get to his hotel. "Ugh…" Malik complains, "this is one of those moments where I wished I'd paid more attention in Spanish. Well, I need to stay calm and keep looking." Suddenly, a man with jet black hair, a mustache, wearing a light blue button down, and brown cargo pants notices Malik walking. The man raises his hand and talks to Malik when he passes by.

"Buenas noches señor, ¿necesita que lo lleve (Good evening, sir, do you need a ride)?" Malik looks to his left and squints his eyes. Although he is somewhat confused, he is amazed at something he noticed back in Africa.
"Somehow, I kinda understand what he's asking me. But how?" Malik walks towards him, pulls up the reservation to the hotel, and converses with him. "Eurostar Madrid Tower," Malik says. "Can you take me there?" The man looks at the reservation, nods, then addresses Malik with eye contact.

"Si. Conozco el lugar. Entra y te llevaré allí (Yes. I know the place. Get in and I'll take you there)." Again, Malik mysteriously understands the man, brings his belongings, and gets in the shuttle.

A few meters away, two shadowy figures look in the distance of Malik and the shuttle. They begin to whisper to each other, as the driver is preparing to leave the airport.

"¿Estás segura de que es la elegida, Esmeralda (Are you sure he's the one)?" one of them whispers.

"No hay duda de que es el moro. Mira sus receptores (There is no doubt he is the Moor. Look at his receptors)," she responds, as her shiny blue eyes give evidence of their presence.

"¿Y ahora qué (So what now)?"

"Los seguiremos hasta el hotel. Luego, nos revelaremos. Entonces veremos si él también está detrás de la espada (We will follow them to the hotel. Afterwards, we will reveal ourselves. Then we will see if he too is after the sword)." The shuttle begins to accelerate, so the shadowy figures begin to follow in the cover of darkness.

"UGH! Eres tan impaciente (You are so impatient)!" Her companion soon follows behind with little enthusiasm but with haste.

The shuttle drives through the lively but rustic streets of Madrid. The large, multi-window buildings blanket the streets while five long skyscrapers oversee the diversity of activity, people, and culture. Malik looks on as the driver continues to maneuver through the streets. The traffic is light, the city lights are bright, and the aroma of enlightenment lifts Malik's mood. "This is a beautiful city," Malik comments. "I actually wish Emma was with me to see this. Even though I haven't spoken to her, I sense that she's in good hands. Anyway, I'll have to worry about that later."

Twenty minutes later, the shuttle pulls up at the Eurostars Madrid Tower. The driver stops the vehicle, looks back, and addresses Malik. "Este es el hotel (This is the hotel), Senor," the man says. Malik gets up, reaches for his wallet, pulls out a €20 and extends it to the man.

"Gracias," Malik says. The man nods and accepts the tip. Then Malik walks out of the shuttle. Malik watches as the shuttle drives away. He takes a deep breath, then turns around. As Malik gathers his things, his keen senses pick up something different, yet familiar. A gust of wind blows, prompting Malik to stop in his tracks. Two mysterious women walk within three yards away from Malik. One of them boldly speaks.

"¿Eres a quien llaman Shadowmoor (Are you the one called Shadowmoor)?" Malik's eyes widen, but he refuses to break his silence. The woman grows impatient and addresses Malik again. "¿Eres sordo o estúpido (Are you deaf or stupid)?"

"Tienes que ser tan dura (Do you have to be so harsh)?" her companion asks. The main woman growls in irritation. Malik knows that he must be careful not to draw too much attention to himself. So, he has little choice but to turn around and face the women.

"*I hope these are not Elite 8 goons,*" Malik wonders. "*If so, I will have to play it cool without drawing too much attention*"

Slowly, Malik turns around. As he faces the mysterious women, he is startled to see what's in front of him. Two beautiful women: one with kinky, black hair, with light chocolate skin, red lips, and an attitude, while the other is similarly dark in complexion, straight black hair pulled into a ponytail, and shorter. Both possess the Avemcernentia which immediately activates Malik's Dracocernentia.

"I can't believe what I'm seeing," Malik exclaims as the main woman walks closer to him. She squints her eyes the closer she gets. She looks Malik up and down, then speaks again.

"Entonces, eres tú. Bienvenidos a España (So, it is you. Welcome to Spain) ... Shadowmoor.

# Chapter 37: Sombra del Fénix (Shadow of the Phoenix)

Malik stares down the women, feeling each other out while looking at the receptor fields. The bright colors of green and red flow within both Malik's and the women's bodies. Despite the lack of deceit or hostility, both parties are a little reluctant to bow down to each other's fluctuation of power. Suddenly, the other woman breaks the awkward silence and speaks to Malik.

"Disculpe, por favor. No queremos hacerte daño (Please excuse her. We don't mean you any harm.)"

"Callate, Triana. Este idiota aún no lo ha descubierto (Oh Shut up, Triana. This idiot hasn't figured it out yet)."

"Hey!" Malik yells. "I'm right here. It's not like…"

"OI!" the main one slaps her head, then slaps Malik upside of his head. "Tú también puedes entendernos, si sacas la cabeza de tu trasero (You can understand us too, if you pull your head out of your ass). Malik's patience reaches his boiling point. His eyes begin to illuminate brightly, his voice gets deeper, and he reacts unexpectedly.

"No sé quién diablos eres pero ... espera un minuto, ¿cómo sé … (I don't know who the hell you are but...wait a minute, how do I know)? The main woman puts her hand on her hip, shakes her head, and responds sarcastically.

"No puedo creer lo lento que eres. ¿Ahora lo entiendes (I can't believe how slow you are. Now do you get it)?" Malik calms down for a moment to dissect his newfound ability.

*"No wonder I could understand those French mercenaries, the driver, and these crazy broads*," Malik reflects. "*Is this some sort of new power of the Dracocernentia?*"

"Escucha, queremos hablar contigo. ¿Qué tal si se registra en su habitación y hablamos un poco más (Listen, we want to talk to you. How about you check in your room, and we'll talk some more)." Malik nods, turns around, and walks inside of the hotel.

When Malik walks towards the counter, the other women sit in the lobby to give Malik some space. As Malik is about to address the host, the women converse on their plan of action.

"¿Sabes algo? Necesitas controlar tu temperamento (You know something? You need to control your temper), Esmerelda."

"Mirate Triana. Sé cómo hablar con la gente, especialmente con este estadounidense (Watch yourself. I know how to talk to people, especially this American)."

"Sigh...No todo el mundo es tu enemigo (Not everyone is your enemy)." Triana responds.

"No, no lo son. Pero créeme, lo entiendo (No, they're not. But trust me, I understand)," Malik interjects.

"Wow eso fue rápido (Wow, that was quick)," Triana says.

"Cuando conoces el idioma, todo parece ir bien (When you know the language, everything seems to go smoothly)," Malik says. "Vamos."

Impressed, Triana gets up and follows while Esmerelda scrunches her nose in irritation. Then, she too follows Malik upstairs to his room.

Moments later, Malik makes it to his room and allows the women to enter first. The room is elegant, wide, and has an excellent view of the city. Malik puts his suitcase by the dresser, while Triana makes herself comfortable. Esmerelda still maintains a distant demeanor and looks at Malik with a certain level of disdain. Malik senses this and decides to break the ice.

"Para una mujer tan hermosa, seguro que tienes mal genio (For such a beautiful woman, you sure do have a temper)," Malik says. Before Esmerelda could respond, Triana laughs then points at Malik. "Hee hee hee, Yo le digo que todo el tiempo. Aunque ella nunca me escucha (I tell her that all the time. She never listens to me though)."

"UGH!!!" Esmerelda grunts as she sits down, crosses her legs, and folds her arms. Malik chuckles as he sits on the edge of the bed. He takes off his shoes and faces the women.

"Entonces, llamarme Shadowmoor probablemente no sea el curso de acción más sabio (So, calling me Shadowmoor is probably not the wisest course of action). Entonces, ¿qué tal si nos presentamos (So how about we introduce ourselves)?"

"Seguro. Mi nombre es Triana. Y esto es (Sure. My name is Triana. And this is...)"

"Puedo presentarme, muchas gracias (I can introduce myself, thank you very much). Mi nombre es Esmeralda."

"Encantado de conocerlos a los dos (Nice to meet you both). Mi nombre es Malik," Malik responds. "Entonces el hecho de que pueda hablar con fluidez. ¿Es ese el resultado de nuestro poder (So the fact I can speak fluidly, is that the result of our power)?"
Before Triana can respond, Esmeralda clears her throat, gives her a mean look, and Malik raises both an eyebrow and a smile.
"Hace mucho tiempo, se dijo que el dragón y el fénix tenían el poder de comunicarse con el mundo. Entonces, en esencia, ninguna lengua, ya sea antigua o moderna, está más allá de la capacidad de aquellos que están en sintonía con su (Long ago, it was said that the dragon and phoenix had the power to communicate with the world. So, in essence, no tongue, whether it is ancient or modern, is beyond the capacity for those who are in tune with their) Fire Line," Esmerelda explains.
"Veo," Malik responds. "Entonces, si puedes hablar cualquier idioma, ¿por qué no hablar inglés (So if you can speak any language, why not speak English)?" Esmerelda breathes hard, closes her eyes, then responds to Malik.
        "¿Quieres que hable inglés, bien (You want me to speak English, fine)! You are a smug asshole that would've been kicked in the face and your poor excuse for balls by now if we didn't need your help. How is that Mr. Entitled-American?"
"I think you are in need of something stiff that isn't in your life," Malik responds sarcastically. When Esmerelda gets the connotation of Malik's analogy, she begins to erupt with rage until Triana steps in to calm her down.
"Right," she says as she guides Esmerelda back to her seat. "I think it is only fair that we speak in a language that you are familiar with. At least until you grasp your new abilities."
        Time goes by. Malik changes his clothes into a t-shirt, pair of Nike shorts, and no show dri-fit socks. The ladies also take off their boots and make themselves more comfortable. "Do you want any room service or food?" Malik asks.
"No thank you, Malik," Triana responds.
"How about you, Esmerelda?" Malik asks again. Esmerelda shakes her head as Malik crosses his ankles.
        "So, why did you seek me?" Malik asks. Triana looks at Esmerelda as she softens up to address Malik's question.

"We belong to the Sombra del Fénix, a group dedicated to preserving our way of life and the artifacts of our ancestors," Esmerelda says.

"But I thought all of the Moors were defeated and banished from Spain during the Inquisition," Malik adds.

"Yes, most of us did perish," Esmerelda continues. "However, a group of Phoenix Moors concealed themselves in the shadows to protect the people left behind while waiting for the next Golden Dragon Moor to appear."

"Golden Dragon Moor! That's the second or third time I've heard this title," Malik exclaims. "What is the Golden Dragon Moor?"

"Apparently, your parents didn't teach you about our legacy, did they," Esmerelda says.

"I... I... didn't know my parents. They were killed before I even knew I was existing," Malik says softly.

Esmerelda changes her attitude. Her face begins to soften, her eyes begin to relax, and her tone becomes more empathetic. "I'm... sorry. I misjudged."

"Hey, don't worry about it. Please continue."

"The Golden Dragon Moor is the man who is destined to lead the people back into prosperity. Only a few men have reached this level, and one in particular did it in the shadows. He created a sword that was to be wielded by the one worthy to be the next Golden Dragon."

"You mean the Harq Alqadr, right," Malik asks.

"Yes," Esmerelda confirms. "The sword is indeed legendary. It is said to have the power to unite the people and draw forth a power unseen in many years."

"Do you know where it is?" Malik asks.

Esmerelda is hesitant in responding. Her head leans down while Malik continues to anticipate the answer. Meanwhile, Triana jumps in to help Esmerelda in her silence. "Truth is, Malik, nobody knows exactly where the sword is. Some say that the sword can only be found by a descendant of Riaahn. Others say, you must obtain the level of the Golden Dragon."

"I see..." Malik ponders. "But that doesn't fully explain why you need my help?"

"There has been an elevated amount of activity lurking in the streets," Esmeralda adds. "Rumors are circling that there is an organization that is creating special weapons."

"What kind of weapons?" Malik asks.

"We're not fully sure," Triana responds, "but they're not ordinary. Somehow, we haven't been able to detect its presence or those who are producing it."

"So, how do you know that there are weapons being created?"

Esmeralda gets up from her chair. She walks towards Malik and stands in front of Malik with her arms crossed. Triana begins to slowly move herself towards the edge of the bed while Malik looks up at Esmeralda. Esmeralda takes a deep breath, sighs, then faces Malik.

"About a month ago, myself, Triana, and another one of our sisters intercepted a message from a young girl who was being trafficked from different countries."

"Is it another sex ring?" Malik asks.

"That's what we thought at first, but when we examined her receptor fields, there was little trauma," Esmeralda says. "Matter of fact, it was as if her senses were… dull. As if she was asleep or paralyzed."

"Paralyzed, but how if she was moving?" Malik asks.

"Well, when we tried to find out, we went to an abandoned warehouse in the north side of the city. Then, a strange smell overwhelmed us and dulled our powers," Emeralda concludes. Then, she lowers her head. Her eyes begin to slump, her shoulders begin to relax, then she turns her head towards the window. Intrigued and concerned, Malik presses on with the debriefing.

"Esmeralda… what happened next?" he asks. Esmeralda says nothing. She rubs her face and sniffs her nose. Her body is consumed with pride, but her heart is filled with regret. After a few tense moments, Triana answers Malik.

"Our sister sacrificed herself to save us. She threw us out of the window and created a fire wave to shield us from detection," Triana continues. "We barely escaped but… we haven't seen her since."

Esmeralda takes another deep breath, looks at Triana and nods. Triana sees the cue, puts her boots back on, then gets up from the bed. Malik looks around and raises his eyebrows at the behavior the women are exhibiting.

"We must go now," Esmeralda commands.

"Wait," Malik pleads. "You don't have to go just yet. I…"

"We will meet again tomorrow night," Esmeralda concludes. "Meet us at the top of the building downtown. We will lead you back to the warehouse to look for clues. COME Triana, it is time to go."

Esmeralda starts to walk towards the door of the hotel room. Triana follows behind, then says parting words to Malik. "It was nice talking to you. We can't wait to see you tomorrow. Have a good night." Esmeralda grunts, shakes her head, then opens the door. The women leave while Malik sits on the edge of the bed contemplating the amount of information that he has gathered.

"Sombra del Fénix… Shadow of the Phoenix…" Malik reflects. "I bet you the Elite 8 are behind this, just like in London. I need to get some rest and recharge my strength. I'll call home tomorrow afternoon. Hopefully Emma is OK." So, Malik gets up from the bed and turns off the lights. Then he makes sure the curtains of his window are shut. Afterwards, he crawls into bed, checks his cellphone for messages, puts the phone down, and closes his eyes.

Meanwhile, back in Florida, Emma watches the sun setting. She looks on as D'Shawn walks behind her slowly. Emma senses his presences and smiles.

"It's OK, D'Shawn. I just like looking at the sky sometimes," Emma says.

"I understand," D'Shawn responds, as he walks next to her. "There's something I want to give you." He hands over her cellphone. Emma looks at it and gasps.

"How did you…"

"Don't worry, I didn't look through it. It was in one of your pockets at the time we rescued you and Asir."

"Thank you. I need to call my grandparents."

"Sure, but use our Wi-Fi first. It has a secure network that makes you impossible to track." Emma nods as D'Shawn walks away.

Emma logs into her phone, applies the Wi-Fi feature, then dials the number. RING… RING… "Emma… EMMMA! ARE YOU OK!"

"Yes Grandma, I'm fine."

"Oh, thank the heavens. What happened to you, child!" Geneva yells as Emma tries to calm her down.

"It's a lot to explain. I'll have to tell you about it when I get home. Have you talked to Malik?"

“Right now, your brother is in Spain.”
“SPAIN???!!! HOW? WHAT’S GOING ON?”
“Emma, listen to me, there is a lot more going on than just the sword. I believe that there is a worldwide scheme that is beginning to take over the world. I can sense it.”
“So, can I. I don’t know what’s going on, but I’m going to find out. Tell Grandpa I’m OK and I’ll see you soon.”
“OK, be careful, my Amira.”
“I love you too.” CLICK

Emma hangs up the phone and continues to look at the sky. Suddenly, a voice echoes behind her. “Your sense is correct, Emma.” Emma turns around and sees Mason smiling.
“I didn’t mean to intrude.”
“No… No… Mason, I’m just worried about Malik.”
“Yes, believe it or not I have an idea where he is and what he’s about to discover.” Emma’s eyes widen and her mouth gasps. Mason puts his hand on her shoulder and relaxes her. “Don’t worry,” Mason reassures. “As soon as the mission is complete, I’ll help him too.”
“Thank you, Mason.” Mason and Emma continue to look on, as the sun begins to set.

# Chapter 38: Operation 1804 Part 1

The winds blow east from the ocean. The temperature is extremely warm, and the sky is setting; painted with the blood of people oppressed past and present alike while mixing with the light of the sun's rays. The men of OBR begin to congregate and mobilize for the upcoming mission. Several vehicles man their equipment, weapons, and soldiers while D'Shawn oversees the operations. Despite his resolve, his mind is cluttered with uncertainty of the enemy's tactics and surprises.

"W.A.V.E. will try to maintain their security without sparking too much attention," he considers. "I don't believe they will be completely oblivious with our intentions or our resolve to attack again. (Sigh) I guess we'll have to fight through it… like we always do." Suddenly, Asir walks by D'Shawn. He is wearing a black, light mitted hoodie, with a pair of jeans and all black Adidas NMDs. Not only has his entire personality changed, so has his attitude. He looks at the surrounding forces with the calmness of a general and the patience of a martial artist. D'Shawn quickly notices and addresses his son.

"Are you OK, Asir?"
Asir looks at his father and responds. "Yes, I am, Dad. I'm actually a little nervous."
"Huh, well you don't look nervous. You look like you're prepared to fight."
"That's just it, I… have never fought anyone before. Except for that time when… I was kicked out of school, but this is different."
"How so, son?"
"For… the first time in my life, I… know what I am... who I am...and it gives me power. Is that weird?"

D'Shawn looks back at Asir and smiles. He leans down on his son and puts his hand on Asir's right shoulder. "No, son. As a matter of fact, the knowledge of self is what white supremacists fear the most. When a Black man knows who he is and where he comes from, regardless of if he has powers or not, he is a threat to the tyranny they reign over. That's why learning to read was illegal, and those of us who prosper would end up destroyed. Do you understand?"
"Kinda; like when we fight back, we're viewed as bad guys."

"Exactly!"

Moments later, Emma walks by but doesn't disturb the moment. She has her on blue hoodie, jeans, and sneakers. She crosses her arms and smiles as D'Shawn and Asir finish their conversation. Emma's presence causes Asir's eyes to illuminate, transforming to the Dracocernentia. D'Shawn sees this, then looks to his left.

"I should've known you were sneaking by," D'Shawn welcomes. "However, you forget that a dragon can sense a phoenix, and vice versa."

"So, it will seem," Emma responds. Asir walks towards Emma. They perform a secret greeting where they slap hands three times, then slap the back of their hands, raise their hands in a gesture saying, "What?!" then cross their arms, tilt their heads, and nod. D'Shawn smiles and shakes his head, partly in disbelief but mostly in genuine admiration of the development of their relationship.

"OK, OK. Asir, Emma will be with you in a few. I need to talk to her," D'Shawn commands.

"Alright. I'll see you in a bit, Ms. Emma." Emma smiles and nods. Asir walks away, down the stairs, then towards their rendezvous site.

"You really love my son, don't you?"

"I'm not the only one who does." He's warmed up in such a short time. Thanks to you, he knows who he is, where he comes from, and how to cultivate the power within him." D'Shawn nods, bites his lips, then looks away. Emma squints her eyes then presses D'Shawn.

"D'Shawn, what's the matter?"

"(Sigh), After today, Asir is going to experience a war not seen in this country in about fifty years," D'Shawn sulks. "I fight so that he wouldn't have to. Unfortunately, he is going to know how much uglier this country...this world will be." Emma looks down, then closes her eyes. She takes a soft, slow breath, then pats D'Shawn on the shoulder, grabbing his attention.

"Then let the world burn. It needs to be purified anyway, and what better way to start the process if the flames were generated from a dragon and a phoenix."

"Right," D'Shawn commands, with a smirk. "Go ahead and meet up with Asir by the black Suburban. It's nearly time to begin." Emma smiles, puts on her hood, then walks away. Afterwards, D'Shawn looks at his tomahawk and activates his Dracocernentia to ignite the resolve within his soul.

Thirty minutes later, D'Shawn mounts the lead military style trucks. A convoy of ten trucks line up behind the vehicle, as the gates open to release the small army. The driver honks as the trucks start their ignition. The collective sounds of roaring engines generate a sound as intimidating as a stampeding herd. One truck after another leaves the gate as they meander through the thick swamps and into the city.

Meanwhile, Asir and Emma are trailing in the black Suburban at the back of the convoy. Emma looks at the window as the driver continues to move through the muddy roads. Asir stares at nothing, yet everything, as his Dracocernentia pierces through the current plain of the present. His silence communicates more than just resolve. Emma taps Asir on his shoulder to calm him down.

"Deactivate your Dracocernentia, Asir," Emma commands. "Otherwise, you'll drain your energy before you get there." Asir nods, closes his eyes, then deactivates his Dracocernentia. "There you go, kiddo. You need to relax. I know what it feels like to have so much power built up inside you, but you have to understand that knowing when to use it is just as important."

"Is that why you stay calm, Ms. Emma?"

"Something like that."

"So, Ms. Emma, did you have an ancestor that taught you about yourself?"

Emma smiles while taking her time to respond. She sits up straight and looks Asir in the eye. "Yes. Her name was… or in our case, is Muqadas. She was a sweet and powerful warrior."

"I would like to meet her sometime."

"(Sigh) I don't think you'll be able to meet her."

"Why not? I mean, if I can meet my ancestors, how come I can't meet yours?" Emma pauses for a moment to think. Asir's inquisitive nature probes Emma like a microscope, waiting for a logical explanation from a woman who possesses powers that were once deemed impossible. Yet, Emma relinquishes her sense of logic, then responds to Asir's profound question.

"Maybe there is a way, but let's focus on the mission first, then we'll find a way. OK?" Asir smiles, leans his hand forward, then Emma responds by doing their secret handshake.

Meanwhile, D'Shawn is sitting in the passenger seat of the lead truck. The rumble of the engine along with the crunching sound of tires over a rough terrain do everything but distract D'Shawn from focusing on the mission. The driver, a Black man with a short, nappy fro with sunglasses asks D'Shawn a question.

"Do you think it's wise to pull directly in front of the building. Snake Sight?"

D'Shawn rubs his beard before he gives an answer. "Once we get on the highway, we are going to split up into three different squads. Three vehicles will park in different, strategic alleyways about ten blocks away from the target. The lone Suburban will park in the rear of the building, so that Blue Phoenix and Asir can sneak in the back entrance."

"So, in other words, we are going to create a distraction by attacking the front," the driver confirms. "So that even if they bring reinforcements, we won't be flanked because of the other squads."

"Exactly! It's possible we'll lose some men in this…"

"We are with you til the end sir!" the driver interrupts. D'Shawn smiles, then faces the front of the road.

Seconds later, an encrypted message pops through D'Shawn's secured cell phone. It comes from an erroneous number with a cryptic message.

"Good Luck. Now I must help our other ally. I will be gone for a while." D'Shawn nods his head, smirks, then puts his sunglasses on.

The convoy enters Highway 17 going northbound. Traveling for about fifteen miles, the trucks begin to break their formation and merge into different lanes. As the series of vehicles continue to drive, some of the vehicles begin to slowly drive towards different exits to separate themselves from drawing detection from any state troopers or police. Meanwhile, the Suburban looks for the exit for I-295 East. While sitting in the back of the vehicle, Emma and Asir remain silent; contemplating the next crucial moments of the mission while trying desperately to maintain their powers.

The driver then strikes up a conversation with Emma to reaffirm the plan of action. "We are going to take the loop to get to the W.A.V.E. building," he states. "Then we'll drop you off about a block away." "Understood," Emma responds. Then the driver takes a deep breath, sniffs his nose, and continues to drive through the light traffic.

Ten minutes later, a sign shows up, signaling the drive to engage the blinkers. The I-295 exit is coming up, and as he carefully speeds up, they exit the highway to merge into the loop.

As Asir looks at the window, he becomes mesmerized by the sight of the city. The skyscrapers begin to light up in the dimming light. The structures of buildings and neighborhoods begin to stir a level of awe in Asir. Emma notices that his attention is fixated at his window, and she begins to question him.

"Asir, are you OK?" Asir hesitates to answer, still lost in his thoughts as he continues to look at the window. Emma carefully places her hand on his right shoulder. Asir closes his eyes, then opens them to respond back to Emma.

"I've… I've never seen the city like this before. I think this is the first time I've been outside of Jacksonville." Emma's eyes soften and moisturize before she responds with calming words.

"You're right to look. The city is beautiful. I know exactly how you feel about not leaving a city. Maybe after this, you can see more of this world." Asir smiles at Emma, then she smiles back.

Suddenly, the driver interrupts the brief conversation. "We're almost towards the exit that leads to downtown." Emma and Asir look at each other, nod, then face the front of the SUV.

"Understood," Emma responds. Emma and Asir close their eyes. They synchronize their breathing and draw from within their Fire Line to prepare themselves to access their power. The driver makes the exit and continues to drive towards the crowded streets towards downtown.

At the W.A.V.E building, Sharon is giving instructions to the police sergeant while directing the movement of documents and furniture. Despite her commanding presence, the hair on her arm begins to raise, small droplets of sweat begin to come out of her pores, and her skin flushes red.

"Are you alright, ma'am?" the sergeant says.

"Oh yes, thank you," Sharon responds. "I'm from the Northwest coast, so the heat is bothering me a bit. Anyway, we just need only about two more hours of your time before the movement is complete."

"Well, we have my best men here to protect you from those thugs who came in the other day. If need be, I can call out S.W.A.T."

"No no no no no, that won't be necessary, thank you." The sergeant nods before heading out towards the doorway.

Meanwhile, the clerk walks towards Sharon while looking at the policeman. She has a stack of documents, folders, books, and charts ready to present to Sharon. "Are you sure you don't want to bring in S.W.A.T, ma'am?" she asks.

"Not with the boys still hidden away. Even with our contacts, the reveal will bring too much attention that we don't need right now," Sharon responds. "Did you get the documents I requested?"

"Yes, ma'am. They're all here."

"Good, get rid of them. Burn them."

"But…"

"We already have the data needed and I sent it to him this morning. Soon he'll be able to perfect the weapon and we'll be rich. Hurry up and go!"

"Yes ma'am," the clerk shrieks before walking the other direction. Sharon takes a handkerchief from her left pocket and wipes her forehead. She begins to hold her head and briefly loses balance. "The aftereffects of the drugs is starting to affect me," Sharon contemplates. "It's getting worse and worse. I know those Black bastards are coming. We need to hurry up and go." Sharon then puts her handkerchief back in her pocket and starts to trek down the hallway.

The black Suburban drives to an alleyway about three blocks away from the W.A.V.E. building. The SUV parks and the engine shuts off. Asir looks at Emma as she looks up at the driver. The driver turns his head while the passenger takes his gun to inspect it. Then the driver addresses Emma and Asir.

"We're about three blocks away from the W.A.V.E. building," he says. "Are you two ready?" Asir takes a small gulp, closes his eyes, then takes a deep breath. Emma turns to Asir and puts her hand on his shoulder.

"Asir… are you ready to go?" Asir doesn't respond. Instead, he scrunches his eyebrows downward, opens his eyes, and activates his Dracocernentia. The driver sees the eyes as Emma feels the energy emitting from his body. "Yes… he is," Emma recognizes.

"Remember, once we get out, we will drive off and meet up with the rest for back up," the driver continues. "Good luck to the both of you." Emma and Asir nod subtlety, then exit the SUV. As soon as they get out, the engine starts, reverses out of the alleyway, and they drive off. Emma then prompts Asir to follow her as she nods at him. Then she puts on her hoodie, activates her Avemcernentia, then with Asir, begins to run towards the building.

Emma and Asir move in synchronized flow through the streets. As elusive as ninjas and just as silent, they stealthily scale the surrounding buildings to avoid any bystanders until they make it to the back of the W.A.V.E building. Once they make it to the roof, they anxiously wait for D'Shawn and his forces.

As they crouch out of sight, Asir begins to whisper to Emma. "Ms. Emma, do you think the other boys are still here?"

"If you… allow yourself to see within the building, you will be able to pick out where they are by the colors they show," Emma whispers back.

"How will I know what colors to look for?"

"Don't worry. Once it starts, you'll see the reactions. Then you'll be able to tell the differences based on the people's attitudes."

"I'll… I'll try," Asir answers. Emma smiles, puts her arm around Asir, and patiently waits for the opening to sneak in.

　　As the squadron of six police interceptors surround the building, the policemen begin to pack in their gear. Growing complacent with the lack of activity, the police sergeant begins to recheck his ranks and ascertain the depth of the situation. As he walks through the officers, he begins to radio to his superiors.

(CLICK) "This is Sergeant Gordon reporting, no negative activity or signs of the boogies."

"ROGER THAT, YOU ARE CLEARED TO DISENGAGE ONCE THE MOVE IS COMPLETE."

"10-4" (CLICK). Then another officer walks up towards the sergeant. "Sergeant are you sure we shouldn't stay around, or call SWAT?" he asks.

"Negative, Officer. They would've shown up by now. Also, we have orders to leave once they finish with their move."

"Understood, Sergeant."

Moments later, a mist of smoke begins to creep towards the squad. The officers in the vicinity begin to look around, suspicious of the erroneous mist that came out of nowhere. As the mist thickens, a lone man begins to walk towards the squad. The sergeant sees the man, keeps his hand on his holster, then gives commands.

"Hold right there! This is a confined space. Please leave this area." The man stands still and does nothing. The sergeant gets impatient, then pulls his revolver, along with the rest of the officers. "THIS IS YOUR LAST CHANCE! LEAVE NOW OR YOU WILL BE FIRED UPON!" The man lowers his head and slowly raises both hands. The officers continue to hold their guns at the man. Then the man lifts his head, activates the Dracocernentia, and creates a silhouette of a fire dragon to surround his body. Emma sees from a distance and understands.

"There's the signal. Let's go, Asir!" Emma and Asir go through the vent in the back of the building.

After seeing the flaming dragon, the officers begin to fire at D'Shawn.
However, the bullet shells melt before they could reach D'Shawn. Then
D'Shawn lets off a roar, balls his fists, then slams them on the pavement,
creating a heat wave so massive that it partially melts some of the cars
while burning a few of the officers. The sergeant quickly opens the door
of a nearby car to shield himself from much of the blast. Afterwards, a
conglomerate of machine guns begins to fire on the officers, killing three
while the rest of the remaining officers take cover to return fire.
Afterwards, D'Shawn with the OBR begins to engage the police for the
long, awaited battle for the freedom of oppressed Black boys.

# Chapter 39: Operation 1804 Part 2

The stampede of noise and commotion commentate the battle. As guns fire from both directions, D'Shawn weaves through the ranks of the cars and dead bodies. As the sergeant tries to mount a defense with his remaining force, D'Shawn grabs his tomahawk and engulfs it with flames. He kneels in front of the remaining officers while they point their guns at him. As the sergeant prepares his men to fire, the remaining OBR members also walk behind him with guns at the ready. Then D'Shawn looks up and flashes his Dracocernentia. The color of fear is so bright in the officers, that they paint the doors of the building with despair and hopelessness.

Seeing the futility of their efforts, the sergeant nods at his remaining force, and they surrender by dropping their guns. Then they hold their hands up as some of the OBR members direct the remaining cops away from the building and in a secluded area. D'Shawn stands up and prompts four OBR members to come to him.

"I suspect that the Elite 8 have heard the commotion and will try to mount their surprise attacks," D'Shawn warns.
"So do we proceed as planned?" one of his officers asks.
"We need to keep the fighting in front of us to give my son and Blue Phoenix time to infiltrate the building. However,"
"However, what sir?" D'Shawn amplifies the power of his eyes to detect any more receptors in the building. Then he addresses his squad leaders.

"There are ten guards directly in front of us. There are two more in the regulator room. That's where they used to push the gas through the building. Then there are three more separate people heading down to the basement. I suspect that's where the missing boys are."

D'Shawn turns around to bring in more men to organize the separation. Each of the men engage by putting on their masks, then reloading their guns. Then D'Shawn points and directs each of his leaders to pursue each agenda.

"You, Black Mamba, will take three men to destroy the gas generator. Once that's done, then report back to the outside to give cover for the remaining men. I know the full force of the Jacksonville PD will come. King Cobra will cover our six with two other men as we take point to engage the main force. After I draw out their fire, you will make your way to the basement to help Asir. The rest will take out the rest of the guards, then set up the explosives. Is that understood?!" All of the men ball their free fist, place it on their chests, then chant together. "WE FIGHT FOR THE FUTURE OF BLACK PEOPLE, AND OUR RESOLVE IS UNCOMPROMISING!" D'Shawn nods, puts on his mask, and leads his men into the building.

Meanwhile, Emma and Asir maneuver through the tightly constructed airways. The gas is still thick and heavy. Asir begins to cough and complain about its effects. "I'm… feeling kinda woozy, Ms. Emma. I don't know what's…" Emma too feels the effects but quickly remembers why.

"That's right, the Reintergon. There's only one way we can fight through it," Emma concludes. "Hang in there, Asir, and just follow me the best way you can."

Emma continues to crawl through the vents with Asir following, until she reaches the vent in one of the closed, locked doors. As she quickly examines the area, the alarms of the building begin to ring. "So D'Shawn is in the building. Perfect. Alright, Asir, this is where we get down!"

Emma punches the vent covering, crawls through the opening, and lands on the floor. Then Asir follows her, and slowly crawls out of the hole. Once Asir lets go of the ceiling, he falls directly towards Emma's arms; she catches Asir to help him land. Then she grabs Asir's attention to instruct him on how to deal with the gas.

"Alright, Asir, listen," Emma whispers. "This gas can dull our senses and keep us from focusing. To deal with this, you may have to hold your breath a couple of times, then take ten deep breaths to keep your energy up."

"What if I have to fight somebody and my powers don't…"

"Don't worry about that. Remember, your dad is going to send some of his men to help you while you locate the other boys. Do you remember how to find them?"

"Yes, I use my eyes to find the colors of fear and confusion. Then go to them."

"Exactly. Now I want you to follow me until it's time for you to go." Asir nods in compliance.

Emma and Asir slowly walk towards the door, unlock it, then open it. Emma cautiously walks out of the door with Asir closely behind down the hallway to find the stairway. As they reach the stairs, Emma and Asir take their time to breathe easily to maintain their powers. "This air stinks, Ms. Emma," Asir complains.

"Don't worry, your dad has sent some men to get rid of the smell."

"I hope it's real soon. My head still hurts."

"Me too." Afterwards, Emma and Asir take the stairs towards the bottom of the building. A group of men with black suits, sunglasses, and guns congregate as Sharon feverishly and frantically addresses her minions.

"What the hell is going on?" she demands.

"They've taken out our escorts and have breached the building, ma'am."

"No… Shit! Dammit!" Sharon yells. "Alright, not a problem. I already took the liberties to have the boys escorted through the basement. In the meantime, kill every one of those bastards you see."

Before the man can respond, a loud crash stuns everyone, causing them to direct their attention towards the incoming OBR Force. As they come closer, the lead henchman yells at Sharon. "GO NOW! WE'LL HOLD THEM HERE!"

"Do you have the…"

"Yes, ma'am. Some of us already took a few doses." Sharon nods, then runs the other way.

D'Shawn sees her and begins to yell. "You're not getting away that easily, you white supremacist bitch!" The henchmen point their semi-automatic guns and begin to fire. Knowing he doesn't have the energy due to the Reintergon, D'Shawn and his men take cover behind tables, desks, walls, and pillars. Then the men return fire. As the shells begin to flash back and forth between lines, D'Shawn looks back, flashes his fist to prompt King Cobra and his squad to slowly move away to divert towards another path to the basement. The battle is furious, as three of the OBR members are shot and killed, while two of the henchmen are hit in the chest with bullets.

Emma and Asir hear the guns and immediately rush downstairs towards the third-floor way. Asir begins to shake with anxiety while Emma remains calm and collected. "Don't worry, Asir. I won't let anything happen to you."

"I know, Ms. Emma. It's just…"

"I understand, but you have to stay focused. Remember who we are and why we are here."

Emma and Asir reach the third floor and open the door out of the stairway. Immediately, they run down the hallway towards the other side of the floor. Despite the thickness of the gas, they continue to huff and puff their way through the vacant rooms. Asir then senses something coming from the opposite direction. The receptors show flashes of yellow, red, and purple. Then he yells to Emma.

"Ms. Emma! Someone is coming towards us!" Emma emits more power in her eyes to ascertain Asir's claims. As she focuses on the receptors, she soon realizes who it is.

When Emma and Asir reach a vacant conference room, they are confronted by a shocked and desperate woman who houses the colors of the receptor fields. Her hair is partly drenched with sweat, her skin is blushing red, and her gaze is as demonic as a hyena to a carcass. Emma and Asir stop running and peer at the woman who is the cause of so much suffering and destruction in the local community.

"It's her, Ms. Emma!" Asir screams as Sharon continues to breathe hard with surprise and disgust.

"Well, well, well, look what we have here. The bastard and his Black bitch!"

"You're one to talk, you evil whore!" Emma responds. Sharon growls, takes the golden case from her pocket, sniffs the entire powder substance then throws the container to the ground. Her nose is covered with residue and sweat while her plunge to insanity is followed by the black rings in her eyes. She takes off her heels, throws them at Emma and Asir but they dodge them. Then Sharon goes into a short rant.

"I'm going to beat you to death. Then I'm going to make your blood into my lipstick and nail polish." She looks devilishly at Asir. "Then he'll be next."

Emma briefly closes her eyes, grabs Asir's shoulder, then opens her eyes. Emma looks at Asir and gives him a command. "Go… NOW!"

"But Ms…"

"I got this. You have a more important job, remember?" Asir takes a gulp, looks at Sharon, then looks back at Emma. He nods, then slowly walks behind Emma. Afterwards, he runs the other direction to find his way towards the basement.

Sharon begins to laugh as she cracks her neck and fists. "He won't be here to save you."

"We'll, it's a good thing I don't need his help," Emma responds. "Now do you mind getting this over with? The smell in here is getting to me."

"Heh heh heh, oh the gas?" Sharon laughs.

"No, my dear. Let's just say someone's cookies are soiled." Emma winks

Enraged by the condescending comment, Sharon rushes towards Emma and begins to throw a barrage of punches and kicks. Emma blocks punches and dodges her kicks, but each hit feels like a boulder. As Emma blocks, the pain from Sharon's strength and attack overwhelm Emma until Sharon catches her off guard with a kick in the stomach.

Emma is temporarily stunned, but counters with a roundhouse kick to Sharon's face. The force of the shoe hitting Sharon's face causes her nose and mouth to squirt blood. The look on Sharon's face darkens, as her rage disregards any pain receptors that are pulsating through her body. Emma's notices this look and then begins to brace herself for what is to come.

Meanwhile, D'Shawn continues to duck in cover from the avalanche of bullets piercing through the air. Pinned down and running low on ammo, D'Shawn sits back while covering himself behind a turned over desk. He begins to take slow, deep breaths, and calms his soul. The noise of the skirmish mutes, his heart beats in rhythm, and the power from within begins to slowly generate.

The henchmen begin to empty up their clips at the opposing squad. Some of them continue to return cover fire while a few take turns reloading their last clips. One of the OBR soldiers breaks his cover and shoots two men in their chests. As they fall to the ground, the lead henchman uses his newly loaded revolver to shoot the OBR warrior in the head.

As the explosion of receptors penetrates D'Shawn's concentration, his sorrow quickly drowns in a sea of rage. His eyes transform into a bloodshed hue, his body is surrounded by reddish yellow heat, and the mighty leader erupts from his hiding place and generates a fire wave so strong and powerful, it partially melts the enemy's guns, knocking the remaining six henchmen back and killing three from the intense heat.

The remaining OBR squad slowly stand up from their hiding spaces and creep behind their leader. The disoriented henchmen attempt to reach for their pockets to grab their containers, but three of the OBR members shoot and kill three of the henchmen in the chest. D'Shawn takes off his mask, showing his blood drained Dracocernentia to the remaining defenders. He grabs his hatchet and engulfs it in fire. Seeing the futility of their defense and weary of their fight, the lead Henchman nods at his remaining followers to drop their weapons. As D'Shawn approaches the man, his eyes slowly turn to its normal brownish yellow color. Then the lead henchman states parting words to his foe.

"You may have won this skirmish," he states, "but you have only ensured that you and your pathetic race will burn. Many more will take our place."

"And we will crush them just like we did you," D'Shawn responds. The henchman begins to laugh as he slowly takes off his sunglasses. He shakes his head and attempts to taunt D'Shawn.

"You will never win. For we control the destiny of…" SWOOSH POW! A cryptic silence emerges after a flaming tomahawk strikes the henchman's chest. As the last remnants of life float into the air, the henchman's eyes roll to the back of his head as he slinks down to the ground.

After witnessing the lifeless body migrate towards the floor, D'Shawn takes the tomahawk from his chest and redirects his attention to the frightened remaining henchmen. As they quiver like naked rats in the snow, D'Shawn shakes his head, then obliges them with his resolve. "Know this before you die…" he confesses, "we are not our timid ancestors who wanted to go along to get along. I come from a lineage that refuses to be conquered by evil men… and this is a new day!"

D'Shawn raises his tomahawk as the remaining OBR members raise their guns.

Asir reaches the bottom of the stairs towards the basement. He sees that there are two henchmen guarding the doorway. Asir becomes anxious and starts to panic.

"I don't know if I can do this," Asir ponders. "What if I can't do it…" Hearing a small commotion, a henchman gets suspicious and begins to walk towards the stairway. Asir's heart begins to pound harder and harder. The beads of sweat begin to flow down as the henchman inches closer.

Feeling trapped and without options, Asir begins to close his eyes. Soon afterwards, a familiar voice from within begins to speak in a calming tone.

"Who are you?" the voice whispers. Asir suddenly widens his eyes as the voice continues to calm him down. "SHHHHH… remember who you are. Fear did not stop your ancestors from fighting back. Fear did not stop you from connecting to the ones you love. Tell me… who are you?"

Despite the henchman getting closer and closer, Asir closes his eyes and takes deep breaths. The room becomes silent, his power begins to flow, and Asir mentally hears the spark of a match. After hearing it, it invigorates his body and the Dracocernentia consumes his eyes. His face becomes determined, his resolved unmatched, and his fists begin to clench.

The henchman reaches the edge of the stairs and pulls out his revolver. As he turns the corner, he sees a deep cloud of grey smoke. He begins to cough and wave away the smoke. Then suddenly, a flash of fire penetrates the mist as Asir lands a flame-engulfed fist in the henchman's face, knocking him unconsciousness.

The other henchman sees the event from a distance and pulls out his gun.

"DON'T YOU MOVE OR ELSE I'LL SHOOT!" he commands. Asir stands above the unconscious man then stares at the other henchman. His eyes glow like a wolf in the night, savoring the moment to strike.

As fear begins to consume the henchman, he slowly begins to squeeze the trigger. Before he could finish the task, POP, the sound is followed by a bullet in his head and blood splattered on the doorway. Asir quickly turns around and is greeted by the squad led by King Cobra.

"Are you alright, Asir?"
Asir nods as his powers begins to grow. "I kinda feel stronger," he responds.
"That's because the machine that produces the gas should be knocked out by now," King Cobra states. "Now, let's go free these boys." Asir nods as he charges both his fists with flames, runs towards the door, and punches them open with fire blasts.

After smashing through, Asir, King Cobra, and the remaining squad find the boys slightly sluggish and enclosed in their containments. King Cobra and the squad begin to open each of the containments, helping the boys up, and leading them out.

One of the boys is so frightened that he refuses to leave the corner. One of the squad members reaches his hand and tries to prompt the shaken boy to come, but he refuses.

"He won't come out!" he states. Asir quickly runs to the room and walks towards the little boy.

"Don't be afraid," Asir says. "These guys are here to help you get home. If you like, you can walk with me. Would you like that?" The shaken little boy slowly reaches his hand towards Asir. Asir puts his hand out and allows the boy to come to him.

After a few, tense seconds, the boy musters up the courage to grab Asir's hand as King Cobra watches. "Good job, Asir," he compliments. "We need to go now." King Cobra, Asir, and the squad members lead the remaining twelve boys towards the stairs and out of the building.

As the battle continues, both Emma and Sharon are covered with bruises, blood, and sweat. The heavy breathing from both combatants echo all around the room as both try to muster up the strength to maintain their stance. Sharon's shirt is nearly ripped in two, partially exposing her bra and red-tainted skin. The rings around her eyes signal a madness that is beyond reform or control.

Emma on the other hand holds her left rib cage with her left hand. Tears slowly fall down her cheek as she desperately tries to manage the pain. Her clothes have spots of blood and grind while her hair is erratic and tangled.

Suddenly, Sharon begins to laugh in a surge of insanity. Her eyes begin to bulge, and her grin becomes intimidating. "Gwahahahahahaha! You actually put up a good fight this time!" she screams. "But now, it's time to kill you...RAAAAAAAAAA!"

Sharon charges forward and balls up her fist. Emma, too weak to move, begins to panic. Her fear is the only thing, besides the pain, that paralyzes her movements. Despite the speed of Sharon's approach, the movements appear to be in slow motion. The sound of the sweat from both foes is as loud as a waterfall. The sound of each breath rings like an avalanche. Then Emma begins to do something remarkable.

Emma closes her eyes and relaxes herself. She focuses on the energy that resides deep within her core. As she generates more power, she begins to remember the lessons that she learned from her previous encounters.

"I remember the first time I was aware of my power," Emma realizes. "How I was once fueled by power, then rage… and then love. Not just love from my brother, my grandparents… but myself." As Sharon draws near, she cocks her right hand, balls up her fist, and throws a right hook.

Like slow motion, Emma is able to mentally see and hear the fist approach her. Her calm state allows her to feel the vibration and the beat of not only her opponent, but her own beat. As the fist comes within millimeters of her left cheek, Emma gracefully dodges by ducking, throwing Sharon off balance.

Surprised, Sharon stumbles towards her left and sees Emma swinging her arms and legs side to side. Enraged, Sharon picks herself up and yells. "I DON'T CARE ABOUT YOUR STUPID DANCE! YOU ARE GOING TO DIE RIGHT HERE AND RIGHT NOW!"

Again, Sharon charges at Emma. This time, Sharon throws a kick. Emma illusively maneuvers away from the kick and swings around Sharon. Then Sharon's rage gets the better of her as she tries to land another punch. Emma again swings her shoulders sideways and moves her head out of the way.

Emma continues to keep her eyes closed and move in the style of Engolo. Sharon continues to throw punches and kicks, hoping to land any blow to her once defeated foe. However, Emma continues to dodge the attacks. With each evasion, Emma's beat allows her to regain her strength. Her pain begins to dull, her wounds become a non-factor, and Emma prepares for the final move.

After a few tired and unsuccessful seconds, Sharon pants like a parched, wounded dog. Her rage breaks a blood vessel in her eye and her nose begins to bleed. Despite this, Sharon lets off a roar and charges forward with reckless inefficiency.

As soon as Sharon gets within range, Emma continues in ginga and prepares to attack. Sharon throws a desperate punch. Emma rolls, turns around, and lifts her left leg. She swings her foot and crashes against Sharon's face. A stream of blood flows in the air as Emma swings around and lands two more kicks.

Disoriented, Sharon holds her head in agony as Emma continues to perform ginga in rhythm. Sharon wipes the blood from her nose and looks at Emma. Her sense of self is now lost, and her blind frustration showcases itself with blood-stained teeth. She lets off one more roar as she once again charges towards Emma.

As Sharon gets closer, the heat from Emma's body begins to take form. The small waves of flames begin to turn blue. Her body illuminates in a brilliant color as Emma continues to move with grace and precision. When Sharon gets within kicking range, Emma's eyes glow bright blue, as the Avemcernentia spots a small window to attack.

Emma quickly does a low sweep kick on the ground and trips Sharon. Then, while she's in midair, Emma torques her full body clockwise, raises both of her feet, and performs an arco iris so fast that she kicks Sharon in the face, causing her to yelp in pain while spinning violently towards the ground.

When Sharon lands, her body becomes numb, her eyes bulge out, and a river of blood flows violently from her nose and mouth. As Emma looks on, she hears a cry from a familiar voice.

"MS. EMMA! MS. EMMA!" Emma turns around and sees Asir with King Cobra, and the rest of the rescued boys. "We have to go now!" King Cobra commands. Emma nods, grunts in pain, then runs behind the squad as they make their escape through the back.

D'Shawn and the rest of his squad begin to walk towards the front of the building. He hears a click on his radio, so he grabs it, pushes the button, and responds.

"Snake Sight here!"

"The package has been retrieved, Snake Sight!"

"Roger that, King Cobra. And my son and Emma?"

"Safe and successfully out of the building!"

"Roger that. We will meet you soon at the hideout!"

"Affirmative. Over and out!" Click.

D'Shawn then nods to his squad and gives out one more command. "Stay close behind me and do not move until I am done." The remaining squad nods, then follows their leader.

Outside of the building, an army of SWAT and police surround the building. An officer with a megaphone gives out instructions. "WE HAVE YOU SURROUNDED. COME OUT WITH YOUR WEAPONS DROPPED AND YOUR HANDS UP! FAILURE TO DO SO AND WE WILL FIRE! YOU HAVE 30 SECONDS!" D'Shawn smiles and closes his eyes. As the constant beeps of the explosives continue to count down, D'Shawn looks back at his men. Then he heats up his body and surrounds himself, along with his men.

The police all begin to load and aim their guns. As they anxiously wait for the order, a huge fire wave in the shape of a dragon blows through their ranks, killing nearly a third of their force while disorienting the remainder. Then D'Shawn and his OBR squad quickly blaze through the partially melted police cars. Despite snipers trying to hit some of the men, the fire shield generates so much heat and protection that the bullets literally burn to nothing.

Soon, the men make their way past the blockade, towards their rendezvous spot, and enter into their well-camouflaged vehicles. Afterwards, they quickly drive off and away from the city block. Afterwards, D'Shawn radios his men while breathing hard.

"Return to base with the boys, locate their parents, then wait for further instructions. We will get them to their families as soon as they are fed and taken care of."

"ROGER THAT!" the microphone responds.

The driver briefly looks at D'Shawn and speaks his mind. "Congratulations on the mission, sir." D'Shawn shakes his head and smiles. He is hesitant to respond, so much so that the driver again addresses him. "Sir, are you alright?"

"This is just a skirmish," D'Shawn responds. "We're now at war, and every Black person is a target. This is only the beginning…"

# Chapter 40: Shadows from Hell

The night covers the skies of the city. The people go through their daily lives without an inkling of worry or concern beyond the scope of their world. As the shadows begin to emerge, Malik posts on the top of a building overseeing the layout of downtown Madrid.

His mind again wonders as the accumulation of information and language press beyond his previous limits of his mind. He shakes his head with discontent. His comprehension of the world is now being questioned, and he feels a sudden dread with running out of time.

"I have been away from home for almost TWO weeks now," Malik complains. "Yet, the more I search, the less I understand." Malik rubs his forehead and controls his thoughts. He briefly takes a breath, closes his eyes, then covers his head with his hood. Afterwards, he opens his eyes and allows the glow of its majesty to alleviate the mental strain.

A gust of wind and a shift of power alert Shadowmoor of a presence. Undeterred, he remains stoic while facing the city. Triana and Esmeralda slowly walk by him with glowing eyes and the yearning for adventure.

"Hola Malik, or should we call you Shadowmoor now?" Triana gracefully greets. Esmeralda rolls her eyes while Shadowmoor chuckles underneath his breath.

"It's good to see you and Senorita Sassy over here," he responds. Esmeralda smacks her lips then addresses the agenda. "If we are done clowning around, as you would say in America," Esmeralda scolds, "we need to search the old warehouse about ten blocks west of here."

"If the place was burned and deserted, what do you hope to find there?" Shadowmoor asks.

"Um… are you aware of your power to trace receptors?" Triana asks.

Shadowmoor squints his eyes and ponders for a second. Then he immediately responds when he understands the reasoning.

"That's right," Shadowmoor says. "Back home, I traced a group of men who killed a boy by the residue they left. So, you're trying to do the same."

"Heh, the American can learn something, other than how to make hamburgers," Esmeralda responds sarcastically. "But because we are used to seeing the same receptor, we think that a fresh set of eyes can weed out the one that can lead us to them."
"Understood," Shadowmoor responds.

Esmeralda struts behind Shadowmoor and Triana as she faces west bound. She smirks, activates her Avemcernentia, and gives the command. "Entonces, ¿nos vamos? ¡No tengo toda la noche! (So, shall we get going? I don't have all night)!"
"Por supuesto (Of course)," Triana nervously responds. "Shadowmoor?" Shadowmoor nods at Triana, then at Esmeralda. "Lead the way, Esmeralda," Shadowmoor says.
"Heh, Intenta mantenerte ... americano (try to keep up...American)."

Esmeralda and Triana jump off the building and down towards a nearby building. Shadowmoor scoffs, then pursues them.

The Moors maneuver through the alleys and streets of the busy night. They camouflage themselves in the shadows while silently refusing to alert their environment of their presence. The rhythm of their jumps, flips, and movements flow like poetry on a rainy day. As Esmeralda continues to lead ahead, Triana treads closely behind while Shadowmoor remains within their proximity.

As the trio draw near to their destination, Shadowmoor moves within earshot of Triana as he sparks up a short conversation.

"Is she always such a hard ass, or is this her personality?" Shadowmoor asks.
"Well, it's complicated. The one we are looking for…" Triana hesitates before finishing, "She and Esmeralda trained together when they were young. They became really close, so close that she was the only one who could control her, you know…"
"Oh! I see. Don't worry, we'll find her, one way or another."

Suddenly Esmeralda begins to shout. "Mira vivo (Look alive), we're here!" Esmeralda lifts her right arm and signals them to stop. The warehouse is completely deserted, with remnants of ash, charcoal, and death while the remaining paint, wood, and ceramic hold the fragile structure by a thread. Esmeralda closes her eyes and begins to take in the aroma of regret and remorse. Triana slowly walks by her side. Before she could say anything, Esmeralda snaps out of it and gives the command.

"Amplify your eyes to see if you can find any clues, Shadowmoor. Triana and I will circle around and do the same." "Comprendida (Understood)," Shadowmoor responds as he starts to walk around the perimeter.

Esmeralda and Triana walk along the borders of the building as they scan around the deserted patch of land. Triana gets on her knees and scraps the ground with her hands while Esmeralda looks up at the building. She stares at oblivion while Triana continues to examine the burn stains on the lawn.

After standing still for two minutes, Triana senses Esmeralda troubled and gets up to try to comfort her.

"Estás bien (Are you alright)?" Triana asks.
"Te sugiero que te preocupes menos por mí y sigas buscando pistas (I suggest you worry less about me and keep looking for clues)," Esmeralda responds harshly. "Cada segundo que desperdiciamos, Eulalia podría ser (Every second we waste, Eulalia could be) …"
"Es gracioso lo duro que intentas ser (It's funny how tough you try to be)," Triana interrupts. "Pero no estás solo. Me tienes a mí y a Malik. La recuperamos (But you're not alone. You have me, and Malik. We'll get her back)."
"OI, the American… I don't know."
"You need to learn how to trust others, Esmeralda," Triana concludes with a smile. "Come, let's keep looking."

Meanwhile, Shadowmoor continues to look around trying to pick up any receptors. Nothing unusual can be seen and Shadowmoor begins to grow impatient.

"Damnit, I don't see anything out of the ordinary," Shadowmoor ponders. "It's strange. Nothing is left. It's as if everything was burned to oblivion and that smell...wait a minute..." The aroma from the sight is distinct and strong. The smell doesn't give off the stench of sulfur and carbon, but something else. Shadowmoor sits down on the ground and begins to concentrate.

"This smell is something different. Maybe if I sync my senses to the aroma, it may give me a trail to follow. Can't hurt to try." Shadowmoor closes his eyes and begins to hold his breath. He becomes one with his surroundings by blocking his mind and ears to everything but the moment. Then he begins to take a slow breath to ignite his Fire Line. After a few seconds, he takes another breath. More time passes, then he takes one more breath.

The area becomes still and enclosed by Shadowmoor. The noise is non-existent and the clouds in his mind dissipate. After taking one, last, deep breath, Shadowmoor opens his eyes and creates a heat wave. The surge of energy allows Shadowmoor to detect particles from a microscopic and atomic state. When Shadowmoor takes a sniff that he identifies as odd, he is able to trace a bluish-purple receptor trail with a chemical compound. When Shadowmoor intensifies the heat, Triana and Esmeralda's eyes illuminate. "Creo el ha encontrado algo (I think he's found something), Triana," Esmeralda suspects. "Vamos a reunirnos con el (Let's meet up with him)."

Shadowmoor continues to pinpoint the chemical component with the receptor. The women come within a few inches of Shadowmoor before he instructs them.

"Sync your eyes with mine," he says. "Then you'll see what I see." Without resistance or sass, both women nod to each other and brighten their eyes.

As the Avemcernentia amplifies, Esmeralda sees the receptor fields and begins to gasp. "I recognize this signature. This is... How did you..." Shadowmoor lowers his heat wave, deactivates the Dracocernentia, and gets up.

Esmeralda becomes soft, reserved, and conflicted with the reveal. Triana holds up her hand for a bit but stands back as Shadowmoor approaches Esmeralda.

"Se como te sientes (I know how you feel)," Shadowmoor comforts, as he slowly and gracefully puts his hand on her right shoulder. "Las receptoras...se mezclan con productos químicos de cloro, harina, hidrógeno y oxígeno. Creo que es algún tipo de anestesia (Her receptors… are mixed with chemicals of chlorine, fluorine, hydrogen, and oxygen. I think it's some type of anesthesia), Shadowmoor explains. "So that means, Eulalia was paralyzed," Triana asks.
"I think so," Shadowmoor responds, then faces Esmeralda. "Don't worry, we'll get her back."

Esmeralda turns her head for a bit as she tries to hide her emotions, then she moves Shadowmoor's hands away. Her eyebrows begin to move downward, her eyes begin to gleam, and her voice becomes raspy.

"Tenemos el rastro ahora. La firma se dirige al oeste de la ciudad (We have the trail now. The signature heads west of the city)."
"¿A dónde podrían llevarla? (Where could they possibly take her?)" Shadowmoor asks.
"Castillo de Aulencia (Aulencia Castle)," Triana adds. "Fue construido por los moros. Es el más cercano a la ciudad (It was built by the Moors. It's the closest one to the city)."
"Then we need to hurry," Shadowmoor states. "Lideren el camino, señoras (Lead the way)." Esmeralda, Triana, and Shadowmoor face westbound, activate their eyes, and begin to trek their way towards the castle.

The trek doesn't take long. The trio move only forty-five miles per hour to conserve as much strength as they can, trying to remain concealed in the shadows. Despite the urgency of the journey, Shadowmoor immerses himself in the countryside while feeling a strange connection to the land.
"It's strange," Shadowmoor contemplates. "Despite growing up in America, I feel like...I've been here before. I know my ancestors built this land more than a millennia ago, but…"
"It's beautiful, isn't it?" Triana asks. "Sometimes my mind wanders too. Especially when the sun rises."
"Yes, it is," Shadowmoor says. "This has been a strange yet fulfilling journey for me."

Esmeralda glances back for a moment but says nothing. The slightest curve of the left side of her mouth escapes upwards as her heart flutters. Her hard demeanor takes a brief break, as she too grows fond of the connections building, even if the progression is slow and calculated. "Hmmm...If he only knew how connected he really is to this land, this world, our people," Esmeralda ponders. "Perhaps he is the one to…" Suddenly, an old, brown structure appears on the horizon. The color is as dark and bland as a bowl of beans. The foundation is as rugged as the mountains of the north, and the winds blowing against it sing tunes of time. Esmeralda quickly refocuses. She grabs Shadowmoor and Triana's attention.

"Mira vivo (Look alive)," Esmeralda yells. "Nosotros estamos aquí (We're here).

The trio stand ten yards from the face of the castle. They sit down to take their time to recuperate their strength while devising a plan of action.

"The receptor fields end here," Esmeralda says, "but I can't see anything beyond the walls."

"That doesn't make sense, Esmeralda," Triana responds. "Our eyes have the power to see through anything. How could this be?"

"It took a lot of power for me to pinpoint the chemicals associated with the receptors," Shadowmoor adds. "If I were to guess, I think there is a chemical compound that can neutralize our powers."

"Which may explain why we couldn't fight back effectively, that night," Esmeralda realizes.

Shadowmoor gets up, then addresses the Phoenix Moors. "Then we need to be prepared for the worst. We need to stick together and keep the power of our eyes to a minimum. We'll need the reserve strength to face what may be in there." Triana nods with compliance while Esmeralda scoffs. Then she closes her eyes, swallows her pride, then looks up at Shadowmoor.

"(Sigh) No me gusta esto ... pero estamos contigo … (I don't like this...but we are with you…) Shadowmoor." Shadowmoor nods, then they all enter the castle doors silently.

The halls of the old castle are dark, damp, and gloomy. Despite the power of their eyes, the Moors still find it difficult to maneuver without alerting their presence. They trek downward towards the base of the castle as they keep closer together. To prevent making any sounds, the Moors communicate telepathically to maintain their silence.

"Why do you think she was led here?" Shadowmoor asks.

"I suspect that the enemy thinks the sword is here," Esmeralda responds.

"Well, is it…"

"I… I don't know."

"What do you mean you do not know?"

Esmeralda hesitates. She begins to rub her arms and comfort herself. Sensing the impatience in Shadowmoor, Triana interjects to explain the reasoning of Esmeralda's apprehension.

"We were never informed of the whereabouts of the sword. We were only sworn to protect certain structures of our ancestors without question."

"So, in other words, they are guessing this may be the location." Shadowmoor asks.

"Si. Only the descendant of the Golden Dragon Moor can open the door. However, it is possible a select few of us know the actual chamber." Shadowmoor stops to think. He chooses not to respond but continues to trek downward.

As they get closer to the base of the castle, there is something in the air that thickens. The mist is wet, it is odorless, but the senses begin to deplete. Triana is the first to notice that something is not right.

"I… feel… dizzy," Triana says. "I feel like…"

"Shhh Triana, you can't talk or else…"

"Esmeralda… I can't…" Triana begins to fall on her knees. Esmeralda stops to desperately try to help Triana. Shadowmoor stops to look around. The brows on his head move downward and his muscles become tense.

"Something's not right…" he suspects. "What is going on here?"

Suddenly, bright lights turn on. Shadowmoor, Esmeralda, and Triana frantically look around to see what is going on. Then, small openings on the ceiling wall expose black tubes that spray a noxious gas.

"Everyone, cover your mouth and run!" Shadowmoor yells.

"But Triana…"

"I SAID RUN!"
"I can keep up, Esmeralda. We have to get out of here!"
So Shadowmoor, followed by Esmeralda and Triana run down the hallway towards the stairs. However, the gases coming out of the valves continue to penetrate their bodies, numbing their muscles and their ability to move. Triana lags as Esmeralda looks back.
"Triana, you need to hurry!"
"Don't worry, I'll be…" POW
A large gunshot moves so fast, it pierces through the back of Triana, then exits out of her chest. Esmeralda's eyes widen as Shadowmoor turns around. Triana crashes towards the ground as Esmeralda screams with agonizing sorrow.
"TRIANA!" Esmeralda extends her arm as Shadowmoor runs back towards Triana. With little strength, Triana slowly tries to get up and extend her arm. With blood dripping down her mouth, she lets out one last, smiling cry.
"I'm ok, I'll…" POW
A single bullet pierces through the back of the neck, then exits through the throat. Both Esmeralda and Shadowmoor's eyes widen and water, as the life of their companion flows out like the blood from her neck. Triana's eyes begin to roll back. Her body floats down the ground, and a low shriek fills the air. "NOOOOOOOOOO! TRIANA!"
Both Esmeralda and Shadowmoor crash down to the ground, trying desperately to revive Triana. As her lifeless body lay dormant, Shadowmoor confirms the worse as Esmeralda emphatically cries while grabbing her hair.
"She's… dead…" Shadowmoor says.
"NOOOOOO!" Esmeralda continues to cry as Shadowmoor looks at Esmeralda.
"Get out of here," he says softly as Esmeralda's long-contained emotions flow out of control. Shadowmoor yells to get Esmeralda's attention. "ESMERALDA, YOU NEED TO GO NOW!"
"But...but…"
"I'll cover you. Go… now."

Esmeralda gets ahold of herself, nods, then responds. "Volveré por ti (I will come back for you) ... Shadowmoor." Shadowmoor nods as Esmeralda musters up the strength to escape down the hall and towards the stairs.

Shadowmoor draws the remaining amount of power from within his Fire Line. He uses the pain from the loss of Triana to generate anger and frustration. His eyes begin to turn reddish, and his body becomes consumed with flames. When a small number of men get within range, Shadowmoor lets off a roar of a dragon and generates a large fire wave. The surge of fire incinerates the men within his view while giving enough heat for Esmeralda to regenerate some of her power. She briefly looks back while she runs up the stairs, wipes her eyes, and makes her escape.

After the spectacle, Shadowmoor collapses towards the ground. His eyes turn back to his normal state. They begin to roll up, and his vision gets fuzzy. Soon he hears footsteps coming towards him. Before Shadowmoor can make out who it is, a familiar voice echoes across the room.

"Aw… you don't look so good," the woman says.

"Baby, I think he needs help."

"Well, my Caramel Candy, I think you're right." Shadowmoor slowly looks up, but his vision is blurred. He sees a familiar form placing her hand on another man's chest while he grabs the small of her back. Then he begins to slur words.

"A… A… Audrey…?" Then Victor kicks Shadowmoor in the face, knocking him unconscious.

"Nighty night… Shadowmoor." Victor snickers as his henchmen grab his body and escort him away.

# Chapter 41: Deal with the Devil

A single drop of water falls from the ceiling. The perpetual cycle gets louder and louder as a man slowly wakes up from unconsciousness. As he opens his eyes, the fuzzy blurring that occupies his sight slowly clears in focus. The heaviness of the gas still surrounds the cell. It pierces through the pores and immobilizes the muscles. Finally, when the eyes open wide, Shadowmoor finds himself ensnared in an uncomfortable bondage. Each arm is raised with each wrist tied to shackles.

Shadowmoor begins to moan and groan. The battle took a toll on his body, but the loss of Triana causes his face to sink.

"Damnit…" he regrets. "Triana… too sweet to even imagine her fighting. I hope Esmeralda got away safely." A single tear sheds and drips down the right cheek of Shadowmoor, as the burden of shame flow through his body as fast as the surrounding gas.

Suddenly, the valves close and retreat back to the ceiling. Shadowmoor notices the change but is unable to maneuver his neck to inspect the ceiling. His breathing becomes hard and heavy, his heart beats hard, and his muscles feel frozen in place. Footsteps come towards the cell. The closer they come, the louder the echoes. Shadowmoor waits with anticipation for those responsible for capturing the Moor.

Then, the echoes stop, and the footsteps face the cell. A key is pulled from the pocket. Then it is inserted into the lock, and the sound of old metal creeks as the door opens. Afterwards, two sets of footsteps walk in the cell.

Shadowmoor's head is facing down. The steps continue to march close to him. A flow of temperature moves through his face as a pair of cold, treasonous hands embrace his cheeks. The hands slowly lift his head, while the right hand removes his hood and mask. Then, the once sweet sounds become venom, as condescending words pour out of the mouth like a cobra's bite.

"Aw… are you OK? I thought you'd be happy to see me?" Shadowmoor looks up with wet, glossy, and hurt eyes. He doesn't have the strength to respond, yet his gaze says it all.

"Well, my Caramel Candy, I think he's still in a bit of shock," Victor says, while smirking at his long-awaited prize.

Audrey looks back, smiles, and walks next to Victor. Both share a kiss, then she looks back at Shadowmoor. The red in Shadowmoor's eyes desperately try to hold back the turbidity of tears only held by his unwillingness to fully concede defeat.

"Say darling, why don't you go get that special thing for me." Victor says.

"But I thought that you would want to…"

"Shhhh… It's my gift to you," Victor interrupts. "Nothing but the best for my sweet chocolate."

Audrey plants another kiss, then responds. "You are so good to me." Audrey then steps away, looks back at Shadowmoor, then blows a kiss to him.

As Audrey walks out of the cell and down the hall, Victor begins to chuckle. He holds a small glass in his right hand while holding his left hand in his pocket. He paces slowly back and forth, taking his time to converse with the disgruntled hero. After pacing the cell for a minute, Victor stops and faces Shadowmoor. He takes a deep breath, closes his eyes, then cracks another smile.

"She is a lovely woman, yes?" he asks sarcastically, as he opens his eyes. Shadowmoor musters up the strength to make eye contact with the devil in the shadows. "Oh, excuse me, where are my manners? Hmm Hmm Hmm, you don't know who I am, do you?"

Victor fixes his brown hair and clears his throat. "My name is Victor Goth. And you, my friend, are the infamous Shadowmoor… or should I say Malik Wilson…" He pauses to take a sip from his glass. "Or… (he points and clenches his lips) should I call you Marshall Benson?!"

Shadowmoor looks up. His eyes squint and his attention is at full alert. Victor notices the micro expressions, then smiles.

"You may wonder how I know about you? (Sigh) Well, let's just say that you have been a thorn on our ass since you had the displeasure of being pushed out by your whore of a mother. It's a shame that he wasn't able to fully indoctrinate you. At one point, we could have been brothers in a common goal...to reach our potential (sip)...to fulfill our purpose...to control the destiny of men…"

Shadowmoor slurs his words before he could regain full control of his motor skills. Victor notices and takes the time to sip more of his liquor. After a few attempts, Shadowmoor is able to make coherent, concise words.

"You're with the Elite 8. You worked with William Benson, and despite what happened to him, kept monitoring me."

Victor smiles, hands one of his body guards his glass, then sarcastically claps. "Well, well, well," Victor compliments, "you are brilliant. So brilliant. Too brilliant." Victor continues to pace back and forth in the cell as Shadowmoor slowly regains his mobility. Shadowmoor spits a squirt of blood from his mouth, then re-engages the conversation.

"Why didn't you kill me? What am I doing here?"

"Straight to the point, are we?" Victor responds. "Hmm… Well, you're right about one thing. Killing you would be practical, but I want to savor this moment of conquest and accomplishment. You see, it was your people who dragged my people nearly to extinction."

"Your people? What are you talking about?"

"(Sigh) For someone who is in tune with his ancestors, you are remarkably ill-informed in history. Oh well, I guess I can give you a short lesson."

Victor positions his body in front of Shadowmoor. His face is pale, his skin flushes red, and his gaze is uncompromising. Then he smiles again before beginning his soliloquy.

"About 2000 years ago, my people fled the barren cold lands of northern Europe and settled in the valley around Hungary and Serbia. However, we were attacked by the Huns of the east. With little resources and the means to defend ourselves, we made a deal. A deal with an empire, a deal with the symbol of complex civilization...but a deal with the devil."

Victor clasps his hands behind his back. He paces back and forth in the cell before stopping once again to finish his story.

"So, the Romans provided shelter, food, and supplies in exchange for giving men to protect the eastern borders from the barbarians. For 500 long years, those greedy, corrupt bastards exploited my people while they grew fat, lazy, and weak." Victor takes a breath to collect his thoughts. Shadowmoor listens with intrigue but says nothing.

"But then, one of my ancestors, a man named Alaric, grew tired of the Roman antics. He decided that power is an all or nothing proposition. Either you have it, or you don't. So, he besieged the Roman capitol and forced them to ensure lands for my people so that we would stop running. But little did Alaric know, after he died, his success paved the way for another great man to complete the task. His name was Gaiseric. He caused the great Roman Empire to collapse under the weight of its own complacency and loss of power. Afterwards, we settled here, on the ground that we stand on right now."
Shadowmoor's eyes widen. He lifts his head, clears his throat, and responds to Victor.
"I get it now. Your people...the history...you're a descendant of the..."
"The people your ancestors slaughtered and built castles like this above the bones of the conquered," Victor sneers as his rage temporarily gets the better of him. He stares down Shadowmoor with bulging, veiny-filled, hazel eyes.
After a few tense seconds of silence, Victor pulls back, fixes his hair, and calms himself down. "(Sigh), I almost admire you; you know that? Your parents… I mean your real ones of course… were essentially murdered. My former mentor adopted you, hoping to exploit your hidden power, much to his disappointment you never achieved," Victor continues while pacing. "Yet, in a stroke of poetic irony, was able to tap in your own power by seeking who and where you come from."
Shadowmoor nods, then responds to Goth. "So, did you keep me alive because of the sword?"
"Oh...much more than that. You see, thanks to your… naivete, and for the record, how could anyone resist such...a beautiful woman, you led us to the sword. However, only a descendant can activate its power."
"So, what makes you think I'm going to help you?" Shadowmoor asks.
Victor bursts out in laughter and points emphatically. He chuckles for a few seconds, then pauses. He stands still for a second and holds his head down.
Then, like a burst from a napalm, Victor cocks his right arm and violently back slaps Shadowmoor in the face. The stream of blood migrates out of Shadowmoor's mouth then settles on the dust covered walls. Victor then grabs Shadowmoor's chin, grits his teeth, and gives a demonic smile.

"We're going to play a game… Once I retrieve the sword, you can either freeze in this cell and die, OR…your eyes will ignite the sword. Either way, I still win." Goth finishes, before letting go of Shadowmoor's chin. "Now, doesn't that sound like a fun game?" Shadowmoor's head slinks downward from humiliation and exhaustion. Victor receives a towel from one of his bodyguards. He wipes his hand, turns around, and walks out of the cell. He then pulls a remote control in his pocket and pushes a button.

Four compartments on the ceiling open, exposing four separate valves. Two valves release the same numbing gas while the other two valves blow freezing, cold air. Goth locks the cell, smiles, then nods at Shadowmoor. Goth nods to his bodyguards as they escort them down the hallway, leaving Shadowmoor to rot in the cell by himself.

Several hours later, Victor is sitting in his office in a skyscraper in Madrid. He picks up a cigar from his desk, gets up from his chair, and walks towards the setting sun. He continues to look at the city lights while basking in his accomplishments.

Suddenly, a knock on the door interrupts his silence. Still dangling his cigar, he addresses the noise.

"You may enter," he says. The door opens, and a man in a black suit, white shirt, and sunglasses walks through. He goes to Victor and whispers in his right ear. Victor smiles and looks at the man.

"Excellent! This is cause for celebration."

"Sir, it is almost time for the council."

"Good. What better way to celebrate than with the council. Log on to our discord and turn on the screens." The man nods, walks to the monitors on the wall, then logs on the computer mainframe.

Victor fixes his collar, his hair, and continues to dangle his cigar. The screens begin to light up. The videos finish buffering. One by one, the visuals and the audio begin to load up, as the council commences the session.

"Council member, this meeting is now in session," the council leader states. "Unfortunately, we must skip the formalities to address the reason for this meeting."

"By all means, council leader, address your grievances," Goth scoffs.

"Victor Goth, you were warned that your operations are causing too much activity. Your methods are jeopardizing…"

"Jeopardizing...why, what do you mean?"

"As you already know, our resources are depleted from the events of last year. You were told not to engage in any activity without this council's approval."

Goth continues to snicker to the accusations. He paces back and forth while the council continues to chastise him.

"We do not find this amusing," Council member #2 says. "If you won't comply, then it is this council's decision to…"

Goth interrupts by lifting his finger. Then he takes his cutter from his pocket. He cuts the tip of his cigar. Afterwards, he pulls out a match, lights his cigar, and takes a huge puff. As he looks at his cigar, he addresses the council.

"You know…as long as I can remember, I have worked hard, gained wealth, and exceeded your expectations. I have created one of the most potent biochemical weapons known to man. I have captured the one man who has thwarted our efforts. AND… I have successfully located, obtained, and will wield one of the most powerful swords ever to be forged by a man...and yet, all you can do is criticize, condemn, and disparage our accomplishment while you sit in your secluded, squeaking, leather chairs doing nothing."

"How dare… you talk this way towards…(GWAAK)" The sound is preceded by the sound of a knife sliding across the throat.

Suddenly, a sea of yelps fills the speakers from all but one large monitor in the middle of the wall. Confused, the council leader looks at the other monitors in horror. Then he looks behind him to see shadowy figures surrounding him. Each of the monitors showcase the lifeless bodies slumped on their desks as their faces drown in a pool of blood. As the council leader cowers, Goth continues to smoke his cigar, then he looks at the monitor.

"Are you familiar with the 48 Laws of Power, Council Leader?"
Council Leader stays motionless while Goth looks on. "No… well, I
love the Laws of Power. As a matter of fact, you know what this
reminds me of? Hmm Hmm Hmm," Goth continues, as he takes a puff
from his cigar. "You know, Law 39 states that you stir up waters to
catch fish. Did you know, that in a certain part of the world, killer
whales will swim deep below a school of unsuspecting fish? Waiting,
plotting, swimming, all while their unsuspecting prey carry along with
their lives. Then, the whales will blow bubbles from the depths with
their blowholes and cause chaos in the schools. As the fish continue to
panic, they coral in a tight ball, falling in their false sense of...security."
Goth takes one more puff before finishing his point.

"Then, when the fish think they are safest, they meet
their...untimely death by entering the mouths of hungry whales. You see,
why you were so fixated and frustrated on my course of action, you
became blind and stupid of your surrounding from your lack
of...mobility. This is the other council members meeting their makers.
Why, you stand powerless in a place YOU thought you were safest?
AND why OUR TIME IS NOW! We have followed your obscure,
inadequate leadership for far too long. The time of the Elite 8 is gone…
and the Elitetion is who truly controls the destiny of men."
"You will not get away with this insurrection, Goth!" Council Leader
responds.

"But I already have. I'm not going to kill you, no no no. Instead,
you will be placed in heavy guard and bear witness to centuries of
planning. You will witness what your decrepit generation failed to do
while my generation will prevail once and for all. And… after we have
control of the destiny of this planet, then… and only THEN…(sigh) will
you die in disgrace."
Goth grabs a glass from his table. He opens a drawer, takes a bottle of
whiskey, pours it in the glass, then walks back to the front of the
monitor.
Goth raises his glass and chants. "For right and reason…"
"WE WILL FULFILL ELITETION!" the rest of the monitors
reciprocate as Goth takes a sip in toast.
"Gentlemen, our time is now. Until next time…"

Afterwards, the monitors turn off and Goth turns around. He finishes his drink, looks at his glass, then throws it on the ground. The sweat from his forehead pours down his face, his lips curve upwards, and his mouth exposes his crooked teeth. Then he laughs maniacally, as the setting sun signifies the turn of the tide.

# Chapter 43: Words of the Father

A day has passed by since Malik has been captured. The prolonged time without food, water, or rest has left Malik at the brink of death. The cell is dark and damp. The surrounding air is unrelenting and chilly. The muscles in Malik's body begin to shiver and quake, as the endless stream of gas and cool air keep the young man suppressed.

In his defeated state, Malik becomes hypnotized by the dripping water from the cool air valve. Each drip is like a signal of time. The soothing sound relaxes Malik's eyes as they draw closer and closer towards the border of his lower lids.

Drip...drip...drip...drip...drip.... Moments later, Malik is drawn into a trance. The surrounding area is pitch black. The perception of space, gravity, and time disappear in the vast sea of emptiness. Only the sound persists. Drip...drip...drip…

Malik sits down in the void of nothingness. His convictions clouded, his confidence shattered, and his Fire Line begins to dim like a flame on a wax less candle. Malik says nothing. He stares at nothing as he continues to sit, only listening to the dripping. Drip...drip...drip…

After seemingly several lifetimes, the dripping is interrupted by a sound of a patted shoulder. Malik slowly changes the apathy showcased on his face. The sound cures him of his insanity and plunge of nothingness. Then, a voice breaks the deathly silence.

"Giving up already?" the voice says. Malik curves his eyebrows in confusion. Then the voice begins to chuckle. "Come on...get up," the voice instructs. Malik slowly turns his head and investigates the source of this seemingly familiar voice. Trusting only his impulses, Malik turns around and sees the source of the calming, deep voice.

"Hey Malik. You have a minute?"
Malik's eyes begin to water, as the voice gives him the kind of comfort denied to him as a child. "D...D... Dad…" Malik stutters. "I expected… I mean…"
The man holds up his hand and smiles. Then he snaps his fingers. Suddenly, the void disintegrates into several pieces like shards of glass. Malik swivels his head back, forth, left side and right as the man continues to stand still.

After several seconds, Malik and his father find themselves on a cliff side overlooking a mountain range. In total shock and awe of the spectacle, Malik remains speechless as his father continues to ease his troubles.

"Beautiful, is it not, son?" Malik remains quiet but nods in acknowledgement. Then his father prompts him to sit on the ground in easy pose. Then, Malik musters up the nerve to speak.

"Dad, what are you doing? I mean, I honestly expected someone like Amir or …"
"Oh, I get it," Michael sneers. "So, your old man isn't good enough to give you some advice huh?"

Malik awkwardly looks away from a moment. He shrugs his shoulders and rubs his arm, then re-engages his father. Michael stares at Malik with the intensity of a heart attack. His brows lower, his eyes sharpen, and his lips begin to curve downward.

After a short moment, Michael bursts into laughter and joy, as Malik looks at him crazy. "Gwahahahahahahahaha… wow… my son is a bit of a stiff," Michael chuckles, "but I guess it can't be helped." Malik nervously chuckles as both men embrace the rare moment of clarity and companionship.

Both men sit down. Malik takes a deep breath as Michael examines his son's mannerisms.

"You don't seem too sure about yourself right now. Tell your old man what's bothering you." Malik crosses his arms in frustration. He closes his eyes and shakes his head in disgust.

"I graduated with honors. I was able to reach pinnacle success in my online business before I turned 24," Malik sulks. "I was able to accomplish things deemed impossible for 95% of our people. So how in the hell did I fall into this trap?"

Michael, again, bursts into laughter as Malik looks at him with a raised left eyebrow and a disgruntled face. Michael shakes his head as he catches his breath.

"I'll tell you why...CUZ YOU'RE SPRUNG! Because you dealt with the only mystery that is ever evolving, even though their basic biology is the same. Because as men, women have the ability to either lower our defenses or put them on high alert."

Malik again, shakes his head in disbelief. Michael returns the gesture with a smile while patting him on his shoulder. "Malik, I've seen through your eyes your triumphs...and your struggles. Have you seen your mother?"

"Only from a few pictures my grandparents have. (Malik sighs) Who would've thought of the things that drive us to make unexplainable decisions."

"(Sigh) Malik, look at me," Michael commands.

As Malik looks into his father's eyes, the reflection shows a pride never experienced by another person towards him. The feeling of unconditional love, patience, and understanding is a feeling strange to Malik, even at his age. Then Malik looks towards the horizon.

"You know, son, I could stare at the sky all day long when I was a kid. Did you know that I once wanted to be a fighter pilot?"

"Yeah, Grandfather told me before he died. How did you get into that?"

Michael clears his throat. He glances at the sky one last time before facing Malik. The softness of his face with his perpetual cycle of smiles puts Malik at ease, as Michael prepares to explain his passions.

"When I was about 12 years old, Mom and Dad took me to the state fair outside the inner city. I remember it being warm despite the cool winds and the slightly turned brownish green leaves. I was walking around the park, trying to ride every ride, play every game, and try every snack."

"I see," Malik responds. "I bet my grandparents were tired."

"HA HA HA… your grandfather complained. He'd say, 'Boy, I have two legs but one set of lungs!'"

Both Malik and Michael laugh at the expression. Tears begin to flow from the side of Malik's eyes, as Michael continues his story.

"Yeah, your grandfather was direct and blunt, but also loving as well as involved. So much so, that I noticed he was leading me to a section of the park."

"Where did you go, Dad?"

"Hold on, son. I'm getting to that part," Michael continues. "So, when we get there, I see a line of people hovering over the most beautiful thing I had seen up to that point. It was a vintage, custom blue paint with yellow stripes running along the plane. It was the first time I'd seen a F-18 Hornet. A squad of four planes called the Blue Angels."

"F-18s? Blue Angels?" Malik asks.

"Yes, sir. Then I remembered one of the pilots walking up as I kept looking at the wings and wheels of the plane. Your grandparents stood by as the pilot walked up to me."

"So, what did he say?"

"Well, he chuckled and said, 'Son, she's a beauty, right?' When I looked at him, I thought that he was the coolest looking person in the world. He was a tall Black man, with a short, curly haircut, and a single thin mustache above his lip. He looked at me and lowered his body towards the ground to talk to me."

Malik looks at his father revisiting his memories. The level of joy of that event invigorates through his pores like mountains flowing with milk and honey. The sparkle in his eyes tingle like stars in a dark night. Malik too feels a sense of pride as his father continues with his story.

"So, he tells me this, 'Hey, do you want to know a secret?' I nod and smile as your grandparents smiled as well from a distance. He continued by saying, 'You know when I fly up there, I'm powerful, I'm fast, I'm…free. Are you going to see the show later?' I shook my head so hard that my head almost snapped out of my body." Malik laughs again as his father continues his story.

"So later that day, I saw the Angels perform their air show. It was the best thing I ever saw how in sync the pilots were, the crashing sound of the engines, and the power of their flight...Almost seemed like a flight of…"

"Dragons…" Malik interjects softly.

"Hmmm… that was the day I decided that I wanted to be a pilot."

"Right," Malik acknowledges as they both sit in a moment of silence.

Then, a flow of dread blows across their faces. Malik clinches his hands as he gathers himself to ask the tough questions he's always wanted to confirm. His voice becomes deep, his breath heavy, and his sorrow consuming.

"Dad… that night… the night that you died. Did you know about your…"?

"You mean the Dracocernentia? Our eyes? And the power hidden behind them?" Malik slowly nods his head with wet and full eyes. Michael takes a deep breath, closes his eyes, and faces Malik. "Later that day of the air show, I started to see strange colors. It was as if I could see the energy of everything around me. I said, 'Dad, everything looks weird.' He responded by saying it was just my excitement. Then he looks back and his face changes. He starts to change his attitude. He grabs my hand. Then he pulled me away from the crowd before I could finish the show."

"Did he explain why, Dad?"

"He told me to keep my eyes closed and not to open them until we got in the car. Soon after that, our relationship changed. It wasn't until I died that part of my spirit resided into you, Malik."

Malik redirects his focus to the key details of the story. His intrigue plagues him with more questions, forcing him to press his father on.

"What do you mean your relationship changed?"

"(Sigh) I remember later that day; I was sitting in my room with my lamp light on. I sat on my bed just looking at the ceiling, trying to figure out what I did wrong. So, your grandfather knocked on the door and walked in the room. He sat right next to me for a while."

"For how long, Dad?"

"It may have been for a few seconds, but to me, it might as well have been the second coming of the dinosaurs. Then he said, 'Michael, you have something special inside you that can get you hurt… if the wrong people know about it.' I said, 'Know what? What's special, Dad?' Then his voice got cold. Really cold, like a man speaking impending death from the mountain top. Then he said this: 'Son, sometimes… it's who we are and what we are capable of that prevents us from doing what we want. I think you should think about doing something else.'

'But Dad, I want to fly jets, just like…'" Michael hesitates for a moment before he finishes the story. "My father yelled at me… like I've never heard him yell before. It was as if he was reliving a painful memory.

'I SAID NO, MICHAEL! THE SAME PEOPLE THAT PILOT WORKS FOR WILL BE THE SAME ONES USING YOU FOR ONLY THEIR GAIN. THEN AFTER THEY'RE DONE WITH YOU, YOU END UP TOSSED OUT LIKE GARBAGE OR WORSE.' I sat speechless. Trembling. I could see the anger in his eyes, like two bowls of burning oil. However, I could also see the tears he was desperately trying to hold back. Then he said this: 'It's for your own good, son. (Sigh) It's your bedtime. Go to sleep, OK?' So, I crawled into bed and looked at him like my enemy. I thought to myself, 'How could he hate my dream, a dream to own the skies?' Then he kissed me goodnight, then slowly walked out of my room."

Malik faces downward as he tries to gather himself with this emotional conversation. As he senses the conversation ending, Malik generates the courage to open up.

"Dad, I wish I could've grown up with you and Mom. I wish I had your outlook on life, and your appreciation for it. How… do… I keep going when it seems that I have nothing left to give?" Michael looks at Malik and rubs his shoulder. He gives a forced smile while grabbing Malik's attention. Then he concludes his talking points to encourage Malik.

"Do you know how a jet engine works?"
"Dad, really… What does that…"
"No no no no no… do you know how jet engines work?" Malik remains silent as Michael gives him a stern, stoic look. "In a jet engine, air flows into a turbo fan. Then it enters a chamber of compressed air, then it mixes with fuel and heat, creating a reaction that propels whatever it's attached to forward. Do you want to know, to me, the most remarkable thing about jet engines?" Malik looks on with anticipation as Michael draws closer. He takes his other hand, extends his index finger, and points to his chest.

"The engine only needs a little bit of fire to fuel the machine. Malik, your struggles, your mistakes, your lack of understanding is what allows you to propel forward. Just like the jet engine, it doesn't rely solely on the little bit of gas, but it utilizes the most abundant source. We are blessed to have a Fire Line. There are three components of fire, son. The first is heat: that can come from anger, fear, or drive. The second is fuel: Sometimes you feel like you have nothing left, until you realize the third component."

"And what is the last component?" Michael doesn't relay the crucial information. Instead, the winds blow around the men as the vision becomes dark. Suddenly, the dripping returns, forcing Malik back into consciousness

Malik gasps for air, as the stampede of sweat flow down his face. He looks up at his wrists and sees the dimming lights enter the cell. As Malik continues to catch his breath, he begins to hear footsteps. As the steps get closer and closer, Malik regains his resolve and ponders the clues left by his father. "What did he mean by the realization of the third component?" Malik wonders before the walking stops.

Then, a set of keys unlock the doors. Two people show up with a golden, jewel encrusted Scimitar and condescending words pollute the air. "Look at what we found," Audrey says.

"Well, well, well, looks like you lose...Shadowmoor..." Victor cackles as the day shines on the cell.

# Chapter 44: Betrayal of Cognitive Deniability

Malik looks on with a level of disgust and rage, as Audrey flaunts the heavy sword in his face. She struts around him, teasing him with her sexual appeal while Victor smiles in triumph. She playfully swings the heavy sword around. Meanwhile, Shadowmoor keeps his composure to verify his suspicions.

"I think I may have figured out a way to get out of here," Shadowmoor schemes. "While they taunt and inflate their egos, I'll breathe carefully and use the air as fuel for my body. If what my dad says is correct, I can counteract the gases numbing my body."

Audrey then walks over to Victor and begins rubbing his back with her free hand. She pretends to bite his ear while Victor begins to speak.

"So, my Caramel Candy, do you think this is indeed the sword he was looking for?"

"Well, baby, I don't know. I mean, legend says that only a descendant or the Golden Dragon Moor can wield it."

"Hmmm… yet you are currently holding it, dear," Victor adds. "Ah… I have an idea." Victor looks Audrey in the eyes. He smirks and nods his head towards Shadowmoor. She returns the gesture with a smile. Then she walks over towards Shadowmoor and holds up the sword.

Audrey positions the sword where Shadowmoor can see the jewel mounted on the base of the cross guard. The gem is magnificent: A ruby shaped like an eye with a single obsidian line mirroring the pupil of a dragon forged in the middle.

As Shadowmoor looks directly at the mineral, the ruby enlivens to a golden reddish color. Suddenly, Shadowmoor's Dracocernentia flares up to match the intensity of the jewel. Shadowmoor becomes plague with flashes of images, signs, and years of knowledge passed down in a split second. The visions are so overwhelming, that Shadowmoor screams in agony. His eyes continue to glow. He is unable to close them. The images of a Golden Dragon begin to flood his vision.

Meanwhile, Audrey uses all her strength to hold the sword with her two hands. Her legs begin to shake. Her arms become strained. The sword produces gale-size winds that knock the bodyguards off their feet. Victor crouches down to maintain his balance. "Magnificent… power…" Victor whispers.

After the chaotic episode, the sword suddenly engulfs itself into flames. Audrey becomes stagnant with wonder and amazement. She softly gulps and chuckles as the power becomes too much for her to handle. Victor slowly walks behind her and carefully caresses her arm and body as she struggles to maintain her grip.

Then, in a flash, Audrey's eyes begin to light up. They transform into a light blue. Shadowmoor barely notices, but carefully doesn't react. "Her eyes are… transforming. Could it be… if so…"
 Audrey catches herself by closing her eyes. Her skin is wet, her breathing is hard, and her stance is weak. As she regains herself, she chuckles a little as Victor slowly moves his hand towards her waist.
"It's… magnificent," she whispers. "All my life, I didn't think it was real but...I have you to thank, my love."
"It was my pleasure, my Caramel Candy," Victor responds. He slowly moves his hand towards hers. Each inch closer is savored as Victor arrogantly looks at Shadowmoor the closer he reaches it.
When Victor's hands finally touch the base, Audrey slowly moves her hand out of the way. The sword reverts to its normal form, as the flames slowly blow away. Victor inspects the sword as Shadowmoor continues to maintain his cool.
"The Harq Alqadr," he continues. "The Burning Destiny… now… in my possession at last. And as for you, my friend, I'm afraid that this stage of our little game is now over." Audrey continues to smirk as she kisses Victor on his cheek. She rubs her hand on his face as she moves her body against his.
"Victor, sweetie. I have something that I want to tell you, my love. Can we go now?"
 "Well, my dear, why wait?" Victor responds gracefully. "I'm sure our friend here would love to hear what you have to say. Isn't that right, Shadowmoor?"
Shadowmoor crunches his eyebrows downward with contempt and disgust. However, he continues to take deep silent breaths.

"Well, Victor, now that you will soon be the master of this world, I guess you'll have a little something to pass down too." Confused, Victor looks at Audrey with a side eye. Then he smiles again in response. "What do you mean pass down?" he asks. Audrey takes Victor's free hand and places it on her belly. Then he looks again at her. She smiles and nods in confirmation as she uses his hand to rub her belly. "That's right, my love," she says. They share a passionate kiss. Suddenly, Victor takes the sword and thrusts it in Audrey's back and through her stomach. Audrey's eyes bulge out. Her shock is only exceeded by the blood flowing down her legs and crotch. The pace of the events gives no time for Shadowmoor to retain his anger. "NNNNNNOOOOOOOO!" Shadowmoor yells, as his strength begins to rejuvenate. Victor continues to chuckle as the life in Audrey's body flows out as fast as the blood. With malicious tone, Victor smiles again. "Oh… I'm so sorry, my Caramel Candy, but I am a descendant of the bastard of King Roderick. So, having my future line tainted with the blood of a Black bitch who betrayed her family and people…. well, not a good look."

"YOU…" Shadowmoor stutters.

Victor laughs as he kicks Audrey to the floor. Then he grabs a rag from one of his bodyguards to wipe the blood off the sword. As Audrey lays on the cold, unforgiving floor, tears begin to flow from her eyes. Shadowmoor's heart begins to sink, as his eyes begin to turn red. Victor smiles, waves at them, then leaves the cell. He walks down the hall as the guard locks the cell back.

Once out of his immediate sight, Shadowmoor closes his eyes. He begins to take heavy breaths. As his breaths get more intense, he yanks his arms forward. With each breath, a simmer of smoke pores out of his veins. Again, and again, Shadowmoor desperately continues to struggle to get free. His rage is uncaged. His breaths begin to flame out. His muscles, once dormant, now light up with each pull. Then, when his eyes open, the entire iris is covered in red with a single sharp pupil. Shadowmoor lets off a roar so intense, so loud, and so powerful, that he shatters his chains and fills the entire castle with a fire blast.

Once Shadowmoor gains his freedom, he rushes towards the floor towards Audrey. He grabs her lower back and lifts her head.

She looks at Shadowmoor with the little strength left in her body. Her eyes are filled with sorrow and her breathing heavy with remorse. The depth of the betrayal has left Audrey with little to no motivation to speak.

Shadowmoor grits his teeth and lets out another roar. A single tear leaves his left eye, but it quickly evaporates before it reaches his cheek. Audrey looks at Shadowmoor before coughing up more blood. Then, in an instance, soft words begin to slip out of her lips.

"Sssss… Say what you want about me… I… have no regret," she says. "Except one…" Still in a drunken rage, all Shadowmoor can do is stare at her eyes. His heavy breathing and flames continue to fuel Audrey's failing body, as she lets go of her burdens.

"That… that is your weakness...Shadowmoor," Audrey wheezes. "You care too much...for the people who don't give a damn about you. You should've done what I tried to do. Go to the winning side."

Afterwards, Audrey's eyes begin to transform from blue to brown. Flashing back and forth as she continues to maintain her breath. As Shadowmoor struggles to regain his composure, he hears some screams and footsteps coming towards the cell.

As Shadowmoor prepares himself, he generates a heat wave to cover his body from the chemicals and cold air that surround the castle. The footsteps get louder and louder.

Then, when the footsteps stop, Shadowmoor is greeted by a familiar and friendly face. Esmeralda comes in with smiles. She quickly engulfs her fist with fire and punches the keyhole of the cell. The opening melts upon contact, allowing Esmeralda to open the door.

She places her hand on Shadowmoor's shoulder and attempts to calm him down.

"Shadowmoor, listen to me. You have to control yourself before you literally explode from your rage." she says.

"But that bastard Victor…"

"You can't stop him, not in this state. Not with her dying," Esmeralda interrupts. "Controle su línea de fuego. No permitas que la maldad de tu oponente contamine tu corazón (Control your Fire Line. Do not allow the evil in your opponent to contaminate your heart)."

Shadowmoor closes his eyes and slows his breathing. He remains still, as the flames that cover his body slowly simmer down. The heat slowly gives way to the cool vents and breeze of the cell. His heart begins to pump at a normal rate. Then, after a few moments, Shadowmoor opens his eyes. They transform back to the golden hue of the Dracocernentia. Then Shadowmoor sheds a tear and smiles. "Si Senorita. Gracias."

"Da nada… Estúpido," Esmeralda responds graciously.

"How did you find me?"

"The fire wave you created ignited my Avemcernentia. I was able to follow your receptors."

"I'm glad you're here. I'm sorry about Triana… and Eulalia. I'm afraid that she…"

"She knew the location of the sword. It wasn't until I talked to someone strange that I realized she was part of a group that helped conceal it. Somehow, they found out about her and… We need to get out of here." Shadowmoor looks at Audrey. Her eyes continue to flicker from blue to brown. "What about Audrey?" he asks.

"She must choose her own destiny now," Esmeralda says. "I'm sorry, Malik. There's nothing I can do."

"COUGH COUGH… You… can go to hell," Audrey says. "Victor will use the sword to destroy you. I… just wish that…"

"You can't mean that, Audrey," Shadowmoor says.

Then Audrey begins to smile with devilish contempt. When the last remnants of life slowly flow out of her, she looks directly in Shadowmoor's eyes. Shadowmoor returns the gesture by giving her his undivided attention.

"You were too predictable… Malik Wilson. You remind me of my grandfather. But he was a fool for thinking he could educate our doomed people back to providence. My grandmother knew the truth and left him. Little did I know that I had the power within me. If I were to choose all over again: live my life pretending to be some mythical being, shunned and overlooked… or to be a bed wench to a man who will control the destiny of men… hee hee hee… well, at least I can safely say I would do the same."

As the last words of Audrey echo throughout the cell, her eyes roll back to the back of the head. With her last breath, a small flame exits her mouth. The flame is blue and takes the shape of the phoenix. Both Shadowmoor and Esmeralda look on as the flaming bird lets off a lowly screech before disappearing in the wind.

Shadowmoor lays Audrey's body to the ground while Esmeralda gets up. She shakes her head, prompting Shadowmoor to get up.

"Que triste y vergonzosa existencia (What a sad, shameful existence). We must go now." Shadowmoor gets up and looks at Audrey one last time. The memories of his first encounter, her voice, her betrayal, and her resolve leave little for Shadowmoor to ponder. "Shadowmoor… MALIK! We have to go now!" Esmeralda yells. Shadowmoor nods in compliance.

Esmeralda and Shadowmoor maneuver through the hallways of the old castle. To combat the amount of Reintergon and cool air, Shadowmoor creates a mini flame ball to encase himself and Esmeralda as they run out of the castle.

"How did you learn this power?" Esmeralda asks.

"I had a vision from my father. He gave me the clue and I just UGH…" Suddenly, Shadowmoor crashes towards the ground with agony. Sharp pains in his head trigger. He holds his head while Esmeralda yells at him.

"Shadowmoor! Shadowmoor! What is it?!" Shadowmoor closes his eyes to help quell the pain in his head. After rubbing the right side of his temple, Shadowmoor opens his eyes.

However, Shadowmoor continues to see flashes of a giant Golden Dragon's head. It has two long horns, yellow bristles on its head, two long whiskers protruding a snout filled with feathery hair, reddish gold eyes, with a single sharp pupil, like the shape of the ruby on the base of the Harq Alqadr. When Shadowmoor shakes his head, closes his eyes, then opens them again, the mysterious figure disappears.

"What is it? What did you see?" Esmeralda asks.

Shadowmoor shakes his head again and gets up. "Let's get out of here. I'll explain later." Shadowmoor reengages his flame ball and continues to trek out of the castle.

Several minutes later, Esmeralda and Shadowmoor make it out of the castle. They gain some distance by moving several miles away towards a solidary building on the countryside.

After reaching it, Shadowmoor and Esmeralda sit down and pant profusely to catch their breath. Their eyes transform back to normal as they lean their heads at the side of the building.

Both look at each other. Drenched with sweat, grit, and nearly completely out of energy, both take their time to regain their strength. As the cool winds regulate their body temperature, Shadowmoor takes the time to formulate his thoughts and debrief Esmeralda.

"You mentioned something about Eulalia knowing about the sword, and that she was part of something bigger," Shadowmoor presses. "What do you mean by something bigger?"

"A man came in earlier today and claimed to have known her. He had information about the men who took the sword and their plans."

"A man? Did you even get his name?"

"No se. Hell, the only reason why I trusted him is because when he mentioned you, his receptors showed that he was telling the truth," Esmeralda responds sarcastically. "As a matter of fact, he told me to meet him here."

"So... how long should we wait until Mr. Mystery shows up?" Then, simple footsteps begin to approach the duo. Shadowmoor notices the noise and begins to yell. "Who's there! Who are you?!"

As the figure appears from the shadow, Shadowmoor's tired eyes begin to draw out in disbelief. He slowly gets up and takes two steps towards the man. Esmeralda follows Shadowmoor but shows signs of concern. Then the man begins to speak to them both.

"It's been a long time, Malik. How are you?"

"So, you know this man, Malik?" Esmeralda asks.

"I… don't believe it," Malik responds. "Mason Richardson… What are you doing here?"

"I'm here for you, Malik. We need to talk now."

"About what?" Malik responds.

"There's more to this than the Harq Alqadr. Come with me, I'll drive you two back to Madrid, and in the morning, I'll explain everything."

Malik and Esmeralda look at each other and nod. Then they follow Mason to his black SUV, get in the vehicle, then drive on the road.

Meanwhile, Victor makes it to his suite in downtown Madrid. He is accompanied by several guards. He is greeted by an older man, wearing a black suit with a white shirt and a black necktie. He keeps an emotionless face as Victor approaches him, sword at hand.

"Congratulations, sir, in retrieving the sword."

"Thank you. Is the machine ready?"

"Right this way, Mr. Goth."

The man escorts Goth towards the back of the suite, where he sees two large cylinders filled with a purple, thick liquid substance, attached to a workstation, a CPU, and a slot to insert the sword. Victor grins with victory as he addresses both the man and his entourage.

"Today, Gentlemen, is the beginning of our reign. Once we insert the sword, its power will amplify the chemicals and cover the globe... like a shroud. And once that happens, the Black threat will finally be eliminated… and we will rule for another 1000 years." Victor then has a servant to bring him a glass while serving the rest of the men in the vicinity.

Afterwards, Victor raises his glasses and chants. "For right and reason…"

"WE WILL FULFILL ELITETION!" Then the chant is followed by a thunderous flow of applause and chanting.

# Chapter 45: The Will of the Golden Dragon

The sun rises in the east. The cool breeze blows against the windows, subtle in its flow but noticeable enough to interrupt Malik's slumber. Malik groans on the couch of his hotel room as Esmeralda is sound asleep in the bed. He slowly moves his sore body on the edge of the couch and sits quietly.

He watches Esmeralda with a focus of a microscope. Her hair blankets the pillow she rests her head. Her breathing is symmetrically soft and mellow. Her eyes are darkened with despair while the light crust forms a line down her cheek. "She must have cried herself to sleep last night," Malik ponders. "I'm sorry, Esmeralda...but I'm glad you showed up when you did."

Suddenly, a sharp pain penetrates the right side of Malik's head. So, excruciating, that Malik closes his eyes and rubs it to relieve some of the tension. He gets up from the couch and walks towards the kitchen overseeing the balcony. When Malik opens his eyes, he keeps seeing the same flashes of the Golden Dragon. "Ugh...What the hell is wrong with me?" Malik complains.

"Good morning, Malik," a voice says quietly.

Malik looks to his right. Sitting on the kitchen table, with a laptop, books, and a cellphone exposed, Mason enjoys the view while sipping a cup of coffee. He has aged little: still has a neat taper fade haircut, with waves covering the top of his head, but now with distinguishing grey streaks in his goatee. Mason puts his cup down and gets up.

"The city is beautiful, wouldn't you say?" he asks as he clasps his hands behind his back, overlooking the sunrise.

"Ugh, what happened to us last night? How did you know I was here? And how did you get here?"

"I know there's so much to explain right now, Malik," Mason answers with a slight smirk. "Come, let's get some breakfast, and then we'll talk."

Moments later, Mason fixes a simple breakfast: buttered toast, scrambled eggs, bacon, with a cup of fresh, mixed grapes, apple slices, strawberries, and blueberries. Once the men fix their plates, they sit down on the table and resume their discussion.

"So, you're wondering how I knew where you were and how to find you," Mason continues. "So, after our last encounter, I retired a few months later from the FBI. However, during those last months, I was secretly involved with a militia group known as the OBR: Order of Black Resistance. I would give them intel of the government's plans, as well as monitoring their surveillance of others like you."

"Like me, you mean those who possess the power of the Moors?"

"Precisely. You see, I had an informant who used to work for the FBI. However, she became rogue, and I was tasked with taking her down. Her name was Eulalia."

"Eulalia, you mean…"

Suddenly, a noise echoes across the suite, as footsteps draw closer towards the kitchen. Esmeralda is rubbing her hair. "Oi, Mi cabeza. ¿Qué nos pasó anoche (My head. What happened to us last night)?"

"Buenos días. ¿Le gustaría acompañarnos a desayunar (Good morning. Would you like to join us for breakfast)?" Mason offers.

"Yeah, there's everything that you'll ever want, except for something long, tall, and gratifying," Malik adds. Esmeralda scoffs at Malik while flipping him off. After she fixes her plate, she sits down on the table and joins the men.

"Gracias Señor Mason. I overheard you mentioned Eulalia. How did you know her?" Esmeralda asks.

"I was about to get to that, young lady," Mason continues. "You see, Eulalia left the United States to come to Spain about fifteen years ago. When my superiors acknowledged the accomplishments with the bust in North Carolina, they tasked me with one last assignment to find her in Spain. So, I traveled to Spain, talked to a few of my leads, and came across a group of women dedicated to protecting something, or someone."

"You mean Sombra dél Fenix," Esmeralda interjects.

"Yes. But before I could find you, Eulalia found me."

Esmeralda and Malik look at each other in shock. Mason finishes his breakfast while taking a sip of his coffee. Mason leans back in his chair while rubbing his stomach. "Man, that was a good breakfast. Now to get back to it, Eulalia confronted me not too far from here."
"What did she say to you, Mason?" Malik asks.
"So, she said, 'Mason Richardson, are you here to bring me back?' I responded by saying, 'Depends on the circumstances and your side of the story. Why did you leave the United States, your career?' Then she said something that blew my mind."
"What was it?" Esmeralda asks.
"She showed me these."
Mason takes out pictures and documents to show to Esmeralda and Malik. As they look through it, Malik's eyes nearly pop out of their sockets. His disbelief is no longer warranted, as the photos show visual evidence of the events that have transpired.
"This is a picture of Hauss… and his family, with…" Malik stutters. "And those photos are of the sword… and that Golden Dragon that keeps flashing… How did she…"
"Eulalia found out that our government was financing the Elite 8 to research biological weapons based on genealogy as well as attacking the melanin compound. Only a certain type of melanin was targeted."
"Which is why the Reintergon attacked only us because of our melanin," Malik realizes. "So that doesn't explain why Eulalia had to die," Esmeralda sneers.
"Because she isn't."
"WHAT!" Esmeralda yells. "Eres un viejo loco. La vi sacrificarse por nosotros (You are crazy, old man. I saw her sacrifice herself for us)."
"What you saw was a formulated plan to get access to the Elite 8's plans. She cleverly switched with a double who sacrificed herself to confirm what Eulalia suspected." Mason answers.
"What did she confirm, Mason?"
"That Riaahn had a living descendant, and guess who that happened to be?"

Then, a flood of emotion overcomes Malik. He relives the moments of the cell, witnessing the color of the Avemcernentia, and the phoenix flying out of her lips before disappearing. Then he gets up to face the balcony while hiding his face. Esmeralda looks on with concerned, soft eyes. Her keen senses pick up the anger that Malik is trying to control. Mason too looks on, as he gives Malik time to take in the news.

"That's why she was able to hold the sword. That's why she had the Avemcernentia...and yet she died denying what her grandfather was set to prove once and for all."

"Yes, the government allowed Willis Hauss to die because he was going to expose the truth about you and our people. They feared that we were going to unify to reclaim the lost glory of the Moors. Hauss purposely secluded himself to protect his family. Apparently, Audrey never knew the truth, so she resented him...and Black people."

"Damnit," Malik yells as he bangs his fist on the rail. "And now Victor Goth has the sword. What is he going to do with the sword?"

"Sigh, I suspect that he is going to use the sword's power to amplify the effectiveness of some new chemical compound. We have to stop him."

"But how? Only a descendant can wield the sword and draw out its full power."

"OR A GOLDEN DRAGON MOOR!" Esmeralda exclaims.

She gets up, walks towards Malik, and places her hand on his shoulder. "I think that the ancestors are giving you visions. You said that you kept seeing a Golden Dragon, right?"

"They come and go."

"Then maybe your journey is not quite over yet. I remember Eulalia once told me a story of how the Golden Dragon was considered a God amongst the people thousands of years ago. There is a temple that is made in its honor. It is said that only a select few can speak to it. Perhaps you should go."

"Where is this temple?" Malik asks.

"It's in a remote monastery in China. It resides in a Shaolin Village guarded by the monks there."

"Then I need to go there and seek the source of these visions."

Then Mason too gets up. He faces Malik with concerned focused eyes. "Are you sure you want to do this? You could be gone for days, weeks, months," Mason says. "If you go home, you can…"
"Mason, I think we both know I can't do that. The only reason I was able to write off the effects of the Reintergon was due to rage. I can't go into every battle with that mindset. I must reach another level. I need to seek out this Golden Dragon."
"I agree," Esmeralda says softly. "Malik, if Eulalia is still alive out there, we need to find her. She may be the key to finally defeat the Elite 8 and bring justice to our people."
"OK, Malik. I'm not going to stop you, but I think there's someone that you need to talk to first."

Afterwards, Esmeralda freshens up, changes clothes and gets ready to leave. Meanwhile, Malik is organizing his clothes and bags while Mason conducts his business on his laptop. Esmeralda walks up to the door and addresses Mason first.

"We will meet again tonight, right?" she asks.
"Yes. Inform your sisters to keep their eyes open and say nothing about Eulalia. We don't want the enemy to suspect anything." Esmeralda nods then looks at Malik.

Malik moves his head up and looks at Esmeralda. She remains stoic while Malik gives a small smirk. "Fue bueno pelear contigo. Me alegro de haber podido ver tu lado hermoso (It was good fighting with you. I'm glad I was able to see your beautiful side). Esmeralda hesitates for a moment. She gulps at the kind words thrown at her. Her eyes glisten. Her lips and cheeks turn red. Then she briefly closes her eyes and looks away. She begins to open the door but hesitates.
The room is still. The air blows through a tense mood. Malik nods, then resumes his packing.

Suddenly, Esmeralda slams the door and walks furiously towards Malik. She catches Malik off guard by giving him a huge hug. She embraces him tight while shedding some tears; she whispers in his ear.

"Para ser un idiota, puedes ser tan dulce. Cuídate (For an asshole, you can be so sweet. Take care of yourself) Malik." Stunned, Malik takes in the moment for a few seconds. Then he smiles, wraps his arms around Esmeralda and whispers back.

"Nos volveremos a ver. Hasta entonces, no tengas miedo de tus emociones (We'll see each other again. Until then, don't be afraid of your emotions)."

After a few precious moments, Esmeralda and Malik let go of each other. Esmeralda wipes her eyes. Puts her hand on her mouth, then blows a kiss to Malik. She waves at Malik before nodding at Mason. He smiles and nods back. Esmeralda turns around, opens the door, and walks out of the suite.

"You sure have a way with the ladies," Mason says. "Wish I had time to tell you how I used to get down in my day. Now we must make our contacts."

"Understood," Malik says. "Let's do it."

Mason prompts Malik to sit next to him on the couch. He clicks on a video icon on his desktop and inputs a password. After typing, the program begins to make a charm sound while waiting for a response.

"Who are we contacting?" Malik asks.

"You'll see," Mason responds.

After four cycles, a video image pops up. Shown on the screen is D'Shawn. "Snake Sight, this is Mason. Can you see and hear me?"

"Loud and clear, mentor," D'Shawn answers.

"Did the mission go as planned?"

"Yes, sir, it was a success. We recovered the lost boys and returned them to their families. However, our activities elevated the BEA policy. Now most authorities in each of the major cities will be looking for us."

"Indeed, but we are quickly gaining the momentum, as long as you keep fighting."

"Understood. So did you find who you were looking for?"

"He's right here."

Mason maneuvers the screen towards Malik. Then Mason introduces them on the video feed.

"D'Shawn, this is Malik Wilson. Also known as the Shadowmoor."

"Wait a minute, Mason..."

"Don't worry, Malik," D'Shawn interrupts. "Covert operations are what we do, and that includes secrets. I am proud to meet and fight for the same cause. Also, there's someone here who wants to speak with you."

"Speak with me?" Malik asks. "Who?"

D'Shawn waves his hand off screen, prompting someone to reveal themselves. After a few seconds, Malik is pleasantly shocked at who shows up.

"ASSWIPE! OH MY GOD!"

"Emma, hey?"

"I didn't know… what's going on?" Emma asks.

"You were right not to trust Audrey," Malik responds.

"Why? Did she blue ball you?"

"No. She was working for the Elite 8."

"Wait...WHAT!"

"We've been tracking their activities for some time now, Emma," D'Shawn says. "Matter of fact, I believe you may have found the new leader."

"His name is Victor Goth. He killed Audrey, took the sword, and left me to die."

"Oh...my god," Emma says.

Mason shifts the laptop to where both he and Malik are visible to the chat. The demeanor of the meeting transitions to that of a strategic battle plan.

"D'Shawn, have your most tech savvy people get with Malik so that they can help him run his business while he is away. We don't want him to appear missing, especially with the Elite 8 knowing his identity," Mason commands.

"Wait a minute," Emma responds. "Malik, what's going on? Why aren't you coming home?"

"I am getting new visions. Visions that may be a key to defeat the Elite 8 once and for all. I have to travel to seek the meaning of these visions."

"But Malik, we need you here. You know that the people need Shadowmoor."

"Yes, but we're at a disadvantage, especially if it's true about their intentions."

"I don't get it," Emma says.

"The Reintergon attacks people who are heavily melanated, meaning it is specifically engineered to attack Black people," Malik explains. "I think that the Elite 8 is planning a genocide under the guise of a pandemic."

"And if they succeed, then we're done for as a race," Mason contributes. "I don't know everything, but I do know that you three have the power to stop this. In order to do that, you must tap the untouched power deep within you."

Everybody remains silent to contemplate the necessary moves needed to proceed to the next step. Emma begins to sulk. Her eyes droop and her voice becomes weak.

"Malik, how long will you be away?"

"It's hard to say, Emma. You know how these things go, especially with us. Take care of Grandma and Granddad. Keep building up your Fire Line and wait for me."

"Will do, big brother."

"D'Shawn, take care of my sister, homie."

"An impossible task, but worth trying anyway," D'Shawn responds. "I hope to see you in person as well, Malik."

"Keep in contact, Snake Sight. Until I return, I trust that you will do what is best for OBR...and our people."

"We fight for the future of Black people, and our resolve is uncompromising. Snake Sight out."

The screen turns off, leaving Malik and Mason to sit for a while to relieve some of the weight of the burden. Malik rubs his face and rubs his eyes. Mason closes his laptop and gets up.

"I got a chance to look at some flights to China," Mason says. "The closest place is Shanghai." Malik looks up, nods, and gets up. Then he walks towards his bag and grabs the rest of his clothes.

"Then it looks like I need to finish packing."

"We'll go in a few hours." Mason says. Then he excuses himself to the other room to prepare for the journey. As the sun reaches its highest point, Malik stops to ponder the journey yet to be completed. Worn out and finding peace in between battles, he takes a deep breath, closes his eyes, reopens them, and finishes packing.

Several hours later, Malik and Mason are standing outside of the check-in terminal of the Madrid Airport. As Malik gathers his things, Mason gives a smile and lasting words of wisdom.

"You know something, you are an extraordinary young man."

"But I lost. I mean, I feel like I'm losing," Malik responds. Then Mason looks Malik directly in his eyes.

"Son, no power in the world makes you immune to failure. My dad failed. I failed. You will probably fail more times than you can stomach. But take a look at yourself. Not just as Shadowmoor, or Malik Wilson, or… even Marshall Benson." Malik raises his eyebrow before Mason finishes. "Your parents, in my opinion, were murdered by a corrupt system of white supremacy. You were raised by THE white supremacist. Yet, what should have killed you mentally, physically, and spiritually ended up becoming the catalyst for the bright future of our people. Malik, I hope that...before this is over, you will realize that the real power isn't the ability to see like a dragon, fight like a dragon, or even spit like one. The real power is this (he points to his head), and also this (he points to his chest). Always remember where the real power lies."

Malik nods, then looks at the terminal. Then he picks up his bag and puts the strap over his shoulder. "We'll see each other again, Mason."
"I expect we will. Take your time, son." Malik extends his hand out. Mason grasps his hand, shakes it, then embraces Malik with a hug. The men hug for about two seconds before releasing their grasp. Then Mason bids Malik farewell. "Good luck." Malik nods and turns around. He walks in towards the counter to check in his belongings and show his ticket. Afterwards, he looks back one last time at Mason, smiles, and walks towards the security gate where one journey ends, and the other journey begins, to seek the will of the Golden Dragon.